THE
APOTHECARY
ROSE

THE OWEN ARCHER SERIES
BOOK ONE

CANDACE

DIVERSIONBOOKS

Diversion Books
A Division of Diversion Publishing Corp.
443 Park Avenue South, Suite 1008
New York, New York 10016
www.DiversionBooks.com

For more information, email info@diversionbooks.com

First Diversion Books edition July 2015.
Print ISBN: 978-1-68230-101-2
eBook ISBN: 978-1-62681-975-7

To Gen, who first got me to England;
to Jacqui, the apothecary;
and to Charlie, who always makes it so.

ACKNOWLEDGMENTS

"The lyf so short, the craft so long to lerne,
Th'assay so hard, so sharp the conquerynge,
The dredful joye, alwey that slit so yerne…"
　　　　　—Geoffrey Chaucer, "The Parlement of Foules"

I thank Lisa Healy for her long-term faith in me and a crucial editing; Paul Zibton for the map, sanity lattes, and a critical reading; Christie Andersen for allowing me the time to write this book; Liz Armstrong for making all my medieval literature courses a joy; Paula Moreschi for keeping mind and body sound through it all; Evan Marshall for turning bad news into good news; Michael Denneny and Keith Kahla for making me feel welcome at St. Martin's; the staffs of the University of York's Borthwick Institute and the Morrell Library; the York Archaeological Trust; Dr. Tom Lockwood, chairman of the English Department at the University of Washington; and, most of all, Charles Robb for providing time, computer resources, food, drink, criticism, enthusiasm, travel arrangements, and organization, for outfitting me for exploring ruins in Yorkshire in a very cold December, and for insisting that a house is not a home without two spoiled cats.

GLOSSARY

archdeacon: each diocese was divided into two or more archdeaconries; the archdeacons were appointed by the archbishop or bishop and carried out most of his duties

jongleur: a minstrel who sang, juggled, tumbled; French term, but widely used in an England where Norman French was just fading from prevalence

leman: mistress

minster: a large church or cathedral; the cathedral of St. Peter in York is referred to as York Minster

summoner: an assistant to an archdeacon who cited people to the archbishop's or bishop's consistory court, which was held once a month. The court was staffed by the bishop's officials and lawyers and had jurisdiction over the diocesan clergy and the morals, wills, and marriages of the laity. The salary of a summoner was commission on fines levied by consistory courts—petty graft formed a large part of his income. More commonly called an "apparitor," but I use the term Chaucer used to call to mind the Canterbury pilgrim he so vividly described.

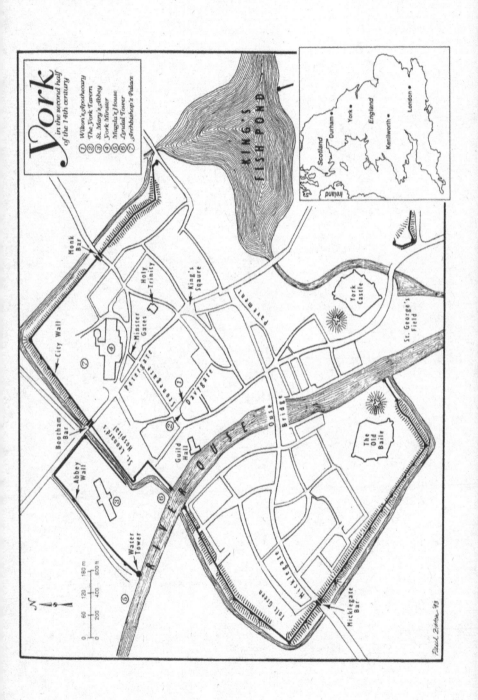

York

in the second half
of the 14th century

① Wilton's Apothecary
② The York Tavern
③ St. Mary's Abbey
④ York Minster
⑤ Magda's House
⑥ Lendal Tower
⑦ Archbishop's Palace

KING'S FISH POND

Monk Bar

Holy Trinity

King's Square

City Wall

Minster Gates

Pavement

Petergate

Stonegate

Davygate

St. Leonard's Hospital

Bootham Bar

Guild Hall

Abbey Wall

OUSE

Ouse Bridge

York Castle

St. George's Field

The Old Baile

Water Tower

RIVER OUSE

Micklegate

Toft Green

Micklegate Bar

Scotland
Durham
York
England
Kenilworth
London
Ireland

N

0   60   120 180 m
0   200 400 600 ft

Paul Bolton '93

PROLOGUE

Brother Wulfstan checked the color of his patient's eyes, tasted his sweat. The physick had only weakened the man. The Infirmarian feared he might lose this pilgrim. Trembling with disappointment, Wulfstan sat himself down at his worktable to think through the problem.

The pilgrim had arrived pale and hollow-cheeked at St. Mary's Abbey. Released from the Black Prince's service because of wounds and a bout with camp fever, the man had resolved to come on pilgrimage to York, his wounds making him more aware of his mortality than any sermon ever had. He'd endured a rough channel crossing and a long ride north that had reopened his wounds. Wulfstan had stopped the bleeding with periwinkle, but the recurrence of the fever caught him ill prepared. The Infirmarian had little experience with the ailments of soldiers, having lived in the cloistered peace of St. Mary's since childhood. He rarely ventured farther from the abbey than York Minster or Nicholas Wilton's apothecary, both within a short walk.

For two days and a night Wulfstan mixed physicks, applied plasters, and prayed. At last, exhausted and sick at heart, he thought of Nicholas Wilton. It was a sign of his hysteria that Wulfstan had not thought of the apothecary before—Nicholas had worked a wondrous cure on a guest of the Archbishop who'd been near death with camp fever. He would know what to do. Wulfstan breathed three Aves in thanksgiving as his spirits soared. God had shown the way.

The Infirmarian instructed his novice, Henry, to keep the pilgrim's lips moist and to prepare a mint tisane for him to sip if he roused. Then Wulfstan hurried through the cloister to ask the Abbot's permission to go into the city. He brushed at the powder and bits of dried herbs on his habit. Abbot Campian was a fastidious man. He believed that a tidy appearance bespoke a tidy mind. Wulfstan knew the Abbot could hardly disagree with his mission, but he found comfort in rules, as the Abbot did in tidiness. Wulfstan believed that if he obeyed and did his best, he could not fail to win a place, though humble, in the heavenly chorus. To be at peace in the arms of the Lord for all eternity. He could imagine no better fate. And rules showed him the way to that eternal contentment.

With his Abbot's permission, Wulfstan stepped out into the December afternoon. Bah. It had begun to snow. All through November and into December he'd awaited the first snow, and it came now, when he had an urgent errand. If he'd been a superstitious peasant, he would have suspected the fates were against him today. But he fortified himself with the conviction that as God had seen him through all the small troubles of his life, surely He could not mean to desert Wulfstan at this late date.

The Infirmarian pulled up his cowl and headed into the wind as fast as he could, blinking and puffing, out the Abbey gates and onto the cobbled street, into the bustle of York. The cacophony of the city startled Wulfstan out of his single-minded hurry. He became aware of a stitch in his side. His heart hammered. Such signs of frailty frightened him. He was behaving like a fool. He was too old to move so quickly, especially on cobbles made slippery with the first snow. Holding his side, he paused at the crossroads for a passing cart. The snow came down thick now, great, fluffy flakes that stung as they melted on his flushed cheeks. *Overheat and then chill. You're an idiot, Wulfstan.* He turned down Davygate, trying to moderate his speed. But Wilton's shop was just past the next crossing. He was so close to his goal. He picked up his pace again, propelled forward by fear of losing his patient.

Wulfstan had grown fond of the pilgrim in a short time. The man was a soft-spoken, gentle knight who identified himself only as a pilgrim wishing to pray, meditate, make his peace with God. He carried with him an old sorrow, the love of a woman who belonged to someone else. He spoke of her as the gentlest, most beautiful woman, whose purgatory on earth was to be tied to an old man who gave her no joy. "What would she think of me now, eh, my friend?" His eyes would mist over. "But she is gone." The pilgrim came daily to the infirmary to have Wulfstan change his bandages. During these visits he had discovered the herb garden, how its beauty comforted the heart, even in winter. "She found solace in a garden much like this." Many a day the pilgrim lingered there while Wulfstan puttered in the beds. He said little, observing the monastic rule of speaking only when necessary. He was ever ready to assist with carrying or fetching, sensitive to Wulfstan's old bones. Wulfstan enjoyed the man's quiet companionship and appreciated his help, though he knew accepting it was sinful indulgence.

So he had taken it hard when the pilgrim collapsed in chapel. The man had been keeping a vigil that night in memory of his love. Brother Sebastian found him in a swoon on the cold stone floor at Lauds. Thanks be to God for the night office, or the pilgrim might have lain there till dawn and caught a mortal chill.

Even so, he was very ill. Wulfstan hurried. By the time he pushed open Wilton's shop door, the old monk was panting and bent double, clutching his side. The dimness of the shop and his own weakness blinded him momentarily; he could not see if anyone was in the shop. "God's peace be with you," he gasped. No answer. "Nicholas? Lucie?"

The beaded curtain in the kitchen doorway rattled as someone stepped through. "Brother Wulfstan!" Lucie Wilton lifted the hinged counter and took Wulfstan's hand. "You look dreadful." She smelled of the outdoors. "Your hands are like ice."

He straightened up with caution. "You've been in the garden." His breathless, shaky voice surprised him. He'd pushed himself even further than he'd thought.

"We wanted to cover the roses with straw before the snow." Lucie Wilton held a spirit lamp up to his face. He blinked in the light. "Come back by the kitchen fire. Your cheeks are aflame. You'll burst your heart hurrying so."

Wulfstan followed her behind the counter and through to the kitchen, where he accepted a bench beside the fire with humble gratitude. Old age and shortness of breath made impossible the polite habit of protesting against kindness. In the cheery kitchen he smiled on Mistress Wilton, who brightened his heart with beauty, gentleness, courtesy. She would have made her father proud at court, he was certain. Sir Robert was an old fool.

She handed him a cup of warmed wine. "Now what brings you out in the snow? And in such haste?"

He told her the purpose of his errand.

"Camp fever. You are tending a soldier?"

"No longer a soldier. With his gray beard and sad eyes, I think those days are over for him." Wulfstan glanced away from the kind concern in her face to the door that opened onto the garden. "I hate to steal Nicholas from his roses. Do you perhaps know the proper mixture?"

"Nicholas has not yet tested me on it."

"I hate to be a bother, but the man is so very ill."

Lucie patted him on the shoulder. "Rest here while I fetch my husband."

Lucie was apprenticed to her husband, a situation not unusual. Wives commonly learned their husbands' trades by working beside them. But Lucie's apprenticeship had been formally arranged by Nicholas to ensure her future. Being sixteen years her senior, and of delicate health, he worried about her comfort after he passed on.

Another man might have looked on her fair face and reasoned that she would remarry. And in Lucie's case, perhaps marry better, closer to her original station in life. For Lucie was the daughter of Sir Robert D'Arby of Freythorpe Hadden; she might have married a minor lord. Had her mother not died when Lucie was young, it would almost certainly have been so. But with the death of the fair Amelie, Sir Robert had become singularly uninterested in his only child's lot in life. He'd sent her off to a convent, where Nicholas had discovered her and vowed to free her into a life more suited to her character. Wulfstan liked Nicholas Wilton for what he had done for Lucie. In the long run the apothecary would be a better inheritance than the settlement she might receive as a lord's widow, and it made her independent.

Nicholas came in, wiping his hands and shaking his head. "The snow was long in coming this year, but how it falls now!" His thin face glowed with the cold, and his pale eyes shone. The apothecary's garden was his passion.

"Have you finished with the roses?" Wulfstan asked. Gardening was the bond between them. And the lore of healing plants.

"Almost." Nicholas sat down with the sigh of a pleasantly tired man. "Lucie tells me you have a pilgrim with camp fever."

"That is so. He's bad, Nicholas. Weak and shivering."

"How long since his last bout with it?"

"Five months."

More questions followed, the apothecary frowning and nodding. "Was he clear-headed when he arrived?"

"Most lucid. While I tended his wounds he sometimes asked about the folk in York. He'd once fought beside Sir Robert in a French campaign."

Lucie looked up at that with a steely expression. She had little affection for her father.

"Now there was an odd thing," Wulfstan said. "He was upset with me when I said you had become Master in your father's place, Nicholas. He insisted that you had died."

"Died?" Nicholas whispered.

Lucie crossed herself.

Later, Wulfstan was to remember that it was then that Nicholas's manner changed. He began to ask questions that, to Wulfstan's mind, had little to do with a diagnosis—the soldier's name, his appearance, his age, his purpose in coming to St. Mary's, if he'd had visitors.

Wulfstan had few answers. The pilgrim had wished to remain nameless; he'd made no mention of home or family; he was gray-haired, tall, with a soldier's bearing even in his illness. No visitors, though he knew the folk at Freythorpe Hadden. And, apparently, knew of Nicholas. "But surely this is unimportant?" The apothecary wasted precious time.

Lucie Wilton touched her husband's arm. He jumped as if her touch had burned him. "Brother Wulfstan must hurry back to his patient," she said, regarding her husband with a worried look.

Nicholas got up and began to pace. After an uncomfortable

silence in which Wulfstan began to fear Nicholas was at a loss for a proper physick, the apothecary turned with an odd sigh. "My usual mixture will not suffice. Go back to your patient, Brother Wulfstan. I will follow with the physick before the day is out." He looked distracted, not meeting Wulfstan's eyes.

Wulfstan was disappointed. More delay. "It is not a simple case, then? Is it the wound that complicates it?"

"It is never simple with camp fever."

Wulfstan crossed himself.

Lucie put a comforting hand on his shoulder. "Is it very serious, Nicholas?"

"I cannot say," he snapped. Then, thinking better of it, he bent and kissed her gently on the forehead. "There's no need for you to stay, Lucie." His voice caressed her. "And no need to worry. You might finish up the last rose bed if you hurry."

"I thought I might learn something by watching you prepare the mixture."

Nicholas took her hand. "I will review it with you later, my love. But the snow will not wait." His eyes were affectionate, gentle, almost melancholy.

Without further argument, Lucie donned her mantle and went out the garden door.

Wulfstan sighed.

"She is a treasure," Nicholas said.

Wulfstan agreed. "You are both blessed in your contentment."

Nicholas looked down at the floor and said nothing. It seemed to Wulfstan that his friend avoided meeting his eyes. Perhaps things were not so well between them. "So you will prepare a special mixture?"

Nicholas clapped his hands, back to business. "And you must hasten back to your patient and ply him with mint to bring on a good sweat."

"I left Henry with sufficient instructions," Wulfstan protested, but seeing Nicholas's odd temper, he took his leave.

A bitter cold return journey it was. Nicholas was right. The first snow made up for its tardiness.

• • •

At dusk, as Wulfstan nodded by the pilgrim's sickbed, he was wakened by a tap on his shoulder. Nicholas Wilton at last. But something was amiss with the apothecary. Wulfstan rubbed his eyes and squinted at the man. Nicholas's eyes were too large in his pale face, as if he'd had a shock.

"You do not look well, Nicholas. You should have sent someone else with the medicine."

The patient moaned. His eyes flickered.

Nicholas drew Wulfstan aside. "He looks worse than I expected," he whispered. Ah, Wulfstan thought, that explained the expression on the apothecary's face. "You must dose him at once," Nicholas said. "Hurry. A dram in boiling water. I'll sit with him."

Wulfstan hastened to the fire.

Apparently the pilgrim woke, for Wulfstan heard him cry out, then Nicholas's voice murmuring some comfort. The sick man cried out again. Wulfstan was not surprised. The gentle knight burned with fever. Delirium was to be expected.

He tested the water, impatient for it to boil. The pilgrim sobbed. At last the water boiled. Wulfstan measured with care, said a prayer over it, stirred well, and hurried with it to the sickbed.

To his surprise, Nicholas was gone. He had left the pilgrim alone. "How odd to leave without a word," Wulfstan muttered.

"Murderer," the pilgrim hissed. "Poisoner." His face was red and slick with sweat.

"Calm yourself, my friend," Wulfstan said. "This emotion does you no good."

The pilgrim's breathing was tortured. He thrashed from side to side, his eyes wild.

Wulfstan did all he could do to calm him, whispering reassurances. "Fever visions, my friend. Visitations of Lucifer to break your will. Pay them no heed."

At last the man's eyes cleared. "He was a nightmare?"

"Yes, yes. There are no murderers here." That was true enough.

Wulfstan held the cup up to the man's pale lips. "Now drink this down. Rest is what you need. A healing slumber."

The watery, frightened eyes moved to the cup, then back to Wulfstan. "You prepared it?"

"With my own hands, my friend. Now drink."

He did so. "Then he is dead. I did kill him," he whispered. The dreadful thought seemed to calm him. Soon, warm and drowsy, the pilgrim drifted into sleep. But shortly after Compline he began to moan, then woke in a sweat, complaining of pains in his arms and legs. Perhaps Wulfstan had been wrong to call it camp fever. But his friend had not exhibited these symptoms before. Wulfstan tried to soothe his limbs with cloths soaked in witch hazel, but the pain persisted.

He summoned Henry. Together they prepared poultices and wrapped the pilgrim's limbs. Nothing helped. Wulfstan was at his wits' end. He had done his best. No one could fault his efforts. The Lord knew how deeply he felt the pilgrim's suffering. He considered sending for Master Saurian, the physician who tended the monks when they were ill, but he had been little help when the pilgrim fell ill, and it was late, and Wulfstan feared Saurian would simply say God's will be done. Of course God's will be done. Wulfstan did not have to drag Saurian out in the middle of the night to be told that. But God's will was not always clear to man.

The pilgrim's breathing became labored. He gasped for air. Henry brought pillows to prop up the sick man's head and help him breathe.

It was a long night. The wind found every chink in the infirmary, and moaned at the door. The hearth smoked and made the Infirmarian's already teary eyes burn. Once, when Wulfstan bent over the pilgrim to blot his brow, the man grabbed his habit and pulled him close, whispering, "He has poisoned me. I did not kill him. I did not avenge her." Then he sank back on the pallet in a swoon.

"It is the fever that burns within you, my friend," Wulfstan said aloud, in case the pilgrim could hear and be comforted. "You would be worse without the medicine." The man did not stir.

How unfortunate that the pilgrim mistook for a murderer the man who had come to save him. A murderer the pilgrim thought he'd killed. Was that why he had been so certain Nicholas Wilton was dead? He had tried to kill him? Gentle Mary and all the saints, no wonder Nicholas took alarm. But as Wulfstan kept watch over the suffering pilgrim, he convinced himself that it was all fever dreams. He could not imagine the gentle pilgrim attacking Nicholas Wilton.

Wulfstan watched in the smoky darkness. His heart sank as the pilgrim's faint stretched on and on. His breathing was shallow, with now and then an explosive gasp, as if he could not get enough air. Wulfstan propped him up higher and prayed. Henry returned from Lauds and knelt with him.

But for all their care, the pilgrim's shallow breathing ceased at dawn. Heartsick, Wulfstan retired to the chapel to pray for his friend's soul.

Henry came to Wulfstan as he nodded over his prayers. Archdeacon Anselm's Summoner, Potter Digby, wished to speak with him.

Wulfstan could not imagine what Digby might want with him. It was a Summoner's dreadful duty to investigate rumors of sinners who'd broken diocesan law, and to summon those he judged guilty to the Archbishop's consistory court to be fined. For this he earned a commission. And for this Digby was disliked among the townspeople, who knew he waited to catch them in marital infidelities, marriage being a sacrament and infidelities his most lucrative charges. The lay clergy seldom had much money to pay for their sins. Many said it was the Summoner's unholy diligence that kept the stonemasons and glaziers busy on the cathedral. Wulfstan thought it a pity that the beautiful minster should be linked to such greed. In truth, he disliked Potter Digby with a sinful energy. As Wulfstan followed Henry to the cloister, he wondered what unpleasantness brought the man to him.

Potter Digby, it turned out, was on private business. He'd found Nicholas Wilton in a faint near the abbey gate the night before and hailed a passing cart to carry him home. Wilton was in such a state he did not recognize his own wife. Digby thought Mistress Wilton would appreciate Brother Wulfstan's presence.

"Nicholas? How strange." Wulfstan thought back on Nicholas's abrupt departure. "He did behave oddly last night. But you must forgive me. I have been up all night. I lost a patient and friend. I cannot come. I would be no good to them."

"Wilton is bad. His wife is frightened." Digby shrugged. "But perhaps Master Saurian—"

"Saurian? He'll be no comfort to Mistress Wilton." Wulfstan wavered. Though trembling with fatigue and a long fast, he could not abandon gentle Lucie Wilton to the cold Master Saurian.

"Then whom do you suggest, Brother Wulfstan?"

The Infirmarian shrugged. "I will ask my Abbot's permission."

Once more Wulfstan braved the snow, his old bones chilled and aching. It did not matter. He could not leave Lucie Wilton alone at such a time.

He need not have worried. Bess Merchet, proprietress of the York Tavern, next door to Wilton's apothecary, met him at the kitchen door. Wulfstan was pleased to see her competent bulk in the doorway. She was a sensible woman, regardless of the brandywine on her breath, and a good friend to Lucie.

"She'll be that pleased to see you, Brother Wulfstan." Bess hustled him in and set a cup of something hot in his hands. "Drink that up and catch your breath. I'll see how things stand up above." She disappeared up the stairs.

Wulfstan sniffed at the mixture of brandywine and herbs, then decided it would do him a world of good. It soon settled his heart back in its caging and dulled the pain of loss.

Upstairs, one look at Nicholas told Wulfstan that he might soon suffer the loss of another friend. "Merciful Mother, what has happened to you?" Wulfstan knelt beside Nicholas's bed, taking the man's hands, which lay limp upon the covers, and trying to rub warmth into them. Nicholas stared ahead, moving his lips but making no sound.

"He has been like this all night." Lucie sat on the other side of the bed, dabbing at her husband's tears. Shadows beneath her eyes bespoke a night as terrible as Wulfstan's. "He left here yesterday afternoon as you saw him, clear-witted and healthy enough to work in the garden, cold as it was, and returned crippled and bereft of speech, tormented by some horror I cannot know and so cannot comfort him." She bit her lip. There was no time for tears.

Wulfstan's heart overflowed with pity for her. He knew his own pain over the pilgrim. How much greater must hers be, seeing her husband like this. He must find a way to help. He tucked Nicholas's hands under the covers and drew Lucie away from the sickbed. "Tell me everything you can."

She could tell him little, only that Digby had helped Nicholas inside, for he seemed unable to support himself on his right leg. The right arm also seemed useless. And he'd made no sound but down in the throat. She clenched her hands and looked desperate for comfort.

But Wulfstan could give little. "It sounds to be a palsy. Whether it be temporary or permanent, only time will tell. It is in God's hands. Perhaps if I knew what caused it." He thought of Nicholas's behavior as he questioned Wulfstan about the pilgrim, and later when Nicholas had glimpsed the pilgrim's state. "He was agitated when he left the infirmary. Perhaps in the dark he fell. A blow to the head could cause such a palsy. Or to the spine. An extreme shock."

"A shock." Lucie glanced at Nicholas, then bent her head away from him so that only Wulfstan could hear. "Could it be the pilgrim?" She asked it in a soft, tense voice.

Wulfstan remembered the dying man's accusations. But he had no proof. And now that the man was dead he could see no reason to frighten Lucie. "My patient's appearance disturbed Nicholas, to be sure. He said he'd not expected the man to be so ill. But that is not shock enough." He looked at Lucie's bowed head. "What is it, my child? What do you fear?"

"It was Archdeacon Anselm's visit this morning."

"Anselm? Came here?"

"They have not spoken in years. Since before we were married. It is odd that he should come today. There he stood in the doorway, so early, before any customers. He'd already heard that Nicholas was taken ill. He expressed concern, for all the world a worried friend.

After so many years. He did not come when our Martin died." Their only child. Dead of the plague before he ever walked.

Something in this disturbed Wulfstan. For last night he had been visited by the Archdeacon. At the time he had given it little thought. The Archdeacon was to dine with Abbot Campian. Before supper he had stopped in the infirmary, curious whether it had changed since he was last bled there. Anselm had been schooled at St. Mary's. Last evening he had been pleasant enough, asking after Brother Wulfstan's health, telling Henry how frightened he had been of Wulfstan, who had been broad in the chest in his younger years. Anselm had asked about the pilgrim, the only patient. It seemed a mere politeness.

Wulfstan drew Lucie down on a chest by the little window. "Tell me about the Archdeacon's visit."

"He had heard Nicholas was ill. He asked if it were serious. I told him I did not know, that I could tell him no more than his Summoner had told him. Nothing had changed. He seemed surprised. He asked why I assumed his Summoner had told him. I told him how Digby had found Nicholas. He did not like that. 'The Abbey infirmary? What was Nicholas doing there?' He said it as if it were an enemy camp, a place Digby should have known not to go."

"My infirmary?" Wulfstan did not like that.

"The Archdeacon alarmed me with his questions. I told him Nicholas had taken a physick to a patient. 'The soldier?' he asked. I said yes, the one who called himself a pilgrim. The Archdeacon's face lost what little color it had. He put a hand on the counter to steady himself. I asked him what he suspected. He asked what had happened at the abbey. Of course I did not know. I suspected that the Archdeacon knew more than I did. I asked him who the pilgrim was. I am sure he knows. He blinked and looked away. 'I have not seen this pilgrim, Mistress Wilton,' he said. It is the sort of half-truth the sisters told to shield us from the world. I persisted. He pulled himself up straight and said he would come back. 'Who is he?' I demanded. 'I will come back,' he said again, and hurried out."

Lucie looked out the window, her jaw set. "Damnable priest. He knows who the man is. Why would he not tell me? I think it has everything to do with the soldier." She turned angry eyes on Wulfstan. "Who is the pilgrim, Wulfstan?"

"My dear Lucie, as God is my witness, I do not know."

"I want to speak with him."

Wulfstan shook his head. "He is dead."

She looked shocked. "Dead? When?"

"Last night. Whoever he was, he cannot help us now."

Lucie crossed herself. It was bad luck to speak evil of the recently dead. "May he rest in peace."

Wulfstan whispered an Amen, his eyes cast down, burning with tears. He was so weary he could not control himself.

Lucie, noting his discomfort, took his hand. "I am sorry you lost your patient."

"It is worse than that. He was a friend." Wulfstan's voice broke. He wiped his eyes and took a deep breath. "Forgive me. I fear I am little use to you."

Gently, she kissed his forehead. Just a touch with her lips, but it was such an affectionate gesture it undid the old monk. He put his face in his hands and wept. Lucie put her arm around him and drew him close.

Later, when Wulfstan had fortified himself with a cup of brandywine, he spoke of his friendship with the pilgrim. Of the man's sorrow.

"He sounds like a gentle man. I thank you for coming in your sorrow. How did you know to come?"

"Digby. He came to tell me of your trouble."

"This is a strange business, Brother Wulfstan. Digby's eagerness to help, the Archdeacon's visit. Do you know, I think if I knew the connection between Archdeacon Anselm and the pilgrim and the Archdeacon and Nicholas, I might understand what has happened."

Wulfstan said nothing. Long ago he had promised Nicholas he would say nothing to Lucie about the past, and he would not. But it bothered him that Nicholas had taken ill while he and Anselm and Anselm's Summoner were at St. Mary's. He found it difficult to see it as a coincidence.

• • •

God created evil in the form of Eve, out of Adam's rib. He took the evil part of man and created woman. So plain, writ so clear, and yet few men heed the warning. And by their blindness they are undone.

Anselm, Archdeacon of York, knelt on the cold, damp stones, trying to push away bitter thoughts and pray for his dearest friend. But the thoughts had everything to do with Nicholas. Gentle Nicholas, undone by his love for a woman, suffering such pain it was impossible he should live much longer. Perhaps that was best.

Anselm shifted uncomfortably. The chill damp had settled in his knees, whence a dull ache moved up to his loins. He offered up the suffering for his friend's salvation. He would suffer anything for Nicholas. He had already suffered for him most of his adult life. But Anselm resented none of it. His prayers for Nicholas were heartfelt.

Nicholas was not to blame for his misfortune. He had not chosen the path of sin. It was his father's choice, his father who had taken him from the abbey school and made him his apprentice in the apothecary, next door to a tavern, close to the heart of the city and its wickedness. It was Nicholas's father who had urged him to look on women, to choose a mate who would bear him a son to carry on the business. Nicholas, always the obedient son, had turned from Anselm and found in his path a woman so evil she would ensnare three men before she was through, bringing all three down with her. And her daughter would seal the deed, trapping Nicholas here until the curse be played out to its horrible end.

Nicholas's father had died as was fitting, with a bitterness in his heart, seeing his son unmarried and with a terrible secret that could destroy all he had worked so hard to create. Such is the price of sin. But Nicholas might have been spared. Beautiful, gentle, loving Nicholas.

Anselm bent his head and prayed for a forgiving God.

• • •

Weeks later, past Twelfthnight, Brother Wulfstan sat beside the brazier in the infirmary, sadly contemplating his hand. First it had tingled, then it had gone numb. With just a fingertip's worth of the physick. Enough aconite to kill by applying a salve. No wonder ingesting it had killed his friend and now Sir Oswald Fitzwilliam. God forgive him, but he had not noticed that he had grown so old and incompetent. And yet here was the proof. Never should an Infirmarian accept a physick prepared by other hands without testing it. But he had. And when the patient died, Wulfstan had not thought to test it even then, but had put it on a shelf, ready for the next victim. God forgive him, it was Wulfstan's own incompetence that had killed his friend, the gentle pilgrim. And now Sir Oswald Fitzwilliam, the Archbishop's ward. Sweet Mary and all the saints, what was he to do?

What did it mean? Nicholas Wilton was respected throughout the county. How could he make such a mistake?

Wulfstan stared at his hand as a possibility dawned on him. Perhaps Nicholas had already been unwell that afternoon and had mixed the physick incorrectly. One powder looks much like another. If he were already sickening, might he not have forgotten which was aconite and which was ground orris root? Wulfstan always prayed for God's hand to guide him as he measured. A medicine could so easily become a poison. And yet Nicholas had shown no sign of illness that afternoon. His color had perhaps been mottled, but he had a weak constitution and he had just spent some hours in the garden during the first serious freeze of the season. There was his odd temper, though. There was that. But, Dear Lord, that was little to rouse suspicion. After all these years of trusting Nicholas.

One thing was clear. Wulfstan must return the unused portion of the physick to Lucie Wilton and talk with her. She must watch over Nicholas when he grew well enough to return to the shop. Nicholas must not be allowed to mix anything until it was clear that he was in his right mind once more.

Wulfstan was so overwrought by the time he arrived at the apothecary that it seemed to him Lucie Wilton knew, the moment her eyes fell on the parcel in his hand, what he carried. But how could she? And her words denied that suspicion.

"A gift for Nicholas? Some new mixture that might change his humours?"

"I wish it were, Lucie, my child."

She frowned at the tone in his voice and led him back to the kitchen, gesturing to the chair by the fire.

Chilled as he had been outside, Wulfstan was now sweating. He mopped at his face. Lucie held a cup out to him. "Bess Merchet brought over some of Tom's ale. You look more in need of it than I."

"God be with you." He gladly accepted the cup, took several long drinks.

"Now, my friend, tell me what is wrong." Lucie's voice was calm, but her eyes were alert for trouble. And he had noted when he took the cup from her that her hands were cold. But of course he had made her nervous, coming here unlooked for, acting so solemn.

"Forgive me. I come from a deathbed. Sir Oswald Fitzwilliam, the Archbishop's ward. And I fear that I might be responsible."

"You, Brother Wulfstan?"

He put the cup down beside him and picked up the parcel. "You see, I administered this to him and then, when he worsened so quickly and dramatically, I examined it. My child, anything but the most minute dose of this physick would be deadly to a mortal man."

Lucie, her eyes on the parcel, asked quietly, "And you bring it here for me to test? Hoping that you are mistaken?"

Wulfstan shook his head. "I am not mistaken, Lucie."

She looked up at him, held him with her clear blue eyes. "Then why have you brought it?"

"It is the physick for camp fever that Nicholas mixed for me the day he fell ill."

At first he thought she had not heard, she was so still. Then, "Merciful Mother," she breathed, crossing herself. "Are you certain?" Her eyes were large with the import of his words.

"I am as careful as I know you are to label everything," Wulfstan said.

"I had no idea there was any left."

"The pilgrim died the very night I administered it. Nicholas gave me enough for several days. It seemed sinful not to keep it."

"But if you knew—"

"Not until today. I never thought to check it until today."

Lucie bit her lip, thinking. "I do not know the mixture for camp fever. What is the poison?"

"Aconite."

"And you are certain that in the mixture you hold the aconite is strong enough to kill?"

"My hand is yet numb with just a pinch of the mixture."

Lucie hugged herself. "Both men had painful limbs?" Wulfstan nodded. "Trouble breathing?" Again he nodded. Lucie put her head in her hands.

"Forgive me for adding to your sorrow, my child. I would not have told you, but I thought you must know to watch Nicholas. You must not let him back in the shop until he is completely mended, in mind as well as body."

She nodded without looking up.

Wulfstan bent to pick up the cup. Lucie's cat stretched beside the fire and came over to rub against Wulfstan's hand. Melisende was a lovely gray and white striped cat with unusually long ears. Wulfstan rubbed her forehead. Melisende purred.

"He must have been ill already," Lucie said.

Wulfstan picked up the cup of ale. Melisende jumped onto his lap and circled about, getting comfortable. "That is what I think. He did not realize that he should not trust himself that day."

Lucie looked up again, her eyes bright with tears. "Could it have been the cold? Should I not have let him work on the roses with me?"

Wulfstan felt horrible. The last thing he intended was to accuse Lucie Wilton of negligence. She had already suffered so much, taken so much on herself. "Lucie, my child, how could you keep him from his garden? You must not blame yourself."

"It is difficult not to. He wastes away."

"Do not give up hope. God will take him only if it is his time."

"But even should he recover—" Lucie touched the tears on her cheeks, as if confused by the wetness there, then blotted them with the cloth with which she'd wiped her hands after pouring the ale. "Poor Nicholas. He will be a broken man if he recovers to find that everything he has worked for is in ruins around him."

"Why should it be in ruins?"

Lucie fastened her lovely, tear-filled eyes on the old monk. "Two deaths. According to the civic ordinances, we can no longer practice. The Guild cannot go against the ordinances. I cannot imagine Guildmaster Thorpe will find it possible to give Nicholas a second chance. We are ruined, Brother Wulfstan."

Wulfstan stroked the cat and silently prayed for guidance. He must prevent such a disaster.

Lucie paced from the fire to the door a few times, then stopped midway, in front of some shelves, and absently rearranged the jars and dishes in front of her.

"It is a terrible business," Wulfstan said, more to the cat than to Lucie.

But Lucie seemed to waken with those words and came swiftly to sit beside the old monk. She took one of his hands in hers. "My dear friend, forgive me. I have been thinking about what all this means to Nicholas and me, but you, too, risk losing your life's work."

"Me? Losing my life's work?"

"Your infirmary."

"My—How would I lose my infirmary?"

"When Abbot Campian learns that you administered the physick without testing it—"

Sweet Jesus, would his Abbot relieve him of his duties? Of course he would. And rightly so. Old age had made him careless.

"Unless we save ourselves," Lucie said quietly.

"Save ourselves?"

"By making this our secret."

"We would tell no one?"

"No one." She looked down at their hands, then back up at Wulfstan. "Would it be so wrong? For my part, I will not let Nicholas mix another physick until both you and I agree that he has completely recovered his reason. And I've no doubt that you will never again administer a physick that you have not tested yourself." She regarded Wulfstan with her clear eyes. Dry now. Calm and rational.

They buoyed Wulfstan's spirits. "I had not thought so far. But of course you are right about the consequences. For all three of us." He drank down the ale.

"Then it is our secret?"

God help him, but Wulfstan did not wish to bring more sorrow to this household. Nor did he wish to lose his infirmary. He nodded. "It is our secret."

Lucie squeezed his hand.

"But when he recovers—" Wulfstan began.

"I will watch out for him." Lucie let go his hand and bent to pick up the package. "According to the ordinance, I should burn this."

Wulfstan nodded. "Do so. I would do it for you, but—"

Lucie shook her head. "No, it is my duty." She leaned over and kissed him on the cheek. "Thank you, Brother Wulfstan. You have been our salvation."

He could not believe that anything so sweet could come from evil. God had shown him the way.

When Wulfstan had left, Lucie paced the room, hugging her arms to herself. She considered the jug of ale. A cup might steady her. But it was early afternoon. There would be customers. She must keep her wits about her. Everything depended on her now.

1

A ONE-EYED SPY

Master Roglio took great pains folding his astrological charts and tucking away the tools he had used to examine the eye. Owen noted a tremor in the physician's hands, the tensed shoulders of a man holding his breath, eyes that would not meet his. Master Roglio stank of fear. Owen glanced at the Duke of Lancaster, who glowered in the corner. An old man, but Lancaster's power was second only to King Edward's. Displeasing him was a dangerous business.

It would be Christian to wait with his question, but Owen had waited three months for this moment, and he could wait no longer. "The flesh heals, but the eye remains dark. You see no change, eh, Physician?"

Roglio's eyes slid to the old Duke, who sat forward, interested. Roglio raised both shoulders in an eloquent shrug. "God may yet work a miracle."

"But you cannot," the old Duke said with a snarl.

Roglio met the Duke's steely gaze. "No, my lord." He managed not to flinch.

The flesh healed, but the eye remained dark. One eye. God had created man with two for a purpose, no doubt. And blinded Owen in one. A purpose to that as well, no doubt.

Owen had made good use of two. Lancaster's prize archer, he had trained the others, drilled them, risen to captain. An achievement for a Welshman. No animal escaped his arrows. Nor man. He'd taken care to kill only for food or in obedience to his liege lord. And all for the honor and glory of God.

Christian charity had robbed him of all that. A jongleur and his leman. Bretons. More independent than the Welsh, Owen had thought. They had no reason to spy for the French. The leman helped herself, flirting with the men. The soldiers would make good use of her. But the jongleur was doomed. The men did not find him entertaining. Only Owen understood the Breton songs, and only with effort. The language was a bastard mix of Cornish and French. The men grew restive. Killing the jongleur, now that would be better sport. Owen argued to release him. And won.

Two nights later, the jongleur slipped into camp and slit the throats of the best prisoners, those who would cost the French nobility most in ransoms. Owen caught him. *Ungrateful bastard. You were shown mercy.* The leman crept up from behind. Owen spun round. A thrust meant for his neck opened the left eye instead. Roaring, he plunged the sword into her gut, retrieved it, and, turning round, did not see the jongleur on his left until he'd sliced into Owen's shoulder. Calling on the bowman's muscles that gave him enough strength to wield a broadsword with one hand, Owen sliced through the jongleur's shoulder and down beneath the neck. Once the Bretons lay in pools of their own blood, Owen slipped to the ground in a hellfire of pain. His last soldierly deed.

Now what?

Everything must be learned over again. He'd not bothered till now, thinking the half-blind state temporary. A passing discomfort, like all his wounds. When an unseen obstacle tripped him up, he shrugged it off, a small penance for his many sins, a lesson in humility. Not an easy lesson. Familiar objects looked foreign. The world appeared lopsided. When he blinked, it winked out.

Owen learned the value of two eyes. With two, a mote in one had not blinded him. It was a mere discomfort. Now it rendered him as helpless as a babe in arms.

Complete darkness. He knew it possible. Death, too, was possible. It changed everything.

• • •

The old Duke argued that Owen's loss of sight did not render him useless—an archer aimed with one eye shut. And the strength would return to his shoulder with work. But Owen saw his blinding as the result of his own faulty judgment and the shoulder wound as the inevitable result of his blinding. A one-eyed man was vulnerable. He would endanger those with whom he fought.

Lancaster let him be for a time, then surprised him. "You are a natural mimic, Owen Archer. In my service you have mannered yourself a knight. Your accent is rough, but the marcher lords carry the accents of their borders. And better than a lordling, you are a free man. No one owns you, you have no family honor to defend, you do not seek power through secret alliances. I can trust you. With a little education I might use you well as my eyes and my ears. What say you?"

Owen turned his head like a bird to study his lord with his good eye. Lancaster possessed a strange humor and was adept at maintaining a level voice, devoid of emotion. But at this moment the old Duke's gaze was level, lacking amusement.

"I would be your spy?"

The old Duke grinned. "Yet another virtue. A blunt thrust to the heart of things."

"A spy with one eye would seem almost as useless as a one-eyed archer, my lord." Best that he say it. Someone would.

"Not to mention how conspicuous you are with your leather patch and angry scar." The old Duke chuckled, enjoying the moment. "Your unlikeliness becomes a disguise."

"An interesting line of reasoning," Owen said.

The old Duke threw back his head and roared with laughter. "Spoken with a lordling's delicacy. Excellent." A sudden sobering. Lancaster leaned forward. "My son-in-law called me a master tactician. And that I am, Owen Archer. Power is not held by attending the King and fighting battles. I need trustworthy spies. You were of great value as Captain of Archers. You can be of greater value as my eyes and ears. But you must know the players and the plots. You must read well both men and their letters. Will you apply yourself to the learning of this?"

A spy worked alone. Owen's incompleteness would endanger no one but himself. It appealed to him. "Aye, my lord. Gladly."

God was merciful in His designs. Owen spent the night in chapel giving thanks. He might yet prove useful.

Two years later Owen stood in the back of Westminster Abbey church, part of the old Duke's funeral retinue. God had lifted him up to strike him down once more. He could not expect that the old Duke had arranged for his future. If the dukedom had passed on to Lancaster's own son, perhaps that might have been. But the old Duke had only daughters. The new Duke of Lancaster, John of Gaunt, was a son-in-law, husband to the old Duke's daughter Blanche, and he was the son of King Edward, which made him a powerful lord in his own right. He could hardly be expected to employ a one-eyed Welsh spy. Owen had thought much on his future the last few days. He had some money earned in the Duke's service. His best plan so far was to arrange passage to the continent and on to Italy. Many princes, much intrigue. Someone would find him useful.

He worked on his aim until his good eye blurred with fatigue and his arms and shoulders twitched. Still a sure shot, almost as strong as before. But vulnerable on the left. He worked on spinning from a crouch, and strengthened his neck so he could turn sharp.

And then John Thoresby, Lord Chancellor of England and Archbishop of York, sent to Kenilworth for him. Thoresby was in London seeing to the King's business. Owen was to join him there.

Owen accepted the proffered cup and tasted the wine. He had not tasted better, even at the old Duke's table. The Lord Chancellor and Archbishop of York treated him nobly. Owen could not think what he might want.

John Thoresby leaned back in his chair. He sipped his wine with quiet pleasure. A fire crackled beside them in the hearth that warmed the private anteroom. Tapestries caught the firelight and lent the warmth of their vivid colors to the room.

With his one eye, Owen could not look at the tapestries without being obvious. It required turning the head this way and that, especially for those on the left. There was only one solution. Be obvious. Praise the man by praising his possessions. He turned his head, letting his one eye span the room. A boar hunt began to the left of the door and continued around the room, finishing with a feast in the great hall, where the beast's head was presented to the victor. The separate tapestries formed a complete set, designed for this room, for the fit was perfect. "The tapestries are exquisite. Norman work, I think. The close weave, the deep green. Norman for certain."

John Thoresby smiled. "Not all your time in Normandy was spent on the battlefield, I see."

"Nor yours in negotiations." Owen grinned. He must not seem cowed by the honor of sharing wine in the Lord Chancellor's chambers.

"You are a bold Welshman, Owen Archer. And adaptable. When the old Duke asked that I take you into my service, I thought his mind muddled with pain. He did not die with ease, as you may know."

Owen nodded. Lancaster had died in agony. Master Roglio said the old Duke's own flesh devoured itself from within so that he could at the end consume nothing but water, which exited his body as a bloody flux. Owen was moved that in the midst of his agony his lord had remembered him.

"He trained you to listen, observe, and retain." Thoresby watched Owen over the rim of his cup. "Is that correct?"

"Yes, my lord."

"So much trust might have overwhelmed an ordinary archer." Thoresby kept his eyes steady on Owen.

The Archbishop was easy in himself. Honesty would be Owen's best ploy. "I lost the sight in one eye, which I thought was death to me. My lord's trust lifted me up from despair. He gave me purpose when I thought I had none. I owed him my life."

"Owed him." Thoresby nodded. "And you owe me nothing. I merely consider honoring an old comrade's request."

"You might have ignored it, and only God would be the wiser."

Thoresby cocked an eyebrow. A grin danced on his lips. "The Archbishop of York would deceive a man on his deathbed?"

"If he judged that it were better for the soul in his care."

Thoresby put down his cup and leaned forward, hands on knees. The Archbishop's ring shone on his finger. The chain of Chancellor glittered in the firelight. "You make me smile, Owen Archer. You make me think I can trust you."

"As Archbishop or Lord Chancellor?"

"Both. The matter concerns York. And two knights of the realm, dead before their times, in St. Mary's Abbey. Do you know the abbey?"

Owen shook his head.

"Good. I want someone who can be objective. Make inquiries, note the facts, report them to me." The Archbishop poured himself more wine and gestured for Owen to do the same. "We serve ourselves. I wished to have no ears but ours this evening."

Owen poured himself more wine and sat back to hear the story.

"I must tell you that the new Duke of Lancaster is interested in you. You might do well with Gaunt. It would be a secure future—more so than with me. Mine are elected positions; he is the son of the King, and Duke of Lancaster for life. I tell you this because you might have cause to speak with him. The second knight in this matter was one of Gaunt's men."

Owen considered this wrinkle. Gaunt was dangerous, noted for his treachery. Owen could well imagine the sort of work Gaunt would give him. To serve him would be an honor, but it would not be honorable. Not to Owen. Surely God had not raised him up from the ashes for such work.

"I am flattered that two such powerful men offer me employment, and I thank you for giving me the opportunity to choose. But I prefer to serve the Archbishop and Lord Chancellor. I am better suited to your service."

Thoresby cocked his head to one side. "Not ambitious, I see.

You are a freak in the circles in which you dance at present. Beware."
His look was serious, almost concerned.

A shower of pain rushed across Owen's blind eye, hundreds of
needle pricks, hot and sharp. He'd taken to accepting these attacks as
warnings, someone walking on his grave. "I am a cautious man who
knows his place, my lord."

"I think you are, Owen Archer. Indeed." Thoresby rose, poked
the fire for a moment, returned to his seat.

Owen put down the wine. He wanted a clear head.

Thoresby, too, set aside his cup. "The puzzle begins thus. Sir
Geoffrey Montaigne, late of the Black Prince's retinue, makes a
pilgrimage to York to atone for some past sin. We do not know what
sin, for while in the service of the Prince, Montaigne's behavior was
beyond reproach. Something in his past, perhaps. Before joining the
Prince's army he fought under Sir Robert D'Arby of Freythorpe
Hadden, a short ride from York. Montaigne's choice of St. Mary's at
York for his pilgrimage suggests that his sin was linked to his time in
D'Arby's service. So. He arrives in York shortly before Christmas and
within a few weeks falls ill of camp fever—the ride north jarred open
an old wound, which weakened him, causing a recurrence of the fever
he'd suffered in France—all this according to the abbey Infirmarian,
Brother Wulfstan—and within three days Montaigne is dead."

Thoresby paused.

Owen saw nothing odd in the story. "Camp fever is often fatal."

"Indeed. I understand that after you were wounded you assisted
the camp doctor. You treated many cases of fever?"

"Many cases."

"Master Worthington praised your compassion."

"I'd had the fever myself but a year before. I knew what they
suffered."

The Archbishop nodded. "Montaigne's death would have gone
unremarked but for another death at the abbey within a month. Sir
Oswald Fitzwilliam of Lincoln, a familiar face at the abbey, making
retreats for sins that were only too easily guessed at by all who knew him.
Shortly after Twelfthnight he falls ill with a winter fever. It worsens. He

sweats profusely, complains of pain in his limbs, has fainting spells, fever visions, and within a few days he is dead. A similar death to Montaigne's."

"A similar death? But it does not sound like camp fever."

"Toward the end, Montaigne was much the same."

"The Infirmarian poisoned these men?"

"I think not. Too obvious." Thoresby took up his cup and drank.

"Forgive me, Your Grace, but how do you come into this?"

The Archbishop sighed. "Fitzwilliam was my ward until he came of age. An embarrassing failure for me. He grew to be a greedy, sly creature. I used all the weight of my offices to get him into Gaunt's service. I did not make friends in doing so. I assume my ward was poisoned. And though I do not pretend to mourn him, I should know his murderer."

"And Montaigne?"

"Ah. As far as I can determine, a God-fearing man with no enemies. Perhaps his death is unrelated." The Archbishop leaned back and closed his eyes. "But I think not. The deaths were too similar." He looked up at Owen. "Poisoned by mistake?" He shrugged. "Or was he merely better at burying his business than Fitzwilliam?" He smiled. "And here's an interesting item. Montaigne did not give his name at St. Mary's. He called himself a pilgrim. Humble and plain. Or sly?"

An interesting puzzle. Owen liked the prospect. "What inquiries have you made so far?"

"A few questions, enough to discover that Abbot Campian thinks they both died of natural causes. Hopes they did, is more like it. He fears we'll wrongly accuse his Infirmarian, Brother Wulfstan. And the Archdeacon of York assures me that if there had been a hint of trouble his Summoner would know of it. I hand it to you, Owen Archer. Disregard them. Begin at the beginning."

"In what guise shall I present myself in York?"

"I think that something as close to the truth as possible will suit the situation. Present yourself as a soldier who has lost his taste for killing and wishes to begin afresh. You are looking for honest work in the city, with a small behest from your late lord to support you in the meantime. My secretary, Jehannes, will doubtless come up with something before you arrive in York. You will of course have all the funds you need. You will go to Jehannes when you arrive, and whenever you have need of anything. The Archdeacon of York would normally arrange all this, but I would rather he not know about your purpose."

"You suspect him?"

Thoresby smiled. "I suspect everyone at this point."

"Everyone but Jehannes."

Thoresby nodded.

"And after I complete this task, what then?"

"We will see."

Owen left with mixed feelings. No need to take ship to Italy. He had an interesting puzzle to solve. But it was a mental challenge, not at all a physical one. Fishing for clues, catching people in lies. Not his best talents. It bothered him a little. What bothered him more was presenting himself as one who had lost his taste for killing. Did the Archbishop think that true? It was not. Given a just cause, he would kill again. He had not lost his nerve. Did the Archbishop think him a coward? His face grew hot.

But no. The Archbishop would not hire a coward. He must push that thought from his mind. Doubts would keep him from doing his best. And he must succeed. Success would secure his future in England. God still watched over him.

2

ENTERING THE MAZE

Owen headed back to Kenilworth the next morning. Gaunt had come to the castle for Christmas and would remain there with his retinue while the roads were too muddy for wagons top-heavy with household items. Owen hoped that of his old comrades-in-arms who had remained in Gaunt's service, someone would have known Fitzwilliam. He was not certain, for he had divorced himself from his old friends when he became a spy, wanting nothing to remind him of the old times.

He arrived late in the day, in time to find his friends resting from a day of training the young recruits. Bertold, who had succeeded him as Captain of Archers, greeted him warmly. With him were Lief, Gaspare, and Ned. The five had fought together in France. It was Bertold and Lief who had found Owen bleeding and delirious with pain near the corpses of the jongleur and his leman.

The four archers sat around a smoking brazier in Bertold's quarters, a small but private room that was one of the rewards for attaining the status of captain in Lancaster's company, enjoying another luxury, a small cask of ale.

"Being Captain's changed you not a whit." Owen tugged at Bertold's shaggy black hair, pulled back with a greasy leather thong, though it curled wildly about his scarred face wherever it could escape.

"No need to put on airs to train archers," Bertold said. "'Tis not the place for lordlings."

"True enough," Owen said.

Doe-eyed Ned lifted his tankard to salute Owen. "You'll never look a lordling with that patch."

"Aye. But the ladies like it."

Laughing, Gaspare made room on the bench beside him. He knew the weakness women had for the right scars. Tall, handsome, broad in the shoulders, he'd seduced many a young woman by asking her to kiss the scar that ran from his ear to his lips, where the knife had left a permanent crease, and then asking if they would like to see where the wound continued on his chest. "You can't be getting much of a chance to try out the ladies sitting at the higher tables. Those ladies are after rank."

"They wed rank. I said nothing about wedding."

They all laughed.

"So you're not hungering for the life of a soldier?" Gaspare asked.

The question was like a blow, but Owen chose to ignore it. "How are the new recruits?"

"Soft as always," Bertold growled.

Lief, a huge man from the north country, frowned at a reed he was hollowing out. Owen looked at Lief's large, thick fingers and was newly amazed at the delicacy with which the man used them. "They come along a bit slower than when you had the training of them. No Welsh fairy tales to inspire them." Lief kept his eyes on his work, but Owen could see the smile beneath the red beard.

Bertold handed Owen a tankard. "You're looking in need of this."

Owen accepted it with thirsty gratitude and drained it in one gulp. His friends cheered and slapped him on the back.

"So. You may talk fancy, but you still drink like one of us. Do you bring us good news?" Bertold asked in a more serious tone. "I'd welcome you to take back this thankless burden. I never asked to be Captain of Archers."

"Sorry, old friend. I'm to leave on a mission to the north country, and I'd a mind to see my old comrades before I started."

Lief blew into the reed, clearing out the dust, held it up to the firelight, squinted into it, then leaned close to Owen, lowering his voice. "So what's Gaunt's business up north, then? The Scots, is it?"

"It's not for him," Owen said. "For the Lord Chancellor and Archbishop of York."

"Thoresby?" Gaspare sounded surprised.

"Aye."

Bertold shook his head. "Churchmen are queer ones to ferret out. How come you to be working for him?"

"The old Duke recommended me to His Grace."

Ned studied him thoughtfully. "The eye's no better?"

Owen shook his head. "Nor is it likely to be."

"You could still be Captain of Archers," Bertold said quietly.

"I haven't changed my mind about that. Nor will I."

Bertold shrugged.

"I did also have news for any of his old mates about Sir Oswald Fitzwilliam. Do you know who they might be?"

Bertold frowned. "News about Fitzwilliam?"

"Aye."

"What's the bastard gotten into now?" Lief snarled.

"He's dead."

Ned leaned forward. "Oh, aye? And who do we thank for that?"

"I couldn't say. Camp fever. Bad case of it struck him down at St. Mary's Abbey in York."

"Pah." Lief spat into the rushes at his feet. "And when was he near a camp, I'd like to know?"

"He'd seen no action?"

Ned laughed. "Depends on what kind you mean. He'd had his fill of hand-to-hand from sticking his nose where it wasn't wanted."

"A spy?"

They all grew quiet.

"I take no offense. I had little time for spies when I was one of you."

Bertold slapped him on the knee. "You'll ever be one of us."

Owen held up his tankard. "Then pour me another."

They proceeded to get bleary-eyed while they talked.

"And so Fitzwilliam's dead, is he?" Ned said, coming back round to Owen's news.

"That's what I heard."

Lief spat again into the rushes. "And good riddance."

"You had trouble with him?"

"Trouble? Pah. Nothing he touched but didn't turn to trouble."

Ned kicked Lief's boot. "Still sore over fair Alice?"

"Hmpf. That whore. I'm better off without her. She would have knifed me in my sleep some night. The type."

Gaspare leaned over to Owen. "Was going to marry her, see. Till he smelled that whore's son in her bed."

Lief got to his feet with a roar, making as if to smash Gaspare's head with his fist. Bertold pushed him back down on the bench.

"Silly girl. She'd have been better off with Lief."

"Fitzwilliam married her?"

"Married?" Bertold grinned. "He's the ward of your new lord. But then you'd know that. Why would he be wanting to marry the likes of Alice, a kitchen maid?"

"Ah."

"I've known worse than him." Gaspare shrugged. "But how'd you come to know him, Captain? He came after you'd gone up the table."

"I heard of him at Thoresby's table. As you say, His Grace's ward."

"What was he doing at an abbey?" Lief asked.

"They say he'd gone on pilgrimage to York."

"Aye," said Gaspare. "He left before Christmastide. Before we left the Savoy."

"That long ago? He arrived in York much later."

Ned shook his head. "Only a fool such as he would travel north in winter."

"Aye," said Bertold. "The Duchess called Lord March mad for traveling that route to fetch his lady."

"Now there could lie a story," Ned said. "Fitzwilliam knew Lord March's lady well. He heads north to see her, the husband follows. Are you sure it was camp fever killed him?"

"'Tis the story I heard. But I know nothing of this lady. He was to see her on his way?"

Ned shrugged. "Who's to say? Lord March has a holding south of York. At Christmastide the Duchess named his lady, Jocelyn, to be part of her household. So he hied himself north to fetch her straightway, though the Duchess said 'twas a cruel thing to make her travel through the freezing mud, that she could come at Easter. But he'd have none of that, greedy bastard. The stipend doesn't begin until she's in residence, you see. He was loath to lose pay while she dallied up north until Eastertide."

Gaspare snorted. "Dally's the right word for what she's about, from what I hear."

Owen felt hopeful. If it proved so easy as this, that Fitzwilliam had gone north, stopped with this Lady Jocelyn, and been seriously wounded by her jealous lord, then his investigation might be concluded with no need to spend February on the road north. "So this Lady Jocelyn is now at Kenilworth?"

"Aye," Gaspare said. "You'll see her sitting high with the other ladies-in-waiting this evening. And Lord March holding forth nearby."

Lady Jocelyn stared off into the ether with a bored expression while a companion chattered on about the weather. Owen would have chosen the pleasant-faced companion over Fitzwilliam's mistress. Lady Jocelyn had a charming, childlike face, rounded and dimpled and dotted with a rosebud mouth, but her eyes were flinty. She regarded him as he approached, calculating his worth to her, Owen guessed. The tiny mouth smiled.

"My Lady Jocelyn." He bowed to her.

She put a hand to her bosom, her dress fashionably low, revealing much, and averted her eyes momentarily, but they returned to regard him with a predatory attention. "You are a guest of the Duke?"

"A retainer of the old Duke, here to collect my belongings. I am now in the household of the Lord Chancellor."

That lit a small spark in the eyes. A member of a powerful household. "Your name, sir?"

"Owen Archer, my lady."

"You sought a word with me?"

"I have a message for you from"—Owen looked at the companion, then back to Jocelyn—"an old acquaintance."

A faint flush. "I am afraid my duties consume my days, from tending to my lady's wardrobe to walking her lapdog in midmorning, out beyond the rose garden. That alone takes up most of the morning till the noon meal."

"Then it is that activity I must praise for putting such enchanting roses in your cheeks, though it keeps you so busy. Perhaps I will have the good fortune to see you on one of your walks. I often walk out to be alone with my thoughts." Owen bowed to her, then to her companion, "My ladies," and withdrew.

Bertold called to him as he moved to go out into the night. "Share a tankard with us."

Owen shook his head, knowing that they would get maudlin about the old days and drink until they could barely stumble back to their cots. He would wake on the morrow with the devil's hammer pounding in his head and a mouth as dry as the sands of Hell. He did not wish to meet with the Lady Jocelyn in such state.

"I can sit no more, my friend. I must walk off the journey so I can sleep lying still tonight."

"A word to a friend, then. Watch yourself with Lady Jocelyn. Lord March is ambitious. He will look the other way if his lady plays with the powerful, but not with a servant of the household, no matter how well you speak."

Bertold had tossed out the right bait. As Owen sat down with his friend, he sent up a silent prayer that he could glean what he needed from Bertold this night and get away before the past came pouring over him in a great wave of ale. Already his head ached from the earlier tankards.

"The lady's a bit round in the face and dull-witted for your tastes, I would ha' thought," said Bertold.

"And where is this Lord March I'm to be wary of?"

Bertold nodded his head toward the table to the left of the Duke's high table. "The bald one with the mouth."

Lord March was the focus of attention at the table, leaning

across it to yell, red-faced, at a smirking companion. He was a tall, lanky man in the latest fashion, sleeves so wide their ends were lost in the rushes at his feet, leggings so tight it was plain for all to see that his argument not only engrossed but aroused him.

"He looks a character."

"At the moment he's favored by the right people, so I for one would not cross him."

"Gaunt favors him?"

"He has a canny mind for contracts."

"I'll watch my step."

The morning sun was hot on Owen's face, though the air was sharp and a brisk wind got under his clothes to chill what the sun could not reach. The scar on his face burned and tugged in the cold, dry air, and the need to squint in the brightness made it worse. He'd a mind to return to the pallet he'd made up in Bertold's room and waste the day away in sleep, but he had his job, he must follow it through. As he passed along the beds of the kitchen garden, Owen sensed eyes on him, but the only person in sight was an old servant raking the path. Owen paused several times to break off a sprig and smell the familiar herbs. He favored spicy, tangy herbs. His mother had fed them a mash of rosemary and sage in winter to keep their blood hot. She'd prepared it in a wooden bowl that carried the scent of the mash year round.

A long time since he'd thought about that. Odd how the scent of a plant could make him feel as if he could reach out and touch his mother's face. Her smooth, soft skin. Her coarse, curly hair, like his, only silver and bronze. Ten years or more since he'd seen her. Her hair would be all silver now, or white. Her cheeks and eyes sunken. She would look old and weary. But he was quite sure she was still alive. He would know if she had died, if his mother's strong spirit had passed from this world. Wouldn't he? Best not to dwell on it.

The paths of the rose garden were wider than those of the

kitchen garden, and edged with river rocks. Here the Duchess would stroll with her maidens and sit on a sunny spring day. The paths twined among themselves and met at an urn that was empty now but for a few dry leaves that skittered in jagged circles within the bowl. In the beds, the brown twigs that would fill out and bloom in summer were heaped with straw. A smell of decay hung in the air. Depressing. He hurried through.

The holly hedge that bordered the rose garden was a welcome goal, its dark green leaves shining and bristling like men at arms awaiting battle. Or were the bright red berries spots of blood? Were they standing at attention at the end of the slaughter, hoping that their lord would notice their many wounds and give them leave to take ship home? Owen shook off the thought. What a gloom this winter garden lay over his soul. Or was it last night's ale?

As Owen passed under the holly arch, he again sensed eyes at his back. And again, spinning round, he saw nothing.

A long way ahead of him, on a pathway between pruned fruit trees, Lady Jocelyn led a dog so pampered that its belly cleaned the path beneath it as it waddled along. It was clear that the dog wished to maintain a much slower pace than the lady permitted, for she tugged at the jeweled leash every few steps. Lady Jocelyn was headed for the maze. Owen hurried, not wanting to lose her. He'd been in the maze only once, and that had convinced him that one walked in a maze only with someone who knew it well. His approach alerted the dog. It pricked up its ears and began to yap, digging its paws into the dirt of the path. Lady Jocelyn glanced back, gave a little wave when she saw Owen, and then inexplicably picked up the yapping dog and hurried into the maze.

Owen halted, perplexed. Had she for some reason changed her mind about granting an interview? Had he misunderstood? Had she misunderstood? His scar was pulling, and the chill made standing still unpleasant. Sleeping off the aftershocks of the ale seemed a better idea all the time. But should he give up so easily? Perhaps he would walk to the entrance of the maze and call her name. If she did not answer, he would turn round and indulge himself.

As he approached, the dog resumed its yapping, farther and farther into the maze. Lady Jocelyn was not waiting for him at the entrance. He almost turned back. What good was it to call to her? He would hardly be heard over the yapping dog. But he must question the lady sometime.

Owen stepped through the sentinel yews and came face to face with the angry eyes of Lord March. He looked much larger in his fur-lined cloak and draped fur hat.

"Are you following Lady March?" he demanded. His voice had a most impressive resonance.

"Following? It was not my purpose, Lord March, but seeing her tugging at the little beast, I thought I might lend a hand."

The face was getting closer. Owen did not like its color. Too red for reason. "You would follow a young woman into the privacy of the maze unchaperoned?"

Owen wanted to laugh. The dog would hardly allow for much dalliance. But he groped instead for a calming comment. It was at such times that he cursed himself for not pursuing his original plan, connecting himself to an Italian noble as a mercenary. That life would not have involved verbal duels. Perhaps humility was what Lord March desired. Owen made a little bow. "Forgive me. I see how it appeared to you. I did not mean to insult Lady Jocelyn's virtue in any way."

Lord March grew redder. His beady eyes were now so close to Owen's face that he could see the red trails of last night's brandywine. "You spoke with her at table last night."

Dear God, here it came. The truth just might get him out of this if it weren't about Lady Jocelyn's dead lover. Owen thought quickly. "Last night. Aye. To be honest, it was that I wanted to apologize for. You see, my mates dared me to seek a word with her, the lovely new lady-in-waiting. They fortified me with ale and sent me off with the lie that she was unmarried. She soon set me straight about that. This morning I feel a fool."

"So you thought to dally with my lady, did you?"

A fist met Owen's face. He couldn't believe it. Lord March had come out here for a brawl? His punch had grazed Owen's chin. Now he seemed to be aiming for his patch. Owen caught the arm that was raised to him and punched Lord March in the mouth. That set him back long enough to give Owen a chance to feel his jaw and reassure himself that any bruising would be hidden by his beard. He disliked the idea of traveling with signs of a recent brawl. One did not get good service at the inn with bruises and an eye patch. Lord March turned back for another go. Owen grabbed the man's arms and was embarrassed by how easily he held him still.

"I do not wish to continue this, my lord. I assure you that you have no cause to fight me. I have not injured your name in any way."

The beady eyes smoldered with resentment. What cursed luck. Owen had hoped to learn enough about Fitzwilliam in this company that he might satisfy Thoresby without journeying north. Now he would have to leave without much to go on, for surely he had sufficiently insulted Lord March with his superior strength that the man would make it his business to get Owen killed. Or at least seriously injured.

"You are Thoresby's man, I hear," Lord March said. "Get you back to London and away from my lady, or I'll have you torn limb from limb."

Owen gingerly let go the man's arms and backed up a few steps, bowed, and tried once more to explain. But it only evinced a howl of rage from the obviously mad Lord March.

Now what? If Owen turned and walked away, the ridiculous man might attack him with a weapon. Lord March did not seem rational enough to care whether he attacked from behind or not. But standing here was no good. And backing all the way to the rose garden seemed unwise.

Owen need not have concerned himself. Lord March decided the next step by lunging at Owen with a knife. Well aimed, too, for a vulnerable spot. His left shoulder.

"Damn you!" Owen cried, kicking the knife out of March's hand and punching him below the belt with all the fury that he felt for the lunatic bastard who'd reopened the wound he'd worked so hard to heal. As Lord March doubled over in pain, Owen drove another fist into the man's jaw. Lord March fell back and lay on the path, bleeding from the mouth. Most likely he'd bitten his tongue.

Owen tossed the knife into the yew hedge and strode angrily away, keeping a tight grip on his wounded shoulder to stem the bleeding.

3

THE ROGUE AND THE LADY

When Owen got to the weapons room, he struggled out of his cloak and his leather vest and was pleased to see that the wound was insignificant, worse in imagination than in fact. It would heal quickly. Gaspare came in while he was there and helped him clean and bandage it, then poured him a cup of brandywine. "For your pride."

"I gave much worse than I got, to be sure. The man was a fool to pick on me. He's a weakling."

"We warned you to stay away from the fair Jocelyn. The man is bedeviled by her. They say that Gaunt had his lady invited into the household to keep Lord March at his work. He was always taking off north to check on her."

"To be honest, she is not so delicious as to warrant such jealous devotion."

"Glad I am to hear you say that, Captain. I'd thought that the loss of one eye had robbed you of your senses in regard to the ladies."

Owen tossed the remainder of his brandywine in Gaspare's face.

Laughing, he headed for Bertold's chamber, where he got out the salve that kept his scar soft and cool and applied a generous portion, then lay down on the pallet. He must have dozed off, for he came to as his head was being gently lifted onto a silken lap.

Lady Jocelyn's rosebud mouth puckered in concern, then widened into a smile. The flinty eyes had softened considerably. "Captain Archer. I am so relieved to see that you are awake. Where did he wound you?"

Her dress was cut dangerously low, in the new fashion, and he could see her breasts heaving with her breath. She was excited. He suddenly saw it so clearly, the chemistry of the marriage. She set up intrigues, March rescued her, she kissed him and tucked him in bed, and then tiptoed off to the wounded bait. Good God in Heaven. Owen wished he were anywhere else in the world right now than here in Bertold's chamber, with no danger of Bertold returning, alone with this woman who would probably get nasty when she discovered that he did not want her. But it would all have been for naught if he did not ask her about Fitzwilliam.

"I am not seriously wounded, though I cannot vouch for your husband's mouth."

"He will have discomfort eating for a few days, but it will heal."

"I do not know why he took such offense, though it did not help that I could not tell him why I wished an audience with you."

"Yes. The old friend—"

"Sir Oswald Fitzwilliam."

"Ozzie?" She put a hand to her white chest. "You have heard from him?"

"More like I have heard *of* him, my lady. Fitzwilliam is dead." Her eyes widened. Owen sat up and took her hands. "Forgive me for the shock my news must inflict, but I could think of no gradual way to tell you."

"Ozzie." She shook her head. "But I saw him—Who killed him?"

Again, the assumption that Fitzwilliam was murdered, that one of his innumerable enemies had caught up with him. Owen began to despair of ever unraveling the mess of the man's life to discover the murderer. "You began to say you saw him. When did you last see him? At Christmas? Perhaps he visited you en route to York?"

She averted her eyes. "He was an old friend."

"A family friend? Perhaps Lord March had entrusted him with a message to you?"

"Yes. Of course. What did you think?"

"Then I could have saved myself a bruise and a wound by telling your husband about Fitzwilliam?"

She looked back at him, frightened. "Oh no. No, I am most grateful that you mentioned nothing. It's—" She brought a dimpled fist to her mouth. Her eyes glittered in the dusty daylight from the high window. "I am most grateful." She reached out to him.

"Lady Jocelyn, I would seek compensation in another way."

She withdrew her hands, as if he'd gotten too hot to touch, and looked at him quietly.

"I want information. Fitzwilliam came to see you at Christmas. What did he talk about? What was he doing penance for at St. Mary's Abbey?"

She said nothing.

"I know you were lovers."

She caught her breath and moved to stand up. He put his hands on her shoulders and made it clear that he meant to hold her there. Her bosom heaved. A part of him found it amusing that he had wasted such a perfect opportunity for an afternoon of pleasure. But mostly he was disgusted with the whole business and wanted to conclude it as quickly as possible.

"I mean you no harm, Lady Jocelyn. I merely want to know what Fitzwilliam was up to just before he died. Whom he might have been seeing in York. Tell me what you know and I will release you without mishap."

"And if I do not tell you?" A teasing tone. She still saw this as a game, a flirtation.

All life was a series of flirtations to her, he supposed. He disliked her kind of woman. Addle-brained. Silly. No good to anyone. "I would prefer not to threaten you, my fair Jocelyn."

He could see from her heightened color that he was right, that she found the situation exciting, that she would be disappointed when he sent her off without so much as a kiss. And he thought it unwise to disappoint this woman. So he leaned over and kissed the rosebud mouth lightly. "You are most lovely. But I do not mean to compromise you."

She dropped her head demurely. "Captain Archer."

"Fitzwilliam's raptures about you fell far short of the truth."

Her laughter surprised him. "Raptures. Fitzwilliam. You are a poor liar, though charming. Quite charming."

Not so silly. "I—"

"Obviously, Ozzie got himself murdered and you've been sent by his guardian, that carrion crow, to find out who dared to spill Thoresby blood, however tainted with common blood it might have been."

Owen felt quite stupid. The flinty eyes had warned him. "Right on all counts, my lady. I am left speechless by your keen wit."

"I'll tell you what I know on one condition."

"What is that?"

"You will leave here tomorrow without questioning any others."

"And how will you hold me to that pledge?"

"My husband will see that you are seriously injured."

"Ah. You will cry rape and he will turn his thugs on me."

"Precisely."

How could he have been so wrong about her? Silly, indeed. He wished now that were true. "Why are you so concerned?"

"I must have no scandal now that I am in the household of the Duchess of Lancaster. It is an honor to be here. It is everything to Jamie—Lord March."

"But you would cause a scandal with your threat."

"I would be the injured party, Captain Archer. It is a commonplace, a woman ravished by a soldier. No one would question it."

"The Lord Chancellor might."

"I'm certain that John Thoresby did not choose you for your virtue. Why should he doubt that you would take advantage of me when I came alone to your chamber to make sure someone had seen to your wounds?"

"That was a silly thing to do."

She shrugged. "People see me as a silly woman. I don't mind. It suits me. Affords me the element of surprise."

"Indeed. Well, I can think of nothing I have to gain by causing a scandal, so you are safe with me."

She smoothed her skirt. "I was with child. Jamie was furious. After waiting for two years, I got pregnant when it was most inconvenient. The Duchess would insist that I stay up north. My stipend would not begin until after my lying-in. Jamie went to Ozzie. Told him that it was probably his child. Ozzie came north and took me to a midwife who, for a fee, halted my future need for her services."

"Was it Fitzwilliam's child?"

"I am not certain."

"What did Lord March use to threaten him?"

Lady Jocelyn looked injured. "He had no need to threaten. Ozzie loved me. He would have done anything for me. He assumed it was his child, and if I did not wish to carry it, he was willing to help me rid myself of it. Safely."

"Lord March does not care for an heir?"

"There will be time for heirs. At the moment he wants to establish his standing with the new Duke."

"And you want to establish yours with the Duchess."

"Of course. They go hand in hand."

"Of course. This midwife. Where was she?"

"Just outside York, on the river. Magda Digby, the Riverwoman. A horrid creature. A smelly shack. But she was good to me. As you can see, I'm none the worse for the experience."

"And Fitzwilliam's pilgrimage to York?"

She wrinkled her nose. "He'd had an unfortunate dalliance with a kitchen maid here. The Duchess learned of it and sent him off to repent."

"What happened to the maid?"

"She will be married to one of the servants."

"Her name is Alice?"

"You know about her?"

"One of my—Bertold's archers was going to marry her before Fitzwilliam got between them."

"I shall mention it to the Duchess—after you have gone quietly. Is there anything more you wish to know?"

"Did he have any enemies in York?"

She gave a little laugh. "A man of Ozzie's spirit had enemies everywhere."

4

THE NORTH COUNTRY

The journey from Kenilworth to York was as unpleasant as a Channel crossing. Owen thought on the pilgrims dead at the abbey and found it easy to dismiss their deaths as the result of traveling to this godforsaken country in winter. By day, the damp north wind howled in his ears, battered his face, chilled him through his warmest clothes. By night, wolves added their hungry cries to the wind's demon voice. The journey would have gone more pleasantly as part of a company of soldiers. Or at least in the company of Bertold, Lief, Ned, and Gaspare. As often as that thought arose, Owen fought it. His soldiering days were over. He must forget that life.

Owen arrived in York weary, cold, and predisposed to hate the city. He entered from the south, through Micklegate Bar, across Ouse Bridge with its stench of fishmongers and public privy, through King's Square and up Petergate, making first for the minster to present himself to Thoresby's cleric. The city was a warren of narrow streets darkened by jutting second stories, stinking of night waste and garbage, much like London and Calais. He wondered how so many fools could be coerced into living in this crowded place, huddled up against the north wind that howled off the moors.

But the minster impressed him. It would be a great cathedral when finished. He stood back and gazed upward, imagining the spires that would crown the two square towers at the front. At least the Yorkshiremen knew how to give thanks to the Lord for seeing them through the long winter.

A dour-faced cleric led Owen to the Archbishop's chambers,

after attempts to direct him failed. Neither could understand the other's accent. As Owen entered the chambers, an odd character slithered past. Short, wiry, with olive skin and lank hair, sly, watery eyes, heavy-lidded. A fishy odor lingered after he'd slipped out the door. Not the sort one expected to find in the Archbishop's chambers.

It was a relief to find Jehannes, the Archbishop's clerk, a pleasant-faced young man with a quiet, watchful air. "His Grace will be pleased you've arrived safely. The Scots are a plague to the winter traveler up here."

"I met few fools out on the road but the thieves in the forest."

A little smile. "Your accent will worry the folk who think all who speak oddly are Scots brigands. I see why Canon Guthrum watched you so closely."

"His Grace forgot to warn me of that. I will try to smooth out my speech."

Jehannes placed two documents on the table. One bore the Archbishop's seal, the other a seal Owen did not recognize. The cleric pushed the latter toward Owen. "Master Roglio provides you with a letter of introduction to the Abbot of St. Mary's. The Infirmarian admires Roglio. This might loosen his tongue."

"So you know of my purpose here?"

A slight nod. "I do not envy you your task. You will not find it easy to wrest information out of Yorkshiremen. Even the city variety."

"And the other document?"

"An introduction to the Master of the Merchants' Guild, Camden Thorpe. I will send it tomorrow. There might be a position for you at Wilton's apothecary, off St. Helen's Square. Close to the minster and the abbey."

"A position?"

"Your disguise. The apothecary was taken ill at Christmastide. Confined to bed with a palsy. His Grace thought you might assist Mistress Wilton. Your experience with the camp doctor makes you credible in such a post."

Owen liked the prospect. "How will I know the Guildmaster's response?"

"I will send word to your lodgings."

Owen perked up. "Lodgings. Now that's a subject I've thought long on. A hot meal and a warm bed. Where might these lodgings be?"

Jehannes looked apologetic. "I'm afraid I am not certain. His Grace thinks it unwise to put you up here, even for the first night. You do not want to be associated with any authority, you see. I suggest you see Bess Merchet at the York Tavern. It's next to Wilton's apothecary. If she has no room to spare, trust her to find you some place where you'll be able to sleep without a weapon at hand."

"A friendly city, is it?"

"Not for strangers. And certainly not for someone with an odd speech."

"You do not make me eager to meet the folk of York."

"It does not help to be overconfident."

"I noticed a singular character exiting."

The cleric thought back to his last visitor. "Potter Digby, Archdeacon Anselm's Summoner."

The match tickled Owen. Summoner was the job of a weasel, and Potter Digby looked like nothing so much as that sly creature. "He looks like he was bred for the job."

Jehannes covered up a laugh with a cough. "I understand I am to provide you with any additional funds."

Hint taken, Owen completed his business without further attempts at gossip, but as he crossed to the door he paused. The name Digby. Could it be a coincidence? "How would I find the midwife they call the Riverwoman?" He would keep the name out of it for now.

Jehannes looked surprised. "What business could you have with her? Have you a woman in distress?"

Owen shook his head. "Fitzwilliam had business with her shortly before he arrived at St. Mary's."

"Ah." Jehannes nodded. "You'll find a footpath that leads down to the river on the far side of St. Mary's. I would go in daylight."

"Oh?"

"Slippery, down there by the river."

"The footing or the folk?"

Jehannes allowed himself a smile. "Both."

"So while I'm watching my step, how do I find this woman?"

"Her shack is out on a grassy rock in the mud flat. When the river rises, she has her own island."

"Does she have a name?"

"Magda Digby. The Summoner's mother."

"Interesting."

"They are an interesting family, yes."

As Owen stepped outside, a sound to his left made him pause, breath held. He turned, ready for an attack. With his good eye he glimpsed a man slipping around the corner of the building. A fishy smell lingered behind. Owen grinned. Seemed he'd kindled the weasel's curiosity.

The York Tavern provided a good living to Bess Merchet and her husband, Tom. The clientele had improved since Bess took over the running of the tavern eight years ago, when she came there as a wife. She beat out the vermin, human and otherwise, and scrubbed and repaired until the inn was clean and respectable. Right away Tom saw her worth and handed over the reins, and the tavern with its modest set of inn rooms flourished.

The stranger came as Bess stirred the last bit of seasoning into the stew she'd made for her neighbors.

Well now, she thought as he stood in the doorway deciding whether to enter, there's a story to him, and a good one, I'll wager. Tall, broad-shouldered, a soldier of some sort. Leather leggings and vest, good boots, a heavy cloak thrown back over one shoulder. He did not come begging, not this one, though the leather patch over the left eye and the scar running across the cheek might make it tough for him to go a-soldiering now. She liked his dark curls and gold earring. There was a bit of devil in him.

"So, stranger, will you be coming in or do you mean to let all the heat escape into the square?"

He laughed and closed the door behind him. "Would you be Goodwife Merchet?"

West Country speech. A handicap, but a strong will and a quick wit could rise above that.

"I am Bess Merchet, proprietress. What can I do for you?" She wiped her plump hands on her apron and adjusted her ribboned cap.

"I need a room. I was told at the minster to try here first. I'd find no better in York."

Bess cocked her head to one side. "Is your business with the minster?"

"My business is to find work before my money runs out. But not to fear, my good woman, I've a tidy sum tucked away, enough to pay for your best room. The Archbishop himself will vouch for that. It was he distributed my late lord's behests."

My good woman indeed. As if the ability to pay were all that mattered to an innkeeper. But the Archbishop. Well now. "What sort of work? You don't look like one trained to a trade or used to a plow."

"You would be right there. I was a soldier until I lost the use of this eye." He touched the patch. "So. Would you be having a room?"

"Not so fast. Bess Merchet makes her decisions in good time." He looked surprised. Used to obedient women. But that was his soldiering. He seemed a decent sort, all in all. "Who was your liege lord?"

"The late Duke of Lancaster."

"Ah. Ousted by Gaunt the upstart, eh?" A source of good stories. She liked that. Good for business in the tavern. "Tell me now, is the Duchess Blanche as beautiful as the ballads say?"

"Oh, aye. And you'd be hard put to find a gentler, more courteous lady in all King Edward's realm."

"So why doesn't the Archbishop find you work?"

He gave her his most dazzling smile. "I promise you I can pay my way."

So he thought he'd turn her head with a smile? Lovely it was, but she was no more fool than he. "You don't want to answer that question?"

He let the smile fade. "I have been the puppet of great men long enough. I envy folk like you who can plan ahead, know what's coming."

Bess sniffed. As if folk had control over their lives.

"As far as anyone can," he added.

More sensitive than she'd guessed. A good sign. "So what kind of work can you do?"

"I'm strong and good with plants. It would suit me to be a gardener. And I know a bit about medicines. I assisted the camp doctor after my injury."

Bess stiffened. She was not one to believe in coincidence. It was no accident brought this Welshman to her door, the very man her neighbors needed. Who had put him on to Lucie's trouble?

"You sound the sort of helper an apothecary would find useful."

"I thought I would talk with some of the guildmasters."

"You've not talked with someone already?"

"I thought it best to find lodgings first."

A cautious man. "What is your name, Welshman?"

His eye widened, surprised. A grin slowly spread across his face. A sincere grin. "You've a good ear."

"Your speech is no challenge."

"I've been warned the folk here might mistake me for a Scot."

"Not Bess Merchet."

Owen pulled the glove off his right hand and extended his hand in friendship. "Owen Archer's the name."

Bess shook his hand. Warm, dry, no fear in the hand he proffered. And a strong grip. Well, an archer. He would be strong.

"Now about that room?"

Bess took a deep breath. Common sense told her this man could be trouble, but the handshake won her. And he did look travel-weary. She nodded, decided. "I've got a room." She led him up the stairs.

Two pallets, a window, and space to walk—a comfortable room. Even a chest in which to store his pack, and some hooks on which to hang wet outer clothes. Bess stood back to let him take a look.

The dark eye swept the room, then paused at the doorway.

"Across the hall. That's a private room?"

That fool Kit must have left the door open when she finished cleaning. "It is. But it's not available."

"I'll pay better than your usual price for it."

There he went with the money again. Bess shook her head. "That would not make up for the loss of business. I save it for a regular customer. Otherwise only for short stays in between. What would I do with you when he returns on Monday next?"

"I'll pay double for this room to keep it private."

Bess frowned. She didn't like folk who threw away their money. Besides, it wasn't right to waste a bed.

"A private room is a rare commodity, Owen Archer. How came you to be so keen on it?"

He said nothing.

She read discomfort in his face. It intrigued her.

"You aren't looking for a place to hide?"

"No."

She waited, hands on hips. A cart rattled by in the street below. A cat padded down the hallway.

Owen grinned. "You would make a good interrogator."

Bess waited.

"It's simple. It's the eye and my years of training as a soldier. Someone sneaks up on my left." He spun round. Bess pressed back against the wall. He thrust with an imaginary sword.

"Merciful Mother." Bess crossed herself.

He retreated, sheathed the invisible sword. "I do not trust myself if I'm awakened suddenly."

"I'll have no trouble here," she warned.

"I will not wittingly cause you trouble." His voice was level. He looked straight at her with the good eye.

Bess smoothed her apron, patted her ribboned cap, suppressed a smile. Oh, to be ten years younger and of a slightly better class. "There is a small room, upstairs in the back. I keep it for family visits. It's plain. But it has a window that looks out on the Wiltons' garden."

The apothecary's garden. Perfect. "I should not put your family out."

Bess heard courtesy rather than honesty in Owen's voice. He wanted the room, her family be damned. It rang true. The thought of the extra revenue pleased her. Her husband, Tom, needed a new pair of boots and she had to purchase a donkey for the cart—Flick was getting long in the tooth.

"Don't worry yourself about my children. Their visits are few and far between. And they grew up in a farmhouse—my second husband, Peter, God rest his soul, farmed near Scarborough. They're used to making do. Let me show you the room."

She apologized for the creaky ladder up to the third floor. She and Tom didn't mind it, but the archer might be used to better.

"I grew up sharing the floor with goats," he assured her.

"Well, you'll not have to do that here." She pushed open the low door. He bent over to step in, straightened up inside, stretched his arms overhead. His fingers just brushed the ceiling. He walked over to the window, pushed it open, leaned out, turned with a smile.

"This will suit me, Goodwife Merchet."

She liked the curl his accent made in her name. She quoted a rate just slightly more than for the double room below.

"More than fair. I'll give you a fortnight's fee today."

Bess ran down the list of house rules and left him to settle himself. She must get that stew over to Lucie. She resolved not to tell Lucie about Owen just yet. Wait to see if the handshake proved reliable.

Exhausted, Lucie Wilton nodded off as she sat in the corner of the bedchamber, her head coming to rest on the shop accounts. The room was tiny and close, and Lucie had not slept well since her husband fell ill. Even now, her nap was interrupted by Nicholas's muttering. But it was good he woke her. She had not meant to sleep. She had closed the shop for the midday meal and a chance to go over the accounts. Things tallied well. They had lost no customers to Nicholas's illness. In fact, the books reflected business as usual.

Even the inventory. Nicholas always kept meticulous records of the medicines they dispensed, so that he might improve the efficiency of the garden. He still had to trade for some roots and barks, and buy some of the minerals and gemstones—ground pearl and emerald were popular with some of their wealthier clients—but they got most of the herbs they used from their own garden.

Lucie had taken pains to spread out the fatal dose of aconite in the records, a pinch in this physick, a pinch in that, over a week's time. The books would arouse no suspicion.

But she worried how long she could keep up her pace. She rubbed the back of her neck, sat up slowly, every muscle aching. It was too much, the shop, the household, the garden. She had asked the Guildmaster for an apprentice. Being an apprentice herself, she knew it was unlikely he would agree. He'd been much too courteous to say that to her face, but she knew how it worked. What was sincere was his praise for her work. Not one customer had been turned away since Nicholas took to his bed.

But Lucie paid for it with a weariness that she could not long ignore. Bess, bless her heart, was only too happy to mother her. She already took care of most of the meals. And she'd taken an armload of mending this morning. No doubt she would clean the house if given a chance. Lucie had given up the fight with dust—a fine layer lay over everything in the house, upstairs and down. But not the shop. That was pristine. She neglected nothing about the shop. Nicholas was proud of her. She was proud of herself. It was one thing to be an apprentice, quite another to be in charge. She enjoyed it, reveled in it, but also feared it. Every minute of every day, with every grain she measured out, she was aware of the trust the people of York placed in her. She held the power of life and death. One slip, one mismeasure could kill. She double- and triple-checked everything, focusing her attention completely on the task at hand.

But she could not keep up such diligence without more sleep. She must sleep. She must have help. If not an apprentice, at least a serving girl.

"Lucie. Are you sleeping at the table?"

She jerked alert and winced as pain radiated from head to neck to arm. But it was good to have Nicholas alert, speaking, knowing her again. His speech was slurred, as if his mouth did not work quite right yet, but understandable. And when the pale eyes lit on her, they saw her, not some phantom, as they had on those first horrible nights.

He had asked if the pilgrim was up and about yet. She had told him that even his physick could not save the man. Nicholas crossed himself and bowed his head. Lucie prayed she never had to tell him the complete truth.

5

THE APOTHECARY ROSE

Up in his room, Owen sat down on the stool beneath the window and ripped off his patch to massage the scar tissue around the eye. He rubbed hard. The skin was tight from the cold ride north, and needle-pricks of pain shot through the eye itself from time to time. Five days he'd traveled, through freezing rain and snow. Only fools traveled north in mid-February. He searched through his pack for the salve that eased the tightness. He had only enough for one day. A natural purpose for visiting the apothecary.

He bided his time, shaking out his extra shirt and leggings, easing his feet out of his boots for a bit. They stank. He stank. He must ask about the public baths.

When he saw no one at any windows opposite, nor down below, he leaned out the window and studied the apothecary's garden. Tidy, laid out in an unusual fashion. More variety than in most such. It looked like a monastery garden. Behind a holly hedge, what must be a potting shed. He could just see the back of the house. A door that led into the garden, one window below, two above. A modest but comfortable house.

Down below, Bess Merchet bellowed an order. Owen grinned. She could be useful to him. And he liked her. Sharp-witted, bold, comely for the mother of grown children—bright red hair, a round but compact body—and a nice sense of humor. Little could get past her. She must know all the gossip worth knowing.

He put on his boots and patch and went downstairs with his salve pot and money pouch.

"You'll be hungry," was Bess's greeting. She motioned to him to sit down at a trestle table. "Kit! A trencher and stew. And some of the new ale."

A man came through the back door, carrying a bucket. He nodded to Owen. "Tom Merchet." Younger than Bess by a few years, burly, with friendly eyes. "You'll be Master Archer."

"Aye. Call me Owen, if you will. I trust I'll be with you awhile."

Tom put down the bucket and went over to fill a tankard with ale. Setting it down in front of Owen, he stood back, arms folded. "Go on. Taste ale. See if it's not better than any in London."

Owen took a good long drink, then set the tankard down with a hearty thud. He nodded, smiled. "I'd heard tales of York Tavern ale, but none did it justice." He meant it.

Tom nodded and went out.

A young woman brought the food. Bess followed close behind. "Go on now, Kit, have your meal in the back." The girl scuttled out.

Owen ate the stew with relish. All the while Bess hovered nearby, moving benches, fussing with cobwebs. He finished, downed the rest of the ale, and pushed the bench away from the table.

"You've made a fast friend, praising his ale so high," Bess said.

"I like to give praise where it's due. I've never had better inn fare. The stew was fit for a lord's table. Archers, even captains of archers, do not often partake of such fare."

"The herbs and some of the vegetables are from the Wilton garden. Nicholas has always been generous with me."

"He's the apothecary?"

"Aye. Round the corner on Davygate."

"A good apothecary?"

Bess sniffed. "The best in the North Country."

Owen noted the qualifier. Not the kingdom, but the North Country. Not an exaggerator. She did not claim there were none better even in London.

"I need a salve for the eye."

A mischievous grin lit Bess's face. "They'll fix you up."

"Why do you smile?"

Bess shrugged. "'Tis nothing. I think of a dozen things at once."

The sly gleam in her eye made Owen uneasy. He had to be careful. "Now let me give you the fortnight's rent before I explore the city."

Bess tucked the money in her apron pocket and smiled to herself. It would not be a bad thing for Lucie to encounter a charming rogue. Have an adventure while her aging, ailing husband was abed. It would warm Lucie's blood, fortify her for the times ahead. Bess knew that Lucie Wilton would catch Owen Archer's eye. She was fair, straight-backed, slender, with clear blue eyes and an engaging smile—a smile seen too seldom these days.

Owen reminded Bess of her first husband, Will, a clerk in Scarborough with an eye for the girls. Bess had snared Will with her coppery curls and bold tongue. It was Will had taught her to read and write. Bright Will. Handsome Will.

Bess knew what it was like to nurse a dying husband and fear for the future. She had buried two husbands, both beloved. The fathers of her children. Poor Lucie did not even have the comfort of children.

Owen Archer might be just the man to lift Lucie's spirits.

But the timing of his arrival disturbed Bess. He suited the Wiltons' needs too well.

Owen did not mean to chat with the apothecary, merely to meet him and get a sense of the man. The door of the apothecary was ajar.

A woman stood behind the counter, measuring powder into a pouch for a customer who paced back and forth, complaining about the weather. The customer was well dressed, though his speech had the rough edges of the North Country. Most likely a merchant. He did not seem at all put out about being helped by a young woman whom Owen assumed to be the apothecary's daughter.

The woman glanced up at Owen. Looked again, with a hint of uneasiness. He was sorry for that, for she was a comely young woman, fine-featured and with clear eyes. But he could imagine what she saw. A scarred stranger in road-dusted leather. Trouble. And perhaps she was right. He waited until the merchant had departed, then approached the counter. She studied him evenly, her eyes pausing on the scar that spread out from beneath the patch across his cheekbone.

"Is the Master about?"

She bristled. "Not at the moment. What can I do for you?"

Stupid. He knew the Master was bedridden. And the question had gotten him off to a bad start with her. "Do you have a salve of boneset and comfrey? My scar tightens and draws with the winter wind."

She reached over the counter and touched his cheek.

He grinned, delighted. "You have a gentle touch."

She withdrew her hand as if he'd burned her. "It is obviously difficult for you, but you must think of me as an apothecary." Her eyes smoldered, her voice chilled.

Cheeky daughter, to call herself an apothecary. "Forgive me. I found your touch disconcerting."

"Sweet words—"

"I did ask your forgiveness."

She nodded. "Honey and calendula. They are the best softeners. Ask any court lady."

"Softening. Aye. That's what it's needing. But something also to soothe the fire that returns now and again. To the scar, that is." He grinned.

She did not. Her blue eyes had a granite glint to them.

He withdrew the grin, coughed. "Sorry again."

"I can add something to cool the skin." She cocked her head to one side, still with the even gaze. "Your speech has an odd music. You are not from the North Country."

"Wales is my mother country. And the scar was got in the King's service."

"A soldier?"

He could see that displeased her. He was not doing at all well.

"No more. I've seen the error of my ways." He beamed his most disarming smile.

"You are fortunate." Spoken without a hint of being charmed.

"It is my excuse for being clumsy with women." York women in particular.

She smiled—politely—and stepped away to mix the salve. Owen watched her, noting how fluid were her movements, how graceful and sure. Her hair was tucked up in a clean white kerchief, baring a long, slender neck. He wished he had two eyes to feast on her.

She bristled as she turned back to him. "Have I grown horns?"

He reddened, realizing how he'd stared. But surely she recognized adoration. He refused to apologize. He'd done nothing to offend her. But he did change the subject. "I noticed the garden gate." He gestured toward the door. "Do you keep bees?"

"Bees?"

"For the honey in the salve."

"No. No hives. I would like to, but I've no time to tend them with my husband ill. We get our honey from the abbey. St. Mary's. You are a gardener?"

Her husband? Surely this was not Mistress Wilton. "I was a gardener in another lifetime."

She looked puzzled. What clear blue eyes she had. How they bored into his soul.

"When I was a boy in Wales."

"Ah. You are a long way from home."

"A long way indeed." He loved those eyes.

She cleared her throat and nodded toward the pot he clutched. "Oh. Aye." He handed it to her.

With a flattened spoon she measured out the salve. Exactly one measure.

"You've a practiced eye."

"Five years as my husband's apprentice," she said with quiet pride.

There it was again. "Then you must be Mistress Wilton." She nodded. How disappointing. Married, and to the man he hoped would employ him. He offered his hand. "Owen Archer. I am staying at the York, so we'll be neighbors for a while."

She hesitated, then shook his hand. A firm, warm shake. "We're pleased to have your trade, Master Archer. The Merchets will take good care of you."

"You said your husband is ill?"

Her face closed up. She handed him his salve. "Be sparing of this. It is a strong medicine."

He regretted the question. "I will be careful."

The shop bell jingled. As the fair Mistress Wilton looked beyond him to the doorway, the color drained from her face.

Owen turned to see what wretch disturbed her. The Summoner, Potter Digby. Owen had acquired a second shadow.

Mistress Wilton did not move. Owen picked up the salve pot. "I've been using what I had twice daily. Is that appropriate for the new mixture?"

The blue eyes moved, focused on him. Color returned to the cheeks. "Twice daily? It must bother you very much. How long since you were wounded?"

"Three years."

The Summoner stepped up to the counter on Owen's left side. His blind side. Sneaking wretch. Owen controlled himself. With a slow, casual air he rested his right elbow on the counter and turned to look at Digby.

The Summoner nodded at Owen, then said to Mistress Wilton, "I inquire after the health of Master Wilton. God grant he is better?"

"He improves with each day, Master Summoner. Thank you for your good wishes."

Owen noted that as much as he had irritated her, she had not sounded nearly so cold as this. He hoped she never used such a tone with him.

Digby seemed oblivious. "I remember Master Wilton in my prayers."

"We are most grateful."

No, they weren't. At least she wasn't, that was plain.

"God be with you." The Summoner bowed slightly and slithered out the door.

A riddle. A visit from the Summoner would be welcomed by few, but Mistress Wilton's reaction was beyond distaste. It seemed she and the Summoner had old business. Owen tucked the incident away to digest later.

Mistress Wilton held on to the countertop, her knuckles white. She closed her eyes. Opened them. Seemed surprised to see Owen still there. He hated himself for bringing that shadow with him into the shop.

"An unpleasant character," Owen said.

"They say he is good at his job."

"Why should a Summoner smell of fish?"

"It's his mother. She lives on the river."

"Oh, aye. A midwife, I think."

Mistress Wilton tensed. "Why would a stranger know about her?"

Damn his tongue. "I encountered the Summoner earlier. I was told he was the son of the Riverwoman."

Mistress Wilton nodded.

"But the fishy smell. Surely he does not live with her? As Summoner he would live close to the minster?"

"Yes, he lives in the city. But, being unwed, he has his mother see to his clothes." Mistress Wilton glanced at the beaded curtain in the doorway behind her. "I must check on Master Wilton."

"Of course. Thank you for the salve, Mistress Wilton." Owen put six pennies on the counter. "Will this cover it?"

"That would pay for six such pots, Master Archer. Two pennies will suffice."

He put out the appropriate change. "I hope your husband truly does improve with each day."

She smiled a wan smile. There was a sadness about Mistress Wilton that he found intriguing.

Outside, Owen paused at the gate that led around back to the garden. If all went well, he would be spending his days near the fair Mistress Wilton. He would exercise all his charm on the Guildmaster to make that so.

Owen returned to the inn to ask directions to the public baths. He expected to need a bath more than ever after his visit with Magda Digby.

• • •

Alone again in the shop, Lucie fought against trembling hands and fears that threatened to distract her from her work. A life was in her hands. Alice Baker's sleeping draught must not be too strong. Lucie must stay clear-headed. But why had the Summoner come? Did he know something? The Summoner could destroy them. Would Archdeacon Anselm allow that? Surely he loved Nicholas too much for that. And Potter Digby was too much a toady to antagonize the Archdeacon. At least she prayed that he was. How wretched to be grateful about the Archdeacon's unnatural love for her husband.

Enough of this. Brother Wulfstan had nothing to gain by telling anyone but her. The Summoner could not know. Nor could the Archdeacon. She forced her thoughts away from her troubles and finished the draught, labeled it. As she put it aside, her hand brushed the honey pot, still down on the counter from mixing the stranger's salve. Reaching to set the pot back on the shelf, Lucie remembered how her skin had tingled as she'd taken it down, feeling his dark eye on her. She had felt the heat of his gaze right through the tightly woven wool of her dress. She had never felt so aware of her own flesh. Thank God he'd kept the other eye covered.

Lucie blushed at her thoughts. Blessed Mary and all the saints, she was a married woman. And this Owen Archer had insulted her. He'd treated her as if she were a silly girl. As if she didn't belong behind the counter. Nicholas had never treated her that way.

Jehannes was right about the mud. While Owen planned his strategy, he watched several people slip and slide down the bank beyond St. Mary's water tower. Then he was rewarded for his wait. A woman with a babe in arms managed the descent without mishap, walking on a path that was not immediately apparent. It zigzagged down the slope among rocks and scrubby bushes a bit away from the tower. Took longer than the other, slippery path, but Owen was not as surefooted as he'd once been. He did not relish tumbling down the slope. So he marked the woman's route and followed it as faithfully as possible. It was slow going with the one eye. He had to sweep his good eye back and forth along the path before him. But at last he stepped down onto the riverbank. Down there the mud had frozen into ridges in places, was soggy in others. Owen understood why people walked past him with their heads down, keeping their eyes on their footing. It was cold enough without a dip in the mud. Owen felt the damp down here by the river through all his leather clothes and his new boots. Surely no one would ever choose to live down here.

He looked round for the house on the rise in the mud. What he saw were rickety compositions of driftwood, mud, and twigs. Close to the abbey walls the hovels crowded together, then thinned upriver. Then he saw it, an odd structure, its roof a boat turned upside down so that a carved sea serpent on the prow peered down at a strange angle. By the door sat a woman swathed in rags of many colors, all mud-bedimmed, whittling at what looked like a mandrake root. This must be the Riverwoman.

Owen had come up with a reason to speak with her on his walk down here, but seeing her with the knife in her hand gave him second thoughts. He considered retracing his steps and returning another day, when he'd prepared a better introduction. But it was too late, she had glanced up and now fixed a keen eye on him.

"Goodwife Digby?" Owen asked, removing his cap.

"Goodwife." She nodded and laughed, a queer, barking sound. Her lungs were probably affected by the river damp. "Naught call me that but want favors. Hast thou a favor to beg, Bird-eye?"

Owen was momentarily taken aback by her blunt reference to his affliction. But why should he expect courtesy in such a place? "Aye, so I do come seeking a favor."

"Lost thine eye in the wars, eh?"

She'd played right into his hands. "Not lost. There's still an eye beneath this patch."

"And thou wouldst know whether Magda can make thee see again?" He nodded.

She rose with some huffing and muttering, stuck the knife in a pouch tied around her middle, and motioned him inside with the hand that still held the root. A welcome, though smoky, fire greeted him. He had to stoop to avoid the roots and plants hanging from the rafters.

"You can dry these down here by the river?"

"The fire keeps it dry. Good for roots, good for bones. It will cost thee for Magda to look at the eye, even if she can do nothing."

He put a silver coin on a table by the fire. "That's for looking. I'll pay in gold for healing."

She looked him up and down. "Thou art well set up. Good clothes, plenty coin. Why come to Magda's sort?"

"A lady friend recommended you. You helped her."

Magda shrugged. "A midwife. Has naught to do with eyes."

"Then I have wasted your time."

"Nay." She motioned him over to the fire. "Let Magda see."

He sat down so his head might be level with hers, lifted the patch, and leaned back.

She bent over him, smelling richly of river and earth. Her hands were grimy. But her touch was gentle. She examined the eye, then stood back with a sigh. "The light's gone from it, though very near wasn't. Thou hast done well to keep the scar from drawing too much. Thou hast done all that can be done."

Her words brought him down so hard Owen realized he had begun to believe his story, that he had come with hope that she might help him regain his sight. What a fool he was. Why would this grimy, smelly hag know more than Master Roglio?

She sniffed. "Thou art angry. 'Tis always the way. And now thou wilt feel Magda is a little to blame for thy blinding. Aye. 'Tis always the way." She snatched up the silver piece.

"You did not ask my name. Or the name of the woman who told me of you."

"'Tis better not to know the names."

"She found you through a friend of mine."

The hag squinted at him in the smoky room. "It's information he seeks, not healing. Magda hears the truth in the voice. Soft, nice voice. Charming Welsh rogue. Arthur's kin, no doubt thou thinkst." She laughed. "Get thee gone, Bird-eye. Magda does not need thy kind."

"I did come for the eye. I have lost my captaincy because of it."

She looked him up and down again, felt his shoulders. "Strong Welshman. Thou art an archer, yes?"

"Was."

"Captain of Archers. Thou'st climbed far. Go back to pulling at the bow, Captain Archer. 'Tis only thy pride keeps thee away. Not as quick and sure as thou mightst have been. Now leave. Magda has charms to carve for folk in need of her."

While Bess waited at the baker's ovens for the night's bread, she considered Owen Archer. He was a man with a mission, no doubt about it. He had that quiet, still look to him, like a cat standing at the edge of a strange garden, sniffing out the danger, sizing up the competition, eye gliding this way and that, nice and easy, don't want to scare the prey. He might be one-eyed, but she doubted much got past him.

So what was his real business in York? He meant to be here long enough that he needed the cover of employment. He'd been a soldier, an archer, a knave with that earring and his good looks, she'd wager. He was Welsh. He knew something of gardens and medicinal plants. And he could read. That was the odd piece of information stuck on the rest. That and his clothes. New clothes, costlier than an out-of-work soldier could afford. But the scar wasn't new. Two years, maybe three years he'd had it. So what had he done since he quit soldiering? Learned to read? Assisted a surgeon? And what in that could bring him here?

He was connected to the Archbishop somehow.

Soldier. Minster. Bess let those two pieces tumble about in her head while she fussed with the loaves. Kit could not be trusted with more than one light basket, she was too busy gawking to watch her step, so Bess had to carry two fully loaded ones. Between the weight of the baskets and Kit's pokiness, it was dusk before they got back to the inn, and Tom was aflutter, setting up for the evening.

"Who's been in while I was gone?" she asked Tom over a cup of ale. It was their custom to fortify themselves for the busy hours ahead.

"Summoner Digby, asking about Owen Archer. Told him he should speak with gentleman himself. Master Archer would be down here for ale sometime, he could be sure."

Bess wished she'd been here. "What did Digby say?"

Tom shrugged. "Just wanted to know if we'd taken in a one-eyed stranger. I asked why he wanted to know. If it was Summoner business. He said maybe, he weren't at liberty to say. Pah." Tom spat into the fire. "Putting on airs. Man stinks of fish. Where's he sleep, I ask you?"

Bess closed her eyes, feeling the heat of the ale and the hearth fire after her afternoon out in the chill. So Owen might have business with Archdeacon Anselm. Most of the Archdeacon's time was spent collecting money to complete the minster.

"And that's all?"

"Aye, he left directly."

"Anyone else?"

"Owen Archer himself came in and left again. Asked about baths. Road dirt. Told him he'd get fever, taking unnecessary baths. Now Digby, he could use one."

"Did he go off to the baths, then?" Bess asked, impatient to know all of it.

"I gave directions. He went out." Tom put down his cup and leaned close to Bess. "Here now, wife. What you be thinking about this Owen Archer?"

Bess checked that they were alone. "I think he's looking for someone or something. Something to do with the minster, I suspect. Maybe some soldier's money didn't make it to the minster coffers?" She shrugged. "I don't know."

Tom grinned. "I know my Bess. You'll have it all figured soon enough."

6

SUMMONING

Archdeacon Anselm smiled at Jehannes to mask his distaste. The young man did not know his place. He was but the Archbishop's secretary, while Anselm was the Archdeacon of York. But Jehannes had a way of making it clear—oh, quite politely, Anselm could not quote a single discourteous word—of making him feel unimportant, an intruder in the day of a busy, important man.

"You had a visit from a one-eyed stranger," Anselm began.

Jehannes put aside the letter he'd been studying and folded his hands, giving Anselm his full attention. "I see your Summoner noted him in passing."

Arrogant boy. The hint of sarcasm in his voice. The smug set to his full, indelicate lips. "The stranger's clothes were those of a minor courtier. An emissary from my Lord Thoresby? Is he to visit York soon?"

Jehannes did not move a muscle. His eyes rested on Anselm with insolent calm and unfriendliness. "You have pressing business with His Grace?"

As if the Archdeacon were to be screened—Anselm controlled himself. "The Hatfield window. He was to discuss the details with the King." There. He was involved in financing York's tribute of sympathy to the King on the death of his young son, William of Hatfield. And the King was to choose the subject of the stained glass.

Jehannes reached for a sheet of parchment and his pen. "I will be happy to write a letter—"

Anselm caught his breath. "I am capable of penning my own," he said with his teeth clenched.

75

Jehannes nodded. "Indeed." He put down the pen. "Well, then, to answer your question, I've no word of an impending visit from His Grace."

Damn the man. He meant to force Anselm to ask the identity of the stranger. Anselm did not have to stoop to that. He had his own means.

Clean and well fed, Owen might be content to sit in the corner with a tankard of Tom's ale, listening to the idle talk around him. But the camaraderie put him in mind of better times, evenings spent with his men, comparing injuries, teasing new recruits, bragging about their prowess in arms and bed. His upper back, hands, and forearms would be stiff from the bow and trembling with fatigue as he lifted his tankard, but his soul would be at peace after a day of hard work. Bone-weary, calm, at ease with his companions. That was contentment.

Not this. Owen sat tensed, ready for trouble to creep up on his blind side, nervous with energy unspent, irritated by random stabs of sharp, hot pain in his left eye. No one knew him here. He was no longer Captain of Archers, admired by many, challenged by none. No one cared that for him it was as easy to lift a man off his feet as it was to scoop up the cat in the corner. It mattered not a whit if he drank himself under the table.

He hated this life. He was no good at it. He'd blundered with the hag today. She knew now that he had come to York fishing for information. He'd almost made it worse. He had almost mentioned Fitzwilliam. It was thanks to her he had not. He could not afford such mistakes.

The door opened and voices hushed, folk shifted on the wood benches as Summoner Digby entered the tavern. Dear God, what must it do to a man's soul to be so greeted? Owen almost pitied Digby. At least it pulled him out of his own self-pity. Owen straightened up. He could not get drunk tonight. He had work to do.

The Summoner noticed him. Owen nodded, unsmiling. He

knew the Summoner had quizzed Tom about him. It was unlikely
Digby had yet spoken with his mother. He would not know yet that
Owen had been to see her. Digby called his order to Merchet, then
came over to Owen's corner. Along the way, no one called to him,
invited him to join them.

"Our paths cross for the third time today," the Summoner said.

"The fourth time. Though perhaps you did not see me as I left
the minster. You were in the shadows."

The Summoner's expression did not change. He extended his
hand. "Potter Digby."

Owen sat back against the wall, arms crossed. "Aye, I know. Anselm's
Summoner." He did not take the extended hand. "Owen Archer."

Digby sat down opposite Owen, taking no offense at the
rebuke. Thick-skinned.

"I don't take to strangers who approach me on my blind side."

Digby shrugged. "In my trade we develop unpleasant habits. It's
best to unnerve the sinner. Drive him to confess." Digby grinned.
An odd grin, limited to his mouth.

"You must do quite well for yourself."

Digby's grin spread to his eyes. "I do. And for the minster coffers."

The candor interested Owen. Digby was not the abject toady
he'd expected.

Tom arrived with Digby's ale. "Aye, now. Told you he'd be
here." He leaned toward Owen. "You'll want to watch yourself with
this one, Master Archer. It's an ill wind blows him in anyone's path."
Though he smiled and winked as he hurried away, it was clear to
Owen that Tom meant what he said.

Owen studied his companion. The hand that lifted the tankard
was steady. The ill will of his fellow men was nothing to the Summoner.

"Don't you miss the days when you had friends in the city?"

Digby put down his tankard, half empty, and wiped his mouth
with his sleeve. "Friends?" He sniffed. "I have the friend I need in
the Archdeacon. But for him I'd live in the shacks beyond the abbey
walls. Vermin city, they call it. How many men make it from there
through the gates of the city?"

Not many. Owen was duly impressed. "How did you come to the attention of the Archdeacon?"

A sly smile. "I gave him information that brought him a tidy sum for the new chapel in the minster."

"What sort of information?"

"Never mind that." Digby downed his ale and rose. "Archdeacon Anselm wants to talk with you. Can I tell him you will come to his chambers tomorrow?"

Bess, topping a tankard at the next table, held her breath.

"Archdeacon Anselm?" So it was the Archdeacon who had set Digby on him. "I would be honored."

As the door closed behind the Summoner, voices rose in volume and warmed.

Bess came over with a pitcher of ale. Owen put his hand over his tankard, but not before Bess saw that he'd hardly touched it.

"One does for me these days." He nodded toward the door. "Did you hear?"

"Some of it. I daresay you've fired Digby's imagination and he's filled the Archdeacon with ideas. You be sure to disappoint him." Later, when Tom lit his way up to the attic room, Owen asked about the Archdeacon.

Tom shrugged. "Some think him a saint. Maybe he is. Most like saints be a bloodless lot—more's the pity." Tom shook his head. "But he's a fair man. You've nothing to fear from him if you've nothing to hide."

Tom lit a taper in Owen's window, then left.

Owen sank down on the pallet and pulled off the eye patch. He stared at the flickering flame. A slight blurring of the image. His pulse quickened. Was it his left eye trying to see? He put his hand over it. Damn. Just the ale blurring his good eye. The second time today he had expected a miracle. He was being a fool. He dug out the salve pot. Sniffed. Calendula and honey. And something else. The honey masked it. He took some on his finger and applied it. Warmth, tingling, then numbness. Monkshood. Must be careful with this. Aconite could kill.

7

MEN OF THE CLOTH

With Roglio's letter in hand, Owen headed for the abbey the next day. A fresh dusting of snow made the cobbles slippery. He was not altogether disappointed when the smooth stones gave way to mud at the abbey gate. Mud might be dirty, but on it he was less likely to lose his footing. It disgusted him that he even thought of that. The loss of his eye had made him a mincing old man.

Roglio's letter gained Owen access to the Abbot, who assured him that Brother Wulfstan would be most gratified to hear that the Archbishop's physician remembered him.

Unbeknownst to the Abbot, Wulfstan was not at all pleased to hear of the visitor. He did not wish to see anyone. He wanted to be left in peace to wrangle with the devil that threatened to rob him of his salvation.

It had begun with the pilgrim. Since the evening of the day the pilgrim fell ill, Wulfstan had known no peace.

It was not because the pilgrim had fallen ill. Many came in such a state. An intimation of mortality turned even the most hardened brigand's thoughts toward God. Perhaps if Wulfstan had not tried to save him. Perhaps that was the error that unbalanced his life. He should have let his friend die peacefully, without fuss. Instead, in his pride, Wulfstan had set out to save him. The man had touched his heart. Wulfstan had not believed the Lord meant his friend to die—else why guide him here, to an Infirmarian with much skill and experience?

What an arrogant old fool he'd been. It pained Wulfstan to think of it. He'd trudged through the snow, warmed by the joy of saving one of God's creatures—and gaining personal glory.

He'd paid little heed to Nicholas's distraction that day, though later he remembered and recognized the signs. How could Wulfstan know that the man was ill and would that very night be stricken with a palsy that would rob him of speech for days and send him to his bed, from which he still had not risen? Nicholas had looked hale and hearty. But the questions he'd asked, his sudden temper, they had pointed to a feverish brain.

And the pilgrim's symptoms after receiving the physick—Merciful Mother, they were so obvious to him now. But then they had puzzled him. He'd assumed he'd misread the signs, that all along his friend had suffered something quite different from camp fever, and that Nicholas recognized that when he arrived and was dismayed. He had perhaps prepared the wrong remedy.

Oh, but the truth was much worse than that. Much worse.

Like a fool, Wulfstan had watched over the dying man, massaging his limbs to ease his pain, helping him sit up to catch his breath. He'd prayed over him, sad that such a gentle knight should take his leave of life in agony.

And then Wulfstan had saved what was left of the physick and administered it to Fitzwilliam, the Archbishop's ward. And watched death come with suffocation and painful limbs, just as it had come for the pilgrim.

Only then had Wulfstan examined the physick. Only then. Such an old fool. What he'd found had broken his heart. A mortal dose of aconite. And he'd administered it. Wulfstan had killed the two men by trying to save them.

Aconite. Monkshood. Wolfbane. In small doses it relieves pain, induces sweating, reduces inflammation. In larger doses it brings terrible pain to the limbs, fainting, a sense of suffocation, and at last death. It was not unusual for a physick to contain aconite. But so much. For Nicholas to make such a gross mistake. Wulfstan had never found cause to mistrust the concoctions of Nicholas Wilton, or those of his father before him. It had not occurred to him to test the physick. But, dear God, it would have been so easy. On the skin it causes a warm, tingling sensation, followed by numbness. When at last he'd tested the physick, his hand was numb through the night.

It was the darkest moment of Wulfstan's life. Never had he thought on the power that he held over men's lives. He could kill. He had killed by his negligence.

Old fool. The apothecary's brain must already have been addled when he prepared the mixture. After all, Nicholas had collapsed just outside the infirmary, only moments after delivering the physick.

Only moments after the pilgrim had called him murderer. This it was that troubled Wulfstan. For the physick contained such a large dose of aconite. Prepared specifically for the pilgrim. Never had he known Nicholas to err so in preparing a physick. He might misdiagnose. And no measurements were ever perfect. But this was such a gross error, so easily detected by anyone who touched it.

And that was why he feared it had not been an error. That Nicholas had meant to prepare a poison. That he'd meant to kill the pilgrim, the man who'd called him murderer, who'd hoped Nicholas was dead, who'd been so certain he'd killed him fifteen years before.

Wulfstan's suspicion sickened him. For surely it was his own guilt he sought to erase by blaming another. Nicholas Wilton could not mean to murder the pilgrim. He did not even know his name.

But Nicholas had asked many questions about the man. Questions that had nothing to do with a diagnosis. And Wulfstan had told him all he knew. Perhaps enough.

No. Nicholas was a good man. It was unthinkable. Besides, what was his motive? Nicholas had everything a layman could want. He was a master apothecary, his shop patronized by the wealthiest citizens of York, married to a beautiful, gentle woman who worked beside him. His only sorrow was his lack of children.

Wulfstan had been taught that his goodness, his innocence, was the source of his skill with medicines. God granted him this most wonderful occupation because he'd shown himself worthy.

But he was no longer innocent. Through his negligence he had murdered two men. And he had chosen to tell no one. No one must know that the men had not died natural deaths. The gossip might ruin the Wiltons and, God forgive him, Abbot Campian's faith in him. He could not do it. Not to Lucie Wilton. Not to himself. He would not destroy her life after she'd been given another chance. And for himself, he knew he would be most diligent from this day forward.

So had he resolved to tell no one of his suspicion but Lucie Wilton. She needed to watch Nicholas. He'd dreaded telling her. But she'd taken it with remarkable calm.

Wulfstan trusted Lucie. But he was tormented by his own guilt in the deaths, his own carelessness.

And in this state, he did not welcome company. Yet he could hardly turn away one who carried a message from the Archbishop's physician.

When Owen entered the infirmary, Wulfstan looked up from his worktable, but his eyes did not meet Owen's.

Owen handed him the letter.

The monk's hands trembled as he broke the seal and read. He had a soft, kind face, red-cheeked and full. But Owen could see anxiety in the pale eyes. It was gone when he looked up from the note.

"Master Roglio. May the Lord bless him for remembering me. I did very little. A physick for the Archbishop." Wulfstan frowned. "I can't remember what exactly. I had all but the mandrake. Don't grow it here, you see. It is the devil's weed." He rubbed the white bristles on his chin, wandering in memory.

"The Archbishop needed a painkiller?"

Pale eyes looked up, anxious once more. "You know something of the craft, I see. Yes, mandragora for pain."

It did not surprise Owen that the monk would be touchy. Two men had died in his care. But he'd hoped the man would be comfortable talking of what he knew. "I am surprised you insisted on mandrake. Surely you grow monkshood—aconite?"

The monk blanched. "Of course. But Master Roglio said the Archbishop's humours were too sanguine. Aconite would overheat him. So I sent to Wilton—he has a fine garden, most complete—for the powdered root and mixed the physick myself. Yes, that's how it went. And for so little Master Roglio remembers me."

"Master Wilton." Owen nodded. "I've met his wife. She mixed a salve for my eye."

"Nicholas Wilton is fortunate in Lucie. She is quite competent."

"I've no doubt. Her mixture was an improvement over what I'd gotten in Warwick."

"You are in good hands."

"My room at the York overlooks Wilton's garden. Do you often do business with him?"

Shoulders tensed. "From time to time." The monk bent to his work.

Owen glanced around the room. Bright and warm, perfumed by the physicks mixed at the monk's worktable and stored in pots and jars on the shelves above. The rushes on the floor were fresh and dry. At the moment there were no patients in the cots against the far wall.

"The brothers of St. Mary's are a robust lot, I see."

"No more than usual. The spring bloodletting is coming up. It is always quiet before."

"No one wants to face the leeches too often."

Wulfstan gave him a slight smile. "You are a student of human nature."

"As Captain of Archers I needed to be." Owen decided to take the plunge. "I am glad to see that this winter's bout of illness has passed over."

The red cheeks blotched. A nervous hand disturbed the pile of orris-root powder. A cloud rose up to Wulfstan's face. He sneezed into his sleeve, wiped his eyes. Coming out from behind the table, he sat down by Owen. "How do you know of the illness here?"

Owen shrugged. "I listened to the gossip at the tavern last night, didn't I? It is the way to learn about a city. Folk make note of two deaths, similar symptoms, within a month. One death means little. It was his time. But two deaths could mean three, four, a dozen."

Wulfstan rubbed the bridge of his nose, eyes closed, a tired, troubled man. "Enough time has gone by that they know not to worry." He shook his head. "In any case, two deaths mean only that it was time for both of them. God in His goodness called both as pilgrims, in states of grace. Two such acts reveal His boundless benevolence."

Owen shrugged. "I presumed their deaths followed from traveling north in winter. I found it a difficult march, and I'm in good health."

The light from the garden window lit the sweat on the monk's face. "Of course that, too, is true. The first pilgrim was in no condition to travel. I think he knew that death might come for him here."

Owen noted emotion in the old monk's voice. "You knew him well?"

Wulfstan bowed his head and closed his eyes for a moment before he answered. "We became friends while I treated him."

"That was the most difficult part for me in the camps. To lose a friend who was under my care."

Wulfstan stared silently at the far wall, his eyes wet.

"Did it fall to you to inform his kin?" Owen asked gently.

"That would be Abbot Campian's place. But as far as I know he came as a nameless pilgrim, an everyman."

"He did not speak of his home to you?"

"He'd been a soldier for so long, I doubt he remembered his home."

Owen nodded. "That is a state I can well understand."

"You are thoughtful for a soldier."

"I have a wound that changed my life."

Wulfstan glanced at the patch with a sympathetic look.

"And the other pilgrim who died? Fitzwilliam. Did he, too, arrive ill?"

Wulfstan shook his head. "A dissolute life caught up with him." Then he looked hard at Owen. "How did you know his name?"

"They spoke it last night. It was that caught my attention. He was in Lancaster's service, too. I was at Kenilworth when news of his death arrived."

The monk tensed. "What did they say of it?"

"That his enemies had been cheated out of killing him. Forgive me. I have brought up a subject that disturbs you."

Wulfstan took a deep breath. "It is not good for the abbey, the death of two pilgrims."

"We heard only of Fitzwilliam's. And we assumed he'd been left for dead on the road by one of his enemies."

Wulfstan bowed his head.

"He was a rogue," Owen said. "There was always talk of him."

"He had a wayward soul. Born under a dark star. That's what the folk around here would say of him."

"Did you know him well?"

"I knew *of* him. He spent much time here. But until this time he had managed to stay out of my infirmary."

"You did not like him."

"I did not know him." Wulfstan's voice had an edge that warned he was at the end of his patience.

"Forgive me. I did not come here intending to pry."

"No matter."

Owen looked out at the medicinal garden. Lavender and santolina edged the beds, whose snowy blankets would be dark earth dotted with green shoots in a month.

He felt the Infirmarian's eyes on him.

"Master Roglio said I must make a study of the two great medicinal gardens in York—yours and Master Wilton's. I thought the medicinal garden at Kenilworth magnificent. Twice the size of this. But Roglio said it offered far less variety."

"We have a long tradition at St. Mary's. But the Wilton garden is the work of one man—Nicholas Wilton. It is his pride and joy. His masterwork, in fact. It was I the Guildmaster brought in to judge Nicholas's worthiness to be raised to Master Apothecary. I had no idea a layman would have access to the books he must have consulted. But I think he was already planning this when he was a student here."

"He went to the abbey school?"

The guard went up again.

Owen wondered what Wulfstan feared he would ask.

"You must excuse me," Wulfstan said. "I have much work to do." He rose.

Owen stood also. "I am sorry to take your time. I look forward to seeing your garden in spring."

Wulfstan frowned. "You intend to be here so long?"

"I have come seeking work." Owen touched the patch. "One-eyed men do not make good soldiers, in my way of thinking."

The eyes were sympathetic. "Master Roglio could do nothing?" Owen shook his head.

"Pity. If anyone could, it would be him. What sort of work do you seek?"

Owen glanced around the room. "I know it is unusual for someone my age, but I hope to apprentice to an apothecary or surgeon."

Wulfstan frowned. "From soldier to healer is a great leap. But if God calls you, He will provide a way."

Owen noted how the monk glanced back at his work. "I have taken enough of your time." He took his leave.

He did not feel much enlightened. What had he learned? That Brother Wulfstan was troubled by the deaths at the abbey and nervous about something. He did not like questions about the deaths or about Nicholas Wilton. Perhaps that meant nothing, but Owen would think about it. And the Infirmarian stuck to the story that Fitzwilliam had died of an illness. But then if the man was murdered in Wulfstan's infirmary it would look bad for the monk, so he was unlikely to admit it.

An unprofitable interview, all in all. Owen decided to take the opportunity to ask some of the other monks what they knew about Fitzwilliam. He gestured to a young monk hurrying past.

"I was hoping to speak with some who might remember a cousin of mine, Sir Oswald Fitzwilliam?"

The fresh-faced monk looked Owen up and down, then grinned. "You are of a different sort than your cousin, sir—?"

"Archer. Owen Archer." He extended his hand.

The young monk gave a slight bow, but did not bring forth his hands from his sleeve. "I am Brother Jonas. I remember your cousin. He was a"—Jonas averted his eyes for a moment, thinking—"he was a character. His death must have been unexpected."

"How he met his death surprised me. With his tendency to collect enemies, I expected he'd meet a violent end."

The eyebrows rose. "I had heard he was one for the ladies. With those tight leggings and short tunics, his intentions were obvious. But that is the worst I had heard of him."

"Was he well liked here?"

"He was not disliked." The monk glanced around, then pushed his hands farther into his sleeves. "I must go about my business now. Shall I show you out?"

"No need." Owen nodded to him and continued up the corridor, then out into the cloister walk. There he met another, older monk. "God be with you."

"And with you, my son," the old monk whispered.

"Forgive me for disturbing your meditation, but I wondered if you were one of the brothers who helped my cousin, Oswald Fitzwilliam. He spoke with affection and gratitude about the peace he found here."

The old monk's gaunt face registered mild surprise. He shook his head. "I can take no credit for your cousin. I have no business with the pilgrims to the abbey." He rose stiffly, made the sign of the cross in blessing, and shuffled off.

"I knew Fitzwilliam," a voice said behind Owen.

Owen turned. A chubby monk with bright eyes and a cheery smile stood rocking back and forth, hands tucked in his sleeves. "I am Brother Celadine, the Cellarer."

"Of course. He would have sought you out."

"Do you have permission to speak with us about your cousin?"

The question surprised Owen. Brother Celadine had begun in a friendly mode. "I do not have permission as such. I came with a letter of introduction to Brother Wulfstan. But I thought as long as I was here—"

"You were close to your cousin?"

"I remember good times."

Celadine nodded. "Most of the brothers tolerated Fitzwilliam because he was the Archbishop's ward. But I was fond of him. It is not easy being ward of a powerful man such as His Grace. Fitzwilliam was watched. His every transgression was noted. He was bound to rebel. But I don't think he was at heart an evil man. Oh, I had no delusions that he would go forth and sin no more, but he tried to be better."

"How did you come to know him so well?"

Celadine chuckled. "I once caught him in the cellars. Partaking of more than was his portion."

"And he repented?"

"He did not repeat the offense."

"How did he seem this last time?"

The monk looked out at the cloister garden, thinking. "Quieter than usual. Pale. I think he was ill when he arrived."

"Was something bothering him, do you think?"

"He never came here by choice."

A door opened at the end of the cloister walk.

The Cellarer glanced over at the door with an anxious look. "I must be about my business," he said abruptly. "God be with you."

Owen turned to see Abbot Campian approaching with a determined stride. The frown on the Abbot's face told Owen the game was up.

"I gave you permission to speak with Brother Wulfstan. Now I hear you are interrupting the brothers' meditations to ask questions about Sir Oswald Fitzwilliam. You take advantage of my hospitality, Captain Archer."

"Forgive me. I thought as I was here—"

"St. Mary's is a place of meditation and prayer."

"I apologize for my transgression."

"I will have Brother Sebastian show you out." Campian motioned a young monk from the shadows.

Owen humbly followed the young monk to the front gate. "Is your Abbot very angry with me?"

Brother Sebastian smiled. "Not angry. He demands order. He expects all to obey the rules."

"He is fortunate to have a world well ordered."

"We are fortunate to have him as our Abbot."

Owen took his leave with a feeling of frustration. He had learned nothing about Fitzwilliam that would explain his death. In fact, the brothers of St. Mary's seemed to find it reasonable that the man died of a winter cold. Owen wondered for the first time whether Thoresby had sent him on a fool's errand.

Perhaps he would learn more from his visit to the Archdeacon.

• • •

An ascetic, Owen thought, as Anselm gestured to him to be seated. Tall, gaunt, dun-colored even to the eyes. A chill to the voice that ensured distance.

"I understand you visited the Archbishop's secretary yesterday."

So this was a territorial matter. Owen relaxed. Thoresby had rehearsed him on this.

"His Grace the Archbishop does a favor for the late Henry, Duke of Lancaster, in providing me with a letter of introduction and the funds my late lord meant me to have. He had me transact the business with Jehannes because it is as Lord Chancellor that he does this favor for the late Duke."

"A letter of introduction? What is your business in York?"

"I seek employment."

The cold eyes looked him over. "What did you do for the late Duke?"

"I was Captain of Archers."

"The present Duke did not wish to keep you on?"

"I am finished with soldiering. I want to learn a trade, apprentice to a master."

Anselm's nostrils flared. "A Captain of Archers content now to become a humble apprentice?"

"It is God's wish that I begin again. I have faith that the loss of my eye was God's sign that I am done with killing. That I am meant to serve Him in another way."

"What do you have in mind?"

"I would like to apprentice to an apothecary."

"From killer to healer?" The voice was amused, but the eyes still cold.

"I assisted the camp physician, measuring out medicines and such."

"I fear there are seldom such apprenticeships available in York. Besides, an archer is not likely to read and write."

"I can do both. The late Duke saw to it that I might be gainfully employed."

"Remarkable." He made the word an insult.

"And God has this very day shown me His purpose. I've heard of Master Nicholas Wilton's situation."

The Archdeacon came alert at the name.

"I've a strong back for gardening, and the experience dispensing physicks."

"Apprentice to Nicholas Wilton?" Anselm rose.

"It is the perfect situation."

The Archdeacon shook his head. "You are wrong. You would be trained by his wife. It is ill-advised to be trained by a woman. And one of questionable background."

"I've heard nothing ill of Mistress Wilton."

The Archdeacon sniffed. "You will. Besides. There would be talk. You are a single man of marriageable age, Mistress Wilton is young and fair, her husband is bedridden. You see the problem."

"I shall board elsewhere."

The Archdeacon bowed to that. "I see that you are eager to find a position. I admire that. But I advise you to stay away from this one. I will do what I can—and my influence is considerable, I assure you—to find you a post. Perhaps not in York, but I assume you are willing to go elsewhere?"

"That is kind of you."

The Archdeacon inclined his head slightly. "Not at all, Captain Archer."

Anselm had encountered men like Owen Archer before, with his honeyed tongue, lustrous curls, and large, liquid, long-lashed eye. Such men carried part of the rib meant for Eve. They were evil, cunning. Attractive to women because the witches recognized themselves in him. This man had been called by Lucie Wilton. Of that, Anselm was certain. Lucie was her mother's spawn. And Bess Merchet aided her. What power must come from that union. Neither woman dropped her gaze in humility when he approached. Bold, unnatural women. Wicked.

And Owen Archer in league with them. He must be watched.

• • •

Bess sat on a stool behind the counter, chatting with Lucie between customers. She took pity on her friend, so tied down with the shop, with Nicholas, and with the house that she never got out into the town to gossip.

"What do you think of Owen Archer?" Bess asked. He had told her he'd been to the shop and met Mistress Wilton. Bess noted with interest the blush that colored her pretty friend's face.

"I am not in the habit of giving opinions on my customers," Lucie said, avoiding Bess's eyes.

Bess snorted. "Just as I thought."

"What is that supposed to mean?" Lucie met her friend's eyes, challenging her.

"He charmed you."

Lucie's cheeks flamed. "He did not. If you must know, he was rude. He took me for a serving girl. Thought he could turn my head with pretty words."

Bess winced. She had not taken Lucie's stubbornness into account when she imagined an innocent romance. Oh, dear. Well, perhaps it was for the best. "Maybe he is a knave. Archdeacon Anselm sent for him. He's been to see him."

"How do you know that?"

"I heard Owen Archer and Potter Digby talking at the tavern last night." Bess didn't like the tightness in Lucie's voice. Or how the becoming blush had suddenly faded. "That worries you?" Bess asked.

"Why should I feel anything at all about the matter? I hardly know the man." Lucie turned sharply and knocked a clay cup off the counter. It split in two as it hit the rushes. Tears filled Lucie's eyes and spilled down her cheeks.

"Lucie, love, what's wrong?"

Lucie shook her head. "I'm tired. Please go, Bess."

"You need help in this shop."

"Tell that to Guildmaster Thorpe."

"Why don't you close up early today?"

"Just leave me alone, Bess. Please."

• • •

Lucie sank down on the stool Bess had vacated and hugged her arms to herself. She did not believe in coincidences. Ever since the night Nicholas was brought home by Digby, the Summoner and the Archdeacon had spied on them. Digby had never brought his custom to her before. His mother was a midwife. She doctored him when he fell ill. But suddenly he was a regular customer. And then yesterday he encountered Owen Archer in her shop and by evening the Archdeacon had sent for him. Was Archdeacon Anselm questioning all her customers? He frightened her. And he frightened Nicholas. Her husband denied it. "He comes as a friend, Lucie. You must not be concerned with his visits." But she knew her husband's moods, illness or no, and he was agitated after the Archdeacon's visits. He did not care for Anselm any more than Lucie did.

8

MAGDA DIGBY,
THE RIVERWOMAN

Owen spent the evening in a corner seat of the York Tavern, watching out for Summoner Digby. He was certain the man would storm in to demand what business Owen had with his mother. But he did not come.

Bess joined him for a drink late in the evening. She settled down across from him, saluted him with a tankard of ale. "I think I deserve this." She sipped, smiled her satisfaction. "He's got the touch, my Tom. 'Tis usually the women who brew the finest ale, but my Tom's the exception to the rule." She took another long drink. "So how are you finding the folk of York?"

"I've not met many. The Archdeacon seems to have taken offense at my connection with the Archbishop. It seemed his sole purpose in seeing me. To find out my business at the minster."

"Anselm's an unpleasant sort. A good man in his way. He's raised a deal of money for the Hatfield Chapel at the minster. That reflects well on us all. I must give him that. When the King comes to the dedication, he'll bring with him a large company. Good for business."

Owen was tempted to mention the Archdeacon's allusion to Mistress Wilton's background, but he did not yet want Bess to know that he had his eye on a job with the Wiltons. He was not sure how Bess would respond. "As for other folk in York, I've met some of the monks at St. Mary's. They seem a pleasant lot."

"Monks." Bess shook her head, making her cap ribbons

tremble. "Hiding away from the world. Pampered little boys, if you ask me. No wonder they're pleasant." She sipped her ale. "You've been up to the abbey, then?"

"I had a letter of introduction to Brother Wulfstan, the Infirmarian. I thought he might know of someone in need of a gardener or a surgeon's assistant. An apothecary's assistant. That sort of work."

She studied him over the rim of her tankard. "And did he know of any such opportunities?" she asked quietly.

Owen had walked right into it. There seemed no way around it. "He mentioned the Wiltons."

Bess bristled. "I'm sure he did."

"The poor man had an unfortunate winter."

"Wilton?"

"No. Brother Wulfstan."

Bess frowned, confused.

"The two pilgrims who died in his infirmary?"

"Oh." She shrugged. "I suppose you could see that as Brother Wulfstan's misfortune. It certainly was the talk for a while. Folk feared the plague. It could happen again. Just that quickly. One day life as usual, next day all your neighbors sickening." Bess sighed. "Doesn't bear thinking about."

"Did you know either of the men?"

"Second one was the notorious Fitzwilliam. Aye. He stayed here once or twice. I had to watch him with the help. A little too eager to plant his seed, that young man."

"He had a reputation down south, too."

"That's right. You would have known him."

"I heard of him. We never met."

Bess shook her head. "A man like him, wasting all his opportunities." She shook herself. "Listen to me. Gossiping about the dead, a man I hardly knew. So what's your next step?"

Owen could not think how to lead back to Fitzwilliam. "I hope to speak with a few guildmasters. See what they suggest. The Archbishop's secretary sent out some letters."

Bess nodded. "You'll soon find something, an enterprising man

like yourself." Bess drained her cup and rose, dusting off her apron.
"Thanks for the company. I must get back to work."

Owen smiled to himself as he watched her move away,
efficiently cleaning away empty cups and wiping off tables as she
went. She'd gotten the information she wanted while seeming to
have a pleasant chat. A professional interrogator. He would do well
to study her technique.

Bess handed Owen a message when he came downstairs the next
morning. "A messenger from the minster brought it first thing." She
gave him a conspiratorial wink. "The Archdeacon won't like this, eh?"

Owen read it while Kit set some bread and cheese and his
morning ale in front of him. Jehannes wanted to see him at once.
Owen ate quickly and set off for the minster.

Jehannes greeted him with an apology for the curt note. "I
had to make sure you came here first. I must warn you, Archer, be
careful with your questioning."

"Someone has complained?"

"Abbot Campian. He wants to know if His Grace sent you to
inquire into the death of Fitzwilliam."

A sharp pain shot across Owen's left eye. "I am not meant for
this sort of work."

"Is anyone ever meant for the work he does?"

"I do not wish to disappoint the Archbishop."

"I told the Abbot that you are asking a few questions in exchange
for the Archbishop's help in finding you a means of support."

"Clever. Thank you."

Jehannes nodded.

"Is he angry?"

Jehannes considered the question. "More a matter of feeling
slighted. We should have trusted him. He says you are free to return
and discuss the matter with him."

"I will do that."

"And he entices you with some information about Fitzwilliam. Some business he had, or might have had, with Magda Digby."

Owen perked up. "I'll go there directly." He rose.

"Have you met the Summoner's mother yet?"

Owen nodded. "A shrewd one, Magda Digby. I came out of that interview feeling a fool."

Jehannes smiled. "Good luck with her. One more thing. Guildmaster Thorpe will see you at midday. He wants to talk with you about the Wilton apprenticeship."

Owen left with a full morning before him. If the Abbot's lead seemed at all worthwhile, he meant to visit Magda Digby before midday. It would be nice to have that out of his way when he met Mistress Wilton again.

Abbot Campian offered him a cup of ale. "To fortify yourself. I expect you will be off to visit Magda Digby. You should have trusted me, you know." He flicked an invisible mote of dust off the table, folded his hands neatly before him, then looked up at Owen.

"I apologize," Owen said. "I am clumsy at this sort of thing."

"You've undertaken a thankless task. But I suppose the interest of John Thoresby is worth it." The fingers fluttered slightly. They were the cleanest hands Owen had ever seen.

"I mean to begin again," Owen explained. "I need the Archbishop's help. Will you tell anyone else that I am his man?"

"Only if necessary." Abbot Campian's eyes were dark pools of calm water. Owen believed him. "Of course this is all a waste of time. Sir Oswald Fitzwilliam was ill. He died, despite my Infirmarian's best efforts and our prayers. It was his time."

His manner made it difficult, even rude, to disagree. But Owen must do what he must do. "The Archbishop wants to be certain."

The fingers fluttered. "One can never be certain."

"No."

They were silent for a while. Owen sipped the ale and let the

Abbot's calm work on him. Finally, Campian spoke. "Fitzwilliam spent his last days in the infirmary, under the watchful eyes of Brother Wulfstan and the novice Henry. I cannot see how anyone might have got to the man."

"He went to the infirmary because he was already ill."

The eyebrows lifted. "Ah. So you think a poison that had a delayed reaction—"

"I am not to think anything, just to collect facts."

"You've come to hear about Fitzwilliam and Magda Digby?"

"Yes."

"It is probably nothing."

"I must know. Please."

"I tell you this in confidence. No one else living knows about the connection with the Riverwoman but the Digbys themselves."

"But if I should have to tell the Archbishop?"

The fingers lifted and fell. "That would be unfortunate. But I wish to cooperate."

"I will tell the Archbishop only if I must."

The Abbot nodded. "I believe you." He looked up at the ceiling, collecting his thoughts, then back to Owen. "I make it a practice to keep the reasons for a pilgrim's penance to myself. Sometimes they choose to share their troubles with others, but usually I am the only one to know. It is not a confession, you understand. I break no sacred bond of silence in telling you."

"I understand."

"The Devil inspires men in a variety of evil. You have heard of the trafficking in bodies for relics?"

"I have heard rumors of such things."

"Fitzwilliam's second visit to us followed his attempt to sell an arm for quite a large sum of money to the wrong person. Needless to say, had he been anyone else—"

"But then the Archbishop knows of this."

"He does not know whence came the arm."

"And you do?"

"Fitzwilliam confided in me. On this last visit. He told me that people are wrong about Magda Digby. That she is a healer and a good woman. She had just gotten him out of a difficulty."

"Why was he telling you this?"

"He wanted to know how he might make reparations for a sin that he had coerced her into committing."

"He coerced her into selling him the arm?"

The Abbot bowed his head and closed his eyes. Owen waited. "I do not know how the incident might be connected with his death. I cannot see how she might have got to him. But perhaps she is one person who wanted him silenced."

"Or the Summoner himself."

"Or her son, yes."

"Do you tell me this to ruin the Digbys?"

The soft eyes opened wide in alarm. "No. *Deus juva me.* I hope that you need not tell the Archbishop. But if you find a connection with Fitzwilliam's death—" He looked down at his immaculate hands. Softly he said, "I do hope you will tell the Archbishop that I was cooperative."

"Why?"

"I am not his man. I became Abbot in the time of his predecessor. He does not know me. Has no allegiance to me."

"How long ago was this incident with the arm?"

"Six years."

"The woman might not even remember it. She would not have known who Fitzwilliam was."

"But her son would. It was about the time he became Summoner. I'm sure he worried that if word got out, he would be ruined."

"What did you tell Fitzwilliam?"

"Tell him?"

"How to make amends with the Riverwoman."

"I told him to pray for her soul." The eyes regarded Owen calmly. This the Abbot was sure of. Prayer was the answer to the world's ills. Sufficient prayer.

As Owen left the peace of the Abbot's presence, he felt grateful to the man for his cooperation. It was plain he had found it embarrassing.

• • •

The upside-down sea serpent greeted Owen alone. The Riverwoman was not outside the hut this time. Owen knocked. Heard a grunt. Took it as permission to enter. When he walked into the dry, hot, smoky room and his eye adjusted to the level of light, Owen thought he had walked into some satanic ceremony. A cat lay strapped to a table by the fire, breathing rapidly but not stirring, as Magda leaned over it with a small, sharp knife. She did not look up at the intruder, but hissed, "Quiet." She made some superficial cuts at the edge of a gaping wound, then put the knife down and picked up a needle and thread. While Owen watched in queasy wonder, she sewed up the wound and then turned to him, wiping her bloody hands on her skirts.

"Bird-eye is come again, eh?"

"You were cleaning the wound of a cat?"

"Little Kate's Bessy. All the world to her, that cat. Cut would fester and abscess. Magda could help." She leaned down to listen to the animal, then straightened. "And thy business this time?"

Owen had resolved to get right to the point. "Six years ago you sold an arm to Sir Oswald Fitzwilliam, the Archbishop's ward."

Magda's eyes narrowed. "Whence didst thou hear this?"

"Fitzwilliam told the Abbot just before he died."

"And the Abbot believed him? The lying scoundrel? Aye. The Archbishop's pup." She spat into the fire.

"You know that Fitzwilliam is dead?"

"Aye."

"And he might have been poisoned."

Magda let go with a barking laugh and sat down hard on a bench by the fire. "Magda poisoned the pup to take back the arm? Is that what thou think'st?" She wiped her eyes on her skirt. "If thou think'st to be ferreting out a murder, thou art working with half a wit."

"Tell me about the arm."

She squinted at him. "Why should Magda tell thee aught?"

"A scandal could ruin your son's standing with the Archdeacon."

"The Abbot would tell?"

"Only if it seems we ought to."

She rubbed her chin. "Thou art the Archbishop's man."

"I am interested in Fitzwilliam's death."

She shrugged. "The pup was a flea. A pest. Not so evil to bring death on him." She gestured to Owen to sit down.

Owen sat carefully on the edge of a stool. "You don't think his enemies might want him dead?"

She laughed. "Pup got caught. Time and again. Folk did not take him seriously."

"Tell me about the arm."

Magda snorted. "Came with one of his little lady loves, quick with child. Caught Magda in surgery, removing a rotten arm. Would have killed the man. Pup asked could he have it. Magda ignored him and put it out in her pit. Gave the pup's lady a potion to rid herself of his quickening seed. Next morning the arm was gone from the pit." She shrugged. "Was Magda to run after the pup? Rotten thing. Stank. Magda wondered. 'Twas Potter told me that churchmen pay for such offal. Put it in a jeweled casket. Folk pray to it." She laughed. "Pray to the rotten arm of a tinker. Magda liked that. She let it be."

"If the Archdeacon had heard of this and misunderstood, your son's post might have been in jeopardy."

"Potter learns much from his mother. Much that takes him to folks' doors to demand payment for their sins. 'Tis not an arrangement Archdeacon Anselm is likely to give up, eh?"

"So your son felt no threat?"

"Nay. Nor did the pup yelp." She shook her head. "'Tis a foolish, dangerous business, summoning. Potter is a fool."

The small patient on the table whimpered. Magda went to see to her. "Bessy, girl, ye be coming along. Rest." Gently she stroked the cat's head between the ears, comforting her, soothing her. In a few moments the cat quieted.

Magda poured herself something out of a jug, came back to sit. "Magda does not offer thee drink. Thou wouldst not take it, eh?"

Owen smiled. She surprised him. He had expected an underworld figure, a renegade, a cutthroat, a liar. But she was a skilled healer at peace with herself and content with her lot, it seemed.

"Why is Potter a Summoner?"

Magda shrugged. "Greedy. Thinks to buy a comfortable perch in his Heaven." She shrugged again. "A good lad. Misguided."

"Fitzwilliam brought a woman to you before Christmas?"

"Aye. Another greedy one."

"Was it his child?"

"Aye, 'twas the pup's child. Lord March is not as he should be."

Remembering the revealing leggings, Owen found that an interesting piece of information. "How do you know?"

Magda shook her head. "Thou art a stranger to York and know'st not the company thou find'st thyself in. Magda Digby, the Riverwoman, is known far and wide. Lord March's mother came to Magda for a charm. And again before the betrothal. No good. 'Twas not meant to be fixed. He might sire a monster. Some such evil."

"Can you tell me anything about Fitzwilliam that would help me understand why he died?"

Magda rose, wiped her hands in her skirts. "Magda told thee about the rotten arm. 'Tis enough to keep my Potter content." She opened the door for him to depart.

9

A CONTRACT

Gray clouds and an icy wind threatened snow. Owen stood behind
Magda Digby's hut, staring down at the river. The chill was a shock
after the hot, dry hut, but he hoped it would clear his head. He must
think. Surely he had learned something in two days of questioning,
something to shed light on Fitzwilliam's death. Something he had
heard must be significant. If only he could think it through.

He felt much as he had when he first woke in camp with the eye
bandaged. He'd kept trying to blink the left eye to bring that side of
the tent in focus. The feeling had persisted. Maddening. Even now he
had walked back to the muddy bank and blinked to bring into focus
the turbulent water to his right, the huts clustered against the abbey
wall to his left. But the huts disappeared until he moved his head.

That was the remedy, dissatisfying as it was. That was what he
needed to do with Fitzwilliam's death. Turn his head. He'd been
searching for the man's enemies, the enemies of a rogue. Everyone
agreed Fitzwilliam had many enemies, but no one could name one
who might be angry enough to have killed him, and taken pains to
do it cleverly. That person might still surface. But what other enemies
might Fitzwilliam have had? Ned had implied that Fitzwilliam was
a spy. Perhaps York was not the place for Owen to look. Perhaps
Lancaster's household was where he should be. Fitzwilliam had been a
spy for Lancaster, son of the King, and the ward of Thoresby, King's
Chancellor. Now there was a different angle. Perhaps Fitzwilliam had
been murdered not by his own enemies, but by those of his lord or
his guardian. John of Gaunt, Duke of Lancaster, had many enemies.

And the Lord Chancellor of England and Archbishop of York surely would have made enemies on his precipitous climb.

Owen resolved to give that possibility more thought.

But now he must hurry to the house of the Master of the Merchants' Guild, Camden Thorpe.

Camden Thorpe looked up through his bushy eyebrows at the one-eyed stranger. He was surprised by the man's appearance. He'd expected someone younger, though the Archbishop had written that the man was Captain of Archers to the old Duke of Lancaster. Still. He'd hoped for someone who looked more trainable.

"The Archbishop recommends you as apprentice at the Wilton apothecary. You are aware of this?"

"I am, and I'm most willing." The tone of voice matched the words.

Thorpe pulled at his beard while he considered the idea. Though Lucie Wilton had not requested it, Camden thought she could use a pair of strong arms around the place. That garden took a lot of work. Spring was coming, and there would be digging and planting and hauling. And this Owen knew something about the business already. He could be trusted to watch the shop for brief periods while she saw to her husband. Such a queer business, Nicholas Wilton's illness. Camden had never seen a man struck so hard, so suddenly, and go on living. It must be Mistress Wilton's excellent care. He'd noted how drawn and thin she looked. Not getting rest, that woman. Probably spending the night beside her ailing husband, dozing in a chair, afraid to miss his call, and working hard all day to keep up the shop and garden. He motioned toward the patch. "You must wear that?"

The Welshman touched the offending patch. "Aye, though it works against me, I know. But as you can see"—he lifted the patch, revealing a puckered lid that would not quite close—"the alternative is not pretty."

Camden sighed. "Poor devil. You must have suffered with that wound."

"I had a taste of Hell with it, aye."

He looked to have been popular with the women before the scarring, for he was handsome otherwise in a dark, rakish way. His Mary would call the man handsome but for the patch. It would turn a woman's eye elsewhere, to be sure. No one likely to gossip about him and Mistress Wilton. All in all, he might just be the solution.

"I've been sore pressed to find a way to honor Wilton's request for an apprentice, you see. Sorely pressed. Trouble was, a parent or guardian would take it as an insult, my apprenticing their boy to an apprentice, don't you see. For, capable as Mistress Lucie Wilton is, she's still not a master, though with a few more months of handling the shop alone she could make journeyman. I mean to put it to the guild members. Even so, it's a better recommendation for a boy to have apprenticed to a master apothecary, don't you see."

Owen shrugged. "My situation is different."

"Well, that it is. That it is." Camden scratched his nose and considered the man. The one eye had a bit of devil in it, to be sure. But it faced him directly with no twitching or sliding away. He could see no harm in him. "Knowing my reservations, you are still interested?"

"Yes."

Thorpe gave the beard one last tug, slapped his thighs. "And you are your own man, I daresay. Well. This makes all the difference. All the difference."

"There is one question, Master Thorpe."

"Ask away."

"Archdeacon Anselm referred to Mistress Wilton's questionable background. What did he mean?"

The Archdeacon, devil take him. Would he never give up on his vendetta? "Questionable? Pah. Old gossip. Nothing to it. To my way of thinking, Mistress Wilton has a most respectable background. Daughter of Sir Robert D'Arby of Freythorpe Hadden." Well, now. Camden saw that that got the Welshman interested.

Owen sat up. "A knight's daughter?"

All men are climbers. Give them a connection with aristocracy, and they perk right up. Never fails. "I know what the Archdeacon's thinking. Her mother was French. Young, beautiful. When she died, miscarriage, the child not his, Sir Robert put Lucie in a convent and went off on pilgrimage. Started much gossip, of course. But Lucie Wilton should not be damned for her mother's sins."

"How does the daughter come to be married to a merchant?"

Thorpe shrugged. "Wilton visited Lucie at the convent. Fell in love. It was the aunt gave permission—D'Arby was still in the Holy Land. The girl likely saw it as her escape. In any case, her background should give you no trouble."

"But how did he come to visit his future wife at the convent?"

"You're uncommon interested in Mistress Wilton." Maybe Camden should be worried.

"An apprentice works side by side with his master. It sounds as if Mistress Wilton would be my master as much as he. I'd like to know something about her."

Thorpe thought about that. It seemed a reasoned argument, all in all. "Lady D'Arby—Mistress Wilton's mother—was a great friend of Nicholas's. Fascinated by the garden, she was. Nicholas helped her repair the maze at Freythorpe Hadden."

"Then Nicholas Wilton is much older than his wife?"

"Aye, but not so much as some." Thorpe stood up. "And now you know as much as you need, Owen Archer."

They set out for the apothecary. A light snow fell, a wet snow that melted as it touched the ground. Owen wondered what Lucie Wilton's reaction would be to the Guildmaster's proposal. She'd not much liked the look of him yesterday.

Mistress Wilton glanced up from a ledger, saw Thorpe, smiled, wiped her hands on her apron, held out her hand.

"Master Thorpe."

"I have good news for you, Mistress Wilton." He shook her hand and stepped aside to bring Owen forward.

Lucie started, then nodded to him. "Master Archer. How is the eye?"

"Better today, Mistress Wilton. I am grateful for your skill."

"Might we go round back and talk?" Camden Thorpe suggested.

Lucie led them through a beaded curtain to the kitchen.

"What is the good news?"

Camden rubbed his hands over the fire, then settled himself at the trestle table nearby. "What would you say to trying out Master Archer as an apprentice?"

"What?"

At least she expressed disbelief rather than distaste, Owen thought.

Camden Thorpe hurried on. "I know he's not what you expected. But consider it. He's got experience gardening and measuring out medicines, though he's had no formal training in either. And he writes a good hand. He could help with the books."

Lucie Wilton flushed. She glanced over at Owen, back to Thorpe. "Master Thorpe, don't play me for a fool." Her eyes flashed. "He's a grown man. Hardly an apprentice. You mean to bring him in to replace me."

Camden looked distressed. "But he is an apprentice, I assure you."

"I expected a boy."

"Well, now, that's been the problem, don't you see. A boy who aspires to being a master apothecary does not wish to start as apprentice to an apprentice, however competent he—or she—may be. But I've told Owen the situation and he still wants the post."

"Why?"

"I've lost the heart for soldiering."

"He comes with a letter of introduction from the Archbishop."

She looked Owen up and down. "It's a lot of drudgery, Master Archer."

"It would be a good situation for me, Mistress Wilton. I am not likely to be offered many apprenticeships. Folks see me, patch on my eye, former soldier, and expect trouble. A boy is more tractable, they think. They're wrong. I've seen the world, don't care for it. Want to find a quiet spot and mind my own business. I am not ambitious. What do I care whether I apprentice to your husband or yourself?"

Thorpe nodded with enthusiasm. "To sweeten the offer, I'll add

Tildy Tompkins to help you in the kitchen during the day. A gift from the Guild for an ailing member. We do owe it to you and Nicholas."

"And where will Owen stay?"

Owen grinned at her use of his given name. Already she thought of him as her apprentice.

"He'll eat his meals with you, but keep his lodgings at the York."

"Then I'll have to pay him."

"I have some money," Owen said. "I can keep myself."

"That might not be necessary." Lucie rose. "Let me see if Nicholas is up to seeing you."

Gray hair, gray eyes, gray skin. Nicholas Wilton did not fake his illness. The little room was shuttered tight and lit by two spirit lamps that made it smell all the more like a sickroom. Owen hoped Lucie did not spend much time up here.

Nicholas nodded at them. "I am"—he frowned, closed his eyes—"most grateful, Camden."

Camden Thorpe hurried over to the invalid and took his hand. "The Lord be thanked, you've recovered your speech, my friend."

Nicholas squeezed his hand. Tears stood in his pale eyes.

Camden gestured for Owen to come forward. "This is Owen Archer. I'm confident he'll be a great help to you both."

Owen took the fragile hand in his. A racing pulse. Damp palms. In his experience, a dying man's palm was dry unless he burned with fever. Nicholas Wilton was frightened. Of death? Of the Guildmaster? Of Owen?

While Owen stared into his tankard, considering the events of the day, Digby slithered onto the bench across from him. He did not look friendly.

"What do you mean, questioning my mother?" Digby demanded.

"A good evening to you, too."

"I mean to know what you're up to."

"Goodwife Digby cleared up the business."

"What business do you have questioning her?"

Owen shrugged. "I'm a curious man."

"She says you work for the Archbishop. Is he concerned about Fitzwilliam's death?"

"Should he be?"

"She said Abbot Campian told you about the arm. Why would he do that? What does he have against the Digbys?"

"What could the Abbot have against you?"

"I mean to know."

"You must have felt threatened by the theft of the arm."

Digby shrugged. "'Tis known the poor use her as a surgeon. The connection could be made. How could she prove she'd gotten no money for it? But I was appointed Summoner shortly. Looked like Fitzwilliam had kept his peace."

"You never thought to make sure he kept quiet?"

Digby squinted at Owen. "What do you mean? That I'd kill him? Shut him up for good? Are you accusing me?" His voice kept rising. Heads turned, then turned quickly away, remembering who sat there.

Owen shrugged. "Becoming Summoner meant much to you. I've been to your mother's house. I can imagine being desperate to get away."

Digby shook his head as if amazed by what he heard. "A daft way to start out as Summoner, murdering the Archbishop's ward."

Put that way, it was a laughable suspicion. Owen gave up the line of questioning. It led nowhere. "The Abbot told me that Fitzwilliam repented what he had done. Realized he could have caused your mother much trouble. And he respected her."

Digby's face reddened. "He said that?"

"Aye. So you've nothing to fear from that old business, I think. Would you like a drink?"

"Nay." Digby sat a moment, concentrating on turning his faded cap round and round in his hands.

"Sure you won't have that drink?"

Digby shook his head, then slipped away, looking confused.

Lucie woke as Nicholas's writing fell to the floor with a crash of paper and pen. She caught the inkpot as it began to slide. Nicholas jerked awake. "I am a burden."

"You are tired. Camden Thorpe's visit exhausted you."

"I am glad of help for you, Lucie."

She touched his hand, his face, smiled for him. "I am glad, too. Now rest. Your notes can wait."

He gripped her hand. "I must finish. Write it all down. The garden. My mixtures."

"There is time." She gently pried loose his hand, smoothed the hair from his forehead.

He sighed. "You are too good for me."

"Nonsense." She kissed his forehead and he closed his eyes. She turned down the lamp and slid in beside him. Tonight she would allow herself the luxury of sleeping in the bed. Nicholas was calm enough.

But it was not like before. Nicholas did not turn and gather Lucie in his arms. Even if he had, it would not feel the same. Lucie did not feel the solace here that she had before. In this bed she had felt protected from the world. No longer. Her future security depended on secrecy. At first it had seemed a small thing. But lately she wondered. Was it that simple? She wished she knew just what had befallen Nicholas at the abbey that night. Whom had he seen? How had the Summoner come to be there? Was the Archdeacon's interest merely a friend's concern? If so, why did it frighten Nicholas?

She smelled danger everywhere. Even the apprentice. She could not even appreciate Guildmaster Thorpe's granting her request.

Instead she wondered what the Welshman was after. Oh, he would be a welcome help, she'd no doubt about that. But what was in it for him? To begin a new life, he said. Perhaps. Her first suspicion had been that he and the Guildmaster planned to wrest the apothecary from her, to help her until Nicholas died, all the while learning the books, the customers, the flow of trade, and then take it from her when he died, saying she was too inexperienced, a woman after all, the daughter of a sinful Frenchwoman. That was why the nuns had tormented her. So well behaved the other girls thought her a prig, she'd been watched constantly for signs of sinfulness because the nuns knew her mother had had a lover, that it was her sin that had killed her. Day in and day out they'd followed her, watched her, listened to her every word, raking through all her words and deeds for seeds of her mother's character.

Once she'd become so sick of it she'd plotted an escape. Her one friend was Sister Doltrice, the Herbalist and Infirmarian, for Lucie's mother had passed on to her daughter a love of gardens and much lore of healing plants. Sister Doltrice did not keep a hawk eye on her. So after breakfast one day, Lucie complained of stomach cramps. She clutched her stomach and let tears trickle down her cheeks. Sister Winifrith hurried her to the infirmary.

The plan was to creep out after Sister Doltrice had tucked her in for the night, slip out the garden door and down through the cluster of sheds and outbuildings to the part of the wall that had crumbled beneath the weight of a falling tree.

While she waited in the infirmary for nightfall, Lucie sipped the minty tisane that her friend had prepared for her tummy, and drowsed in the warm room as Sister Doltrice puttered with her chores. In the early evening the nun declared Lucie's color better and let her sit up a little, keeping her occupied with stories of her large family and their busy farm up near Helmsley, a farm cradled between heathery hills beside the cool clear water of Trilicum Beck. They were merry tales, full of silliness and love, and Lucie lost herself in them, gradually nodding off and slipping down into the soft bed, where her sweet dreams kept her until dawn.

As she'd left for her morning lessons, she'd turned and asked Sister Doltrice why the other sisters were so hard on her.

"Because of your mother, child. Because they do not understand that your mother was very young and frightened by the wildness of the North Country and found her solace in a gentle man who loved her and made her smile."

"Can't you tell them to stop?"

She snorted. "And let them wonder how I could understand such a thing?"

Lucie looked into the Infirmarian's face and saw what a beauty she'd been—still was, in a comfortable sort of way—and realized what she was saying.

Sister Doltrice took her hand. "And now we have shared secrets that we must swear never to reveal to a soul."

"What secret do you have from me?"

"That your tummy aches when you need a day of Doltrice's minty concoctions and endless stories. Much better than running away, don't you agree?"

"You knew?"

The Infirmarian knelt down and took Lucie in her arms. She was warm and smelled of flowers and herbs. "To be a good healer, one must read the heart as well as bodily wastes."

"It's our secret?"

"Our secret, little one. And you're always welcome."

Lucie had trusted Sister Doltrice as she'd trusted no one since her mother died. Only Nicholas would later earn such trust.

And the apprentice? She thought not. She'd once asked Sister Doltrice how to tell whether a stranger was trustworthy. "Look them in the eye and ask them," she'd said.

Lucie had been disappointed with that answer, which seemed no answer at all.

She still thought it silly. And unwise. For one who asks such a question reveals that she has need of discretion. And she did not want the Welshman to get curious. Especially with his connection to the Archbishop and the Archdeacon. She wished there were a way to refuse him as her apprentice. But she needed help. Who knew how long the Guildmaster would take to replace him? And to refuse the Guildmaster's offer when she had made such a fuss about needing help would arouse suspicion.

10

THORNS

Nicholas Wilton disturbed Owen's sleep. The man's condition struck him as more than a palsy. It was not that Owen could point to this or that and say this was what was not right about Wilton's condition, that a palsy would not cause the hair to turn gray, the flesh to wrinkle, or the palms to sweat. A palsy might do all that. His suspicion was all in his gut and too vague to be useful.

At dawn he dressed and headed for the Wiltons' garden. His breath smoked in the frosty air. His boots crunched on the snow. He made his way along the paths and through the holly hedge to the woodpile. In the shed beside it he found an ax. He took off his tunic. Though chilly now, he intended to work up a good sweat. He would want his tunic dry when he cooled down. A habit from his old life on campaign. With the singlemindedness he'd used in archery, he attacked the woodpile, pretending it was the Breton jongleur. *Ungrateful wretch.* He hacked at him. *I fought for your life.* Another blow. *I risked the ridicule of my comrades.* He hacked. *You and your gypsy.* Another. *She unmanned me.* Crack. *Breton bastard.*

At first his injured shoulder was painfully stiff, but as his muscles warmed, it loosened up and he rediscovered the satisfaction of physical labor. His mind calmed and cleared. His movements became rhythmic and fluid.

A cough interrupted him.

"You begin the day with remarkable energy." Lucie Wilton handed him a cloth. "You'll want to dry off and get dressed. There's a warm breakfast in the kitchen."

THE APOTHECARY ROSE

It was plain she'd heard him and hurried out to investigate, thinking him an intruder. Her hair was loose, covered only by a shawl. The pale morning sun caught red-gold strands and caused them to shimmer with life. Dear God, how he would love to touch that hair. Yet even as she stood here, radiant and vulnerable in the morning light, he was aware of a bristly guardedness with which she maintained a cautious distance.

He remembered the cloth in his hand. And suddenly he felt how the cold penetrated. And he was uncomfortable standing before her, stripped to the waist. He dried himself quickly and donned his shirt.

"You've cut enough wood to last a fortnight," she said. "And all on an empty stomach. You'll win me over yet, Owen Archer." Teasing words, such as his sisters might have used with him.

But she'd misunderstood him. He had not cut this stack of firewood to impress her. "I needed to move," he said. It sounded ridiculous.

Lucie Wilton nodded, not interested enough to note the awkward comment, and led the way back through the snowy garden.

While he ate, she quizzed him on his experience and his knowledge of medicines and gardens. His answers appeared to satisfy her. Her questions impressed him. She was indeed ready to graduate from apprentice to journeyman, if he was any judge. She was quick, like Gaspare. She absorbed information and used it at once, asking questions off his answers. It was plain she knew more than Owen did about both medicines and gardens. Far more.

The questions dwindled and she grew quiet, staring down at her hands on the table. And then those cool, level eyes lifted to his. "I can believe that you might be through with soldiering and want to learn a trade. But why in York? Why not in Wales, close to your family? You speak of your mother and the land with affection."

Why indeed? He explained that the old Duke had asked Thoresby to assist Owen in entering a trade. But it sounded hollow and rehearsed to his ears. Surely it must to hers.

Lucie Wilton sighed, got up, busied herself at the hearth. She looked proud and noble standing there, though her dress was simple, with darned spots, most of them unraveling. An impatient

113

seamstress. He wondered why she had not arranged for help before. Wilton's business could certainly support such help. The room was substantial for a merchant's kitchen, beams, shelves, trestle table, and chairs of oak. The crockery on the shelves was simple but well fired. Little of it appeared to be used. Most was covered in dust. In fact it was easy to see what took precedence in this house. From the beams, herbs hung to dry and shed their debris unchecked, so that dried flowers and leaves mingled with the dust on the shelves and were crushed underfoot, starring the packed dirt floor. Odd, when the shop was as dust-free as was humanly possible.

Lucie sat down again. Her mouth was set in an angry line. "Soldiers are a cold, unnatural lot."

It was not at all what he'd expected her to say. He had to think about where their conversation had left off. "I'm condemned for not returning to Wales?"

"You are a free man, with funds enough to keep a private room at an inn. Funds enough to let your people see that their prayers were answered, that you are alive. Did it not occur to you to see them before you took up your new life?" Angry tears stood in her eyes. The emotion brought color to her face.

Apparently aware of how readable she was at that moment, Lucie looked down, flicked invisible crumbs from the table.

Owen could think of no answer to her outburst. To be honest, he'd never considered his family. They'd been part of his boyhood. Wales was the past. But he did not say that. He said nothing for a moment, wondering about the source of this attack. A possibility occurred to him. "Your father was a soldier, I hear."

She stiffened, eyes cold.

He'd guessed the source, but it was a misstep, for sure. "I do not mean to pry." It seemed as though prying was all he did these days.

She did not warm to his apology. "You'll begin the day by sweeping the shop doorway and lighting the lamps. Then you can stack the firewood outside the kitchen door. Later I'll show you around—"

A rush of cold air sucked the warmth out of the kitchen as Bess Merchet opened the outside door. "I thought I might find you here." Her cheeks were rosy. She paused to catch her breath, her eyes taking in the remains of breakfast. "You're off to an early start, the two of you. And so's the Summoner. He's just been to the inn to say the Archdeacon wants to see you, Owen Archer. I sent Digby off with the promise I'd tell you at once."

Owen glanced at Lucie.

She looked pale, but said calmly, "Get the shop ready before you go."

The Archdeacon smiled. An unpleasant experience on his face, but a smile nonetheless. "I suspect you thought yesterday's promise mere courtesy, Archer. But God has granted me the grace to fulfill my promise in one day. I have heard this morning of an apothecary in Durham who needs an apprentice." Anselm sat back, elbows on the arms of his thronelike chair, his fingertips meeting in a satisfied steeple.

Owen had not foreseen this turn. He did not respond at once as he thought how best to relay the bad news.

The Archdeacon chuckled. "I see that I have, indeed, surprised you."

Owen decided to act simple. "Oh aye, that you have, Archdeacon. As you said yourself, posts such as that are rare. And I took that to heart yesterday and—well, I signed a contract with Master Nicholas Wilton."

The steeple crumbled as the Archdeacon's hands descended to the arms of his chair, which he clenched with enough strength to turn his knuckles the color of bleached bone. "You did what?"

"You see, I decided I'd best settle for whatever I could get, apprenticing to an apprentice though it is, else I might starve before I heard of another post."

"You—" The Archdeacon checked himself. "Most unfortunate." Anger tightened his throat.

Owen stood up. "I'm grateful to you."

Anselm's eyes burned into Owen's, then glided away. He nodded.

"'Tis a binding contract—" Owen said.

"Go." Anselm breathed the word as if expelling poison.

Owen obeyed, hurrying away before he made matters worse. He paused in the minster yard, committing the Archdeacon's reactions to memory. It was to be expected that Anselm would be annoyed to have wasted his time on Owen. But why had he done so in the first place? In case it might please Thoresby? Perhaps. But Owen could not think of a way Anselm could have sent queries to Durham and received a reply in the hours between their two conversations. That made it very likely a bogus post. To what end? With the hope that Owen would be attacked by Scots on the road? And eliminated. Anselm's anger, then, had more to do with Owen's working for Nicholas Wilton than with Anselm's having wasted his time. And his anger had made him reckless. Owen did not like that.

Owen sat across from Lucie and ate his meal in silence. Once she caught him watching her, and he quickly looked down at the stew in his bowl. She had an uncanny effect on him, as if he'd taken up the role of little brother. It irritated him, and yet when he met that grave, level gaze, instead of confronting her he looked away, confused, as now.

They'd managed to pass the day in peaceful cooperation. He'd learned the lay of the household, shop, and garden. Much impressed he was, too.

He finished his meal before Lucie did, and got up to stoke the fire.

"Don't build it up so late," she said.

"It will go out in the night."

"I want it to. I mean to clean the hearth first thing in the morning."

"Then you'll have to rebuild the fire."

"'Tis always so when I clean the hearth." She looked at him as if he were simple.

"When will you have time to do it?"

"Before dawn."

"How will you know when to rise?"

"I'll sleep beside it. When the fire dies, I'll wake with the cold."

"Let me do it."

"No, this I do myself."

"Then the serving girl." She was to come the next day.

"No."

"Why is it so important that you have a clean hearth?"

"Because I want it clean."

"I'd like to help."

"You'll have enough to do. Besides, what could you know about cleaning a hearth?"

"A man learns many things on campaign."

"There are no hearths on campaign."

She exhausted him. "You'd be right about that." He caught her watching him with a puzzled frown.

It was her turn to look away. "It's odd for a soldier to offer such help," she said.

"I was not always a soldier. I helped my mother as a lad."

"Did your mother teach you to clean a hearth?"

"Aye. She did that. And many other things besides. Didn't yours?"

"My mother died when I was young," Lucie said.

"And then it was the sisters."

"Yes." Her guard came up. "Who told you that?"

"Camden Thorpe. I asked a few questions. Natural curiosity. He said that your mother was fond of Nicholas's garden."

"It reminded her of home." There was a breathless tension in her voice. He trod on dangerous ground.

He tried to make her comfortable. "My mother believed that tending a garden was the highest form of devotion to the Lord. She made all her children work in the garden."

It worked. She met his gaze. "And did it bring you closer to God?" she asked.

He tried a smile on her. "It showed me what a lot of work He'd made for us."

The corners of her mouth twitched. So she had a sense of humor. "Well, then, you can see the work ahead of you." She went back to the fire, quiet for a while. "And did your soldiering teach you anything?"

"That I loved to make an arrow sing through the air and hit its target straight and true, but that war is not confined to the armies who fight it."

He'd spied a lute in the corner. Now he picked it up. Lucie started as the strings hummed with the motion. About to reprimand him, she was silenced by his gentle, sure touch on the strings. He brought the lute to life with a doleful tune and began to sing. He'd been told by many a woman that he had a beautiful voice. Lucie did not want him to see that it affected her. Though tired and aching to sit for a while, she got up and tidied the kitchen while he sang. She tried not to look at him. He lost himself in the song, letting the story move him.

The music rose to a shivering cry and stopped.

They were both quiet, lost in the echo of the music. The fire crackled and hissed. A branch scraped against the house.

Lucie shivered. "What a beautiful language."

"Breton. I learned it from a jongleur," Owen said. "It is close to the language of my country. Though at first I did not understand all the words, I understood the heart of it."

Lucie sat down tentatively, acutely aware of how little she knew this man with whom she was to share her days. "What is the song about?"

"Across Brittany are great cairns—they call them dolmens— built with stones so immense only giants could have moved them. They are said to be the graves of the old ones, the people who came before. In one of these lives a gentlewoman who has vowed to save her people from the routiers of King Edward."

"Routiers," Lucie whispered.

Owen thought she was asking for a definition. "Soldiers our noble King strands across the Channel without pay. The people say there are hundreds of them roaming the countryside, raping and looting. Perhaps they exaggerate."

"My mother told me about them."

"Your mother was French?" He had seen she did not respond well to his knowing about her.

Lucie nodded. "There are hundreds of routiers."

"They are the scourge of the French."

"My mother said that war was the scourge."

"Aye. Well, she would think so. It is different for us here, on an island. Our wars are fought on foreign soil. When our King is victorious, those who return come with booty. When our King is defeated, those few who return come with empty hands. But in France, whether the French king wins or no, the people suffer. The soldiers on either side burn their villages and towns to starve the enemy. It makes no difference to a homeless, starving child whether he starves for his own king or another's."

Lucie watched him, seeming to see him for the first time. "You do not speak like a soldier."

He shrugged.

"How does this woman save her people?"

"Acting the part of a defenseless gentlewoman lost in the forest, she lures the routiers, then surprises them with traps she has laid, and with her skill wielding a knife. She tells them she has lost all and wishes to join them. To prove herself, she will lead them to a noble house at the edge of the wood, where much treasure and wine are to be found. She has prepared an ambush. That is the part all Bretons know. What follows changes with each song. This one tells of her compassion for a routier who stands apart from his fellows, troubled by what he has become. As the company approaches the hiding men, the gentlewoman is moved to spare him. Calling to him, she leads him away from the party to a circle of standing stones on a hill. As the cries of his fellows reach them, he is incensed by what she has done. 'You are free to choose death,' she tells him. 'Say it is your choice, and I will set my men against you. Or look into your heart and admit you have no stomach for slaughter without honor.'"

"Which does he choose?"

"The song does not say."

Lucie looked disappointed. "Is it a true story?"

"I do not know."

"It cannot be. Else the jongleur would have been betraying the savior of his people by singing the song."

"Perhaps that is why he sang it in his own tongue."

"You understood it. Many of your archers would be Welsh, too."

"And like me they keep their peace."

"And the others. Did no one ask you what it meant?"

"I told them it was 'Aucassin et Nicolette' in Breton."

"You protected him?"

Owen sighed. "And in return for my protection, he blinded me. Or rather his leman did."

Lucie reached across the table and touched the scar. "Why did his leman blind you?"

"She was protecting him."

"From you? I don't understand."

He told her the story. "I was a fool. And for my pains I must begin again, find a new path in life. I was already disgusted with soldiering." He'd said it so many times it felt true. "But what they did to me I cannot forgive. They betrayed me when I'd done everything to help them."

Lucie watched him a few minutes more. "You feel crippled without the eye. But you do not seem crippled to others. I don't suppose it helps to know that."

"Kind words. I thank you for them. But you cannot imagine what it is like to lose half your sight."

"No, I cannot." She stood up. "I must take Nicholas his supper, then sleep for a while."

"You won't let me help?"

"Not with this."

Owen saw that she meant it, and wandered back to the inn in a thoughtful mood.

Bess called to him as he entered the tavern. "You've a visitor." She nodded toward the back corner. "It's been a long time since Guildmaster Thorpe gave us his custom. You're good for business, Owen Archer."

Few heads turned, no conversations died as Owen passed among the tables. That was a good sign. He'd been accepted as a regular. He was pleased.

But his pleasure faded when he saw the Guildmaster's expression. The man's round, comfortable face was creased with worry. "Archdeacon Anselm made a fuss about your appointment. Wanted to see the letter Jehannes sent. Asked all sorts of questions. Alluded to your not being who you say you are. It's worrisome, it is."

Owen told him about the apprenticeship in Durham.

Camden Thorpe pulled at his beard. "Now isn't that queer? He never said a word about that to me. On the contrary. He sounded as if he suspected you of being some sort of outlaw, lying low for a time."

"I wonder how Archbishop Thoresby would take the implications of that?"

Thorpe frowned, unsure of Owen's meaning.

"The letter of introduction?"

"Oh, aye." The Guildmaster smiled. "The Archdeacon is confused, isn't he?"

Owen managed to reassure Camden Thorpe all was well, but he was not at all certain that was so. The Archdeacon exhibited an odd concern over Owen's apprenticeship. He obviously saw through his guise. But how much did he guess, and why did it disturb the Archdeacon to the extent that he would risk making a fool of himself with the Guildmaster? In Owen's mind, that spoke of a desperate man. And such men were dangerous.

But why the Archdeacon?

Lucie dreamed she ran through the maze at Freythorpe Hadden, stumbling now and then, breathless with laughter. She feared he would catch up. And she feared he would not. She tingled with the expectation of his hands around her waist, pulling her to him, kissing her neck—

She woke shivering. The fire had gone out. Yet her face was hot. She'd dreamed of Owen Archer. She must be mad.

• • •

Anselm paced. He'd underestimated Archer. He'd moved much faster than Anselm had thought possible. Archer must be Archbishop Thoresby's man. Thoresby had sent Archer, had arranged for him to insinuate himself into the Wilton household. To inquire into the death of the Archbishop's ward. Of course Thoresby would. How stupid of Anselm not to have predicted that. Considering Fitzwilliam's character, of course the Archbishop would suspect murder. Damn Fitzwilliam. Damn Brother Wulfstan, that bumbling monk. If Fitzwilliam had not died, no one would have cared about the other. But now John Thoresby, the most powerful man in York, was involved.

How odd that the Archbishop should care about a ward who brought him only trouble. Anselm's own father would care not a fig if Anselm died in mysterious circumstances. He would make no inquiries. He would forget the death in no time. He whose son had risen in the Church to the rank of Archdeacon of York. It was not just that Anselm was the second son, marked for the Church. His father had rejected him because he had no taste for violence. Once Anselm had shown his colors, he could do nothing to win his father's respect, much less his love. But the Archbishop, a mere guardian, wanted to know how the odious Fitzwilliam had died, a young man who had aspired to break all the commandments as often as possible.

What a lucky fellow, Oswald Fitzwilliam. Doubtless he had been sheltered as a youth, and hence his appetite for sin. Man craves the unknown. The mysterious. Anselm had learned early about sins of the flesh. All curiosity had been wrung from him by the slime his father trained as soldiers, the curs among whom his whore of a mother had thrown him. The quiet virtue expected at the abbey school had been a welcome relief.

11

DIGBY'S DEAL

Long after the Guildmaster had gone home to his bed, Owen sat in the corner, vaguely aware of murmuring voices, the sour smells of ale, wine, and unwashed bodies, the draft that wrapped around his legs when a customer opened the door to the street. He rubbed the scar on his cheek and stared down at the tavern floor, thinking. Not of Fitzwilliam, but about his home. It was difficult, like peering through a mist, to remember. And so long ago, so much had happened—to them as well as to him, no doubt. Life was difficult in the village. Every journey sent one up mountains and through forests, in and out of every season except summer. Work broke the back and the spirit. There were no physicians like Roglio, or even apothecaries like Wilton. Folks had their remedies—his mother had many—but mostly they soothed rather than cured. Illness and injury meant death more often than not. Would Lucie believe him if he told her that the reason he had not returned was that he could not bear to find them all dead? His mother, her smile, her voice, her spirit, rotting underground, feeding the roots of the oak and ash, feeding the worms. And his sisters—Angie with her snapping eyes, Gwen with her slow, dreamy ways—so many young women died birthing. He crossed himself.

Lucie Wilton had sent him into black thoughts with her anger. Working for her was not easy on his heart.

Better to think on the death of Fitzwilliam. That was what he'd come to York to investigate. The faster he answered the Archbishop's questions, the sooner he might leave. And leave he must. He was losing his heart to a woman who would never care for him, even if Nicholas died. She had rejected Owen before she ever knew him. Unfair, but, there being no one to complain to, he must accept it.

Accept it. Owen looked up, caught Tom's eye, lifted his tankard.

Tom ambled over. "You're looking gloomy, Master Archer," he said. "Bad news from Guildmaster?"

"Nothing to do with him. Missing the old days."

Tom frowned with sympathy. "Aye. Captain of Archers. Not many rise so high."

"Fortune smiled on you when he gave you a living you could keep into old age, Tom. And a bonny wife."

Tom's face brightened. "Aye. The Lord's been good to me." He nodded and moved on among his customers with his pitcher of fine ale.

Owen took a long drink, appreciating the oiliness of the brew in his mouth. Tom Merchet was an artisan of great skill. His art brought comfort to his fellow man. A far cry from Owen's lost art—killing, maiming. Perhaps his apprenticeship would be his redemption.

He imagined himself and Lucie working side by side, like Tom and Bess. Running a tavern. Lucie would lend a different character to the place. Bess was saucy. The men met her eye boldly, called out to her. And she gave as good as she got. But men would lower their eyes to Lucie, like boys addressing their best friend's mother. Their voices would soften. And he—

Pah. Owen could not imagine her married to him. Murdering oaf. One-eyed, clumsy—

He slammed his tankard down on the table. His neighbors glanced up with curiosity. When they saw his apologetic flush, they shook their heads and went back to their business.

But they were soon interested in the Summoner's appearance. He stopped at the counter, then wound his way through the customers with his tankard in hand. He sat down at Owen's table.

His arrival did not help Owen's mood. Hoping rudeness would discourage the Summoner, Owen looked not at him but down at his ale. "Don't tell me the Archdeacon wants to see me again?"

"Not as such."

Owen nodded without looking up.

Digby fidgeted. He'd meant to intrigue Owen with his reply. He leaned closer. "He wants me to follow you. Find out who sent you and why."

Owen glanced up. "Is the Archdeacon always so wary of strangers?"

"Nay."

"Why me?"

Digby grinned. "He didn't say. But I know. He thinks the Archbishop sent you to look into the death of Fitzwilliam."

"And how do you know the Archdeacon thinks that?"

"Because I think so, too." Digby took a long drink. He had gained confidence since last night.

"Surely the Archdeacon did not mean for you to tell me?"

Digby laughed. "Course not."

"So why are you telling me this?"

"Because I want to know what you want to know."

"You mean if I was sent to York by the Archbishop to inquire into the death of Fitzwilliam?"

"Aye."

"Now what, might I ask, is there to question? They say the man died of a winter chill."

Digby snorted. An unpleasant sound. "Not Fitzwilliam. He wasn't that sick."

"You knew him?"

"Aye. I knew him well. An easy source of revenue for the minster fund. Muck clung to him like cobwebs to a cat."

"Stealing the arm from your mother's pit was not his worst offense?"

"Pah. That was nothing."

"You think he was murdered?"

"Aye. That's how it always is with his sort."

"In the abbey infirmary?"

"That's where he died."

"One of the brothers?"

"Not likely. But perhaps. They're not all saints."

"Like the Archdeacon."

Digby snorted again. "Him least of all. They're all born with original sin, same as you and me."

Him least of all. A tantalizing comment.

"What you're saying is that both you and the Archdeacon think this Fitzwilliam was murdered, and that I'm here to find the murderer. You hope I find him, but the Archdeacon doesn't. Is that right?"

Digby grinned.

"Odd that you would work at cross purposes to your employer."

Digby looked down at his tankard. "I don't feel good about it."

"Why are you so interested?"

Digby frowned at Owen as if he couldn't believe the question. "I'm a Summoner. 'Tis my duty to bring sinners to justice. Someone committed murder on hallowed ground. I mean to find out who."

"But the Archdeacon doesn't care?"

"He's protecting someone."

"Who?"

Digby looked away. "Don't know enough to make an accusation. Don't know the connection." He met Owen's eye with a solemn resolve. "But let me give you something to think on. They talk of two deaths. Nay. Two murders." He lingered on the last word.

Owen considered it. "You mean the first one, with no name?"

Digby winked. "Think on't. Honest men don't refuse to give their names. Involved in one of Fitzwilliam's shady deals, I suspect."

"This gets interesting. But what's to make me believe it was murder? What do you know?"

Digby drank down the rest of his ale. "Thirsty work, this talk."

Owen caught Bess's eye. She poured another drink for the Summoner. "Put it on my bill, Bess."

She grinned. "Takes more than a drink to bribe the Summoner, Master Archer."

Digby bristled.

"It's just to afford me his company for a while longer," Owen said.

Bess shrugged and moved away among the tables.

Owen noted Digby's irritation. "I thought you had a thick skin."

"I don't mind them resenting me for snooping. That's natural.

But I'm not corrupt. The Archdeacon wouldn't keep me if I were."

"You speak well of him. But you think he's covering up for a murderer. Make up your mind."

"Everyone has a weakness. Something or someone that they'd risk everything for."

"And his is?"

Digby glanced around, leaned closer. "Nicholas Wilton."

Owen did not like that answer. "What do you mean?"

"Old friends. Went to school together."

"The abbey school?"

"Aye. You know the sort. Always in trouble together. Each quick to come to the other's defense. But they fought over something years ago. Didn't speak to each other all that time. And then, the day after Wilton collapsed, the Archdeacon showed up at the shop. A regular visitor now. You'll see him now you're apprenticed there." There was a funny light in Digby's eyes.

Owen ignored it. "And the Archdeacon sends you to check in on his friend when he's not able to?"

Digby shook his head. "He knows naught of my visits. Nor should he. I'm being honest with you."

Their eyes met. Owen nodded. "I believe you are. What's your game, that's what I'm wondering. Why do you visit the shop?"

Digby grinned. "To see if Mistress Wilton's nervous to see me."

"Anyone would be."

"I mean more nervous than usual."

"And is she?"

"I make the lovely Mistress Wilton very uneasy indeed."

Owen wanted to wipe the sly smile off Digby's face with his fist, but he controlled himself.

"You said the Archdeacon was covering up for someone, implying Nicholas Wilton. And Mistress Wilton knows something, too. So you think Nicholas Wilton killed the two men?"

Digby shrugged. "It all adds up to that, hard though it be to believe. You see, I was there, wasn't I, the night Nicholas Wilton took the physick to the abbey."

Owen sat up. "Took the physick?"

Digby preened with the attention. "For the first pilgrim. He had camp fever. Everyone knows Nicholas Wilton has a secret concoction that is particularly effective for it. Brother Wulfstan went for some. I met him on the way. He returned without it. Wilton was bringing it later, he said. Had to make it up special."

"You believe he poisoned the pilgrim?"

"That's what I'm saying."

"Why?"

Digby sighed. "I don't know. Wilton's not the sort to make trouble. So I reckon there's something we don't know, something the stranger did to him, say. Not knowing who the man was, I can't figure it." He leaned even closer. "But I'll tell you this. I saw Wilton come from the abbey that night. Man looked like he was caving in, that's what he looked like. Then he began to twitch and jerk, and then he fell down in a faint."

"What did you do?"

"Hurried to the infirmary for Brother Wulfstan, but he had his hands full with the pilgrim. Man was flailing around and yelling. So I went back out to see to Wilton. I couldn't rouse him, even with snow on his neck. Hailed a farmer passing on a donkey cart and took Wilton home in it."

Owen looked long at the man. "So what is your weakness?"

Digby grinned. "I'm no fool to tell that, Master Archer." He took a drink. Sat back. "Told you more than you dreamed I knew, didn't I? Seems you owe me something in return."

Here it came. "What do you want?"

"As I said, I want to make sure a sinner confesses and does penance."

Owen wondered why it was so difficult to believe the man took his position seriously. Took pride in ferreting out sinners. His appearance was against him, for certain. But so was Owen's. Odd thing was, having met the man's mother, Owen wanted to trust Potter Digby. Maybe it was time to trust his instincts. Thinking had not gotten him far. "How about the first pilgrim's name? If I tell you that, will you tell me what you find out with the information?"

Digby's face lit up. "I swear."

They both leaned forward. "His name was Sir Geoffrey Montaigne."

"Montaigne," Digby whispered, "Geoffrey Montaigne. Now that stirs a memory somewhere."

"I hoped it might."

Owen had also hoped Digby would leave with the information, but instead he sat there frowning into his ale.

Oh, well. Owen settled back to consider what Digby had told him. Nicholas Wilton had mixed a physick for Montaigne, then fallen ill himself. Digby was witness to that. Owen sat up. "What was your business at the abbey that night?"

Digby's eyes slid to Owen's, then away. "I'm Summoner. My business is everywhere."

Owen could tell Digby was lying. It was encouraging that he could tell. So maybe the rest was true. "A clever answer. What are you hiding?"

"I've offered you my help."

"Then you should tell me all you know."

"I don't want you getting the wrong ideas."

"You were there for suspect reasons?"

"I was waiting for the Archdeacon. I had to speak with him."

"He was at the abbey?"

"He dined with the Abbot that night."

"The night Nicholas Wilton, the Archdeacon's old friend, collapsed outside the abbey? The night before he resumed his friendship with Nicholas Wilton?"

Digby looked worried. "It's not how it sounds. I'm sure of it." He shook his head. "Montaigne. Geoffrey Montaigne." He grew quiet again.

If Owen believed Digby, he might have the answer to why he had not got far. He'd been looking at it all wrong, focusing on Fitzwilliam and what he'd been up to right before his death. But if the trouble had begun with Montaigne's death, not Fitzwilliam's... Perhaps there was something much more intriguing being hidden than the death of the Archbishop's ward. And the pilgrim Montaigne was the key to it, not Fitzwilliam. Could that be?

What did he know about the man? Montaigne, considered a virtuous, chivalrous knight by all who knew him, had come to York to atone for a past sin, and the journey brought on a recurrence of camp fever. Such fever can kill, and the long ride had opened a recent wound, which had weakened him, making it even likelier that the fever would kill him. The Infirmarian thought Montaigne had known he might die at the abbey.

But Brother Wulfstan was uncomfortable. He might feel responsible for Montaigne's dying in his infirmary, but Owen did not think so. The monk would not have survived as Infirmarian if he blamed himself for every death in the abbey, no more than a captain could function if he blamed himself for the loss of men in battle. You taught them what you knew, and then it was up to them and God. Wulfstan would have done all he could.

Still, Wulfstan was uncomfortable. According to Digby, after Wulfstan had exhausted all his knowledge, he had gone to Nicholas Wilton for help. And Nicholas Wilton had collapsed outside the infirmary after delivering the medicine he had mixed specifically for Montaigne. While the Archdeacon was dining with the Abbot and Digby was lurking around outside. Thorny.

Poisoning can look like a fever. But if the man was near death, why bother?

Because waiting was hard. Especially when one's life hung in the balance. Be patient. Owen had drummed that into his new archers. Do not rush. Wait for the best moment to let fly the arrow. Do not let fear or desperation loosen your grip too soon. Nothing is changed by your panic, only your ability to reason. But some forgot the lesson when tested in battle.

If Montaigne had been poisoned, it was because someone had panicked. He would have died anyway, but perhaps more slowly. Owen could see the how. If Brother Wulfstan did not sense trouble, he would not examine the physick. And that was what made Digby's suspicion plausible. Brother Wulfstan would not have gone to Nicholas Wilton for help if he had suspected him of wanting to poison the patient. So when the physick had not worked, Wulfstan had taken it as a sign that the Lord wanted Montaigne now. The monk would accept that. It was Church doctrine.

That was, perhaps, the how.

But the why? Owen stared at Digby, who was nodding to himself with a pleased look on his face.

"So?"

"I've placed Montaigne. Lady D'Arby's lover, he was. Folk said 'twas his babe killed her."

The name sounded familiar, but he could not place it at once. "Lady D'Arby?"

"Your Mistress Wilton's mother. You might speak with 'em up at Freythorpe Hadden. Dame Phillippa and Sir Robert."

"He was the lover of Mistress Wilton's mother?"

Digby nodded. "The beautiful Amelie. Sir Robert's war prize."

"And Montaigne's baby killed her? So there was a scandal?"

"Lots of talk, but no action taken. She died. Montaigne disappeared. Lord D'Arby went on pilgrimage to the Holy Land."

"Who is Dame Phillippa?"

"Sir Robert's sister. Looks after him."

"Where is Freythorpe Hadden?"

"South of here. Ask your new mistress." Digby drained his tankard, rose, extended his hand to Owen.

Owen cupped his hands around his drink. "Unwise for us to look friendly, Summoner."

Digby shrugged and walked away.

Leaving Owen in an even worse mood than he'd found him in. Montaigne was the lover of Lucie's mother. Owen did not like that at all.

12

KNOTS

Owen lay awake, bothered by all that Digby had told him.

Montaigne and Amelie, Lady D'Arby. There had been a scandal. As Lucie's husband, Nicholas Wilton might have wished to avenge his wife's family's shame. But surely that was an old story. On the other hand, Montaigne's return to York would reopen old wounds.

Owen thought of the wizened old man lying in the sickroom. Nicholas hardly seemed strong enough to hatch such a plot and see it through.

And then Owen had an awful thought. He tried to discard it, but he could not. Lucie Wilton could have prepared the physick. She was knowledgeable. She could concoct a poison as well as her husband could. Digby had said Wilton delivered the physick to the abbey, but the Summoner could not know who had prepared it.

Perhaps Lucie Wilton. She might have reason to hate Montaigne. She had a marked antipathy toward soldiers. Owen had assumed it was her father, sending her to the convent and going off when the mother died. But perhaps it was Montaigne. And though Montaigne had not identified himself, that might not matter. Children noticed much. Lucie might have seen him, recognized him from the past. Owen must find out if she had been to the abbey while Montaigne was there. The possibility sent pain across the blind eye. He rubbed beneath the patch.

There was no escaping it. Lucie Wilton might be guilty. Her being a beautiful young woman should not cloud his judgment. He knew full well that a woman could be as ruthless as a man. It was not the jongleur who had blinded him.

But what a sickening suspicion. It was an ugly, unredeemed world that could make Lucie Wilton betray her calling to heal and use her God-given skill to murder.

And yet suspecting Nicholas Wilton of the same crime had not made Owen sick at heart. He disgusted himself. He was smitten by Lucie Wilton, and was allowing it to color his judgment. It was not impossible that Lucie might avenge her mother's ignoble death in such a way. Given her training as an apothecary, it was the likeliest way for her to strike back.

Of course, all this assumed Digby was right, that Montaigne had been poisoned. But where did that leave Fitzwilliam?

It was still possible that Digby was wrong. The evidence lay in the grave of Montaigne. All the evidence lay in the grave of an unknown pilgrim. Were such graves marked? What words would the monks of St. Mary's speak over the grave of an unknown pilgrim? How would they mark it? A gentle pilgrim who met his end on such-and-such a day in the thirty-sixth year of the reign of King Edward the Third of England?

The grave was where his clues lay. Owen flipped over on his left side, sending a shooting pain through his shoulder. With a curse he rolled back on his right side.

What unpleasant tasks this sleuthing necessitated—tussling with Lord March, opening a grave. And to disturb consecrated ground was a sacrilege. Would God blame him for it? No point in worrying about that yet. He might not have an opportunity to find out. Abbot Campian would probably refuse to cooperate. And Thoresby might reject evidence got in such a way. Owen did not like this prying into people's lives. It made him no different from the Summoner.

Next morning, Owen sought out Digby. He discovered him standing in the shadows near the marketplace, watching a maid and a soldier who stood at the edge of the stalls, their heads bent close together, speaking in hushed voices.

"Looking for sinners?" Owen asked Digby.

The soldier glanced over at them, whispered something to the maid.

Digby backed farther into shadow and put a finger to his lips.

The couple parted, the maid wandering over to a stall, the soldier hailing a comrade.

"I have a mission for you, my friend," Owen said, grinning.

Digby gave him a disgusted look. "So we're friends now, are we?"

"You've made it rather plain we're meeting at the tavern."

"Have I caused trouble for you?"

"I hope not. Time will tell."

"Well, you've ruined my morning. What do you want?"

Wulfstan smiled at Henry's attempts to tie the rag around the monk's head. Michaelo had one of his headaches this morning, and Wulfstan thought to use the opportunity to teach Henry the treatment the monk responded to best. Feverfew steeped in a warm cup of wine, to mask the bitterness of the herb, then a cloth soaked in minted water bound around his head. Wulfstan suspected that Michaelo enjoyed the extra wine and the chance to sit and dream while the cure took effect, but it seemed a harmless vice. It was not as if he appeared every week with his complaint. Twice a month, and not at regular intervals, so it might be a legitimate complaint. At worst a moderate vice.

Henry had done well with the feverfew-and-wine concoction, and the soaking of the cloth. But his fingers were all thumbs with a knot.

"No fisher folk in your family, I see," Wulfstan said.

"I have never been out on the water, Brother Wulfstan. Nor tied a knot. Am I very stupid?"

"I do not think the tying of knots renders one intelligent, Henry. You will learn." Wulfstan showed him again. Henry tried once more. "Better. Much better, God be praised." Wulfstan undid the loose, partial knot and handed the cloth to Henry. "Soak this once more and give it another try."

Brother Michaelo was wondrously patient through all this, quietly sipping the wine and humming. The wine obviously worked its magic. Indeed, that must be the key to Michaelo, Wulfstan thought, he loved his wine. He thanked the Lord that Michaelo had not been apprenticed to him in the infirmary.

Henry's next attempt at the knot was interrupted by Brother Sebastian's breathless entrance. "Summoner Digby to see you, Brother Wulfstan."

Digby's name burned in the Infirmarian's stomach.

"The Abbot said to show him back here. Is it safe?" Sebastian, a healthy man, associated the infirmary with bloodlettings and death.

"Quite safe," Wulfstan assured him, though he wished he could say otherwise and deter the Summoner. Merciful Mother, let Digby not bring bad news this time. "Show him in."

Wulfstan looked down at Henry's work. "Why, Henry, that will hold well."

"Tie up a boat like that, and the first wave would sweep it downriver."

Brother Wulfstan recognized Digby's voice. "Brother Michaelo's head is in no danger of being swept away," Wulfstan said, angry that the man undid his praise.

Brother Michaelo sniffed and opened his eyes. "What smells of river water? It cannot be the cloth?"

Wulfstan pulled Digby away. Henry assured Michaelo that he had soaked the cloth in well water. The Summoner followed Wulfstan to the small hearth at the other end of the room.

"Forgive me for interrupting your work."

Wulfstan closed his eyes and hardened himself for bad news. "What is your news, Summoner?"

"No news. A question, if it is not too much trouble. It is for the diocesan records."

"My Abbot would be more appropriate in a question of records."

"Forgive me, I thought you would be the one to ask. You see, it is about the pilgrim who died in your infirmary—in this very room—the night of the first snow."

Deus juva me. Wulfstan's old legs threatened to collapse. "I forget myself. Sit down by the fire and rest yourself." He sat likewise, gratefully, gripping his knees through the coarse wool of his habit to keep them from knocking. "The pilgrim. Yes. What is the question?"

"Did you bury him on the abbey grounds?"

Wulfstan pondered the question. Or what it implied. Why would the Archdeacon care where someone had been buried? To be sure he had been buried? Wulfstan had heard there was a brisk trade in bodies for relics. Surely the Archdeacon had no cause to suspect the monks of St. Mary's of trafficking in false relics. No. More likely they questioned the cause of the pilgrims' deaths. They hoped to dig up the body here in York and have Master Saurian examine it. Wulfstan had heard of such things—digging up the dead. But surely the Archbishop would not desecrate consecrated ground in such a way? Merciful Mother. Wulfstan was not sure whether anything could be told three months later. But if the poison were evident... They would blame him. Dear God. And he would have no choice but to point his finger at Nicholas Wilton. And Lucie would lose her security. And he the infirmary, for—as Lucie had wisely pointed out—how could Abbot Campian trust him not to make such a mistake again? They would declare him too old to be competent.

"Brother Wulfstan?" Digby leaned forward, frowning. "It requires a simple yes or no."

True. And he could not think of any reason not to answer. "My thoughts are on Brother Michaelo this morning, Summoner. Yes. We buried the gentle knight on the abbey grounds, as he had requested."

"Ah. Then he made a behest to the abbey?"

Wulfstan nodded. "The Abbot can tell you the amount."

"And what name did you inscribe on the stone?"

The question puzzled Wulfstan. "No name, just 'A Pilgrim,' as he had wished."

"But the behest. From whom will that be collected?"

"He brought it with him. Spoils of war, he said. Truly, these are not questions for an Infirmarian."

The Summoner rose. "You have been most helpful."

Wulfstan showed him to the door, where Sebastian waited to accompany him out.

The Summoner caught the door as it was about to close on him. "But surely he told you his name. Or there was something in his possessions that identified him?"

Wulfstan shook his head. "I can vouch for that myself. He never said, and there was nothing to suggest who he was."

"Did he have any visitors while he was here?"

"None."

"No one from the city?"

"No one at all, Summoner Digby."

The Summoner shrugged and left.

Wulfstan went back to his instruction, but his mind was in turmoil. The Archdeacon must have sent Digby. But why? What was he getting at? Perhaps the minster collected a portion of such behests. Such matters were none of his business. Yet he had told the Summoner about it. Surely Digby had not come to the Infirmarian for information like that. Unless the Abbot had denied that the abbey received a behest in order to keep the money at St. Mary's, where there were always more expenses than money. The orchard wall needed mending, an exquisite chasuble had been torn beyond repair, and dry rot had weakened several of the tables in the refectory. But would his Abbot lie? Wulfstan doubted it. He had never known the Abbot to hide behind a lie. Indeed, Wulfstan devoutly hoped he was not wrong about his superior. He had always held him up as a model of men.

Whether the pilgrim was buried at the abbey and what his name was, those were the Summoner's questions, now Wulfstan thought of it. His name. A missing person, perhaps? That was it. But if someone was traveling in disguise, he would not go by his own name. And Digby had not asked for a description. In any case, the pilgrim had seemed such an honest man.

"Brother Wulfstan, you've cut yourself." Henry lifted the knife from Wulfstan's hand and dabbed at the blood welling from a cut on the hand beneath it.

Wulfstan stared at his own red blood for moments before

seeing it. "Oh my." He'd been chopping parsley for a morning tonic. Chopped right into his hand and never noticed, no more than any of his other aches and pains. He crossed himself and said a prayer of thanksgiving. It might have been much worse. "Well, there you see the danger of daydreaming while working with sharp instruments, God be praised." He made light of it to lessen dear Henry's concern.

"Let me wash it out for you," the novice offered.

Wulfstan accepted his ministrations, then went to ask the Abbot for permission to go into town.

"Does it have to do with the Summoner's visit?" Abbot Campian asked.

Wulfstan could withhold facts, but he could not lie. "Yes. I wish to know why Archdeacon Anselm sent him to me. He did ask for me?"

The Abbot nodded. "I wondered about that, too. What did he want?"

Wulfstan told him.

The Abbot sighed. "Most unfortunate. Had he asked me, I could have told him the pilgrim's name. Montaigne. Sir Geoffrey Montaigne. I suspect that the Archdeacon wants to strike him from his list of infidelities, now that both parties are dead."

Wulfstan shook his head. "I do not understand."

"Just give the Archdeacon the name, Wulfstan, and that will be an end to it."

Wulfstan turned to go.

"Surely you do not mean to go out in sandals, Brother Wulfstan?"

The Infirmarian looked down at his dusty toes. He'd put on his cloak and forgotten his boots. "Of course. I was in such a hurry."

Abbot Campian put a hand on Wulfstan's shoulder and looked deep into his eyes. "Are you up to such an errand, my old friend?"

"Oh, quite. Of course. I was simply rushed." Wulfstan scurried back to his cell. Perhaps all this trouble was God telling him that he was, indeed, too old to be trusted with the lives of the monks of St. Mary's.

But his memory was intact. Sir Geoffrey Montaigne. He would remember that.

A warm sun had already turned the snow on the streets to slush, and it was not yet midday. The icy wetness penetrated the leather of Wulfstan's old boots. His feet were frozen by the time he stood in the hall waiting to see the Archdeacon.

"Brother Wulfstan." The Archdeacon smiled as the Infirmarian was shown in to his chamber. "How can I help you?"

How to begin? Wulfstan felt unprepared. He'd spent the entire walk fretting over his cold feet and chanting the pilgrim's name so he would not forget it. "I—" When in doubt, trust to the truth. "About the Summoner's visit today, I—well, you can imagine how disturbing a soul finds a visit from the Summoner. And his questions. They were so odd. I wondered, as did my Abbot, what was the purpose of asking them of me?" There. He had forced it all out.

Archdeacon Anselm picked up a parchment, set it down, pushed an ink pot a little farther to his left, touched his brow, then, at last, said, "This is the first I have heard of my Summoner visiting you, Brother Wulfstan. But perhaps I simply do not connect you with one of his inquiries. If you told me what he'd asked—"

"It was about the pilgrim who died at the abbey just before Christmas. He asked had the pilgrim been buried at the abbey, and what was his name."

Anselm leaned toward him, far more interested than he had been at first. Wulfstan did not know whether to be pleased or not. "And what were your answers?"

"He has not told you?"

"Not yet. As I said, I did not know of his visit."

"Oh. Yes."

"Your answers, Brother Wulfstan?"

"The pilgrim was buried at the abbey, as he'd requested. But the pilgrim's name I could not give him."

"And he did not say why he asked these things?"

Wulfstan shook his head. He noticed that the Archdeacon shared Brother Michaelo's habit of flaring his nostrils when he thought. Like a horse. An odd habit for humans. "So you did not send him to quiz me?"

"I assure you I did not, Brother Wulfstan, and I apologize for any discomfort his visit might have caused you."

"Strange." And now Wulfstan wondered whether he must tell the Archdeacon the name of the pilgrim. After all, he said he had not sent Digby, so it must be the Summoner who wanted to know, not the Archdeacon. Wulfstan had a queer feeling in his stomach about this whole business. A protective feeling toward his dead friend. Geoffrey. His friend had not wanted his name known. But Abbot Campian had told him to give the Archdeacon the name.

The Archdeacon rose, and so did Wulfstan.

"You said you could not give him the pilgrim's name," the Archdeacon said as he led Wulfstan to the door. "You mean that you did not know it?"

Oh dear. Could he disobey? "No, Archdeacon, I did not know the pilgrim's name." Which was true. He had not at the time.

"Anonymous to the grave."

Wulfstan nodded, his heart in his mouth.

Out on the street, he felt weak and lightheaded. And cold. His joints and his extremities ached. He thought of Lucie Wilton's cozy hearth fire. The apothecary was closer at this point than the abbey. And he did feel dizzy and chilled. He decided to pay her a visit, ask after Nicholas.

He had not foreseen that the apprentice would be minding the shop. "I—I came to see Mistress Wilton. To ask after Nicholas. I was out and—"

Owen nodded. "Mistress Wilton is in the kitchen. She will welcome your company, I am sure."

Brother Wulfstan went back.

Lucie sat by the fire, darning. "What a pleasant surprise." Then her smile turned to a concerned frown. "What is the matter, Brother Wulfstan? You look as if you've had a fright."

He had not meant to mention it. But her solicitous manner made him want to confide in her. After all, they were in this together, in a sense. "Summoner Digby paid me a visit today. Asked questions about the pilgrim who died the night Nicholas took ill."

Lucie sat him down and poured him a cup of wine, adding spices and heating it with a hot poker. "Now," she said, handing him the cup and resuming her seat, "tell me what he wanted."

"He wanted to know if I had known the name of the pilgrim, if he'd had any visitors, where he was buried. It must mean he suspects that a sin was committed. That is the Summoner's business."

Lucie looked thoughtful. "But such questions are not to the point, are they?"

"I don't know why he asked them. And why he asked them of me. The Archdeacon could not tell me."

"The Archdeacon? You spoke with him, too?"

"I went to him. My Abbot thought it best. That is why I am out in the city. But the Archdeacon seemed to know nothing of the visit."

"And were you able to tell Digby the pilgrim's name?"

Again, forced so close to a lie. "I—no. I could not tell him."

Lucie studied his face. "You would have told him had you known, wouldn't you?"

"Charity is difficult for me with a man such as Summoner Digby."

"You would lie?"

Wulfstan flushed. "Not that. I would try to—avoid telling him."

"And is that what you did? Avoid it? Do you really know who the pilgrim was?"

If he said yes, the next question would naturally be the pilgrim's name. Again, the old monk was loath to reveal his friend's identity. And what good would it do Lucie to know for whom Nicholas had mixed the fatal physick? "I could not tell Digby, that is the truth." Narrowly, but it was the truth.

Lucie seemed satisfied. She picked up her darning. "Some unfinished business, perhaps. We have nothing to worry about, my friend. He would have no way of discovering our secret. Drink your wine. Let it warm you."

Wulfstan sipped it. It warmed him most pleasantly. He sipped again, sat back, and let himself relax. Of course Lucie was right. They had shared their secret with no one else.

As he sat by the fire watching Lucie's lovely face bent over the darning, Wulfstan noted how much like her mother she looked now. The hair was not raven like Amelie's, and the mouth was firmer, the chin squarer, but—Geoffrey Montaigne. He remembered now. Lady D'Arby's lover. It had been such a scandal, even Wulfstan had heard about it. The beautiful Amelie, Lady D'Arby, and the fair young knight who had guarded her on the Channel crossing. She had been with child by him when she died. Sir Robert had been in Calais too long for it to be his. Geoffrey Montaigne.

"*Mon Dieu*," he whispered. Lady D'Arby had been Geoffrey's only love.

Lucie looked up, frowned. "What is it?"

Wulfstan flushed. Shook his head. Thank heaven he had not told her the name. He should not stir up bad memories for her. Indeed, who knew how much an eight-year-old had been told. He knew little about the raising of children. "It is nothing."

"You did not look as if it were nothing."

"It was simply—I thought how much you look like your mother. The way you held your head just then."

It was Lucie's turn to flush. "I am not half so beautiful as my mother."

Saint Paul said that it was unwise to flatter women. That they put too much stock in appearance. But poor Lucie had so little joy these days. "I think you are more beautiful than your mother."

Lucie gave him a perplexed smile. "Brother Wulfstan. You are flattering me."

"I am a silly old man, my dear Lucie. But I know beauty when I see it." He rose, fumbling with his sleeves to hide his flushed face. "And now I must hurry back for Vespers."

She took his hand. "Thank you for coming."

"I am glad you could take the time for me."

He nodded to Owen as he went out through the shop. Wulfstan felt Owen's eye on him all the way out the door. That man did not belong as an apprentice in Lucie Wilton's shop. Wulfstan did not like to think of him there, with that predatory eye fixed on her innocent beauty. An apprentice should be a young man. A boy. An innocent.

. . .

From the shadow of the neighboring house's second story, Digby watched Wulfstan leave the shop. Then he went in.

Owen held up his hand to keep Digby quiet while he listened to Lucie's movements in the kitchen. She was speaking with Tildy, the new serving girl. She would not overhear them. He nodded. "So what did you learn?"

"I might ask you the same. I just watched him leave the shop."

"He spoke with Lucie about your visit."

"Why did he come here?"

"You tell me." Owen fixed his eye on Digby until the man flushed.

"He seemed disturbed," Digby said, "very disturbed by my questions about Montaigne's grave. But he knew nothing about who Montaigne was. And according to him, the man had no visitors."

"So we still don't know what makes the good Infirmarian so nervous. Did you believe him?"

"Aye. He's an innocent, for all his age. Takes his vows seriously."

"Montaigne's grave is at the abbey?"

Digby gave him a worried look. "I won't disturb a consecrated grave."

"I would not ask that of you. Thank you, Digby. You're a good man."

When Digby left, Owen paced the shop. *He would have no way of discovering our secret.* Holy Mother in Heaven. And yet it seemed she did not know the pilgrim's identity. Could it be a code between them? In case they were overheard? Or might they have some other secret? Sweet Jesus, let her be innocent.

But she had a secret. One shared with Wulfstan. One that Wulfstan feared the Summoner might discover. And it had something to do with Montaigne's death. That did not sound innocent.

13

DIGBY'S WEAKNESS

Brother Michaelo glided into the room. "Your Summoner paid a visit to old woolly-head today while I was taking my cure."

"I know."

The young man's eyes widened, an alert look unusual for him. "You have another friend at St. Mary's?"

"How charming for you to be jealous, Michaelo. But it was the Infirmarian himself who told me. The old fool worried why he'd been singled out. He's going to slip, Michaelo. I cannot have that."

Michaelo shrugged and yawned. "Why you fuss over Nicholas Wilton, that worn-out man, I cannot understand. An apothecary. A merchant, really." He sighed and slumped down in a chair.

"He was as fair as you once, my young buck."

"But now he's palsied."

"Youth makes you cruel."

"I doubt that you'll worry over me when I'm old and palsied."

"I will be long dead."

"But would you? Worry over me?"

Anselm looked away. Of course not. Michaelo came to him out of greed, not love. Anselm was Michaelo's chance of escape from the abbey. It had been different with Nicholas. He had loved Anselm. Until the Abbot frightened him. And even afterwards, there had been a tenderness. There would never be anyone like Nicholas. There could never be. But Anselm needed Michaelo's loyalty. "Of course I would worry over you, Michaelo. You mean very much to me."

Michaelo stretched contentedly and stood up. "Am I to do

something about old woolly-head?"

"He does worry me."

"And what do I get in return?"

"A word in the Archbishop's ear. About how useful you might be to him as Lord Chancellor's secretary. That is what you want, is it not? To see the court?" Michaelo was suited to that life. He would go quietly mad at the abbey, where he felt trapped, where his only recreation was the Infirmarian's wine.

Michaelo glowed. "What about the fishy one?"

"I'll deal with my Summoner."

"He's been seen with the one-eyed Welshman. At the York Tavern. And elsewhere."

Anselm pretended not to be surprised. "Digby is a scoundrel."

"He's quite handsome, the Welshman."

Anselm ignored the comment. Michaelo was too lazy to be promiscuous. But not so lazy that he would not take care of Wulfstan. He knew better than to disappoint Anselm. He could not afford to have Anselm telling Abbot Campian or Archbishop Thoresby of Michaelo's petty thievery and the bribes he paid to escape work. Such behavior would not recommend him for the post he desired.

"The abbey is an unhealthy place this winter, my young buck. Take care that you do not catch a chill yourself."

Michaelo pouted. "You grow tired of me."

"Not at all, Michaelo. I am concerned about your welfare."

Michaelo took his leave.

Anselm paced his room. Digby had betrayed him. Potter Digby, raised up from the slime by Anselm, set in the path of grace. Meeting Owen Archer in that bitch's tavern. Plotting with him. Against the man who had brought him out of the vermin city and certain damnation with that witch of a mother. Cur. Ungrateful monster.

Brother Wulfstan made his way back from the Wiltons' in a daze.

Gentle Geoffrey had been Lady D'Arby's lover. The man who

seemed an innocent. When Wulfstan had heard of the adulterous affair, he had imagined a rakish knight. A Fitzwilliam. An Owen Archer. Glib, clever, careless of the feelings of his fellow man. But Geoffrey was nothing of the sort. He was God-fearing, kind, well spoken, considerate. How could Geoffrey have betrayed Sir Robert D'Arby, the man he had served? Were Wulfstan a farmer instead of a monk, would it be clear to him? He had never dreamed that Geoffrey had lain with the woman he remembered with such tenderness. A married woman. That must be the sin that had brought Geoffrey here to make his peace with the Lord.

But he had also spoken of killing someone. Wulfstan had thought nothing of that. The man had been a soldier. He'd mistaken poor Nicholas for someone else. Or had he?

Nicholas Wilton is Master? Son of old Paul? No, it cannot be. You are mistaken. Nicholas Wilton is dead these fifteen years.

Geoffrey had been almost angry, insisting on it.

Wulfstan had told Nicholas that.

Dear God in Heaven. Sweet Mary and all the saints.

But why would Geoffrey have tried to kill Nicholas? Jealousy? Nicholas and Lady D'Arby had been friends.

Wulfstan went to the chapel. *My dearest Lord,* he prayed, kneeling on the cold stones, *Help me to understand. Tell me what I should do.*

He stared at the statue of Mary, Mother of God, the Virgin Mother. He knelt there he knew not how long, his thoughts in turmoil. It did not make sense. And what of the Archdeacon? He had been Nicholas's friend at the abbey school. More than a friend. If Geoffrey had tried to kill Nicholas, and Anselm knew of that... It was too much for Wulfstan to contemplate.

He picked himself up off the damp stone, brushed off his habit, and went to seek out Abbot Campian.

Owen asked Lucie if he might go out after Vespers. It was time for another talk with Wulfstan. If he let the old monk think too long about Digby's visit, he might talk to the wrong people. Whoever they might be. And he must discover the secret Wulfstan shared with Lucie.

Owen did not look forward to the interrogation. His questions would upset the old monk. He did not enjoy hounding Wulfstan. But better to upset him than let him walk into a trap.

Abbot Campian was puzzled. "You are Brother Wulfstan's second visitor today. Has this anything to do with Summoner Digby's earlier visit?"

"I know of his visit."

"That is intriguing. The Archdeacon did not." Campian's usually calm eyes were troubled. "The Summoner's questions regarded Sir Geoffrey Montaigne. I presume you know who he was?"

"Yes, I do."

"And your inquiry into Fitzwilliam's death has led you to question Montaigne's?"

With so little information Campian had put together the truth. It was plain to Owen why the man had achieved the position of Abbot. "It is essential that you keep my secret."

"And to Brother Wulfstan? What do I say to him? He was alarmed by the Summoner's visit. Now you return. He is an old man. The deaths in the infirmary distressed him deeply. Especially Montaigne's."

"When I have learned from him what I need to know, I will tell him my purpose."

The Abbot bowed his head for a few breaths, then looked up. Owen read calm resolve in Campian's eyes. "Tomorrow the Archbishop arrives. I intend to speak with him about this."

"May I talk to Brother Wulfstan?"

"Not until I speak with His Grace."

"Come with me to speak with the Archbishop's secretary, Jehannes. You will hear that His Grace would wish me to do this."

The Abbot did not blink. "I will speak with His Grace tomorrow."

• • •

Digby dressed himself with care and made sure to tell his landlady, Widow Cartwright, that he would dine this evening with the Archdeacon.

"He must be pleased with you to extend such an honor." The widow considered whom she ought to tell first. News of the Summoner was always eagerly received. All folk liked to keep track of his career. Good times for Digby meant trouble for someone. It was good to know when to watch your back.

Digby hurried to the minster yard over frozen mud and slippery cobbles. As dusk descended, the sun-thawed streets refroze and a mist rose up from the iced puddles, mingling with the damp river air. Digby was chilled through his wool cloak by the time he arrived at the Archdeacon's chambers.

While warming himself before the fire, Digby drank down a goblet of mulled wine and poured himself another. He felt aglow by the time they sat to eat, and looked forward to a pleasant evening. The Archdeacon seemed in an expansive mood, speaking of the minster windows and Digby's critical role in raising the funds. They toasted their successful partnership and cut in to an excellent roast. Perhaps it was the wine, which the Archdeacon encouraged him to enjoy, or perhaps the praise, that loosened Digby's tongue. He chatted about this and that, working his way into a confiding mood, and at last he brought up the one blemish that troubled his otherwise perfect contentment—that he suspected Wilton of poisoning the pilgrim at the abbey and was reluctant to bring him to justice because of the Archdeacon's friendship with the apothecary. Of course Digby stopped short of accusing the Archdeacon of protecting his friend. Indeed, he apologized for shocking him with such an idea. But people changed over time, got caught up in situations that twisted their thinking and led them astray.

Anselm looked puzzled. "You make a serious accusation, Digby. My friend led astray. Indeed it might happen as you say. But Nicholas. I have seen no hint of evil in him." The Archdeacon twisted his goblet round and round in his hands. "But as my Summoner you have always judged with a fair reasoning. Perhaps you might enlighten me."

The praise, even more than the wine, buoyed his spirits. Digby gave him all the details he had put together. Except, again, his suspicion that Anselm wished to cover up for Nicholas. For he was certain now, as he sat across from the man and saw his quiet, pious countenance, that Anselm could not be guilty of such a thing.

Anselm put down his cup and nodded when Digby concluded. "I thank you for discussing this with me. And so honestly. I will consider this tonight, Digby, and give you my decision tomorrow."

Throughout the rest of the meal, Digby sensed that the Archdeacon was distracted, which was no surprise. He would not be much of a friend, were he to take such a suggestion calmly. Digby took his leave directly after the savory with a warm feeling of having done the right thing.

But as he made his way home, the damp, icy air began to sober him. And as he sobered he grew afraid, thinking about what he had done, thinking of the rather quiet manner in which the Archdeacon had received the accusation of his friend. He had frowned, but he had not exclaimed. He had shown no surprise.

And it came to Digby that he had been unwise to blurt it out. He began to tremble. He knew it was partly the aftereffects of the wine that jangled his nerves, but he was afraid, and too troubled to go directly to bed. So, icy though it was, with a soft snow falling, he headed down Lop Lane, then Footless Lane, past St. Leonard's Hospital, to Lendal Tower. The smell and the rush of the river often calmed him.

He stood on the walkway beside the tower, looking down at the rushing water, the river swollen from the beginning of the thaw, and tried to let the familiar sound soothe him. But the movement beneath him made him dizzy and fluttered his stomach. When he closed his eyes, the rushing water was there, but now spinning in a whirlpool. He tasted bile, and his head pounded. Too much wine. Oh, sweet Jesus and all the saints, he was drunk as a lord.

He felt a hand on his shoulder. "Are you unwell, my friend?"

Digby recognized the voice with a shiver of shame and fear. He took a great gulp of air and grasped the rough stones of the tower before he opened his eyes.

"I am afraid my hospitality was overmuch," Anselm said. "The wine has made you unwell."

It was too dark to see the Archdeacon's face, but something in his voice frightened Digby. Oh, he meant to sound sympathetic, apologetic, but there was a chilly edge to it. Perhaps it was just disapproval.

"Forgive me. I have been foolish…" Digby's tongue felt thick and woolly. He was terribly thirsty.

The Archdeacon put a protective arm around Digby. "Come. I will help you home."

"I can manage."

The Archdeacon patted him. "Please. Let me perform my Christian duty." He began to lead Digby, one arm at his back, a hand at his elbow. The walkway was indeed slippery. Digby was grateful for the Archdeacon's support. He forgot why he had been afraid. They came to the end of the walk and the Archdeacon paused, facing the snowy bank that fell away down beneath them, from bright snow to shadow to the glitter of the rushing Ouse. The water was deep here.

"God's greatness manifest, is it not, Digby?"

The drop-off and the motion of the water brought on another wave of dizziness. Digby turned his back to the river. "I must get home."

"Home. Yes. What is it they call your mother? The Riverwoman? Yes. The river. That is really your home, is it not, my friend?" Digby wondered why the Archdeacon went on so. It was a simple matter. He must get home. But the Archdeacon kept talking. "Even on a night such as this, you had to stop here, listen to its singing. What does she say to you, Digby? What does the river whisper to you?"

Digby shook his head and leaned against the Archdeacon, burying his head in the coarse wool cloak.

"Do you turn your back on her, Digby? Foolish man." The voice roughened. "Never turn your back on a woman. You must see the eyes. Look into their depths. See the treachery. Yes, you look away and she sounds comforting, she murmurs to you, but turn, Digby, and look. Look deep, Digby. See her treachery."

Strong hands turned Digby around. He clutched for the cloak, but there was only air. The silvery, rushing Ouse dizzied him. He cried out.

A hand went over his mouth, his feet were kicked out from under him, and he was lifted, swung back. No, dear God, no! Digby swung forward, out over the bank, and fell, first through the icy air, then slipping down the snowy bank, hidden rocks tearing at him. So cold, so horribly cold, the snow burned on his cut hands as he tried to grasp a rock, a bush, anything to stop him. The thunder of the river warned him of its nearness. The water rose up to clutch him, embrace him. He fought back up to the cold, but the drink and the pain weakened him. He kept sinking into the warmer depths, which were comforting, soothing. No. This was madness. He had to get a breath, must not breathe down here. He struggled up, up. His head came crack against something. Had he dived by mistake? He changed direction, but it felt wrong. He panicked. What was up, what down, he could not tell. His chest was being crushed. *I am dead*, he thought. *He has killed me.* A great sob rose up from his soul, and he gave himself up to the river.

14

PURGATORY

The in-between time as the earth warmed gradually to spring always brought on much illness. The shop was busy, and Lucie was glad of Owen's help. She could leave him while she sat for a while with Nicholas, knowing that Owen would come for her if he was uncertain how to proceed.

This morning she had used this new freedom to creep up the stairs after the Archdeacon and eavesdrop on his conversation with Nicholas. It was a sneaky, distasteful thing to do, but she must somehow discover what was between them. Why the Archdeacon visited. Nicholas did not wish to speak of it, and she was afraid that if she pried too much, he would grow secretive.

She did not hear the beginning. And what she heard did not clarify much. But it did frighten her.

"—but what has he to do with it?" Nicholas asked in a querulous voice. "You said no one knew. You promised me."

"He is a slippery creature, Nicholas."

"He must not—"

"Shush, Nicholas, shush." A quiet moment. Lucie held her breath, fearful of being discovered in the sudden silence. Her head was against the door, her wimple pushed aside so she might hear. "You have nothing to fear," Anselm finally said. "He will learn nothing, tell no one. I promise you."

"How? You say he is slippery." Lucie did not like the pitch of Nicholas's voice. He had improved a little. This would set him back. She yearned to interrupt them, but she could not.

"I have"—the Archdeacon paused—"set him on a new path. Something that will consume his time."

A long silence.

"I cannot live with this," Nicholas suddenly cried.

"You would have done better to come to me." The Archdeacon's voice was cold. "But it is done." His voice softened. "Rest now, Nicholas. I will leave you. I must not weary you."

With that, Lucie turned to go. She took one step down and saw, there in the gloom at the bottom of the stairs, Owen, silently watching her. Dear God. Behind her, footsteps approached the door. Her heart raced. She feared Anselm far more than she feared Owen Archer. She stepped down, in her panic forgetting to lift her skirts, and tripped on her hem. She felt herself begin to fall. *Foolish. Stupid.* Strong arms caught her. Owen scooped her up and carried her down to the kitchen. Tildy was scrubbing the table. Her eyes opened wide at the sight of her mistress in the arms of the apprentice. Owen set Lucie down quickly.

"Mistress Wilton tripped on the ladder in the shop, Tildy. Make sure she sits still for a while, and get her something to drink."

"Oh dear. Oh yes. Sir. Ma'am." She led Lucie over to the bench by the fire, and helped her readjust her wimple.

Owen returned to the shop. The Archdeacon stood in the doorway, dabbing his face. When he became aware of Owen's presence, he nodded and departed.

Lucie welcomed the shawl that Tildy draped over her shoulders, and the warmed ale. Her hands shook as she lifted the cup to her lips. Tildy exclaimed over the torn hem and sat down right there to mend it. While Tildy worked, Lucie tried to forget the feeling of Owen's arms catching her, picking her up. The smell of him. The warmth.

Why had he been standing there? How long had he been there? Those were the important facts to find out. Not how it felt to be in his arms.

And then the conversation between the Archdeacon and Nicholas. *Who* was slippery? *What* could Nicholas not live with? Her spying had gained her nothing but a fright and an embarrassing tumble into Owen's arms.

"There," Tildy said, rising and nodding at the patched hem. "'Tisn't pretty, but it won't trip you again." She blushed at Lucie's thanks and shuffled back to her scrubbing.

Lucie took a deep breath and went into the shop. Owen was with a customer, so she waited, fussing with jars and spoons, trying not to look at him. When at last they were alone she asked, "Had you come looking for me? Was there a problem?"

"Aye. A question about Alice de Wythe's unguent."

"I heard Nicholas raise his voice. I did not want the Archdeacon upsetting him."

"I'm sorry I frightened you."

"I owe you thanks for breaking my fall. My hem—" Her face grew hot under his regard. The one eye seemed to see right through her. "What was the question?"

He started, then grinned. "A safer subject, to be sure." She wanted to slap him for his insolence, but he wiped the grin off his face and got down to business without another comment.

Not that the incident was forgotten. Throughout the day she caught him watching her with an intensity that made her uneasy. Not the shy, cautious watching that meant attraction, but a wary watchfulness. He was not fooled by her explanation of why she'd been standing there, her head against the door. Or perhaps her own fear colored her judgment. But he was wondering. Oh yes, he must be wondering why she would eavesdrop on her husband and a visitor. She must be more careful.

And yet it was not just she that seemed to distract Owen that day. When he took his eyes off her movements it was to watch the shop door, as if he expected a visitor.

At last she asked, "Did someone promise to come today? You watch the door as if your anxious eye might make the person appear."

"I—no, I expect no one."

• • •

Owen paced his room that evening, trying to forget the feel of Lucie in his arms, her heart beating against his chest, her arms around his neck. All evening down in the tavern he'd caught himself thinking about her. The scent of her hair, her slenderness. More to the point, he should be thinking of a way to find out what she had been doing there, obviously listening in on her husband's conversation with the Archdeacon. Did she suspect something? Or was she worried that they knew something?

Today had been hell on earth, trying not to think of her and waiting for permission to question Wulfstan. Owen was worried about the monk. He should have told the Abbot that he was concerned. Perhaps that would have gained him an audience.

And this evening Owen had waited for Digby down in the tavern, but the man had not appeared. It was irksome, his not coming. Owen needed to tell him that Brother Wulfstan had told the Archdeacon of his visit. And he needed to make sure he knew all that Digby and Wulfstan had said before he spoke with the Infirmarian.

He tried to stop pacing, but it was agony to sit still. It was not an unreasonable hour. Digby might yet appear. Perhaps Owen had given up too soon. But he'd found the wait tedious. Bess was too busy to talk with him, and Tom was not a conversationalist.

Besides, all the sitting had made Owen restless. He felt a dull ache in his lower back from sitting too long on hard wood benches. Even a saddle was better for the muscles. He would take a walk. In the direction of Digby's rooms, now there was an idea. If the house was dark, he would walk on by. But if not, he would see if the Summoner might talk with him. Then he would rest easier.

The snow on the streets had refrozen in icy ridges. Fresh snow fell, stinging his face and blinding him as the flakes thawed on his warm eyelashes and dripped into his eye. Owen cursed, blinking away the moisture. He knew he would have the same problem if he had both eyes. He knew what bothered him was the lack of a second line of defense to put to work when one eye failed. He might stumble in that moment of blindness and crash down upon the frozen ground. It did not help to know what bothered him. Pah. He'd become an old man, plagued by fears.

Few people were about. Perhaps the hour was less reasonable than he'd thought. He doubted he'd find Digby's landlady still up. Well, he'd needed the walk.

He came upon the house, which was well lit on the lower floor. The front door gaped wide. A small cluster of folk stood across the street, watching the house. Some raggedy children lurked by the door.

The light from the house glinted in the eyes of the watchers as they considered him and then stepped farther back into the shadows. The children moved away from the door as he knocked.

"She won't hear you," observed a boy, his feet wrapped in rags, matted hair dusted with snow. "She's crying over the body."

"Whose body?" asked Owen.

The children ran away.

Owen entered the small shop where Widow Cartwright did fancy sewing. Two men stood in the doorway to the back room. Beyond them, a woman wailed in the rhythmic chant of a mourner.

As Owen entered the room, the men hushed and stood back from the doorway.

The black-clad mourner was visible through the doorway now, bent double, hands to head. Owen moved toward her. A body lay on a trestle table, pallid and swollen. Digby. The stench of death already overwhelmed the man's characteristic fishy odor. Someone had placed coins on his eyes.

In a corner sat Widow Cartwright, weeping noisily. The mourner was Magda Digby. Owen spoke her name. She did not hear. He touched her shoulder. Her wailing chant faded. Slowly, as one rousing herself from sleep, she unfolded herself and turned eyes on him so red and swollen that he doubted she could see. But he was wrong.

"Bird-eye. Look at my son. River took him. The river." She squinted at Owen as if she expected him to explain. Her eyes moved over his face, then came to rest on the hand that lay on her shoulder. She put her rough hand over it. "Thou art good to come."

"I mourn with you, Goodwife Digby. He was a friend."

"Magda will remember thy kindness."

"Why did they bring him here?"

"Potter wanted Christian burial, not his mother's way. So Magda brought him here. Anselm will bury Potter as he wished. 'Tis his duty. But he would not from the Riverwoman's house. Nay. Such as Anselm think 'tis cursed. He would not come. So Magda came here. She does her part. No one will deny a mother's sorrow."

She nodded, then folded herself up once more and resumed her wailing.

Owen backed out of the room. The two men watched him.

"How did he die? Did he drown?"

One of the men pulled himself up, thrust out his chest. "And who be you to ask?" he demanded.

"I was a friend."

The other sniffed. "Friend of Summoner?" He spat in the corner. "And I be King of France."

"Who is in charge here?"

"Archdeacon Anselm," said the first one. "We're waitin' for him."

The other stepped closer, peering up into Owen's face. "You're Wilton's apprentice. They do say you sat with Summoner in tavern—" His eyes stopped on something in the front doorway, behind Owen. "What are you doing here?"

Owen recognized the cold voice of the Archdeacon. He faced him. Anselm was not someone to have at his back. "Where did this happen? When?"

"He was fished out of the river this evening." Anselm's voice was calm for someone who had come to visit the dead.

"But he was accustomed to the river."

"Accustomed, yes. Overconfident, perhaps. What do you think, Owen Archer? And how do you happen to be here?"

"He says he was Summoner's friend," said the man who had spat in the corner.

"Indeed?" The Archdeacon's voice softened, grew oily. "An odd choice of a friend. Guaranteed to make a stranger suspect."

"I did not know any better. Rome is but a quiet presence in my country. We have no Summoners." There seemed no reason to linger. "I will leave you to your business." He took a step toward the door.

The Archdeacon stepped aside.

Owen's legs felt heavy, tired. Something should be said. Some kind words about Digby, who had befriended him. Odious the man might have been, but he had believed he served God in his weasellike way. Owen paused next to Anselm. "I would like to be one of the pall bearers."

The Archdeacon's nostrils flared, an eyebrow lifted. "We will bury him without ceremony. He was of humble origins."

"When will you bury him?"

"Tomorrow morning."

"Where?"

"At Holy Trinity off Goodramgate."

Owen left, resolved to rise early and attend the funeral.

Back up in his room at the inn, Owen shed his boots and leaned back on the bed. Pain pulsed through his head in giddying waves. He rubbed his temples, hard, harder, too hard. He put his head in his hands. When he closed his eye he saw Digby lying on the table. Heavy with river water. A fleshy sack of river water. The coins glittering on his eyes.

Owen felt responsible. Digby had thought he was doing the work of the Lord. As Owen had thought of his own mission for the Archbishop. They were not so different. He had sent Digby to sleuth for him, and Digby was dead. A coincidence? Or did Owen's new occupation make him obsessive about plots and motives? He was too tired to know.

But just how reliable had Digby been? He'd guessed wrong about Montaigne being in league with Fitzwilliam; the Archbishop would have mentioned a connection between them. And could Owen credit Digby's suggestion about the relationship between Wilton and the Archdeacon—that Wilton was Anselm's weakness? To a soldier the implication was clear. But an Archdeacon? What about Montaigne and Lady D'Arby? Was it likely that was true?

Sharp pains coursed across Owen's blind eye, making his head ache. Perhaps that was why his thoughts were such a muddle. He needed sleep. A good rest often calmed the eye. He still had some brandywine from Thoresby's London cellars. But he was tired of drinking from flasks. Tired of living like a soldier on campaign, traveling light, ready to move. He was no longer a soldier. He wanted a cup for his brandywine. He went downstairs in search of one, taking the flask with him.

A light drew him into the kitchen. Bess Merchet sat at a small table near the hearth. On the table were a jug, a cup, and a small lamp. One hand on the cup, Bess stared at the embers in the hearth.

Owen paused in the doorway. A line between Bess's brows suggested that she, too, found her thoughts holding off sleep. She lifted the cup to her lips, sipped, put it down, then cocked her head, as if just now she'd heard him. She turned, nodded to him. "Obliging of you to appear just now, Owen Archer."

He thought it an odd greeting. "I came for a cup." He held out the flask. "The last of the Lord Chancellor's fine brandywine. I thought it would help me sleep."

Bess grinned and held up the jug before her. "I wonder if it's as good as the Archbishop's." She nodded to the bench across from her. "Get a cup from the board to your right."

After they'd established that Thoresby kept a slightly better cellar as Archbishop than as Lord Chancellor, and sat back, warm and companionable, Owen asked, "You were thinking about me?"

Bess frowned, sipped from her cup. "I was over the Wiltons' this evening, after hours. I'm worried about Lucie. Got home, couldn't sleep for worryin' about her. Came down to think. I do my best thinking over a jug of brandywine. I must decide what to do, you see, for I cannot rest easy in my bed until I know you mean her no harm."

"Lucie Wilton?"

"Aye."

"You would warn her against me?"

"She's accepted you, I know. What's done is done. But I want answers, Owen Archer. You arrived well informed. What are you up to?"

"I have told you."

"How'd you come to know about Lucie needing help?"

"Jehannes told me—the Archbishop's secretary. There is nothing mysterious or underhanded in that. When I arrived, he said the Archbishop had written a letter of introduction to Camden Thorpe—my late master had asked the Archbishop to assist me in finding a post."

"You're sniffing about, that's what I say. Asking questions. Something to do with the minster."

Owen grinned. "You followed me."

"No, I never. But the Archdeacon sends for you. The Archbishop provides for you. I'm not simple."

"I had a small behest from my late lord. Administered by the Archbishop. I visited the Archbishop's secretary first thing to arrange for the payment. Anselm did not like that."

Bess sniffed. "True, no doubt. But not the whole truth. Not by half."

She was a formidable opponent. With bow and arrow Owen might better her, even with one eye. But he could not best her with words. Bess would sniff and scratch around every word, gesture, deed. He had to watch himself.

"I cannot think how to assure you that I mean your friend no harm."

"You can't." She leaned forward. "But be warned, Owen Archer. Your charm does not blind Bess Merchet. You bring the Wiltons trouble, and I throw you out. And worse." She sat back, smiling grimly, satisfied that she had made her threat.

Owen believed her. And it was quite possible that she would have the opportunity to carry out her threat. The Wiltons looked terribly guilty.

Unless Digby's death had been no accident. Poisoning was one thing, but he could not imagine either Wilton throwing Digby in the river.

"You are close to Lucie Wilton."

"Poor chit. She's not had an easy time of it, daughter of a knight though she may be. My own Mary had more love and security. When her father died, I made sure my next husband was the sort who would love her as his own."

"Tom's a good man."

"Not Tom. Peter. Tom's my third." Owen could not help but grin. He could well believe she would outlive a pair of husbands. She would probably outlive Tom, too. Bess sipped her brandywine. "I've tried to be a mother and friend to Lucie." She sighed into her cup, then looked up at Owen. "But what keeps you awake? You went up early tonight."

"And went out. Walking. I'm accustomed to a more active life."

Bess sniffed. "You seem plenty active to me. I've seen you at the woodpile."

"I happened to pass the house where Digby boards. Something was up. Too well lit, folk crowded around."

Bess sat up. "Trouble at Widow Cartwright's? I warned her not to board that man. He's a slimy creature. No good will come of him."

"Certainly that possibility is past. He's dead. Drowned. They dragged him out of the river tonight."

Bess crossed herself. "Why didn't you tell me that straightway? You let me say an unkindness about the dead." She shivered and crossed herself again. "You might have saved me that."

"Forgive me."

Bess took a drink. Sighed. Gave Owen a good, long look. "Are you bothered by his death?"

"I am."

"That's why you needed the brandywine?"

"Aye."

She shook her head. "Troubled by the Summoner's death. Odd for a soldier."

"Aye. You would think a soldier saw too much death to let it trouble him. But Digby meant to be a good man. He believed he was doing God's work. And I—"

Bess suddenly sat forward, alert, sniffing the air.

"Fire!" someone yelled.

Bess jumped up, knocking over her cup. "That's Tom."

Owen followed her through the dark tavern. He could smell the smoke.

Tom met them coming down, reeled back, shocked.

"What is it, Tom? Where?"

He nodded to Owen. "His room. Blessed Mary full of grace, I thought you were a dead man, Master Archer."

Owen hurried up. Smoke billowed out of the room. Owen's pallet smoldered. Flames licked at the wall beside it. Owen managed to get the pallet to the window and toss it out. Better char something out there than inside, where people slept. He tossed the greasy torch that had started the blaze out after it. He'd look at it in the morning light.

Tom huffed in with a bucket of water. Bess rushed in with blankets. In a moment the fire was out.

"I was afraid you were trouble," Bess muttered.

Tom scratched his bristly cheek as he stared at the damage.

Bess sighed. "It will take a day to tidy this up and air it out. Owen can sleep in one of the other rooms tonight."

"I doubt I'll get much sleep."

Tom nodded. "Doubt you will."

Bess turned, fixed her eyes on Owen. "Do you know who did this?"

He shook his head. "Who knew which room was mine?"

"Aye, that's the question." Tom scratched his head. "Me and wife. Kit. Stable boy, he has his nose in everything." He shrugged. "Some of guests, mayhap. Hard to say. Folk have eyes."

By now the other guests had crowded about on the landing below, demanding news.

"Best to keep this quiet," Owen said. "Say I tripped with a candle. Likely enough with one eye."

Tom frowned, glanced over at Bess.

"Go tell them, Tom. Just as he said."

Tom thought about it, nodded, and went down to tell the tale.

Owen gathered his things, which had been on the opposite end of the small room.

Back in the doorway he looked down at the soggy, blackened floorboards, the scorched wall. "It did not burn long."

Bess was quiet. Owen turned so he could see her with his good eye. Arms folded across her chest, she glared at him. "I've a mind to send you packing, but it would look bad for business. I think you'd agree you owe it to us to tell the truth. What you're doing here. What you're after."

Smoke lingered in the room. Owen's eye burned. That made him uncomfortable. "In your room. Can we talk in there?"

Bess led the way. Tom, who'd calmed the other guests, was close behind.

It was a large, airy room, with a feather bed at one end, a table piled with record books at the other. Owen dropped his things inside the door and crossed over to the table. Tom and Bess joined him. He studied their faces. Honest, both of them. And decent to let him stay. He did not for a moment believe that it was just for business. He decided to tell them the truth.

Bess grunted with satisfaction when he told her his mission. "I knew it. Didn't I say he was more than he seemed, Tom?"

"Oh, aye." Tom blinked, fighting sleep.

"And now Potter Digby's found belly-up in the Ouse, and someone puts a torch to your bed." Bess's eyes shone with excitement.

Tom came alert. "Digby? That fishy scoundrel drowned?"

"They found him tonight."

"He was snooping for you?"

Owen nodded.

Tom shook his head. "Sounds to me like you've made a mess of it."

After Tildy had gone to her little closet for the night and Bess had returned to the inn, Lucie sat up by Nicholas, listening to his labored breathing, searching her memory for some concoction she might yet try to soothe him. It was the struggle for breath, she was certain, that weakened him. He got no rest. How could he rest, when every breath was such a struggle? How could he heal if he did not rest? *I cannot live with this.* Did he know what he had done? Had he deliberately—No. She would not let herself even think that.

Bess thought Nicholas was dying. That was why she had talked so much tonight about Will and Peter, her late husbands. She wanted Lucie to be prepared. To know that life would go on. To begin to look around for Nicholas's replacement. And who better than Owen Archer? Dear Bess. If only life were that simple.

Owen Archer. The enigma. But Lucie admitted he was a hard worker. He never complained. No job was too humble. And he needed instructions only once. He always remembered. And that voice. The way he played the lute. He did not have the soul of a soldier. Perhaps he really had taken the loss of his eye as a sign to turn to a more godly life. He had given her no cause to distrust him. His only fault was the way he made her feel. He could not help that. That was her own sinfulness. It was because Nicholas had been ill so long.

Well. Nicholas was not dying. Lucie would not let him. So she would have to keep fighting her feelings for Owen. But it did not mean she had to be uncivil.

She would try to be more pleasant with him.

Lucie must have drowsed at last when a commotion outside drowned out Nicholas's gasping breaths and roused her. She went to the window. Across the way was a sight terrifying to a city dweller. Fire. Smoke billowed from the upper floor of the inn. Sweet Jesus. Bess and Tom—did they know? Were they awake? Something large plummeted from the window and landed with a thud in the snow below. It seemed to be smoldering. A torch followed, hitting the snow with a smoky hiss. Then faces appeared in the window. A boy ran out into the yard. Lucie hurried outside, her heart pounding.

She called to the boy.

"What is on fire?"

"The top room. Captain Archer's." The boy nodded toward the smoldering heap on the ground behind him. "'Tis his pallet."

Lucie clutched the fence. *No. Not Owen. Please God.* "And Master Archer?" Her throat was so tight the boy could not hear her. She asked again.

"He weren't in his room. Lucky, eh?"

"Was anyone hurt?"

"No one's I could see."

Lucie thanked him and walked away while she still could. Her legs were feeling untrustworthy.

Back in the house she sat down in the kitchen, not wanting to return to Nicholas just yet.

Her reaction to the news that it was Owen's room on fire shocked her. Sweet Mary, it was as if—No. Not as if. She would not lie to herself. She was in love with Owen. She had thought herself so strong. Strong indeed. Falling in love with a one-eyed soldier. A handsome scoundrel had been Bess's first impression of him. A favorite with the ladies. Lucie could not believe it. A soldier. Trained to kill. And he had trained others to kill. Soldiers belonged to a brotherhood of death. It made them unfit for life. Her own father was a cold, unfeeling man. He had pushed her from him the moment her mother's back was turned by death. Only a simple child fell in love with a soldier.

But Owen did not seem like her father. He was more like Geof, her mother's fair-haired knight.

Owen said he had done with soldiering.

A ruse. A posture by which he meant to win her. She must remember he had been a soldier.

But her body remembered how he had caught her. He had perhaps saved her life.

Because he had been watching in the dark at the foot of the stairs. What of that? What was his purpose? His purpose still might be to wrest the apothecary from her when Nicholas was gone. All he needed was to reveal a scandal. And it was there for him to find. The ordinance said nothing about a second chance. Said nothing for exceptions due to illness. He could ruin them with such a small piece of information.

She had lost her wits, to think such things of him and love him at the same time.

Lucie lay her head down on her arms and tried to calm herself, tried to tell herself that he was only an apprentice, that she had worried for him as she would for anyone with whom she spent so much time, that she could not possibly love him, that she must not love him. Her life was in turmoil enough without that.

• • •

Anselm lay prostrate before the altar, trembling with fear. If he were to die at this moment, he would burn forever in the fires of Hell. He had murdered twice now. He, who had rejected the life of the sword, had taken two lives in as many nights. He felt calm about the second, the burning of the one-eyed devil. He was quite sure that in sending Owen Archer to the fires of Hell he was carrying out God's will. And though Archer was Thoresby's man, Anselm was not afraid. The Archbishop would have no reason to connect Anselm with Archer's death.

All in all, Anselm was content with his dispatching of Archer. But Digby's death was different.

"Sweet Savior," Anselm whispered, "I am your—" he hesitated, uncertain how to proceed. He could not think how to pray, what to pray for. He had killed Potter Digby. No amount of prayer, no matter how heartfelt, would change that. Anselm had murdered his Summoner, the man who had worked hard for him, brought him far in his goal to complete the Hatfield chapel, never cheated him. Anselm had murdered Digby because of a rumor. Because he had suspected Digby of changing his allegiance. Because he had feared the man would accuse Nicholas Wilton in public, so that Anselm could not ignore it, would be forced to condemn his friend, his dearest friend.

But killing Digby was a mistake. Anselm had known that even as he walked from the river. Digby had not betrayed him. He had told Anselm of his suspicion. He had presented the facts to Anselm and would have accepted Anselm's decision. As always. So why had Anselm murdered him? What devil had taken hold of him and twisted his reasoning, pushed him to such an act? "Sweet Savior, forgive me. *Mea culpa, mea culpa, mea maxima culpa.*"

Perhaps this had been God's will? Perhaps Digby would have told someone else? Would have betrayed Nicholas? And God meant for Anselm to protect Nicholas. It was for that purpose that God had brought Anselm and Nicholas together at the abbey school.

Ever since Anselm had first seen Nicholas, he had understood that his own role was to protect him. Brilliant, humble, beautiful and fragile as an angel. Of course Nicholas was one of God's special sons. Destined to sit beside God through all eternity.

And Anselm had been called to protect him.

Anselm knew all about the need for protection. His father had used the manor as a training camp for young soldiers. Anselm had disappointed his father, he was quiet and studious, slender as a girl, his father said with disgust. Only his mother had fussed over him. His older brother was like his father. His sister was a horsewoman. Anselm was his mother's comfort.

And then she pushed him away to dally with one of the young men. Pushed him out. Fool that he was, he sulked around the stables and came to his father's attention. His father put him in training. Wrestling. Swordplay. Archery. His performance was hopeless. The young men laughed. His father was humiliated. One night, after too much wine, he dragged the boy out of his soft bed and gave him to his men. "That's what comes of boys who hide behind women's skirts."

The next morning, in pain and ashamed, Anselm hid. Eventually his mother asked for him. He told the tale, ashamed though he was, for he felt certain she would sympathize, somehow intercede for him. But she waved away his horror. "It is the way of men, my weakling. I cannot protect you from the world."

He tried to explain the pain, the horror.

She laughed. "And do you think it is any different for me, you little fool? Watch next time your father comes to my bed. Watch."

He did. His father beat her, and then used her with such fury that she screamed in pain. Afterwards she wept, crumpled in a little ball.

Anselm came to her, tried to comfort her. The stench of his father was strong in the room.

He vowed to kill his father next time he came to her. Anselm watched. But it was the young soldier his mother fancied who came next. And she shamelessly showed herself to him, pulled him to her, urged him on. They were rutting animals.

When the man left, Anselm crept in with her. There was the

smell of sex all over her. Anselm pressed his head to her breast. She pushed him away.

"I saw."

"Little sneak. Get out!"

"You told me to watch."

"That once. Only then."

"Let me love you as he did."

"Dear God!" She sat up, pulling the covers around her. "Your father is right. You are unnatural."

He saw loathing in her eyes. She, who had loved him. The only one who had ever loved him. There was some mistake. He reached for her.

She yelled for her maid. The heartless bitch. She coddled and caressed him as long as it amused her, and when she had made him totally dependent on her love, she discarded him. He lunged for her and tried to scratch her eyes out. He was pulled away and sent out to the soldiers. They had their fun with him until he found a protector.

Oh yes, he understood the need for a protector.

And then he'd been packed off to St. Mary's. And his turn had come to protect. And he was good at it. The Lord knew he had done his best. Even his father might be proud. And that bitch. She would have learned to fear him.

But had he gone too far? Could he be wrong about God's purpose? He could no longer remember the sign with which God had shown him his path in life. That frightened him.

Poor Digby. Anselm was sorry for that. He wished he had not had to kill Digby.

15

A PIECE OF THE PUZZLE

Tom's words haunted Owen the next morning. *Made a mess of it.*
Aye, he'd done that. Owen walked through the awakening city to
Holy Trinity Church. Overnight the wind had changed, bringing
warmer air that had turned the refrozen streets to slush. He slogged
through the icy mush, which seeped through his boots and made his
feet ache with cold. Chill mist clung to his face and neck. Wretched
North Country. How much colder must Digby have been, plunging
into the rushing waters of the Ouse. Owen shivered and stepped
into the candlelit church. It smelled of beeswax, smoke, but, most
of all, of damp stone. The flickering candle flames bothered his eye.
He moved off to the side, into the darkness.

The priest's heart was not in the words he spoke over the coffin.
He acknowledged the need for Summoners, spoke of God's grace
in pulling Digby up so far from his beginnings, out of the vermin
city and into the minster. Saying this, the priest cast uneasy glances at
Magda Digby, who stood on the other side, glaring at the small group
of mourners. Across the church stood Archdeacon Anselm's clerk,
representing the Archdeacon. Near Owen was Jehannes, representing
the Archbishop. Widow Cartwright, draped in black, stood directly in
front of the pulpit. Perhaps ten more, mostly the white-haired women
who attend every service in a parish, made up the congregation.
Their responses echoed hollowly in the stony space.

Out among the graves, the river mist cast a proper pall over the
mourners. The priest said a few words, dropped dirt on the grave,
and withdrew. To a warm breakfast, no doubt. The others departed,

all but Magda Digby, who knelt by the gaping hole to drop dried leaves, twigs, flowers on the coffin. She whispered as she worked.

Owen watched, filled with a heaviness he could not account for. He'd made a mess of it. That must be what bothered him. He'd been clumsy, obvious. Though unpleasant, he could live with that. What he could not abide was that his ineptitude had cost a man's life. Even in war, one despised the maneuver that cost more lives than necessary. But Digby was no soldier. This was not war. No one should have to die here for Owen's mistakes. He'd been wrong to use Digby. Wrong. Lazy. Arrogant. He had considered the man a thing to be used. A Summoner. Already dirty. Already guilty.

Magda, one gnarled hand pressed to her lower back, one on the muddy ground, struggled to rise. Owen offered her his hand. Dark, shadowed eyes peered at him.

"Thank ye. Magda knows about thee. Potter explained. Thou'rt Thoresby's man, just as Magda said."

Owen looked around, worried that someone might hear. He saw no one, but the mist could deceive. "I am Wilton's apprentice," he said loud enough to reach all ears.

"Oh, aye." She chewed on her gums, considered him. "Magda's lad helped thee. Potter judged thee a good man." She nodded, patted Owen on the shoulder, and shuffled away.

"I am sorry about his death," Owen said to her retreating back.

She glanced back over her rounded shoulder. "Thee and me. The others care not a whit." She chewed air, shrugged. "Potter should've stayed on the river with me. I named him for the craft I meant him for. Summoners are dead men." She hitched up her cloak and shuffled off into the mist.

As he watched Magda disappear, Owen considered her words. She believed the Archdeacon's interest in her son was to blame for his death. The Archdeacon. He'd tried to get rid of Owen. Had he rid himself of his Summoner when he found out the man was asking questions about Montaigne? Could Owen have prevented his death if he'd told him that Wulfstan had gone to the Archdeacon? Owen prayed that was not so.

Archbishop Thoresby, Lord Chancellor of England, leaned back in his chair and closed his eyes. "You were wise to come to me about this, Campian. It would not do to share your Infirmarian's concern with others. Or yours."

"I knew of your interest in Fitzwilliam's death. But the Summoner questioning Brother Wulfstan. That disturbed me."

"You say Archer knew of the Summoner's visit."

"He did."

"I question his choice of assistant."

"He did not say he had sent Digby."

Thoresby bowed his head a moment, thinking. He either trusted Archer or he did not; he could not support him piecemeal. "You might encourage Brother Wulfstan to speak with my man."

"He distrusts the Welshman."

Thoresby raised an eyebrow. "Perhaps the Infirmarian shows better judgment than the Archbishop."

They smiled at his little joke.

"I will encourage Brother Wulfstan."

"It is interesting that Anselm's Summoner would express such interest in Montaigne. And no questions about my ward?"

"Nothing about Fitzwilliam."

The Archbishop closed his eyes again. It disturbed him that he had forgotten the knight's connection with Lady D'Arby. This was an intricate knot he was untying. All because of the rascal Fitzwilliam. How odd if his ward had been an innocent victim. Much was odd in this matter. The Summoner had involved himself. Why? And now he, too, was dead. Questioned the Infirmarian, dined with the Archdeacon, and then drowned. A man who had grown up on the river, drowned. Thoresby did not like it. It meant trouble for the minster.

"Why does Brother Wulfstan distrust Archer?"

The Abbot winced apologetically. "I confess I have no idea. He keeps to himself. We are quiet men. It is the rule."

"Tell me this—has my man Archer visited the infirmary?"

"Yes. He carried a letter from Master Roglio, the old Duke's physician."

"Roglio is also my physician."

Campian flushed, realizing the implication that had escaped him until now. "And yours. I am quite an innocent in these matters, Your Grace. But of course your ward died in Wulfstan's care."

"I do not think your Infirmarian is a murderer, Campian. Perhaps not as sharp as he once was, but no killer."

Campian wiped his brow. "God be thanked. He is my oldest friend." He sipped his wine. His hand trembled. "But then you knew Archer visited—"

"He told me nothing of the visit, so I wondered. Wulfstan's distrust might simply reflect his own feelings of guilt, his suspicion that Archer was investigating the deaths."

Campian nodded. Then, in a tentative voice, with his eyes averted, he said, "There is another matter, Your Grace."

Mon Dieu, another little scandal?

"These questions about Montaigne's grave. You would not mean to exhume him?"

"Why should we do that?"

"To look for signs of poisoning?"

What now? Had they sold the body for relics? Thoresby did not know Campian as well as he should. The Abbot had been in place when Thoresby rose to Archbishop. Campian was not one of Thoresby's men. He seemed forthright, but Thoresby knew many accomplished actors. He did not want any chance of scandal. "I do not believe even Roglio knows enough about these fleshy shells to pronounce a cause of death without qualifying every step in his analysis. It is the soul that reveals the man. The deed."

Campian wiped his brow again. "I am much relieved. The peace of St. Mary's has been disrupted too much already. The two deaths did not go unnoticed. Some of my boys were ordered home. Several of the older brothers have become reluctant to use Wulfstan's balms for their aching joints. Many dread the spring bloodletting more than usual. Poor Wulfstan knows this and is distraught. It seems only Brother Michaelo still frequents the infirmary."

"Michaelo? I do not know him."

"A pretty young man. Lazy. Always devising ways to escape work. Which reminds me of another item. Michaelo was in the infirmary when the Summoner came to speak with Wulfstan. And later that day he asked permission to visit the Archdeacon on family business. His family has donated considerable sums for the Hatfield chapel. They seek the King's favor."

Michaelo. A link. "A pretty young man, you say?"

Campian sighed. "I suspect that Anselm has failed in his resolve to give that up."

"I never believed he would give it up, Campian. I did not choose him for his virtue." Thoresby rose. "I am increasingly uncomfortable about all this. I must consider what to do."

Campian rose also. "I will leave you to it, Your Grace. If I can be of any assistance, please let me know."

"Meanwhile, allow Archer to question Brother Wulfstan."

Abbot Campian bowed, said, "Your Grace," and took his leave.

For a long while Thoresby stood at his window trying various connections. Then he summoned Jehannes. "It is time to invite Archer for a cup of wine. Tonight, Jehannes. Before I dine."

Owen was halfway to the apothecary when the messenger from St. Mary's caught up with him.

"God be with you." The boy pressed his palms together and bobbed his head, then peered up at Owen. "Captain Archer?"

"A fair guess. How many one-eyed men are there in York?"

The boy screwed up his face, reckoning. "Seven I know of. Nay. Cowley lacks both. But—"

Owen waved him quiet. "'Tis no matter. What is your message?"

"The Abbot says you may speak with Brother Wulfstan this morning, Captain."

Abbot Campian greeted Owen solemnly. "His Grace tells me to trust you. I have encouraged Brother Wulfstan to confide in you. You may go to him."

Owen thanked him. "One question. Does Brother Wulfstan know the identity of the first pilgrim?"

Campian nodded. "I told him after the Summoner left. I thought that might be what Archdeacon Anselm had sent Digby to find out. I told Brother Wulfstan to tell the Archdeacon his name."

Owen groaned. "And did he?"

"No." The Abbot's expression was bemused. "Brother Wulfstan disobeyed me. Not that he lied to the Archdeacon. Wulfstan is incapable of lying. He has always been so. The Archdeacon did not ask him the name directly."

"God be thanked," Owen said, and headed for the infirmary, tucking that bit of information away. Wulfstan was a bad liar, but not above misdirection. And another interesting fact. Wulfstan had known the pilgrim's name by the time he spoke with Lucie Wilton, but he had evaded her questions also. Even Lucie Wilton. They shared a secret. But not all secrets.

The novice Henry sat at a table, studying a manuscript. Brother Wulfstan dozed by the fire.

"He is tired," Henry whispered when Owen entered. "Can you see him another day?"

"No, I cannot."

Henry went over and woke Wulfstan with a gentleness that Owen found touching.

Wulfstan's sleepy eyes slowly focused on Owen. "Oh. Yes. Abbot Campian said you were to come."

"Could we speak alone?"

Henry looked at Wulfstan, who nodded. "Go meditate on what you have read this morning. We will discuss it this afternoon."

"He is a good boy."

Owen sat down across from the old monk. "Forgive me for being abrupt, but you must know why I am here, so I see no point in games."

Wulfstan assumed a cool, almost hostile expression. "It is you who have played with me. You are the Archbishop's man. You might have said so."

"I hoped I need not say anything. Did your Abbot warn you to keep your silence about this?"

"I need no warning."

The old monk's hostility disappointed Owen, but he could not blame Wulfstan. He would feel the same. Best to get the worst behind him. "The matter is this. I believe that Geoffrey Montaigne was poisoned. And perhaps Sir Oswald Fitzwilliam."

Wulfstan looked down at his sandals, but Owen could see the sweat on his forehead.

"I am not accusing you, Brother Wulfstan. I believe someone used you. I suspect that you discovered the treachery and are worried that someone will blame you."

Wulfstan said nothing.

"If you tell me what you know, it may save St. Mary's from more disruption."

The Infirmarian looked up with frightened eyes. "What sort of disruption?"

"Exhuming Montaigne's body."

"No. Sweet Heaven, no. Please. Do not disturb Geoffrey."

"I would rather not. Will you tell me what you know?"

"I thought the Archbishop wanted to know about Fitz-william's death."

"I think the two deaths are connected."

Wulfstan sighed and gazed down at his hands.

"Who are you trying to protect?"

The old monk got up and poked at the fire. "My Abbot wishes me to cooperate. But it is hard." He fussed with the fire. "Who is to know what you learn?"

"That would depend on what I uncover, eh? Perhaps I need tell no one but His Grace."

"And you will not disturb Geoffrey?"

"No."

Wulfstan returned to his seat. He clasped his hands tight and bowed his head. "I am certain that it was an accident."

"What was?"

"I did not discover it until after Fitzwilliam—I had no idea that the physick was deadly." He lifted frightened eyes to Owen. "He was already ill, you see. He must have been."

"Nicholas Wilton?"

Wulfstan closed his eyes. Nodded once.

"Tell me exactly what happened."

With much wringing of hands, Wulfstan told him the story. Most of the story. He did not mention Nicholas's odd questions when Wulfstan had gone for the medicine. Nor did he mention having spoken with Lucie Wilton about his discovery.

What Owen did hear was a revelation to him. "You thought nothing when Montaigne called him a murderer?"

"He was delirious with fever. I am accustomed to discounting things said in such a state."

Owen got up and paced for a few minutes, thinking about what he had learned. Wulfstan sat with his hands in his sleeves, gazing at the fire. His face betrayed him, sweaty, flushed. He had not told all he knew. Owen was not surprised. He had not expected it to be easy.

"What did you do when you discovered how much aconite was in the physick?"

"I disposed of it."

"Where?"

"I—" Wulfstan closed his eyes. Obviously he searched for a safe response. "I had it burned."

"You had your novice burn it?"

"I—No." The monk could not lie. Owen counted on that. He just had to be patient.

"Then who?"

"A friend."

"So someone else knows of this?"

"They will speak to no one."

"You are still playing games with me."

The flush deepened. "You know that you need not exhume Geoffrey. You know what killed him. Is that not enough?"

"Are you certain that the dose of aconite in the physick was an accident?"

"How could it have been otherwise? I did not know the pilgrim's name then, so I could not have told Nicholas Wilton." *But Nicholas asked those questions. He knew for whom he prepared it.* "He had not been to the abbey while Geoffrey was here, so how could he know? And why would he poison a stranger?" Sweat dripped down Wulfstan's back, making him squirm. What if he protected a murderer? What about that? Lucie Wilton was innocent. He must protect her. But what of Nicholas's questions? And the palsy. Might it have been brought on by the shock of seeing his victim, the weight of his intended sin pressing on his heart?

"I asked if you were certain that it was an accident, Brother Wulfstan."

Wulfstan dabbed his forehead. Shifted on the bench. Closed his eyes and covered his face with his hands. Owen could hear him murmuring to himself. The arrow had struck the target, he was certain.

At last Wulfstan sat up and looked Owen in the eye. Owen read fear in his flushed face. "One cannot see into another's heart. I have always found Nicholas an excellent apothecary and a good man. But I confess I do not know what to think about that day. He asked questions about the patient, questions that I did not think"— he frowned, searching for just the right word—"that had nothing to do with diagnosing the man's condition."

Owen led Wulfstan through the questions gently, until it was clear that Nicholas Wilton had heard enough to guess who the pilgrim was. "Forgive me for putting you through this. I do not like hounding you."

Wulfstan nodded. Tears shone in his eyes.

"Tell me this. Can you be certain that the physick you tested was the one Nicholas made up?"

Wulfstan sighed. "I am certain."

"No one could have switched them on you?"

"I marked it with care."

"And you would have noticed if it had been switched?"

Wulfstan slouched, defeated. "I think I would have. I suppose I cannot be certain."

"It is unfortunate that you did not keep it."

"I wanted to be rid of it. I was frightened who else might unwittingly take it."

"So others have access to the physicks?"

"No one else has permission. But if something were to happen to me—"

"Who burned it?"

"I told you. A friend."

"Here at the abbey?"

The eyes flickered this way and that. "No."

"In the city somewhere?"

Wulfstan lifted his chin resolutely. He would not betray an innocent. "I did not see where it was burned. I cannot know for certain where it was burned." He took a deep breath.

Owen wondered who it was the old monk protected with such stubborn loyalty. Who might inspire such heroic silence? In whom might the old monk have felt comfortable confiding his discovery?

And then it came to Owen. The one in whom Wulfstan had confided his most recent discomfort. The one with whom he shared a secret.

"You told Mistress Wilton about your discovery."

Wulfstan bowed his head and made the sign of the cross. He struggled against the desire to curse the one-eyed monster.

"You felt she should know. So that the error might not be repeated."

Still, not a word from the old monk.

"I must know who knows," Owen said gently. "You see, if the murderer is not Nicholas, if the murderer is loose, anyone who might give evidence is in danger. I am warning you. I must warn your friend."

Wulfstan looked up, his eyes uncertain. "In danger?"

"In a situation such as this, knowledge is dangerous."

"*Deus juva me*, I had not thought of that."

"Was it Mistress Wilton?"

"Now that I know, I can warn my friend."

"Think. I am working in Wilton's shop. If I know that Mistress Wilton is in danger, I can protect her."

He could, Wulfstan thought. This broad-shouldered man could be Lucie's protector. And what could Wulfstan do? How was he to protect her? "Yes, I told Lucie Wilton so that she might watch over Nicholas. And I had her burn the physick."

"It must have been a difficult thing to tell her."

"I did not like doing it."

"She must have been shocked."

"Lucie Wilton is a courageous woman. She took it calmly. Understood at once why I told her."

"She did not cry or wring her hands?"

"That is not her way."

"You must have been relieved. You would not have much experience with a woman's faint."

"I would not have told her if I thought she would be silly about it."

"So she was not at all shocked?"

Wulfstan frowned. The question led in an uncomfortable direction. "I do not think she would let me see if she were shocked."

"Does Mistress Wilton know the identity of the pilgrim?"

"No."

"Are you certain of that?"

Wulfstan shrugged. "As certain as a soul can be about another."

"He was her mother's lover. Did you know?"

Brother Wulfstan blushed. "I realized that."

"And no one in Mistress Wilton's family, her husband or her father, knew of Montaigne's presence at the abbey?"

Wulfstan shook his head. "I do not see how they would."

Enough. "I am sorry to have put you through this. Mistress Wilton is most fortunate to have you as a friend, Brother Wulfstan. I will pry no further." Owen rose. "I thank you for this information. I will use it only to discover the truth."

Brother Wulfstan thanked him and followed him to the door.
"Remember. Be watchful. Trust no one."

"Not even Abbot Campian?"

"No."

"Or Lucie Wilton?"

Especially not her. "Keep it simple to remember. Trust no one. And when I know the truth of the matter, I will tell you that you can let down your guard."

"You will watch over Lucie Wilton?"

"I promise you."

Wulfstan believed Owen. But it did not make him feel any less a traitor. He knelt down in front of his little altar to the Blessed Mother and prayed.

16

MANDRAKE ROOT

The wind carried the scent of the river. Owen slogged through the snow and ice, his heart heavy. Wulfstan had wished to protect Lucie Wilton. Owen wished to protect Lucie Wilton. Nicholas most likely wished to protect her, too—she was his wife. Everyone wished to protect lovely, gentle Lucie. But what if behind that facade she laughed at all of them and used her power over them as a protection? Could it be that Lucie had overheard the details about the pilgrim and taken revenge? That was the question that weighed on his heart. Had she mixed the physick and given it to Nicholas to deliver?

Lucie was with a customer when Owen got to the shop. He nodded to her and went into the kitchen. The serving girl scrubbed the stones in front of the hearth under Bess Merchet's critical eye.

"Say good morning to Owen, Tildy."

Enormous eyes in a pale, thin face, pretty but for a wine-red birthmark on the left cheek. She started to rise.

"No need for that," Bess said. "Just say hello."

"Mornin', Master Owen." Directed down to his feet in a breathy, trembling voice.

"Not 'Master,' Tildy. He's an apprentice."

Owen grinned. "Good morning, Tildy. I can see you're busy. I'll try to stay out from underfoot."

Tildy smiled gratefully.

Bess sniffed.

Tildy hunched her shoulders, expecting a blow. When it didn't come, she bent over her work, scrubbing with enough energy to dissolve the stone.

"Perhaps I should look in on the Master," Owen suggested.

Bess clucked at the flying water, sighed, shook her head at Owen. "No need. The Archdeacon is with him."

Lucie called to Owen from the doorway. "Watch the shop for me, Owen. I must see to Nicholas."

He went into the shop, glad to escape Bess's watchful eye. Now that he'd confided in the Merchets, he was nervous to be around them in company, worried one of them would slip and reveal his true purpose. And Bess had a discomfiting way of watching him, as if she knew his sins, knew him for a scoundrel. He pitied Tildy.

Lucie, frightened but determined, crept up the stairs. Pushing her wimple to one side, she leaned against the door.

"He was a dying man, Nicholas."

"Montaigne and now Digby. Oh, Anselm, where will it end?"

"You are upsetting yourself, Nicholas. Forget about them."

"You are so cold."

"Is your memory so short? Geoffrey Montaigne once attacked you and left you for dead."

"When he saw me that night. Oh, Anselm. His face."

Lucie choked back an exclamation. Geoffrey Montaigne. Her mother's knight. She sank down on the top step. Geoffrey Montaigne and Nicholas? What in heaven's name did they have between them? And why mention Geoffrey now? He had disappeared when her mother died.

She leaned back against the door. Someone wept. It must be Nicholas. She could not imagine Anselm weeping. That monster would undo all her nursing. Anselm was murmuring something.

"I—Don't. I am fine," Nicholas said. "Just—I must—there are things I must say."

Montaigne and now Digby. What was the connection? Lucie sat in the dark, trying to make sense of it. *Geoffrey Montaigne once attacked you and left you for dead.* Wulfstan had told Nicholas that the pilgrim could not believe he was Master Apothecary because he thought Nicholas was dead. And the pilgrim had fought in France with her father. That must be it. The pilgrim was Geoffrey Montaigne. Dear God in Heaven. What did it mean? Why had he and Nicholas fought? Why had she not heard of this?

"You must not harm her, Anselm."

"We do not speak of her."

"Anselm, you must promise me."

"They have destroyed you, Nicholas. First her mother, now her. She-devils."

Lucie was stunned by the venom in the Archdeacon's voice.

"Lucie is a good woman."

"She has blinded you. And now she's down there with her one-eyed lover, waiting for your death."

Monster. Lucie wanted to run in there and scratch out his eyes. *No, Nicholas. Don't listen to him.*

"It is you who are blind, Anselm." Nicholas's voice sounded weak. She should go to him. But if Anselm suspected she'd overheard—Dear God, he spoke with such hate. She felt as if he could see through the door and follow her with his eyes, with his cold, inhuman eyes. She fled to the kitchen.

Tildy looked up as Lucie leaned against the doorway, out of breath. "Mistress Wilton!"

"Lucie, what is it?" Bess was quick to her side.

She shook her head. "Nothing. I was—" She shook her head. "I must get back to work."

"Nonsense. Just look at you."

"It's nothing, Bess. Please." She hurried through the shop door.

Owen also wondered when he saw her. Her wimple was pushed askew. Hair tumbled out at the temples and curled damply on her cheeks. "You need not have hurried."

"I want some jars off the top shelf. It will be easier if I can hand them down to you." She was breathless.

"Perhaps you should sit down a moment."

She surprised him by sinking down on the bench behind the

counter. Shadows marred the pale skin beneath her eyes. Guilt, or worry over Nicholas's illness? Owen hoped worry and overwork. She rubbed one of her elbows as if weary to the bone.

"Can I get you something?"

She shook her head. "Just help me with the jars."

"Let me climb," Owen offered.

Lucie sighed. "If we're to work together, you must stop debating my orders and just accept them. Can you do that?" She tucked her hair in, yanked the wimple straight.

"I thought—"

She stood up. "I know what you thought. A woman should not climb ladders or lift heavy jars. If you watched a woman clean house, you'd see what nonsense that is."

She was angry. Perhaps Bess had not told her where he'd gone. "I went to Digby's funeral."

Lucie nodded. "You've a right. Bess told me about your mishap last night, knocking over the candle."

"You see why I gave up soldiering."

She shook her head. "I've watched you work. The eye does not trip you up. Was it because of Digby? His death disturbed you?"

Her eyes were so clear. Honest. He did not want to lie to her. "Death in peace is different from death in war. When many die each day, the heart hardens to the news. But Digby did not expect to die."

She regarded him, trying to take in the answer. *Montaigne and now Digby*. She shook her head. Must put that out of her mind. "Once again you surprise me, Owen Archer. Perhaps a man can change his nature. I would like to think that."

"What was my nature before?"

"That of a soldier."

"And what is the nature of a soldier, I ask you? Do you think that I chose to be one? That I had a taste for killing? That I wanted to kill and be killed for my King? I did not choose that. I was chosen by the King's men because of my skill with the bow."

"And when you developed that skill, did you not see where it would lead?"

"No. It was a game, like any other a child plays. I was good at it, so it became my favorite game. And so I became even better."

She turned away from him. "There is work to do."

"Why are you like this? Why can I do nothing to please you?"

"You are not here to please me."

"Of course I am. I'm your apprentice. Your opinion is everything to me."

Everything to me. The words echoed between them. Lucie looked at him, startled out of her anger. He wanted to grab her stubborn shoulders and shake her. *You are everything to me.*

She looked away, brushed some dust from her apron. "My approval of your work is all you need worry about. So let us get down to it."

Owen gave up the fight and followed her to the ladder, staying at its foot and saying not a word when the weight of the clay jars made him wonder how she could trust her balance under such a load. Once she stumbled and he grabbed her around the waist. Such a slender waist. He felt her hold her breath. She glanced down at him, for just a second, with an odd, frightened look, then resumed her work.

As she returned to ground level she said, "Again I must thank you for catching me. I would have fallen."

He just nodded, fearing he would say the wrong thing.

"Nicholas wants to see you after his midday meal. He has some books for you to study."

"I look forward to that. I understand the Archdeacon is with him now."

Lucie was quiet while she measured chamomile onto a slip of parchment. Owen noticed a set look to her mouth. Her hand trembled slightly.

"His visits bother you?" Owen asked.

"They agitate Nicholas. It cannot be good for him." She handed him the jar of chamomile. "You can put this back."

While Owen was up on the ladder, a boy entered the shop. It was the stable boy from the inn by Micklegate. A horse was lamed and could not be spared at the moment.

Lucie asked questions, which the boy answered carefully. Owen knew horses. And the treatment Lucie recommended was exactly what he would have chosen.

He watched her prepare the mixture. Practiced and sure of herself. In skill he suspected she was as capable of mixing an effective poison as her husband. But did she have the stomach?

"Not to worry, Jenkins," she said, watching the boy's pacing out of the corner of her eye. "This salve will keep her going." She covered the jar and set it on the counter, holding out her hand for payment. The boy counted out the coins, relieved when she corrected him from shortchanging himself.

"Much obliged, Mistress Wilton." He flushed in the glow of her smile. Owen knew just how he felt.

"And don't give up on her, Jenkins," Lucie said, handing him the jar. "This will give her a chance to heal."

The boy looked doubtful.

"Not all lamed horses need to be destroyed. Just give her time." Lucie leaned over and patted the top of the jar he held close to his greasy tunic. "That's my husband's special blend."

"They say he's poorly."

"He is that, Jenkins. But his medicine's as good as ever."

The boy nodded and shuffled quickly from the shop.

"You'll notice I insisted on payment before I handed over the physick," Lucie said. "Jack Cobb has to pay his bills immediately. Most folk are trustworthy—or deserving of charity. But Jack Cobb puts bills off, hoping merchants will forget them. A rich, selfish man. He doesn't get away with that here."

A strong-willed woman. Certain of her judgment. If she believed that a man deserved punishment for her mother's death, would she just as coolly see to the punishment?

"I will remember about Jack Cobb. Are there others who do not—"

Lucie had turned suddenly to the doorway from the kitchen as the Archdeacon came through. Owen, who had not heard Anselm's steps on the stairway, realized that Lucie must have been listening for them. Which meant she was more anxious about the visit than he'd guessed.

"How is he?" Lucie asked.

"He is tired, so I thought it best I leave." Anselm noticed Owen in the corner. "Good day to you both."

Lucie wiped her hands on her apron. "Owen can show you out, Archdeacon." She hurried from the room. Owen heard her light step on the stairway.

"I can show myself out," Anselm said. And did so.

After a midday meal served shyly by Tildy, who then sat down to join them, Lucie led Owen up to the sickroom. Nicholas lay propped against pillows, several small bound books on the covers beside him.

"Lucie is—pleased with you." Nicholas struggled with the words, groping for them, breathless and beaded with sweat after a sentence. "But I fear Anselm is right. We are wrong to keep you to your contract."

"What are you saying?" Lucie knelt beside Nicholas to dab his sweaty face with a sweet-scented cloth.

"Apprentice to an apprentice." Nicholas shook his head. "Not good for him."

Lucie's color rose. "Nonsense. Where else would he have access to books such as yours? Not to mention the garden. He's apprenticed to the most successful apothecary in the North Country." Her eyes snapped with indignation.

"Lucie, my love"—Nicholas reached for her hand—"a Master in Durham has need of him."

Owen felt like an eavesdropper. He reminded them of his presence. "I chose my situation. All is as it should be."

Nicholas shook his head. "It is not a good post for him. Anselm is right."

Lucie closed her eyes against Nicholas's pleading look. "You wanted to give Owen something to study."

"Lucie."

She leaned down to him. "Must I remind you of our agreement, Nicholas? I am in charge of the shop while you are unwell. I make the decisions."

The apothecary looked down at his hands and shook his head.

Like a child, Owen thought. One who has been naughty and is doing his penance.

"Good." Lucie moved away and gestured for Owen to go over to Nicholas.

The apothecary's hands shook as he showed Owen the books, the critical passages. He stank. Not just of the sickroom, but of fear. A smell a soldier knows well.

"You should heed the Archdeacon," Nicholas whispered to Owen when Lucie had left the room.

"He does not want me here, that is plain." Owen looked into the sick man's eyes. Rheumy, red-rimmed. Fear added a disturbing intensity. "Why, Master Nicholas? Why does the Archdeacon want me gone?"

"Anselm watches over my soul."

"I can scarce believe I endanger your soul."

Nicholas said nothing, his watery eyes flicking here and there, pausing on anything but Owen's watchful face.

"I am just what you need here. You know that."

"Anselm...sees it otherwise."

"Why?"

"I am selfish to use you in such a way."

"Nonsense. I came of my own free will. I am content. This is exactly where I want to be."

Nicholas took a deep, shuddering breath and closed his eyes. "Potter Digby. You knew him?"

"A little. Why?"

"He should not have died. None of them should have died."

"None of them?" Here at last, a confession? Owen leaned closer. "What do you mean?"

Nicholas's eyes opened wide. "I—" He shook his head. Tears welled up, ran down his fevered cheeks. "Protect her." His head fell back on the pillow. He struggled for air, his bony hands clawing his throat. Owen called for Lucie.

She ran up the stairs. "Merciful Mother." Nicholas twisted and turned on the bed, fighting to breathe. The smell of sweat and urine filled the room. Lucie knelt down and grabbed one of the clawlike hands.

"Nicholas, love. What do you need?" He moaned and pressed her hand to his chest. "Your chest? Is the pain there?"

The watery eyes fluttered. "Breathing. Mandragora."

Lucie sat back, frightened. "You need something so strong?"

Nicholas drew a great, shuddering breath. "A pinch. In the milk. You know."

Lucie hesitated. But when he doubled up, she turned to Owen. "Watch him. If his eyes start to roll or he begins to choke, call me at once."

Nicholas calmed. But just as Owen thought how much better he seemed, Nicholas threw his head back and arched in a paroxysm of pain.

Lucie, back with the physick, brought the small table with the spirit lamp over beside Owen. "Watch me," she said in a tight voice. Her eyes reflected her husband's pain. "See that I do exactly as I say."

Owen watched.

Lucie held up a tiny silver bowl, smaller than a thimble. "Powdered mandrake root, just this measure, no more." Her hands trembled as she dipped the bowl into a heavy crock on which was painted a root in the shape of a man. Owen steadied it for her. She poured the thimble's contents into a larger bowl. "Dried milk of poppy, this amount." She lifted a larger measure, and Owen tilted the second crock for her, on which was painted a delicately pleated flower. "Boiling water to two fingers beneath the edge." Her voice was calmer now. She poured the water. "And mix well over the lamp, then cool, still mixing, until I can keep my hand against the bowl for three breaths. I must not scald my patient's gullet."

"Can I mix it for you? I'm sure Master Nicholas would rather you held his hand."

Lucie nodded and changed places with Owen. With her apron she dried the sweat from Nicholas's face. "Peace, Nicholas, you'll soon sleep without pain."

Owen stirred the liquid and followed her instructions under Lucie's watchful eye. When she'd seen him keep his hand to the bowl for three breaths, she nodded and he handed it to her, then lifted Nicholas's head, holding him while he coughed up phlegm and fought to catch his breath. When Nicholas was quiet, Lucie helped him drink. Within a few minutes the moaning ceased.

"Bless you," Nicholas said. The effort to speak cost him a cough. He winced with pain.

"No more talk, Nicholas, my love. Sleep now."

Owen lowered him to the bed.

"Do you need a priest?" the Archdeacon asked from the doorway.

"Anselm!" Nicholas gasped and clutched at his heart.

In two strides, Owen was at the door.

Lucie dropped to her knees beside Nicholas, whose eyes were wide with terror. "I did not call him back, Nicholas." She held him close to her, trying to calm him.

"My master is in need of rest, Archdeacon," Owen said, pushing Anselm out the door with him. "Your prayers are appreciated, but they'd be best said elsewhere." He closed the door firmly behind them.

"Anselm is mad, Lucie," Nicholas whispered, clutching her hand. "Stay away from him."

"I will, my love. Now rest. You must rest." She smoothed his brow and watched with relief as the milk of poppy quieted him. "And I will keep him away from you. He is killing you."

On the stairs, the Archdeacon demanded, "What happened?" As if he had a right to know.

Owen led him down to the shop without a word. Once there, he said in what he hoped was a controlled, emotionless voice, "Nicholas Wilton is in much pain. Your visits do not calm him. You must let him rest."

Anselm glared at Owen. "You overstep your place, Owen Archer. You are not the master of this house."

"If you are his friend, leave him in peace. He had a spell, requiring mandragora to relieve the pain. He must sleep now."

The Archdeacon's face changed. The eyes warmed to honest concern. So he did care about Nicholas. "Mandragora. Then he is worse."

"I think so."

"I did not know. Of course I will leave and let him rest. He must get well. You must do everything possible to make him better." Anselm paused with his hand on the door. "I do not like trusting him to you, Archer. A Summoner stands apart from the people. He must, in order to impart a fair judgment. To befriend a Summoner is the act of someone buying favors."

"You suspect me?"

"I merely warn you."

"I will get no favors from him."

"God rest his soul."

"You show an unusual interest in my welfare."

"You are apprenticed to my friend. I do not want you to bring dishonor upon his house."

"I will not."

"See that you do not." The Archdeacon swept out of the shop.

He had not said what was on his mind, of that Owen was certain. But that he was worried for Nicholas was clear. Worried and angry.

After the evening meal, Owen perused Nicholas's books. Lucie mended and Tildy shelled beans. Lucie spoke softly to Tildy of the morrow's work.

Now and again Lucie would look up with anxious care, as if her eyes could see through the floorboards to the sickroom. Owen could not help but wonder what that old, dying man had to offer her. He could not even give her a living child. What made the lovely Lucie so loyal to Nicholas Wilton? Was it that he had killed for her?

Or that he had delivered the poison for her? But if he was merely the unwitting messenger, what had caused his collapse? A poison with a delayed effect?

One poisoning. Two poisonings. One meant to kill, the other to silence. Had she poisoned Nicholas to silence him?

Owen looked up from the book he'd been pretending to read. Lucie was listening to Tildy repeat the ingredients of tomorrow's soup pot. "...after the barley boils, that bit o' pork from yesterday, winter savory, salt, a stalk of fennel…"

"Not fennel, Tildy, lovage." The voice soft, the manner gentle. She tucked a wisp of hair back into Tildy's kerchief. The girl smiled. Lucie patted her hand. "You're a good girl, Tildy. You're a big help to me."

Such a woman did not injure her husband and kill her mother's lover. How had such thoughts come to him? He watched as Lucie showed Tildy which pot to use, where the spices were kept, how to interpret the labels. She was patient and thorough with the girl, as she was with him.

He tried to imagine her, in her patient, thorough way, planning the poison, how it would be delivered. Thinking about her lovely mother, the babe that had killed her, how Lucie was then sent off to the convent, and now she'd heard that the man was back, that he was dying at the abbey, that Nicholas had been asked to make a physick to save the man's life. Gently she would offer to mix the medicine. Or to wrap it while Nicholas dressed warmly for the walk. A few extra pinches of aconite, and it was ready. Who would notice?

One poisoning to kill, the other to silence. Fitzwilliam an accident. And then, when Brother Wulfstan discovered the deed, she agreed to burn the rest of the poison and keep quiet. How tidy.

Could she have done that to Nicholas? Was that why she was so solicitous? Guilt?

"I'll say good night, then, Owen," Tildy said, standing over him with her candle. He was startled by her nearness. He hoped his head had been bent over the books.

"Good night, Tildy."

When Tildy was gone, Lucie said, "Something bothers you."

So much for his subtlety. "It is so much to learn. I hope that I don't fool myself, thinking I can learn it so late. I'm no child. Not the usual age of an apprentice."

"You are doing well. You have no need to worry."

He wished she were not suddenly kind to him. He must take the opportunity of being alone with her to find out what she knew. What she would admit to. He must approach it slowly. She must not guess his purpose. "It is very different here from the camps. Childhood illnesses, pregnant women, the very old—I saw nothing of this before. There it was mostly wounds and camp fever."

She did not react as he had hoped, relaxed and ready to talk shop. Her face reddened. "I hope you do not find the work here tedious."

Dear God, he could not even make small talk with her. "Not at all. I have already learned so much. Master Nicholas has a unique mind. They do say he has an excellent physick for camp fever. We experimented with many mixtures. What does he use?"

She yanked at a tangled thread and cursed as it snapped. "We are not in a camp."

"But surely there are men in York who contracted the fever as soldiers. It recurs. That's the curse of it."

"Nicholas has not discussed it with me." Her tone closed the subject.

Owen let it go. It was enough for now to know she found the topic disturbing. He went back to his reading.

After a while he noticed that Lucie stared into the fire, her mending forgotten on her lap. The firelight shone on tears spilling down her cheeks.

He closed the book and went to her. "What is it? Can I help?"

She shook her head. Her shoulders trembled as she worked to compose herself.

When she seemed calmer, Owen asked, "It was unusual for Master Nicholas to ask for mandragora?"

"He prescribes mandrake root only when the danger of an overdose is outweighed by the pain. He is in great pain." She wiped her eyes. "Thank you for your help this afternoon."

"I was glad I could do something for you."

"His condition frightened me. All I could think of was that he might die. One mismeasure of mandrake." She looked down at her hands. "What we do. We possess the power of life and death."

"Better than a soldier, who holds only the power of death."

"No." She touched his hand. "No, listen to me. You must never forget that about what we do. We could as easily kill as heal." Her eyes held his.

What was she telling him? "But the amount of mandragora you gave the master was safe."

"Yes, of course." She pressed his hand, then withdrew hers with an embarrassed blush. "I am not myself."

"This cannot be easy for you."

"Perhaps you should go."

"Whatever you wish."

"I wish none of this had happened. I wish—" Her voice broke. She ducked her head, dabbed at her eyes with the corner of her apron.

Owen took her cold hands in his and kissed them.

"Owen—" Her eyes were soft, not angry.

He put his hands on her shoulders, drew her to him, and kissed her. Her lips were warm. She responded. A warm, urgent kiss. Then pushed him away. She looked down at her hands, her face flushed.

"Know this, know this always, Lucie Wilton," Owen whispered, not trusting his voice, "I will do anything I can to help you. I cannot do otherwise. I will not press myself on you. But if you have need of me, I will do whatever you ask."

"You should not say such things." She still did not look at him. "You do not know us."

"I cannot help what I feel."

"You must go now."

Owen kissed her hands again, then hurried away, out into the fog, feeling foolish, angry with himself, and yet relieved. She had not withdrawn her hands. She was not angry. She had kissed him with the same hunger he felt. Lucie Wilton did not find him, one-eyed and starting over again like a boy, repulsive. He had held her, kissed her, and said to her what he had ached to say ever since he'd first seen her. And she had not pulled away. He felt lightheaded. Triumphant.

And disgusted with himself. For against all reason he had fallen in love with a woman who might be a murderer. Whose crime he was honor-bound to expose. She had the knowledge to poison Montaigne. She had said as much tonight. *We could as easily kill as heal.* And perhaps she had a motive. Or a motive to persuade her husband to commit the sin, which was worse than committing it herself. She would condemn Nicholas to Hell with her.

And that other sin he had thought of. Could she have brought on Nicholas's illness? He thought about them together, up in that stuffy room. Her tender nursing. No. To carry that off would require a most devious mind. He could not believe that of her. He would not.

And Anselm. Where did he fit into the scheme? Why was he so threatened by Owen's presence in his friend's shop?

Owen tried to concentrate on that question. But his mind turned back to Lucie. Twice today he had held her. She was beautiful. Responsive. Dear God, let her not be a murderer.

Anselm closed his eyes and swung the knotted thongs against his bare back, again, again, mortifying the flesh, offering it to his Savior in return for Nicholas's deliverance from the evil that surrounded him. Nicholas must live. He must live long enough to recognize the error of his life and come back to Anselm, his protector. He must understand. God had given Anselm this task. Why could Nicholas not understand? What had they done to him? Anselm beat himself until his body was on fire with divine light. He would succeed. The Lord smiled on him.

17

AN ACCOUNTING

A funeral, an interrogation, a sickbed, a profession of love, and no answers. Owen knew himself a failure at this new life. And he had chosen the easy life. As a mercenary in Italy, he would have been called on to use much more of his wits. But also his training as a soldier. His body. Perhaps this life of spying made him lazy. It disgusted him even more that he planned to take a tankard of ale up to his room and dull his thoughts enough to sleep. He had lost all his honor. Better if he were truly the Wiltons' apprentice. He could throw himself into his work. Devote himself to his new profession. But the knowledge that it was temporary held him back. He hated to let Lucie Wilton become dependent on him, for she would lose him soon enough. Whenever the Archbishop realized he was getting nothing from him. Then he would send him away, probably on an errand from which he would not return. With such black thoughts, Owen returned to the York Tavern.

Bess was waiting for him, hands on hips, impatient. "So there you are at last."

"I hope no visitor awaits me tonight, Bess. I have no energy for conversation."

She looked him up and down. "I can see you've lost some spark. But the Archbishop's secretary came for you. You are wanted at the minster."

"It is late."

"He said whenever you came in."

Perhaps it was a good sign. Perhaps the Archbishop wished him to give up the inquiry. And wished to give up on him. Then Owen could settle in as apprentice to Lucie Wilton. And when Nicholas died—

Jehannes answered the door. The Archbishop was comfortably enthroned beside the fire. Owen could not imagine Thoresby doubting anything. His life was set, his goals clear. Men such as he, highly placed, did not see their lives whittled away piece by piece, a limb, an eye, a stomach wound that prevented them from eating properly. Only if they were foolhardy did they put themselves in vulnerable situations. They might be murdered, but their attackers would make sure it was successful. Death was a clean end. Of course Thoresby was comfortable. He would never stand here wondering whether his fate had been decided, what was to be next for him.

"Well, Owen Archer. I judge it about time we discussed your progress."

With no warning, of course. Left him alone to hang himself, then suddenly demanded a report. On a whim, no doubt. Still, perhaps it would lead to his freedom. "Your Grace. I confess I have no definite answer to how Fitzwilliam died. Only new questions."

Thoresby motioned Owen to the seat across from him, with his good eye facing away from the fire. At least he had been that considerate. Or Jehannes had set it up that way.

Jehannes handed Owen a goblet of wine. Owen lifted it toward Thoresby, then drank. "This is most welcome, Your Grace. My day has been unpleasant. It began with a funeral and ended at the sickbed of my dying employer." Owen downed the wine with relish.

Thoresby smiled. It was not as friendly a smile as Owen might have wished. Thoresby must suspect him of something, had heard something not to his liking. This was not the time to be evasive.

"You said you had new questions?" Thoresby's voice was silky. Dangerous.

Owen set his cup beside him, sat forward. "To be brief, I have lost the man who was assisting me in my investigation. Digby the Summoner. He drowned. Not by accident, I think."

Eyebrows lifted, but they did not fool Owen. The Archbishop's eyes expressed no surprise. "Why the Summoner?" Thoresby asked.

"Why would you trust the man least trusted in all York?"

"He offered his services to me in exchange for information. I had no reason to distrust him."

"His being a Summoner was enough for most men."

Owen shrugged. "I'm a Welshman. I struggle against the current by nature." He grinned.

Thoresby returned a ghost of a smile. "This information you gave Digby, did he find it useful?"

Not good. "A poor choice of words, Your Grace. He, too, was interested in the deaths at the abbey. He wished to help. I told him the identity of the first man. He was able to tell me why the man came to York."

"And that was useful to you?"

"I think it will be." Owen picked up his cup, which Jehannes had unobtrusively refilled, and sipped the wine, trying to think how he might modify the story to protect Lucie Wilton. But Thoresby's expression hurried him into the truth. "Digby, you see, was at the abbey the night Montaigne died."

Now the eyes were surprised.

"He found Nicholas Wilton in a swoon outside the infirmary. Wilton had just delivered a physick for Montaigne." He paused. "It would have been helpful had you told me of Montaigne's connection with the late Lady D'Arby."

Thoresby regarded Owen coolly. "I did not think it important in the investigation of Fitzwilliam's death."

"Digby thought it important. He thought it was all connected. He just didn't know how."

"Curious that Digby would be interested."

"Digby was a curious man."

"If he told you this much, most likely he told you why," Thoresby said. "It appears that he trusted you."

The Archbishop's eyes moved over Owen's face as if the truth that he tried to hold back were written there.

How cool, Owen thought. How secure in his world.

"I am not sure you will find it plausible," Owen said.

"Try it out."

Owen took a deep breath. "Digby suspected Archdeacon Anselm of protecting Nicholas Wilton. It disturbed him that the Archdeacon might be implicated in a murder."

Thoresby closed his eyes. When he opened them, he did not look at Owen, but rather frowned into the fire. "That connection again. But what had Wilton done that Anselm should need to protect him?"

Owen wished he could get up and pace. He was in way over his head. The Archbishop obviously knew of the closeness of Anselm and Nicholas. He had no idea what else the Archbishop knew. He might know everything already. Owen wished this were a duel with swords. Better yet, a sweaty wrestling match. He did not know where he stood.

"What had Wilton done, Archer?" Thoresby asked quietly.

"Digby thought he had poisoned Geoffrey Montaigne. His wife's mother's lover."

The Archbishop considered the fire for a moment, then sighed and put down his cup. "So he thought, and presumably you think too, that Wilton poisoned Montaigne for his wife, who wanted to avenge her family's honor, and the guilt is killing him?"

"I do not think Mistress Wilton knows the pilgrim's identity."

Thoresby regarded him closely. "Do you fancy Mistress Wilton?"

Owen's stomach turned. He felt like the cat in the corner, unable to read this man from a different world, who had complete control of his destiny. "She is my employer, Your Grace."

"Indeed. But also beautiful and soon to be widowed."

"You doubt my judgment. But hear me out. There is an additional twist. Your Archdeacon. Although they had once been close, Anselm had not spoken to Nicholas Wilton for years. The morning after Nicholas took to his bed, the Archdeacon appeared, expressing much concern. He visits Nicholas regularly now, even though his visits disturb Nicholas—so much so that today it nearly killed him."

Thoresby silently took that in. Then he shifted in his chair. "All intriguing, Owen Archer, but I employed you to inquire into the death of my ward Fitzwilliam."

"The two deaths are connected, Your Grace, I am certain of that. And I think that Fitzwilliam's death was the accident, not Montaigne's."

"A poison made for Montaigne given to Fitzwilliam?"

Owen nodded.

"And Digby suspected this?"

"And is now dead."

"Nicholas Wilton could hardly have killed Digby."

"Perhaps the Archdeacon?"

Thoresby considered Owen with a grave expression. "Is that what you believe?" he asked at last.

"It fits with Digby's suspicions. And a clumsy attempt on his part to rid himself of me."

"Oh?"

He told him of Anselm's claim to have arranged, in less than a day, an apprenticeship for him in Durham. "He hoped I might not return, I think."

"Interesting. What do you know of Anselm?"

"Very little. What should I know?"

Thoresby smiled at the question. "You are a bold Welshman. The old Duke chose his men well." He nodded to Jehannes, who filled his cup, and freshened Owen's. The Lord Chancellor's chain of office glittered in the firelight as Thoresby toyed with it. He nodded to himself, picked up the cup, tasted the wine, nodded again.

"Do you know the duties of an Archdeacon, Owen?"

"Primarily fiscal, are they not?"

Thoresby nodded. "As Archdeacon of York, Anselm must raise money for the cathedral building. You can see that it is not finished. A long, expensive process, this expression of York's devotion to the Lord. And the King. The Hatfield chapel is close to the King's heart." He sipped. "Thus the paradox of the position. The Archdeacon must be a cleric and yet worldly—not usually a virtue in a man of the cloth."

Owen nodded, but he wondered where Thoresby was leading.

Thoresby chuckled. "Your one eye is quite expressive. You think I wander. Too much wine, perhaps." He put down his cup. "You would be wrong to think that, my friend. John Thoresby never wanders."

"I would not make the mistake of thinking that, Your Grace."

"I chose Anselm—and it has proven to be a wise choice—because he did not show great piety. A good scholar, a persuasive speaker, with a solemn air about him—the pinched face, the gauntness—but poorly suited to an abbey. He has a weakness for young men, you see."

"I had heard that he and Nicholas were good friends at the abbey school."

Thoresby smiled. "You see Nicholas at the end of his life, on his deathbed. But he was a handsome young man—in a delicate way. Magnificent blue eyes. And he was a listener." Thoresby shook his head. "Anselm was smitten. There was a scandal. Not because two boys were discovered in bed together. A common occurrence in abbey schools—you must be used to it in the army. But Anselm was Abbot Gerard's prize novice. Gerard was grooming Anselm for high office in the Church. He was furious. And anger opened his eyes. He saw the signs of Anselm's nature, realized that it was his protege's doing, that young Nicholas had merely been flattered—and flustered, no doubt—by the attention of the older boy. And perhaps comforted to share a bed with another. Anselm was harshly reprimanded. He became rather an ascetic. But Gerard knew it was a mask."

"He offered Anselm to you as Archdeacon to get him away from the novices?"

"It was Anselm's request. To be removed from temptation."

"Admirable."

"You smirk as you say that. But Anselm is a fine man. I have had no cause for complaint. Or did not till now. It was his misfortune to be a second son, bound for the Church. Had he been a layman, his nature would not have mattered. Oh, he might have found it unpleasant siring his sons, but as long as he saw to that in an acceptable space of years, he would have been free to pursue his pleasures where he would. You must pity Anselm. The Church was not his choice."

"It is difficult for me to pity a man who tried to trick me into a dangerous, perhaps fatal journey."

"I find it hard to believe he would be so…clumsy."

Not that he would not do it. Owen said nothing for a few minutes, absorbing that. "I take it the Archdeacon never got over his passion for Nicholas Wilton?"

"They were great friends. I think no more than that on Wilton's part. But that ended with the death of Lady D'Arby."

Owen sat up. This was more what he wished to hear. "Why?"

Thoresby shrugged. "He did not like Nicholas's friendship with Lady D'Arby. But why they fought after she died, I do not know."

"I wish I had known all this when I began."

"I hardly imagined my ward had been poisoned by accident. He had so many enemies."

The two men regarded each other for a moment.

"Do you have any proof?" Thoresby asked.

"Not exactly. I have Brother Wulfstan's word that he gave your ward the physick made for Montaigne. After the second death, and only then, Wulfstan tested the medicine and discovered too much monkshood. Enough to kill. Looking back, he realized that their deaths had been similar, with all the symptoms expected of poisoning by monkshood."

"He is certain of this?"

"Yes."

"Why did he not tell anyone of his discovery?"

"It was too late to save them."

"Where is the physick now?"

"Burned. So that no more harm could come of it."

"Belated caution." Thoresby sighed. "Did Brother Wulfstan confront Nicholas Wilton with his discovery?"

"The man is dying, Your Grace."

"So he did not." Thoresby seemed irritated by this turn. "Have you said anything to Wilton?"

"No. Do you wish to pursue this further?"

Thoresby sat back, gazing up at the ceiling, his hands pressed together, lips pursed. "It is difficult for me to accept, when I was expecting a clear case of revenge and my ward to be the intended

victim. It is the motive that eludes me. Too weak. Not good enough
for me, Owen Archer. Let us see this to the finish, shall we?"

Owen nodded, rose to leave, then hesitated, frowning. "I might
wish to exhume Montaigne's body."

"To what purpose?"

"To look for signs of poisoning. Since Wulfstan destroyed the
physick."

"I think not, Archer. I want no more upset at the abbey."

Withholding information, tying his hands, what did the man
want of him? "Then what would you suggest, Your Grace?"

"Look to the living for your answers, Archer. You have
uncovered quite a complicated knot. Now unravel it."

Lucie sat by Nicholas, turning the few facts she had around in her
mind. If Nicholas were not so ill, she might mention Geoffrey, see
his reaction. But he was so weakened by today's attack. And if what
she suspected was true, if his poisoning Geoffrey was no accident, it
might kill him to know that she knew. But what could drive Nicholas
to murder?

She was frightened.

She-devils. She and who? Her mother? What could the
Archdeacon have against them? Of what vileness did he suspect them?

But of course. Her mother with Geoffrey, and—he had accused
her of it today—she and Owen. But it wasn't true.

And why would Geoffrey have attacked Nicholas?

She must know more. Geoffrey Montaigne, her mother,
Nicholas, Archdeacon Anselm, Potter Digby. What connected
them? Who might know? It must go back to her mother's time.

Her Aunt Phillippa. Of course. She would send for her in the
morning. She would say Nicholas was dying and she needed her
aunt's support. And she did. The house would feel much safer with
her Aunt Phillippa in it.

18

LUCIE JOINS THE DANCE

Nicholas slept. His breathing was ragged, but regular enough to assure Lucie that the pain had diminished. She lay down beside him, the room dark but for the tiny flame of the spirit lamp. The cat climbed up on her chest, a welcome warmth. Lucie petted Melisende absently as she stared at the ceiling, wondering how to approach her Aunt Phillippa. To ask about her mother would not be unusual, but to ask about Geoffrey and Nicholas—Her aunt's guard would go up. Phillippa was always careful talking about that time. Lucie knew there was much her aunt chose not to tell her. She would want to know what Lucie had heard, what she was fishing for. Perhaps if Lucie did not make much of it. Something overheard, that Geoffrey and Nicholas had argued. But if she made light of it, so might her aunt. She must say enough that Phillippa would want to separate truth from rumor. Perhaps she might say she had noticed an odd entry in the shop records.

The shop records. Lucie had not thought of them till now. The Archdeacon had said Geoffrey had attacked Nicholas and left him for dead. Then Nicholas had been wounded. Perhaps she could find a reference to it in the records. Her father-in-law had been as meticulous as Nicholas in recording all transactions. Might there not be an entry in the log for dressing a wound, for a salve to quicken the healing?

She sat up, waking Melisende, who hissed and moved with slow dignity to Lucie's feet and began circling in preparation for lying down in a new spot. Lucie disturbed her once more as she pulled her feet up and out onto the cold floor. The old shop records were kept up here in their bedchamber, in a heavy oak chest beneath the front window. She lit the oil lamp from the spirit lamp, wrapped a shawl around her shoulders, and went over to the chest.

It was Lucie's wedding chest, and her mother's before her. Out of this chest Lucie had pulled mementos of childhood when she carried Martin. How happy she had been. God had smiled down on her, allowing her joy. And in his short life Martin had given her much joy. Through him she had remembered her own girlhood, had seen her own mother, with her dark hair and pale eyes, bent over the chest, bringing out treasures, many of them gifts from Geof, her handsome knight. He had brought Lucie presents, too. A carved doll with silken hair, a small cart in which he pulled her through the maze. He had the sunniest smile and the gentlest voice...And Nicholas had poisoned him? The thought burned in the pit of Lucie's stomach. She told herself she had no time to dwell on that now.

She lifted out an armful of sewn books, each painstakingly illustrated on its cloth cover with an unusual herb, and set them aside. These were Nicholas's. Beneath them were older, leather-bound books, their covers dry and cracking. Lucie leafed through them, pausing over meticulous sketches of astrological signs, heavenly portents. Paul Wilton, her father-in-law, had been more interested in that part of his work than in the botanical work that Nicholas delighted in. She found it confusing to follow her father-in-law's chronology; he would go through several books and then go back and fill in blank areas in all of them before moving on to a fresh book. Or sometimes he would interrupt one book to return to another. Lucie was uncertain what date she sought, though she knew it had to be within the range of her mother's marriage and the time Geoffrey was in York. She knew that Geoffrey had come after she was born. She'd asked her Aunt Phillippa about that long ago, when she'd had a romantic idea that she might be Geoffrey's daughter. "Oh no, my little love, you are my niece, you are Robert's child. Never doubt that."

Her Aunt Phillippa did not understand how lovely it had been, imagining that she was the child of her mother's happiness, that her father was the fair-haired knight who made her mother laugh. She did not want to be the daughter of the grim man who shouted and called her "little lady." It hurt her more than her father's scolding that Sir Robert never said her name. As if he could not be bothered to remember it. It had frightened her. If her father could forget her, God could, too. Geoffrey had remembered her name. And her favorite color. And secrets she'd told him...

Lucie shook her head. She had sat and dreamt over the same notebook long enough that needles prickled in the hand poised to turn the page, and one of her feet had gone to sleep. She picked up the record books that she guessed covered the years of her mother's marriage, and moved over to the table and chair by the garden window.

Slowly she made her way through the books, pausing at all mention of "N," which was Paul Wilton's code for Nicholas. There were no complete names in the records, just one or two initials, enough to distinguish one customer or supplier from another. Most of the entries mentioning Nicholas referred to his purchase of cuttings and seeds for the garden. Occasionally, more frequently as time went by, Nicholas helped his father in the shop. His responsibilities grew.

And then she found it. An entry about the time of her mother's death. She had almost stopped before she reached it. "MD cauterized wound, bandaged. Stayed the night to see what N's eyes looked like when he woke. Left salve and tisane. AA, D'Arby and DP agree N has done his penance." And in the accounts were entered a generous payment to MD for services rendered and a gift to the minster fund, the size of which made Lucie uneasy. For surely "AA" was the Archdeacon, D'Arby was her father, and "DP" Dame Phillippa. They agreed that Nicholas had done his penance for what? What sin required such a large offering to the minster fund? Did it have something to do with her mother's death? And who was "MD"?

Owen woke at dawn from a light drowse that had taken most of the night to achieve. His stomach burned and his head felt crowded with demons chattering incessantly in voices pitched to hysteria. Too many questions, few answers, too many constraints. He could not exhume Montaigne, he could not question Lucie or she would know he suspected her, he could not question Nicholas because the man was dying. Anselm was a madman. Thoresby—what of John Thoresby? The comfortable, confident Lord Chancellor of England and Archbishop of York sent Owen out to inquire into his ward's death, yet Owen felt the man pretended ignorance where he knew the facts. Why? Did Thoresby not trust Owen? If not, then what was Owen doing here? Not that he was certain anything would be proved by exhuming Montaigne, but for Thoresby to so summarily deny him...

Such thoughts got him nowhere. He must think where he might get some answers. He needed to talk with someone who knew something of Lady D'Arby, Montaigne, and Nicholas. Bess had not lived long enough in York to know anything but rumors about that time.

Magda Digby. It was a long shot, but Owen suspected that little occurred in York that the Riverwoman did not hear about. He applied some salve to the eye, put on his patch and his boots, and crept out of the inn. He could speak with her and be back before Lucie was ready to open the shop.

After her wakeful night, Lucie was anxious to send Owen for her Aunt Phillippa. She put away the records and slept for a while, then rose shortly after dawn and broke her fast with Tildy while they discussed the girl's chores for the day. By then Lucie expected Owen, but he did not come. She checked for him out at the woodpile. The air was frosty, and snow clouds glowered overhead. Under the holly hedge, spring crocuses pushed green shoots through the thinning snow. It made her heart glad to see the first sign of spring. But her irritation returned when she found no trace of Owen anywhere in the garden. Now that she had resolved to send for her aunt, she could not bear the delay.

She would go to the York Tavern and fetch Owen. Tildy could listen for Nicholas and come for her if he woke.

• • •

Tom was measuring the contents of the casks. He looked up with a smile when she entered. "Lucie Wilton. Welcome, neighbor." He noticed her agitated state. "Is it Nicholas? Is he worse?"

She nodded. "I want to send Owen for my Aunt Phillippa."

"And you thought to find him here? Nay, he was off at first light."

Bess's voice rang out from up above, barking orders.

"Do you have any idea where he went?" Lucie asked.

Tom scratched his beard, then shook his head. "He said naught to me. I didn't think but he was coming to you. Go on up and see if Bess knows aught."

"She sounds busy."

"Oh, aye. Trying to put Owen's room to rights. She won't rest till fire is scrubbed away. But go up. She'd want to see you."

Bess stood in the doorway of the small room, hands on hips, one toe tapping. "I don't know, Kit. I just don't know what to do with you. You're all elbows, girl. Nothing is safe when you're near."

"Bess?"

Bess turned, her face as red as the hair tumbling from her cap in tight, damp curls. Her sleeves were rolled up to the elbows, revealing muscular forearms. "Oh, goodness me, you catch me in the midst of teaching this child the art of scouring a floor. Can you believe she's made it to fifteen years without learning the trick?"

Normally, Lucie would have smiled at her friend's tirade, but this morning she was too intent on her mission. "Have you seen Owen?"

"He's not with you? When he left so early this morning, I thought you'd ordered him there at dawn."

Lucie turned toward the ladder. "Damnable man."

The set of her friend's jaw, her lack of humor, and the frustration in those two words alerted Bess. She caught Lucie's arm. "What is it, love? Has Nicholas taken a turn?"

Lucie nodded.

"And you need someone to watch the shop while you sit with him?"

"I want to send Owen for my Aunt Phillippa."

"Your aunt? Whatever for? What good has she done you, I ask? I'll watch the shop."

"You have your work here."

"Kit can do it."

"I need my aunt. It's time she helped me out."

"Well, I won't disagree with you about that. But why send Owen? Send John, my stable boy. He's a good lad, rides fast, he'll be back and forth in no time."

"I don't need to burden you, Bess."

"It's no burden, love. I want to help."

Lucie looked down at her hands. "I wish you could."

Bess folded her arms across her chest. "As I thought. It's more than sending for your aunt that's worrying you. Come now, downstairs with you, tell Bess all about it."

"I can't stay, Bess," Lucie said as she followed her friend down to the tavern.

"Then we'll talk at your house. It's all the same to me."

"No. I can't talk there."

Bess led her into the kitchen, set her down in a chair, tsking at the bony shoulders. "You're not eating right, Lucie. Everything seems worse when you're not eating right." She poured a cup of ale for Lucie and one for herself.

Lucie found herself swept up in Bess's assumption that she was about to confide in her, wondering where to begin, how to explain what she feared about Nicholas. But it seemed disloyal to admit even to her best friend that she feared her husband had killed someone.

"I have to talk with my aunt, Bess. I need to know some things, that's all."

"That's all, is it?" Bess took off her cap and reworked the pile of curly red hair, stabbing horn hairpins into it with a brutal impatience that made Lucie wince. Bess tested her work with a vigorous shake and, satisfied when that did not undo it, put back her cap and leaned across the little table toward Lucie, her eyes fixed on her friend's. "Now why don't you just begin at the beginning?"

And Lucie, despite herself, poured it all out to Bess, what Wulfstan had discovered, what she had overhead, the entry in the records.

"Merciful Heaven," Bess muttered at the end of Lucie's account, "you have carried a load of worries on those delicate shoulders. Have you asked Nicholas about all this?"

Lucie rubbed her temples, a weary gesture. "How could I do that? He's so ill. To upset him with questions that brought back disturbing memories—"

Bess nodded. "Well, at least you've given it thought. I tell you what, you have in your household someone who ought to hear all this. I'm sure that he could help you."

Lucie shoved the cup aside and rose. "You're pushing me at Owen again. Do you think of nothing else, Bess? Why would I confide in my apprentice? He's almost a stranger. How do I know I can trust him?"

"I know you can, love. I'm not suggesting it to play at matchmaking, not this morning. Not when you've such trouble."

"I'll take care of this myself."

"John will go for your aunt."

"No. I'll send Owen."

"Please, love. It makes sense to send John. He knows the way. He knows where the Scots lie in wait. We've sent him hither and yon for supplies, and he's never failed us. He's young and fearless. He thinks it's a lark."

Lucie saw that Bess's argument was sound. "All right. Please send him. And thank you, Bess."

"You're like my own, child. I could not do less."

Lucie hugged her friend. "Forgive my temper."

"You have good reason to have your feelings so ready at hand. I've taken no offense."

"If you see Owen Archer, send him to the shop. He's more than late."

Owen had to wait while Magda dressed a man's wound. Every moment he waited made him later getting to the shop. It frustrated him. But if he gave up, he would have wasted the trip, and if Lucie was to be mad at him, he wanted it to have been worthwhile. At last Magda sent the man on his way and joined Owen by the fire, wiping her hands and nodding with satisfaction. "'Tis a good mornin's work, saving Kirby. A good fisherman. Best eel catcher on the Ouse."

"How was he wounded?" The man had a gash across his stomach.

"Folk come to Magda knowing she'll not tell their sins. The man cut his gut, 'tis enough for thee to know." She sliced some bread from a hard loaf on the table beside her, and spread it with a ripe cheese that turned Owen's stomach. "But thy business, now, what might that be?"

"I can trust you to keep as quiet about my business as you are about the eel catcher's?"

"Aye. Thou wert Potter's friend. Potter's friend, Magda's friend. Except for the one he thought a friend who was never anything like. That Archdeacon. Carrion crow. 'Twas him killed Magda's boy."

"You know that for a fact?"

She spat into the fire. "Magda has many friends. There were eyes by the tower that night. They saw the crow push Potter down. Too far into the mead bowl he'd dipped. And the crow took the chance."

"Why?"

"Thou know'st why. To protect his sweetheart. The soft-eyed Nicholas."

"You know what Potter thought Nicholas had done?"

"Oh, aye. And Potter came too close to knowing all the truth." She wiped her hands on her skirt, cut another hunk of bread, and spread it with the cheese. "'Tis good cheese. Thou art a fool to sniff at it." She grinned.

"What was the connection between Nicholas and Geoffrey Montaigne? Why would Nicholas kill him?"

"The lady's fair knight once tried to kill Nicholas. Mayhap he would try again. Or stir up trouble that had been put to rest."

"I need to know about this, Goodwife Digby. I need to know who else Anselm might want to silence."

She shrugged. "Magda. Sir Robert D'Arby and Dame Phillippa.

Perhaps even the girl Lucie. Married to soft-eyes, isn't she? Phillippa was silly to agree to that. Magda told her. No good would come of that."

"Why would no good come of it?"

Magda peered at him. "Digging deep, Bird-eye. What's an archer to do with such history?"

"Potter told you my purpose."

"Mighty Thoresby wants to hear all this?"

"It seems that Fitzwilliam's death came from all this trouble. He means to understand it."

"Back to Cain and Abel, eh? But Fitzwilliam's death cannot be undone."

"He would not want that, in any case. His ward was an embarrassment. But he must make sure there is nothing in this that could endanger his own person."

"He need not fear."

"Why was the marriage a mistake?"

"Thou know'st the history of Anselm and Nicholas? That Anselm of the visions took the pretty, sickly boy Nicholas under his wing and into his bed?"

"Anselm had visions?"

Magda laughed. "Canst thou look at the crow and see a comely boy in him? Nay, he lured him with stories of Mary, Mother of God, and the boy Jesus. Anselm was to befriend Jesus and care for him. Clever, eh?"

"Abbot Gerard knew of this?"

"A fool. He would have bought the rotting arm from Fitzwilliam."

"So what are you saying about Nicholas and Anselm? That they continued to be lovers?"

Magda shook her head at him. "Nay. If 'twere so, none of this would happen, eh? Nay, Nicholas had not the nature for it. But he believed the crow's visions."

"So Anselm could influence him."

"Magda has watched folk crawl on bloody knees where their saints beheld visions, Bird-eye. 'Tis powerful stuff for some."

"You told Dame Phillippa of this?"

"Aye. Much good it did."

"You were friends?"

"Oh, aye. Magda helped her deliver the girl Lucie. Amelie D'Arby had been foolish. But thou carest naught for women's complaints. 'Tis enough to know the soft-eyed boy was bewitched by Lady D'Arby. So she used him instead of Magda when the fair-haired knight's babe quickened in her. Poor, foolish soft-eyes. Magda would not have been so foolish. The lady killed herself with his help. And Montaigne blamed Nicholas Wilton. 'Tis that simple."

An abortion gone wrong? Was it that simple? "Tell me about Amelie D'Arby's complaints."

Magda shrugged. "Lord D'Arby brought home a war prize. A pretty French girl to breed. A year passed and she did not grow big with child. Lord D'Arby lost his temper. The girl's silly maid brought Lady D'Arby to Magda. She must bear him a son or he'd find a way to be rid of her. Magda did not doubt it. Gave her pennyroyal and madder. And a mandrake root to bury beneath her lord's window. Not that any man needed encouragement to lie with Amelie D'Arby. A beauty she was."

"Did it work?"

"Nay. So she sought out soft-eyes. Thought he could do better."

"She did not go to Nicholas's father?"

"Aye. But he sent her to church to pray. So she teased help from the boy. Foolish girl."

"And she had Lucie."

"Oh, aye. 'Twas only a matter of time. Child had suffered much in the war. She needed time to forget her brother's head on a pike. But the birth almost killed her. Nicholas trusted her to be cautious with the potions. The lady was too frightened to be wise. Magda could see that. But soft-eyes was young and bewitched." Magda shook her head.

"And he still hadn't learned when she went to him to prevent a birth later?"

"Soft eyes," Magda pointed at her eye, "soft head." She tapped her head. Cackled.

"Why did she not want the second babe?"

Magda shrugged. "Phillippa could tell thee."

"You never asked?"

Magda snorted. "Every day they come to Magda. How can she care about them all?"

"You said Nicholas was bewitched by Lady D'Arby. Do you mean he was in love with the mother of the woman he married?"

Magda grinned. "Too rich for thy taste, eh?"

"Why did Potter never summon Nicholas Wilton to answer for this?"

"Potter did not know so much. Wasn't safe for Potter to know. Magda promised the crow never to breathe a word."

"What power did the Archdeacon have over you?"

Magda shrugged, spat in the fire again. "Magda must not make enemies. She has no protection. The crow could burn down Magda's house, take away her power to heal. Ruin Potter."

"And yet you're telling me."

"When the crow killed Potter, he forfeited Magda's silence. He must be punished. Thou'lt see to it. Magda knows."

Owen felt like a fraud. He had no intention of taking the law into his own hands. If Archbishop Thoresby decided to punish Anselm, that was another matter. But chances were Thoresby would overlook his Archdeacon's crime. "Nicholas Wilton should not be trusted as an apothecary."

"Soft-eyes is weak, not evil. Such a fool to poison Montaigne. Man was dying. All this trouble for lack of mother wit to tell him when to wait."

He had to ask. "Is it possible that Lucie Wilton mixed the poison? To avenge her own mother's death?"

Magda frowned. "How so? 'Twas her husband killed her mother, not Montaigne."

"How could Lucie agree to marry Nicholas Wilton?"

"Phillippa told the girl little, to be sure." Magda laughed at the look on Owen's face. "It sickens thee, this story. But the lady asked for the death soft-eyes gave her. 'Twas her own doing."

"Do you think he loves Lucie? Nicholas, I mean."

Magda peered at Owen until he felt the need to shift in his seat.

She snorted. "As much as Bird-eye loves the girl?" Magda laughed afresh at his attempt at denial. "Thou'rt too far gone to hide it. Magda can see." She shook her head, her sharp eyes merry. "But aye, Nicholas loves her well enough."

It was late morning by the time Owen left Magda's house.

When Lucie returned from the York, she was furious to learn that Owen had still not arrived, but she bit her tongue and thanked Tildy for her watchfulness. "Master Nicholas did not wake?"

"I heard him greet the Archdeacon when he went up, but—"

A shiver ran through Lucie at those words. "Archdeacon Anselm is up there with him?"

"Yes, ma'am."

"Did you not tell him that your master slept?"

Tildy nodded. "I did so, but he would go up. You did not say he could not." Her eyes were wide with the fear that she had done the wrong thing.

"You are quite right, Tildy, I said nothing to you of the Archdeacon. You've been a great help. Go on now with your chores."

Lucie climbed the steps. Nicholas's voice was raised in a frightened whine. "We are cursed," Nicholas cried. "You have cursed us."

It was not good for him to get so excited. He would be worse for it. The Archdeacon would surely kill him with his visits. Lucie could not stand back and let that happen, no matter what Nicholas said. She opened the door. Anselm was kneeling beside the bed, clutching Nicholas's hands and whispering something to him.

Two red spots stood out on her husband's death-white cheeks. His hair was damp with sweat.

"No, Nicholas, sweet Nicholas. You must not say such things." Anselm cooed at him as if he were a fretful child.

Nicholas tried to retrieve his hands, but Anselm held tight. "You have killed me, Anselm," Nicholas whimpered.

"How can you say that? I am your protector."

"Leave me."

"Get out of here," Lucie said.

Anselm started and turned toward her. "Leave us alone, woman."

No name. Just "woman," spat out like a curse. And the sickening, cloying way he entreated Nicholas. God help her, but she despised the Archdeacon. It gave her strength. "You would tell me what to do in my own house? He is my husband. I have done everything I know to make him better, and you come in here and undo it all. Look at the effect you have on him. He said it himself. You have killed him. Get out of here." She was shouting. She trembled with rage.

Anselm rose. Dun-colored and fleshless, like a desiccated corpse. He sickened her. "Nicholas would not be in such a state if it were not for you," he hissed.

"What do you mean? What do you know of this?"

"Anselm, please," Nicholas cried. "Leave us."

Anselm turned to Nicholas. "Is that what you want? Do you want me to leave you with her?"

"Yes."

"Then you are a fool. I will leave you to your doom." Anselm swept by Lucie, but paused in the doorway, turning his sunken eyes on her. "I go at his request, not yours."

She stood there trembling until she heard the shop door slam. Then she sat down on the bed beside Nicholas, who lay back with his eyes closed, his hands clenching and unclenching on the covers. She took the cloth from the bowl of scented water and cooled his face, his neck, loosed the hands from the covers and wiped them. "You are too kind to me," he whispered, opening his eyes.

"What is this about, Nicholas? You cannot expect me to go on believing that you welcome the Archdeacon as a friend. You told him he had cursed you. How, Nicholas? What is between you?"

Nicholas shook his head. "Forgive me."

"For what? What have you done?"

He closed his eyes. "He hates you. Beware of Anselm."

"Why, Nicholas? If I must beware of him, I should know why."

But he merely shook his head and turned away from her.

19

BESS INTERVENES

Owen entered the shop rehearsing his apology for being so late. But Lucie gave him no chance to recite it.

"Watch the shop while I go out. If you are uncertain about anything, leave it for me. You can save your excuses until I return." And with a snap of her cloak, Lucie was out the door.

She had every reason to be irritated with him. But her abruptness surprised him. He poked his head into the kitchen and asked Tildy if she could give him something warm to drink. She jumped up, all smiles, happy to be of use. "You should not be too kind to me, Tildy. Your mistress is cross with me."

"She has not been herself today, sir. She's that worried about Master Wilton." Tildy shook her head and sighed. "Archdeacon Anselm came and upset him, you see. Mistress Wilton shouted at him and made him leave."

"She shouted at him?" Owen had never heard Lucie raise her voice.

"I could not help but hear, sir, it were so loud. Everyone shouting. Master Wilton sounded so pitiful. Is there trouble, sir?"

"Do you know where your mistress was going just now?"

She shook her head. "But I hope she's going to complain about that Archdeacon. He has no cause to come here and upset the Master."

"Or over to talk with Bess Merchet?"

Tildy shrugged. "She went there looking for you and stayed awhile before. That was when the Archdeacon came."

So Anselm had watched the shop? What was he up to? "Thank you for the broth, Tildy. Now get on with your work and I'll mind

217

the shop and together we'll try to make the rest of Mistress Wilton's day go smoothly."

Where could she have gone in such a hurry after ordering Anselm out of the house? He could imagine the state she had been in, if she'd heard Nicholas shouting at Anselm.

Brother Wulfstan was puzzled to hear that Lucie Wilton was here to see him. She sat in Abbot Campian's receiving room, holding a flat parcel. As he entered she lifted a pale face to him that spoke of a sleepless night. "What is the matter, Lucie?"

"I am trying to find out, Brother Wulfstan," she said wearily. "That is why I'm here." She unwrapped the parcel. It was a book with a cracked leather cover. "This is one of my father-in-law's record books. I have come across an entry that I want to understand. It is about Nicholas."

"And you think that I can help?" Merciful Mother, let it not be about Anselm and Nicholas.

"I overheard something the other day that has me frightened. The Archdeacon and Nicholas were arguing. Something about Geoffrey Montaigne. You know, my mother's lover. Did you know that he was the pilgrim who died here?" She saw the truth in his eyes. "Why didn't you tell me?"

"It was not until the Summoner, God rest his soul, came to question me about him the other day that my Abbot told me who he was."

"He wounded Nicholas. And by this entry I think it was the night of my mother's death. Do you know anything about that?"

"Nicholas wounded? By Montaigne? But why?"

"That is what I must know."

Wulfstan nodded to the book. "What does it say?"

She handed it to him.

He read, puzzling over the initials. "D'Arby—of course that would be your father."

THE APOTHECARY ROSE

"Yes. And Archdeacon Anselm and Dame Phillippa, my aunt. I need to know who 'MD' is. Or was. Can you guess?"

"'MD cauterized'—Magda Digby, could it be? Nicholas's father had commerce with her. It was Nicholas who decided to have nothing to do with her. She is an able surgeon, from what I hear, though not in a guild. Who would sponsor her? People use her when they want secrecy. What is this about, Lucie?"

"I don't know. I fear—" she shook her head and made a motion as if to brush away the thought. "No. I will say nothing until I know more. Do you think Magda Digby would come to me? To talk with me?"

"You don't think—You aren't thinking that Nicholas meant to poison Montaigne?" The old monk had tried to push aside his suspicion. For if Nicholas had willfully prepared a poison, Wulfstan had been most cruelly used.

"What do you know of my mother's friendship with Nicholas?"

Wulfstan gave her a puzzled frown. "What could that have to do with this?"

"Were Geof and Nicholas rival lovers?"

"Rival? Oh. I—Oh, Lucie, what are you thinking?"

Lucie had taken the book and was rewrapping it. "I must speak with Magda Digby and my Aunt Phillippa. I must know. Can you send someone for the Riverwoman?"

"No. That is, we are not to associate with her. There is a question whether she is even Christian."

"But her son was a Summoner."

Brother Wulfstan shrugged. "He did not accept her ways."

"I must speak with her."

Wulfstan sat down and took her hands in his. "Lucie, my child, do not pursue this. There is nothing we can do about the past. What God wills is done. Trust in Him that all happens according to His plan."

The old monk's hands were hot with anxiety. Lucie squeezed them, sorry that she had involved him. But at least he had identified "MD."

"I will be careful," she promised him.

• • •

Bess sat in Owen's purged room and fought with herself. Lucie's visit this morning had so disturbed her that she'd set Kit's little brother to following her friend. He'd told her about the Archdeacon's angry exit from the shop and Lucie's hurried trip to the abbey. Lucie was back now, working in the shop with Owen, busy because they had opened late. But how long would she stay put? She was on the trail of trouble, which could bring her nothing but trouble. What to do?

Having a boy follow Lucie would do little to protect her. If only Lucie would trust Owen. He could protect her. And he needed to know what Lucie had heard. They needed to talk to each other. Bess could tell Owen what Lucie had told her, but then she would lose Lucie's trust. That would be unwise.

She must think.

Lucie had said little to Owen since she returned from the abbey. He had tried to find out more about her encounter with Anselm, but they were interrupted by a customer. Lucie wondered about Bess's assurance that Owen could be trusted. Why would Bess be so sure?

At dusk the shop finally grew quiet. Owen told Lucie what Tildy had said about the Archdeacon's visit.

"Tildy should not tell tales."

"She was worried for you. So was I."

"Why?"

"Because he might have hurt you."

Lucie regarded Owen closely. "You think the Archdeacon would hurt me? Why would you think that?"

Clever, Owen. Walked right into it. He thought fast. "When voices are raised, it means people are excited. Anything might happen."

Her smirk reflected his own chagrin at his weak response. "The whole truth would be a pleasant change from you."

God help him, he expressed concern and she turned it into an argument. "I don't know what you're talking about."

"No, I don't suppose you would. You can go. I'll close up shop."

He began to leave, but he had to try to make it up. "I don't know how I always manage to make you angry with me."

"It doesn't matter."

"It does."

"Where were you this morning?"

"I had to see Jehannes about my money."

"Tom Merchet said you left quite early."

"I couldn't sleep."

"Come early tomorrow. I've sent for my Aunt Phillippa. I'll need to prepare a place for her to sleep, so I'll need you in the shop."

"You've sent for your aunt?"

"Nicholas is worse every day. I need her here."

"Who did you send?"

"Bess's stable boy. She offered."

Owen would have liked to go. Dame Phillippa was someone he would like to talk to. Alone. Away from Lucie. "Why not me?"

"I need you here," she said, but her tone did not make it a compliment.

Owen headed for the minster. He wanted to tell Thoresby what Magda Digby had told him about Potter Digby's death. The Archbishop stood at a table, studying an array of maps.

"What is it?" Thoresby asked.

"You suggested when we last spoke that Anselm may have murdered Digby."

Thoresby inclined his head. "I think it possible. The Summoner dined with my Archdeacon the night of his death. I know that Anselm did not care for Digby's company. So why that night?"

Again, withholding facts, playing with Owen. "Magda Digby has learned that someone saw the Archdeacon push his Summoner into the river."

"I am sorry to hear that. I wanted to be wrong." Thoresby left his maps and walked over to the fireplace. He stood before it with his hands behind him. "You did not come here just to tell me that."

"If he did murder Digby, what's to keep him from trying again? Mistress Wilton and Brother Wulfstan might be in danger."

"He does present a problem."

Jehannes had come in with a flagon of wine and cups. Now he cleared his throat.

Thoresby turned to him. "You have an idea?"

"There is that business in Durham. A financial concern, really. Appropriate for your Archdeacon. Sir John Dalwylie's bequest?"

"Durham? Dalwylie?" Thoresby frowned, then grinned. "Ah, Durham, yes. Excellent." He took the cup of wine Jehannes handed him. "Archdeacon Anselm will leave for Durham at first light. The roads are quagmires at this season. Two days, perhaps three, each way. A day for business. He will be gone for at least five days. Unless, of course, he meets with an accident."

Bess joined Owen at his table. "This is an honor, so early in the evening," he said.

"I've something on my mind."

"So do I."

"Oh yes? And what is your trouble? Where did you slip out to, so early this morning?"

"To see Magda Digby."

"Still digging into the deaths at the abbey?"

"That's what I'm here for."

"And what of Lucie Wilton, eh? When you're finished with your digging, will you leave her without an explanation?"

"It might be best."

"You disappoint me, Owen Archer."

"What am I supposed to do?"

"Did it ever occur to you that she has a right to know what you're up to?"

"It's best she knows nothing about it. She's stubborn. She

would insist on getting involved. She might walk into danger. I can tell her nothing."

"And do you think it won't touch her in some way?"

"I am watching out for her."

"Oh yes? And where were you this morning when Anselm arrived, eh?"

Owen closed his eye. "I have taken care of that. It will not happen again."

"And how is that?"

"The Archdeacon will be leaving York for a while."

"A while. How lovely. Long enough for you to stir everything up and then leave. Have you considered the fact that she'll still be there when you leave? When the Archdeacon comes back?"

"I do not think he will be back."

Bess looked at his solemn face as that sank in. "Oh. Well, then."

Owen rubbed the cheek below his patch. "She is so quick to offend. I never know what will set her off."

"You argued?"

"Every conversation is an argument."

"She has a lot on her mind. A great deal of trouble and responsibility. You could help more, you know."

"How?"

"Confide in her as you have in me. Let her know why you're here, what you know."

"I cannot."

"Prepare her for the fact that you won't always be here."

"It's best she knows nothing."

"So you think she knows nothing, do you?"

He straightened up at that. "What have you told her?"

"Me? Nothing. But she has eyes and ears."

He thought about that. Remembered her at the top of the stairs. "The Archdeacon and Master Wilton. She's listened to their conversations?"

Bess shrugged. "And what if she has?"

"It's dangerous, Bess."

She rolled her eyes. "You think I don't know?"

"What has she heard, Bess?"

"I can't be telling you. She'd know."

"I won't tell her."

Bess shook her head. "She'd know. You must confide in her. For her safety, Owen. You must."

"I cannot."

"Why, for heaven's sake?"

"How do I know I can trust her?"

"What do you think she'll do? Tell Nicholas?"

He stared into his beer.

"That's ridiculous. You must trust her. Let her know she can trust you. She'll walk into danger if you don't. She's about to do it."

"Is this why she's sent for her Aunt Phillippa?"

"What do you think? That she's suddenly decided to depend on her family?"

"Perhaps. With Nicholas on his deathbed."

"You're a fool, Owen Archer. I was that worried about her this morning, I had Kit's little brother follow her. She went to the abbey to see the Infirmarian. She's getting ideas. Ideas about the night the pilgrim died. And she's poking around, trying to find out what happened. Potter Digby did that and wound up in the Ouse. What do you think of her chances of survival?"

"I told you. The Archdeacon is being sent away."

"Ah. So it's he threw Digby in, eh?"

"I didn't say that."

"Talk to her. It's too dangerous to leave her in ignorance."

"So why didn't you tell her everything?"

Bess pulled herself up, indignant. "I swore to you that I wouldn't, didn't I? What do you think I am?"

"She went to the abbey today? Why?"

Bess rose. "I've done my part. It's up to you now." She moved off among the tables.

"Damnable woman," Owen muttered. The eye was pulling and aching. He took his ale up to his room.

• • •

Lucie sat at the table by the garden window, staring down at the record book. MD. That was who she must talk to. She had to find a way to see Magda Digby. It was not so simple as finding the time to go. She needed a guide. A young woman had drowned last spring when she lost her footing going down below the abbey wall. That was probably how the Summoner had fallen into the Ouse.

She looked over at Nicholas, who lay with his back to her. His breathing was too irregular for him to be asleep. He had turned that way when she'd tried to talk with him about her mother. "Why is she suddenly not to be mentioned, Nicholas? We always talked about her. It's been a comfort to me to talk about her with you."

"I cannot." And he'd turned away from her.

How much easier it would be if he would answer her questions. "I know that Geoffrey Montaigne wounded you after my mother died." She watched his spine stiffen, but he did not turn, he did not speak. Damn him.

So Lucie sat, staring down at the record book, at once angry with Nicholas and frightened by his behavior. He had changed so much. Was it just the illness? No. That would make him more tender, more confiding. His behavior was that of a man with something to hide. A guilty man. She was more and more convinced that he had poisoned Geoffrey Montaigne. But why? She needed to know what had been between them.

It had been a long day. At last even her worries could not keep her awake. She was nodding over the book when something hit the wall behind her. She sat up straight, listening. Again, stones against the outside wall. She got up, looked down into the yard. Someone in black, hooded. Brother Wulfstan? When he saw her, he moved quickly away, to the back of the garden. Too quickly for the old monk. Lucie lit the oil lamp and went downstairs, got her cloak, went outside. Something flickered in the dark garden. Again. The potting shed. A fire. Her heart raced. Someone had seen it and tried to rouse her. Thank God. She put the lamp back inside and grabbed a bucket instead. To the well. She drew up the bucket, filled the one she carried, and lugged it to the shed. The fire was inside, at the back of the shed. She would have to go in to douse it. The door was open. Perhaps the person who'd warned her was already at work on the blaze.

"Are you in there?" she called at the door. She looked in, but could not see through the smoke. She stepped in. She would heave the bucket at the far corner and run out for more water. But from the shadows an arm wrenched the bucket from her hands and threw it out the door. "Idiot!" Lucie cried. She wiped her eyes and focused on the moon-pale face of the Archdeacon. "That was water for the fire, for pity's sake." She turned to retrieve the bucket and go for more water.

He grabbed her. "Burn, she-devil. Succubus. Whore of Babylon. Burn." He laughed, then threw her over toward the blaze and rushed out of the shed, closing the door behind him.

Lucie screamed and rolled away from the burning corner. Her hem had caught fire. She beat at it with her hand.

Once up in his room, Owen pulled off the patch and rubbed in some salve. He lay down on the pallet, but he knew he wouldn't sleep. Maybe a walk. He got up, looked out the window. The stars glimmered in a clear sky. It was the first clear night he'd seen in York. He stared at the stars, trying to remember Gaspare's names for them. Now there was someone he'd like to talk to right now. Gaspare always made sense out of things.

A movement down below caught Owen's attention. Down in the Wiltons' garden. Someone ran past the kitchen door, which stood open, a lamp flickering on the floor just inside. Who was out in the garden? Could it be Tildy? The figure ran toward the street. Too tall for Tildy. Then he noticed the glow. Dear God.

"Fire!" Owen yelled as he raced downstairs and through the tavern. Tom and several customers took off after him. Tom yelled for someone to get the extra buckets in the stable. Owen had the first bucket up out of the well by the time Tom arrived with another.

They set to work on the back of the shed.

But where was Lucie? Surely the lamp and the open door were a sign that she'd come out to fight the fire. Owen went round to the door of the shed. A bucket was upended in front of it. He pushed on the door. It would not budge. He put a shoulder to it and broke it down. She lay just inside, coughing weakly. He gathered her in his arms and hurried for the house.

One hand was blistered, a corner of her skirt singed, and she had a cut on the side of her head where she must have fallen. Bess arrived with a flagon of brandywine. Owen lifted Lucie's head and Bess poured a little brandywine down her parched throat. Lucie coughed it up and pushed Bess away, but Bess forced more down her. This time it stayed down.

"Not bad. She'll be fine," Bess said with relief. She helped Lucie sit up.

"Who was it, Lucie?" Owen asked. "I saw someone running from the garden. Did you see who it was?"

"I thought he—" A coughing fit shook her. She took the cup of brandywine Bess handed her and drank without argument. "I thought someone had seen the fire and had come to warn me. He threw stones against the house. I did not see the fire until I went outside. He was in the shed. He threw me down and cursed me."

"Who?" Owen asked.

"The Archdeacon."

Bess and Owen exchanged looks. Hers clearly accused him of not protecting Lucie.

A banging began on the floor above. Lucie put down the cup. "That's Nicholas. I must go to him."

"No. I'll go to him," Bess said. "Then I'll see that they take care of the shed. You've much to talk about, I think."

Owen realized how badly Lucie had been shaken when she did not argue, just slumped back in the chair. Bess nodded and left. Lucie's hands trembled as she picked up the cup. "He meant to kill me," she whispered, as if trying out the words. Her head was lowered, her eyes staring at the floor.

Owen cursed himself. Magda had said Lucie might be in danger, and now she'd almost been killed. He should have watched the house. He'd been so caught up in suspecting her—and he'd been wrong. Almost fatally wrong. He had not really made an effort to protect. "It's all right. Anselm's being sent away tomorrow."

Lucie looked up at him. "How do you know—" Her eyes widened. "Sweet Jesus."

He put his hand up and discovered he'd forgotten his patch. Damnation. He turned away.

"No," she said. "Please. Forgive me. I'd never seen it uncovered."

"I am sorry I frightened you."

"No. I have seen much worse." He still did not face her. "Please, Owen. Don't turn away from me. Nicholas turned from me tonight. Did he know what the Archdeacon planned?"

The despair in her voice touched Owen. He knelt before her and took her hands. "I cannot believe that Master Nicholas could bear to have you hurt."

She touched the puckered lid gently, the eyebrow, the scar beneath the eye. "Bess says I can trust you. And now you've saved my life." She studied his face. "I need your help, Owen."

20

PLAIN TRUTH

They both started at a sound out in the shop. Owen rose, motioned for Lucie to stay still, walked silently across the kitchen, peered into the shop. "What are you doing in there?" he asked. Lucie was relieved to hear his puzzled but friendly tone. He would not speak that way to an intruder.

"Nicholas wanted me to give Lucie the eyewash cup and medicine." Bess's voice. "Here it is." She came through, holding the items high, as if proud of her find. She set them down on a table by Lucie. "See you use these now."

"Did you tell Nicholas who lit the fire?" Lucie asked.

Bess straightened up, hands on hips. She gave Lucie an impatient look. "I did not. If you want him to know, it's for you to tell him. All he knows is there was a fire in the potting shed, you got trapped inside, Owen rescued you."

Lucie was relieved. "Thank you, Bess."

"'Course, he's no fool. He knows you were upstairs, and fires don't start themselves." Bess shrugged. "But he asked only after you. How you were. If you were injured."

"How is he?"

"He had me give him a tisane to help him lie easy. The one he takes before he sleeps."

"He's being sensible." Lucie noticed that Bess had the lines around her mouth that she got when she was worried. "I will be fine, Bess, just as I'm sure you told Nicholas. Would you like something to drink?"

"Nay. Must be going. Fires make the customers thirsty. Tom

will have his hands full. You'll stay and watch out tonight, Owen?"

"I will."

Lucie noted that Bess and Owen exchanged some sort of wordless message. "You two seem cozy."

Bess laughed. "Comes of sharing a bottle of brandywine or a tankard of ale every night. You two should try it. Fare thee well, now."

Owen stood in the doorway chuckling as Bess left. "She has plans for us, I think."

Lucie stiffened. She had almost confided in him. How could she have forgotten her first impression, a rogue. "I did not mean I needed you *that* way."

His smile faded quickly enough with that. "I did not mean that I think that. It's Bess. She makes no secret of her fondness for pairing off the world."

He found everything funny. Lucie had been about to tell him that her husband had murdered someone. He would have laughed at that, too, perhaps. "You find this amusing." She was so angry with him she wanted to cry. But she would not. He would surely find that amusing, too.

"What did I say to anger you?" He sat down beside her.

The eyelid, puckered and red, was lifted toward her, a vulnerable counterpoint to the good eye. She noticed that the eyelashes were as long, silky, and dark as those on the good eye. How beautiful he must have been. How it must pain him to see himself now. "Perhaps I am too quick to take offense tonight," she said, rubbing her eyes. She'd been exhausted even before the fire.

"Wash your eyes. Our talk can wait."

"I'm simply tired, Owen. I'm always tired these days. Let's talk while we're at peace."

"Your eyes look red. You might have a cinder. Rinse your eyes first, then we'll talk."

He exasperated her. "Why do you always question my judgment?"

"I'm worried about you."

She could see the concern in his face, hear it in his voice. "I am fine, Owen. I do not need to be bullied to take care of myself."

"Bullied? I worry about you, and you call it bullying? Is it because I'm a soldier? Did I forfeit all human feeling when I took up arms for my King?"

Lucie dropped her head to her hands. It was impossible for them to talk.

"Now I'm doing it, eh?" Owen sighed. "Can we try again?"

Lucie raised her head.

He touched her hand. "I want to help. I do not mean to bully you. Tell me what I can do."

"I would not burden you with it, but I'm frightened, Owen. What happened tonight is just a small part of something that I need to understand, or I might lose everything. Though I might lose everything anyway. The shop, this house, the respect of the people—everything. That is not comforting to hear, I know."

"I am not worried about myself."

"Well, you should be. An apprentice often goes down with his master."

"Why might you lose everything?"

"It is very complicated." She wished it were easier to explain. She was so tired. "It began the day Nicholas fell ill. Brother Wulfstan came for a physick that afternoon, and as he told Nicholas about the patient—Nicholas began to behave like a stranger. His questions were inappropriate. And afterward, while he worked in the shop, he was so secretive. He has been so ever since. It is not just the illness. I know the difference between melancholy and secretiveness. That night the Summoner brought him home. The next day the Archdeacon came to see him. Two people who had not set foot in our home since our marriage. And Nicholas can give me no better explanation than that the Summoner happened to be at the abbey, and the Archdeacon is concerned for him."

"Master Nicholas has been secretive? Is that what troubles you?"

"I wish it were only that. Nicholas has been good to me. I owe him much. But if he did what I fear he did..." She could not say the words. "The Nicholas I thought I knew could not have done it."

"What do you think he did, Lucie?"

She stared down into the cup, trying to form the words. "I think..."
She took a deep breath. "I think that Nicholas willfully poisoned
Geoffrey Montaigne, the pilgrim who died at St. Mary's. Geof, who was
my mother's lover, tried to kill Nicholas, years ago. When my mother
died. I do not know why. Nor do I know why, after all these years,
Nicholas struck back. But he did. You are apprenticed to a murderer."

"You say he has been secretive, yet he confessed this to you?"

"No. I have found out by listening at doors, reading old shop
records." Owen was frowning at her as if trying to read her face. But
he did not look surprised. "You are not shocked?"

He shook his head.

She clutched the cup so tightly with her blistered hand that her
palm stung worse than before. She took a drink and put the cup aside.

"Say something."

"I know Nicholas poisoned Montaigne."

It was the last thing she had expected to hear. Owen knew?
How could he know, unless he had been involved? How could he
have been involved when Geoffrey had died before Owen arrived
in York? "Why do I have this feeling that you are also about to turn
into a stranger?"

Owen did not answer at once. He spent a while staring into the
fire. She could tell by the tension in his face, his whole body, that he
was struggling with something.

"Is it so hard for you to tell the truth?"

"You always think the worst of me. All right, then, I will tell you
the truth. It is not the wisest thing to do right now. You need my help,
and it may make you refuse it. But I will not lie to you anymore."

His words did not make her feel triumphant.

"I am here under false pretenses, as you have suspected all
along. His Grace the Archbishop sent me to York to inquire into
the death of his ward, Sir Oswald Fitzwilliam."

The cut of his clothes, the cost of a private room at the York,
his implausible humility in going from Captain of Archers to an
apprentice, it all fit now. "How much better for me if my first
impression was wrong." Lucie felt terribly alone.

Owen reached for her hands. She shrank away from him.

"I knew nothing about you when I agreed to come here," he said. "His Grace knew of your need and wrote a letter recommending me to Camden Thorpe."

"Why? Why us?"

"You had need of an apprentice, and it was a job I could do. I had to have an occupation so I might stay here without arousing suspicion."

"Was the Guildmaster in on the deception?"

"No. He took some coaxing."

"How do I know whether to believe you?"

"You have my word."

"For what that may be worth." She reached for the brandywine, then changed her mind. It would only make it harder to think clearly.

Owen looked pained. What on earth did he have to feel pained about?

"How could you think I could trust you after this?"

"I knew the risk of telling you this tonight. I knew you might never trust me, once you knew how I came to be here. But you should trust me, Lucie. You need to. I can protect you."

"From whom?"

"Archdeacon Anselm, for a start."

How was she to judge? He sounded sincere, but did she just want to believe him? Of course she did. So her judgment was clouded. "So you connected Fitzwilliam's death to Montaigne's and somehow discovered that my husband had poisoned Geoffrey?"

"Yes. Digby set me on the right track, though I did not believe him at first. The Archbishop was so certain that his ward's enemies had caught up with him."

"It would have been far better had you told me this sooner. Why did you wait so long?"

"Because—I would have told you sooner, Lucie. I never wanted to lie to you."

"Why now?"

He hesitated. Lucie steeled herself for another unpleasant revelation. "Until tonight I thought you might have poisoned Montaigne."

She felt it like a blow. It was the sort of thing Owen might say with a laugh, but he was not laughing. Not even smiling. He looked apologetic. All this time she had flattered herself that Owen respected her work and even cared for her, and the truth was he thought her a murderer. "Why would I have murdered him? And how could I? It was not until last night that I knew who the pilgrim was!"

"If you had known, what would you have done?"

"I would have gone to him. He was good to me, Owen. He took the shadows from Maman's eyes." Lucie fought tears, failed, wiped at them impatiently, furious that her own body betrayed her. "I would sooner murder Sir Robert." A foolish thing to say. "So the Archdeacon's attack was my good fortune? It exonerated me?"

"Lucie, please. Montaigne was your mother's lover. He had brought shame to your family. You could as easily have poisoned him as Nicholas. And, to my mind, with more reason."

She had never considered how it might look to others. The reasoning was sound. Lucie could not argue with it. It frightened her.

"I am happier than you can know that you are innocent," Owen said softly.

Lucie did not want to pursue his feelings. "So what have you discovered? Obviously you don't know why Nicholas poisoned a dying man, or you would not have suspected me until now." She would express her worst fear. "Were Nicholas and my mother lovers?"

At least Owen had the courtesy to look embarrassed. "Lovers? I believe not, but I cannot know for certain. I do not understand it all that well."

"Just tell me what you know."

"It is an unpleasant story, Lucie."

"I do not imagine that murder is ever ennobling."

"Magda Digby thinks that Nicholas did it to keep Montaigne quiet, so that you would not lose your standing with the Guild when your husband dies. That, at least, is noble."

"Quiet about what?"

"That Nicholas gave your mother the abortifacient that killed her. Gave her too much at once."

Lucie felt sick to her stomach. "He administered a mortal dose?"

"No, she took too much herself."

"And he should have known better."

"So I think in his mind Nicholas was redeeming himself through you."

"Am I to find that comforting?"

"No. None of this will be comforting."

Lucie took a good swallow of brandywine. "Tell me the rest."

"I wish I could spare you this, but after what happened tonight, I think I should begin with Nicholas and Anselm."

Lucie listened quietly as he told her about her husband's relationship with Anselm at the abbey school.

"It explains much of Anselm's behavior," she said when he paused. "What else have you learned?" She could see in Owen's eye that her calm response reassured him. He relaxed and told her about Digby's suspicions, about Magda Digby's information. At dawn they still sat there.

"*Deus juva me*," she whispered when he had finished. "My life is ashes."

Owen said nothing.

"My mother…" Even if the Riverwoman was right that Nicholas had not understood her mother's weakness, he was still guilty. "My loving husband gave my mother the means to kill herself. He should never have become Master Apothecary. How was it concealed?"

Owen shook his head. "I do not know. Perhaps your Aunt Phillippa will enlighten us."

"Aunt Phillippa encouraged me to marry Nicholas. She encouraged me." Lucie got up and went to the garden door, opening it to the pale morning light. "Is she my friend or my enemy?" Lucie whispered, hugging herself. "She could arrive today. I was going to get her bed ready first thing."

"You should sleep awhile."

Lucie spun round. He was so blind. "Lie up there next to that stranger and think about all you've told me? I'd go mad. I don't know whether to hate him or pity him."

"I will find out all I can for you."

"You mean for the Archbishop."

Owen got up and came to her, taking her hands. "I mean for you, Lucie." She could not help looking at his face, uncovered, vulnerable. The scar had reddened. Shadows underlined his good eye. He was as exhausted as she. "Can you forgive me, Lucie? Can you ever trust me?"

"I don't know. Help me get to the bottom of this wretched story, Owen, then we'll see. But your future is up to His Grace, isn't it? I'll be looking for an apprentice. Well. Work will keep my mind busy." She left the room.

Upstairs, she checked on Nicholas. Force of habit.

His eyes flickered open. "Lucie? Are you hurt?"

"Not really." She had leaned down to see if he was feverish.

He touched her face.

She recoiled.

"Lucie?"

Her mother's murderer. She wanted to hurt him. "It was Anselm who started the fire, did you know? He called me she-devil. Succubus. Whore. The fire was for me, Nicholas. I was to burn. Then he could have you all to himself."

"He is mad. What did he say to you?"

"You call him mad? But he is your friend, Nicholas."

"That was long ago, Lucie."

"Really? Of late he has been a welcome guest. Ever since you poisoned Geoffrey."

"No!" Nicholas hissed.

Lucie moved to the foot of the bed. He sickened her with his lies. "Even now you cannot tell me the truth?"

"It isn't what you think."

"You poisoned him, Nicholas. You used the skill God gave you to murder Geoffrey Montaigne. He was a good man. Gentle. He loved my mother. Did you? Were you jealous of him?"

"Lucie, please. She was my friend, nothing more."

"And so you killed her?"

"I did not—I did what she asked."

"And did she ask you to kill Geoffrey?"

"I did that for you."

"For me? You damned yourself for me? You say that as if you expected my gratitude. I never wished for Geoffrey's death. It was not Geoffrey who killed my mother."

"You blame me?"

"I do."

"Who has told you this?"

"You should have, Nicholas. You should have."

"I—I am guilty of poor judgment. I was very young. But I tried to make it up to you. The shop. You would be Master Apothecary. No one could take that away from you. Except Montaigne. If he told someone what I had done—Please, Lucie."

He would not even take the responsibility. "Go to sleep, Nicholas. Leave me alone."

"I love you, Lucie. I did it for you. But to tell you—I could not."

For her. He really thought he had murdered for her. Her entire body trembled as she walked out of the room.

Next door, in the tiny room that had been Nicholas's as a boy and would have been Martin's, she made up a pallet for her Aunt Phillippa and one for herself.

21

THE GIFT

Anselm's clerk jumped up when the Archdeacon arrived to see to some business before he said Mass. "His Grace the Archbishop is waiting to see you."

"His Grace?"

"He said to come at once."

"At his house or in his chambers?"

"His chambers."

Anselm hurried away. It was not often these days that he was summoned to the Archbishop. He wondered whether the Archbishop could have learned about the fire. Unlikely. The only witness was dead. And if the Archbishop did learn of it—might he not approve? They were, after all, the shepherds of the flock. And he had eliminated a she-wolf who threatened one of their dearest lambs.

Jehannes showed him in to the Archbishop's chamber.

John Thoresby did not rise to greet Anselm, but motioned him to a chair in front of the table where he had been examining documents.

"Your Grace. I am honored to—"

"I did not call you here to exchange pleasantries. I need you to go on a mission for me."

So it had nothing to do with the fire. "Out of the city, Your Grace?"

"To Durham."

It was an honor to be needed by the Archbishop. But Durham. That was impossible right now. He must be near Nicholas in his time of need. "Forgive me, Your Grace. A good friend is ill. On his deathbed, I fear. I hate to leave him right now."

"Nicholas Wilton, is it?"

The guess surprised Anselm. And flattered him. That the Archbishop would bother to learn so much about him. "He is my oldest friend. And so alone now."

"I know of your friendship. I understand that this is a difficult time for you to be apart from him. But he is hardly alone. Wilton is in good hands, and I need you in Durham. Sir John Dalwylie is contemplating a gift to the minster fund. A considerable gift. We must pay him respect and encourage him with an account of similar gifts. I entrust you with this mission, Archdeacon. It is an honor. Are you going to make me regret my faith in you?"

"No, Your Grace. It is an honor. I am most grateful. But could it not wait?"

"No, it cannot. I need you to leave today. As soon as you can ready yourself."

"I say Mass—"

"I have seen to that."

Anselm bowed. He knew when not to pursue his excuses any further. "I will not fail you, Your Grace."

"Good." Thoresby rose. "You will instruct your clerk on any business you might expect in the next five or six days. Jehannes will explain the mission and provide you with letters of introduction."

When Anselm came out of the Archbishop's chamber, the intrusive Owen Archer was conversing with Jehannes. They spoke too softly for Anselm to hear the matter of their speech, and they broke off as soon as they became aware of him.

"Archdeacon," Jehannes said. "Please, sit down while I announce Captain Archer to His Grace." Jehannes slipped into the other room.

Anselm felt the cursed man's eye on him. "You are out betimes, Archer."

"I had a sleepless night."

Anselm noted the man had a most malevolent look in the one eye. Perhaps the Lord had blinded him in the other as punishment for that bold look.

"Trouble sleeping? You have been unwell?"

"No."

Jehannes returned. "His Grace will see you at once, Captain Archer."

Thoresby stood as Owen entered the room. "Jehannes tells me there was a fire."

"Your Archdeacon was eager to send Mistress Wilton to her final reward, Your Grace. Had I not been at the window, had I not tried the door to the shed, Anselm would have succeeded."

"You are certain it was he?"

"Mistress Wilton is certain."

Thoresby nodded, sifted through the papers, chose one, read it over, took a pen and signed it with a flourish. "I have just signed his death warrant, Archer. You need not worry about his return."

"When does he leave?"

"At once."

"I must get back to the shop, then. To make sure that he does not stop to say his farewells."

"He will not, Archer."

"I will make sure of that."

The moment Lucie entered the room she knew something was not right. Something about her husband's inert body. She opened the shutters to get more light, her fingers clumsy with panic. Saliva dribbled from Nicholas's mouth. His breathing was shallow and uneven.

"Nicholas, can you hear me?"

He did not respond.

She felt his pulse. It was weak and erratic. "Jesu mercy." Another attack. She had wanted to give him pain. But not this.

• • •

When Bess came over to see how Lucie was recovering from the night's scare, she was puzzled to find her friend sitting at the foot of the bed, staring at Nicholas.

"What is it, Lucie?"

"Nicholas had another attack. He's dying, Bess."

"Oh, child," Bess sat down beside Lucie and smoothed her hair from her face. "He's been dying all this time, love. It's best you accept that and look to yourself. There's nothing any of us can do to save him." Lucie's skin was ice cold. "For heaven's sake, child." Bess threw a shawl over Lucie's shoulders and led her over to the table.

"I've killed him, Bess."

"And how did you do that, for pity's sake?"

"I told him it was the Archdeacon who caught me in the shed. I told him what he'd called me, what he'd said. I told him what I told you, my suspicions." Lucie looked up at Bess, her eyes red from the fire and no sleep. "I wanted to cause him pain. I brought on the attack."

"Oh yes, of course. And how about the night at the abbey? Did you bring that on, too? Nonsense. The man has something on his conscience, and it's killing him. It's nothing to do with you. How is your hand? Let me see." Lucie winced as Bess unwrapped it. "You should know better than to let it dry out like that, Lucie. Why does your training fail you when you are the patient, eh?"

Lucie's thoughts were elsewhere. "You knew Owen was not who he said he was, didn't you?"

Bess started to deny it, then thought better of it. "I did not know until the night his room caught fire. Then he owed it to us to tell us why someone was trying to kill him."

"The fire wasn't an accident?"

"No more than the fire last night, child."

Bess had never seen Lucie's eyes so dead, her posture so defeated. "Did you sleep at all?"

Lucie shook her head.

"You and Owen talked?"

"Yes. I suppose you know all of it?"

"I doubt it. But no matter. I would not put you through it again so soon just to enlighten me."

Downstairs, the shop bell rang.

"I must go down," Lucie said with weary resignation.

Bess hugged her. "I'll sit with Nicholas—though much good it will do."

Dame Phillippa arrived at midday. She was not the bent, white-haired old woman Owen had expected. Dame Phillippa was tall and straight-backed and walked with a healthy stride. Her eyes were deep-set and knowing. Her wimple was snow white and her simple dress and veil spotless. She gave Owen a firm handshake, looked around the kitchen, and frowned. "As I thought, Lucie needed to call for me long ago, but tried to carry it all on her shoulders."

"That is not why I sent for you, Aunt," Lucie said from the shop doorway. She hesitated, then crossed over quickly to her aunt and took her hands in hers. "You are good to come, Aunt Phillippa."

Phillippa gave her a hug, then stood back and studied her niece, the bandaged hand, the red eyes. "There is more to this than your husband's illness, I can see."

"Let me show you where you can put your things."

Phillippa followed Lucie up the stairs. She noted the second pallet. "I did not bring a servant."

"It's for me. I was going to sleep in here with you. But Nicholas took a turn last night. He is much worse."

"He is dying?"

Lucie nodded.

"That is why you sent for me?"

"That is part of it. We must talk, Aunt Phillippa."

Her aunt nodded. "There is trouble here. I can smell it. Tell me, Lucie."

"Tonight. I must get down to the shop now."

Her aunt shrugged. "I will watch over Nicholas." She took off her cloak and hung it on a peg.

"That would be kind. Bess Merchet is sitting with him now. I'm sure she cannot spend the day up there."

"Bess Merchet?"

"The owner of the York Tavern. Next door."

"She works for you?"

"No, Aunt Phillippa. She is my dearest friend."

The eyebrows lifted slightly. "Do you ever find it difficult? This is not the life you were born to."

"I am finding this life most difficult at the moment, Aunt Phillippa, but it has nothing to do with my station. We will talk this evening." Lucie hurried away before she began something she had no time to finish right now.

News of the fire the night before brought more customers than usual to the shop, hoping for details. Lucie and Owen worked until Phillippa called them for the evening meal.

Phillippa had brought a game pie and a delicately seasoned soup of winter vegetables and barley. Lucie and Owen ate silently.

As Owen pushed himself from the table, Lucie suggested that they sit by the fire with brandywine. "And Aunt Phillippa will tell us about Nicholas, Geoffrey Montaigne, and my mother."

Dame Phillippa looked confused. "Whatever for?"

"I need to understand why Nicholas poisoned Geoffrey Montaigne at Christmastide."

Dame Phillippa looked from one to the other. "Blessed Mary, Mother of God," she whispered, crossing herself. "Will that sorrow never cease?"

Wulfstan squinted toward the open door. It was difficult to make out faces at a distance when he'd been doing close work for any length of time. He recognized the graceful movement of the hand on the door. "Brother Michaelo. Another headache so soon?"

"No, my savior. I would like to share something with you. In appreciation for all you have done for me. A liqueur for which my family is known in Normandy. My mother sends just a few drops, for fear more would be a temptation to the messenger. I do not offend you by offering spirits?"

"Not at all, Michaelo. They aid digestion admirably, which is a blessing at my age. Please. Sit down."

Wulfstan fetched two small cups.

Michaelo's dark eyes shone with a luster that Wulfstan did not see when the monk had one of his headaches. They were moonlit pools in his pale, slender face.

"It is pleasant to see my patients when they are well."

Michaelo smiled as he poured. He gave Wulfstan twice the amount he poured himself. Even so, it was very little. He held up his cup. Wulfstan lifted his.

"To Brother Wulfstan, in whose hands resides the healing touch of Our Savior."

What a pleasant young man. Wulfstan flushed with pleasure and sipped. An odd assortment of flavors confused his palate.

"Oh my. Now there is a talent. To mix so many herbs. The monks do something like this at Pridiam. Twenty-six herbs, I think." He took another sip.

Michaelo's eyes shone. "I knew that you could appreciate it, knowing the ingredients as you do." He touched the cup to his lips.

Wulfstan's tongue moved the heavy liquid around in his mouth so that he might taste all the nuances. Delicate combinations. Yet there was a false note. Something that did not belong. The Pridiam concoction was better balanced. Pity Michaelo's family added so much of the offensive plant. An odd, powdery taste.

"Something is not to your liking?"

Michaelo's dark eyes swam before Wulfstan. "Dizzy." He sank back against the wall, his hand on his heart, which pounded against his hand. Slow and strong. Dizzy. Powdery taste. "Too much foxglove." He shook his head. The room tilted.

• • •

The bells chimed for Compline. Henry waited in the cloister for Brother Wulfstan. If there had been a patient in the infirmary, he would have relieved Wulfstan for the service. But when there were no patients they attended service together. Oddly, the kitchen workers beat Wulfstan this evening. The Infirmarian had been acting distracted. Perhaps he was unwell. It would be like him to hide it. Henry went after him. The silly Michaelo darted past, from the direction of the infirmary.

So Michaelo had delayed Wulfstan with another headache. Henry ducked into the infirmary to see if he could help.

"Henry?" Feeble, faint, he could just hear his name. Henry turned round and round. Merciful Mother, Wulfstan lay on a cot, clutching at his heart.

Henry dropped to his knees beside him, felt his brow. A cold sweat. "What has happened?"

Wulfstan lifted his head to speak, choked, leaned off the cot to vomit. Henry went for towels and a basin. Wulfstan lay back on the cot while Henry cleaned him. Then Henry helped him sit up a bit.

"Do you know what it is?"

"Foxglove. In drink."

"What drink?"

"Mic—" He closed his eyes. Shivered, then bent double. Henry smelled the diarrhea.

Dizziness, slow, pounding heartbeat, vomiting and diarrhea. Foxglove poisoning.

"Michaelo gave you something to drink?"

Wulfstan nodded.

It would have to be a strong dose. "Where are the cups?"

Wulfstan pointed a shaking finger at a small table. Henry smelled the little cup. It had been rinsed. He looked around for the water. Saw a damp spot by the garden door. Brother Wulfstan had been in no condition to rinse out the cups and take the water to the garden. And lazy Brother Michaelo was not so fastidious.

Unless he wanted no one to examine the evidence.

Wulfstan began to choke again, and Henry hurried over.

Dear God, what was he to do? To call for help was no use. All the brothers were at the evening service. Wulfstan might choke if Henry left him to find help. And he must clean him. The poor man could not be left to lie in his own excrement.

But Michaelo might escape.

22

AMELIE D'ARBY

Dame Phillippa stood in the kitchen doorway watching the icy rain, silver threads in the darkness. The air was different from the air at Freythorpe. Here the spicy fragrance of the moors was muted by the damp river air. Perhaps she had been wrong to let Lucie come here. Not just because of the air. No, that was a minor worry compared with what Lucie and the apprentice had just told her.

Nicholas Wilton had murdered Geoffrey Montaigne. It was difficult to accept. Phillippa had never imagined Nicholas Wilton capable of harming anyone. That is why she had been able to forgive him for Amelie's death. She thought of the frail man up in the sickroom. His illness was the clue to understanding it all. What he had done was killing him. He was a good man who had been driven to commit a sin he could not live with. Phillippa could not believe anything else of him. And she had to convince Lucie of that. Lucie had to realize that if Nicholas had indeed committed murder, he had done it to save himself. Or to save Lucie.

Phillippa turned back to Lucie and Owen, who sat quietly, waiting for her to rejoin them. Lucie stroked her cat, who had curled up in her lap as if she sensed Lucie needed comforting. Blessed Mary and all the saints, with her husband dying upstairs and her past revealed as a knot of lies and half-truths, the child did need comforting. The best comfort Phillippa could give Lucie now was to tell her everything.

"When you were little, you had a cat much like that one. You called her Melisende, the queen of Jerusalem."

"This one is also Melisende," Lucie said. "She is as stubborn and beautiful as the other."

Phillippa was glad. "So you do not remember only the sorrow. That is good."

"My memories of Freythorpe before my mother died are good memories, Aunt."

Phillippa nodded. "Then perhaps what I say will count for something. I want you to understand Nicholas. You must not condemn him, Lucie. Or your mother. I will tell you what you need to know." Phillippa sat down, poured herself a generous measure of brandywine, and took a mouthful of it before she began. "You must first understand Amelie. She was only seventeen. Given away to a stranger who took her far from her family, her country." Phillippa shrugged. "But it's the way things are done. Daughters are chattel. And then they say we cry too much. As if we had no cause." She looked at Lucie. "I vowed it would not happen to you. You must believe that I permitted this marriage only because you agreed to it—indeed, seemed set on it—and it gave you the chance to become your own woman."

Lucie said nothing.

Phillippa sighed, took a sip of her brandywine. "Amelie clung to me, pathetically relieved, when I spoke court French to her. Other than Geoffrey Montaigne, a young squire in my brother's company who had been very kind to her—more than kind, I could see—she had had no one to talk to, no one in whom to confide her fears. I need not tell you, Lucie, that your father was no comfort. That is what he's spent these years repenting, of course. She never should have been brought here, so far from her home. A war prize, Robert called Amelie. Can you imagine?" Phillippa looked at Owen. "I'm sure you've no trouble imagining that, being Lancaster's Captain of Archers all those years."

"He's not like Sir Robert," Lucie said in a quiet voice. "Let him be." To Owen, Lucie said, "You must not blame Aunt Phillippa for her discourtesy. She has known little pleasure with men." Owen swallowed the retort he'd prepared.

Dame Phillippa merely shrugged. "I want you to understand

Amelie's—Lady D'Arby's—unhappiness. My dear brother was angry when a year passed and the marriage bed produced no son— or daughter. And he made his anger known. Poor Amelie. Robert's behavior made matters worse. You see, her monthly flux had stopped, I'm sure from unhappiness and fear and loneliness and whatnot. I told Robert it was his own doing, that from such fear as she had for him there could come little good, but of course he could not believe me. His pride could not accept that he might be to blame. Men are so arrogant about their seed. Amelie was to blame. He had to believe that. And he convinced her. She brooded over it. She wanted nothing more than to have a child, a babe to love. She was ripe for all sorts of nonsense. That was when her maid took her to Magda Digby.

"Poor child. She had hope, but the concoction ran out and still no monthly courses. Amelie asked me about the herbs in my garden. I began to show her. And I'm afraid I told her of Nicholas's garden, and that they were of an age, and he already hard at work learning his trade. His garden was a masterwork of plants that would yield common and exotic medicines. I never thought..." Phillippa shook her head.

"Much of what I tell you now was got from Nicholas himself. He came to me and told me all before he asked for your hand. I think he wanted to be refused. He sought penance."

"For her death?" Lucie asked.

Phillippa waved the question away. "But I liked him. Now, after I tell you all this you may say, 'Silly old fool, how could you like him after knowing what he'd done?' And to that I say, 'How could I not?' He did all with the best—"

"Aunt Phillippa, please get on with it!" Lucie said.

"Well." Phillippa straightened up. "So." She brushed an imaginary crumb off her skirt. "Amelie came here, sought out Nicholas, saying she wished to see the garden. Nicholas was a charming young man. Gentle, not strong. But that raven hair and those piercing blue eyes. Like hers, but with a different mood. Where Nicholas was angelic, Amelie was tragic. There was something in her eyes." Phillippa paused, thinking of those eyes.

Owen glanced at Lucie and saw that the sad memory held her, too.

Phillippa sighed and shook herself. "Do you know, but for that difference they looked like brother and sister. But the difference was so marked. I can imagine them there in that lovely garden, bent over the creeping thymes while he ticks off the names—she leaning over to brush the mounds with a fingertip, sniffing, praising, and he blushing all the while. She had that French way about her that men find disarming. He adored her, it was plain."

Lucie flushed at the comment. Owen was uneasy at the direction of this tale. Not that it did not seem the most natural consequence in the world, but what would this mean for Lucie? What had possessed Nicholas to marry the daughter of the woman he adored?

"On that first visit Amelie asked Nicholas for cuttings of angelica, pennyroyal, and madder. He asked why. She told him she wished to begin a garden. To show Robert she meant to play the proper lady of the manor. He suggested prettier plants—lavender, santolina, poppies, mother of thyme. No, no, she wanted just what she asked for. He argued that angelica archangelica was an ungainly plant, a huge seed head, no flower. She told him that at the monastery of San Martin they strewed angelica on the floors and were delivered from a visitation of the Devil.

"He grew bold, hoping to show off his knowledge. 'You fear that the Devil prevents you from bearing a child?' She blushed, but met his eyes, rewarding him with just that look of admiration he'd hoped for. She plainly thought he could read her mind. Merciful Heaven, it must have been her maid put such a foolish idea into her head." Phillippa looked down into the fire. "Or perhaps I was foolish not to see that she was, indeed, bedeviled." She shook her head and her eyes returned to Lucie.

"Nicholas proudly explained how he had guessed. Pennyroyal and madder were to bring on her monthly flux in case it was not the Devil who prevented it. He asked why the Devil would do this to her. Amelie said she deserved to be cursed. She did not love her husband, which was a great sin. 'But you wish to have his child?' 'Oh, but it is most important. I am no one if I do not have his child. If I disappoint him, he will cast me aside.'

"The poor boy. He was outraged. He must protect her. Save her from Sir Robert. How could he refuse her? But it would take too long to begin the plants. So Nicholas gave Amelie the prepared medicines—he sneaked them out, knowing full well he should not do this without his father's advice. Nicholas swore that he gave her careful instructions. He told me that Amelie's eyes shone when he brought the medicines to her, and he felt like a king." Phillippa nodded to Owen. "You've only to look at her daughter to understand. Though Lucie's soul is different—she has my backbone. Amelie would be alive now if she'd our blood in her."

"Did no one in your family ever die in childbirth?" Lucie demanded.

Her aunt closed her eyes, drew back into herself. "Your mother's death was unnecessary," she said softly. "It was not God's choice."

"You do go the long way round," Owen said.

"I want you to understand, that is why. You must understand. The garden enchanted Amelie. She and Nicholas became friends. Because she was content, by midsummer Amelie was with child." Phillippa looked up and noticed discomfort in both faces. "Sir Robert's child, you understand. Nothing of that sort ever passed between Nicholas and Amelie."

"Merciful Mother," Lucie whispered, crossing herself.

Owen hated this eavesdropping. He was not cut out for it. He yearned for a practice field. A battle. The slaughter of strangers seemed easier on the stomach than this prying. Dearest Lucie. What must she be going through? And this slow, opinionated woman dragged it out.

"It was a difficult birth. Magda Digby helped. We walked Amelie all night. She was in such pain, even the birthing chair was agony on her skin. But a magic lit her face when she was delivered of a healthy girl. Magda said it was a good thing Amelie was pleased with you, for she doubted she would have another after such a difficult birth. I disagreed.

"But Sir Robert had heard Magda's prediction. A brother will always listen to a stranger before his own sister." Phillippa sniffed at Owen's warning look. She would choose her own pace. "Within months my brother was off to London to resume his service with King Edward. My brother, the old fool." She leaned over and took Lucie's hand. "You know, I feared that Sir Robert would neglect you. A daughter is important only in helping with the young ones who come after, and in creating alliances through marriage. But Robert would win more support in King Edward's service than he'd gain by marrying you into a noble family. And Magda said there would be no more young ones. I swore then that I would watch over you. See that you had a chance at happiness."

"Surely Maman also would watch over me?"

Phillippa patted Lucie's hand. "If she were not such a child herself." She sighed.

Abbot Campian, noting the absence of Wulfstan and his assistant in the refectory, sent Sebastian to inquire. It was like Wulfstan to forget to ask for assistance. Campian was not surprised to see the novice Henry return. Sent by Wulfstan to make his excuses as usual, he guessed.

But Henry made no excuses. He looked distraught and spoke with breathless haste. "Brother Wulfstan has been poisoned. I had to stay with him. Brother Michaelo. You must confront him. He gave him a drink that contained a large dose of foxglove."

His old friend. Dear Lord, not his old friend. "Where is Wulfstan now?"

"In the infirmary. I left Sebastian with him. Told him not to let anyone in but you or me."

"Good. Good." The Abbot scribbled something, went to the door, and called for his secretary, Brother Anthony. "Take this to Jehannes, the Archbishop's secretary. He will know what to do. As you leave, tell the porter to look out for Brother Michaelo. He must not leave the abbey."

Anthony left without a word.

• • •

Melisende leapt off Lucie's lap to investigate a movement in the corner of the kitchen. Lucie got up, checked the soup that simmered for tomorrow, sat back down. "In my wedding chest I found an herbal with my mother's mother's name in it. I could not remember the book. Or Maman giving it to me."

Phillippa shook her head. "Nicholas never showed it to you? How like a man not to realize what it would mean to you. Amelie presented it to Nicholas when he became a journeyman. Her mother had given it to her. It was wondrously illustrated and bound in soft leather. She had it by heart and thought he might enjoy it."

"It sounds as though they had a pleasant life, those two," Owen noted.

"Ah. But then trouble appeared. Amelie changed. Her feet skimmed the earth. Her eyes sparkled. She spent hours in the maze, but without Nicholas. It was Lucie, seven years old and very curious, who told me her mother had a friend in there with her, a fair-haired prince."

Lucie looked horrified. "I betrayed her."

Phillippa rolled her eyes. "Nonsense. You simply understood me better than your mother did. My brother was a lout. If this man could bring Amelie such joy, I saw no harm in him, none at all. And if that shocks you, so be it.

"So I told Amelie I wished to meet the young man. And I did. Oh, but he was handsome. Blond, tall, courtly. I could find no fault with him. And he had come for her. He'd found a patron in Milan and meant to take her with him. No one would know she was not his wife.

"That gave me a start. Milan! I'd heard tales of the soldiers in service with the Italian nobles who fight endless wars among themselves. Such a soldier did not bring with him a wife and child. I reasoned with them. But they had answers to all my protests. Lucie would go to a convent there. After all, her mother had been educated in a convent.

"But in France, I reminded her, where they spoke her language. Shared her customs. 'Oh, but they will speak French. All educated people speak French.' She was such an innocent. I reminded her that Italy was nothing like Lucie's home. Sunny and warm. The voices soft and slippery. A child is frightened by such change. And then to be apart from her mother. Oh, dear God, what was she thinking?" Phillippa paused a moment to calm herself. "But she was decided. And once Amelie decided, God and all His angels could not change her mind. It was her undoing." Tears glittered in Phillippa's eyes. She watched Lucie, but it was plain she saw Amelie sitting there before the fire.

Phillippa shook herself. "I digress. As you can imagine, Nicholas now saw little of Amelie. But at summer's end, Geoffrey went off to arrange his life in Milan, and Amelie once more sought Nicholas's company. She was jealous of the time he spent in the shop and out in the garden. His father had opened his purse for Nicholas, encouraging him to send far and wide for seeds of exotic strains. The lad was torn between pleasing his father and indulging Amelie. To his credit, his work usually won.

"Which made it all the harder for me. I had all I could do to keep my patience with her that winter. She paced the great hall, snapping at you, poor child, for the slightest thing, picked at her food, complained about everything.

"In spring, Geoffrey returned. He went to Nicholas and thanked him for being a friend to Amelie. And he assured Nicholas and myself that he'd arranged a home for Amelie, though Lucie was still to be put in a convent for a time. Oh, my love, my heart went out to you. An Italian convent. Geoffrey swore that the sisters knew French, that they were quite civilized. He asked Nicholas and me to be Amelie's support for a while longer. He must go to his family in Lincolnshire to make his farewells and settle his affairs. The calm before the storm.

"Amelie's mood darkened, but so gradually that she was completely caught up in it before I could see what was happening. She grew secretive. I learned from Nicholas that she'd come to him one morning, earlier than usual, alone, frightened. She was with child. She wanted him to help her. He did not understand. For so long she had wished for this very news. She said Geoffrey would not take her with him if she was pregnant.

"Nicholas urged against drastic measures. She might conceal it long enough. But it was July, and already the swell of her stomach was noticeable. And Geoffrey had been delayed. He could not leave before Michaelmas. Two months. She said that she had quickened with child because at last she was happy. So it would happen again. Later. When it would not mean the death of all her joy. She begged Nicholas for something that would pass the child from her. He was frightened. He knew that it was a mortal sin and that it would be dangerous for her. She had such a difficult time with Lucie's birth, and now she was distressed, her humours in turmoil. In such a state, already weak, a medicine could quickly become a poison. He refused.

"She fell to her knees, begging him, weeping and threatening to dose herself with rue from my garden. Fell to her knees and wept. He was almost undone. He begged for some time to pray over his decision.

"He went to his old friend Anselm to ask his advice. Anselm advised Nicholas that Amelie would get what she desired from someone, so if he was concerned about her, it ought to be him. He was the best apothecary in Yorkshire. He would one day be a master apothecary. He was the son of a master."

Lucie could see Anselm's motivation. "The Archdeacon hoped it would kill her. He was jealous of her. And if Nicholas was guilty, he would struggle to forget her. Then Anselm might have another chance."

Phillippa shrugged. "I knew nothing of their relationship. I only knew that Nicholas respected Anselm's opinion and trusted him to keep the matter to himself. Since Anselm's counsel was to give Amelie what she wanted, Nicholas did so. He mixed her a potion of rue, juniper, tansy, and wormwood, the dosage low enough to ensure that it would work gradually and could not poison her. As much as mortal man can ensure such things. He told me what he'd given her, what was the safe dosage. No one of the ingredients could be guaranteed to abort the child, but it was a rare case in which none of these worked. I thought it clever, but my heart misgave me. I watched her like a hawk, making sure she took the smallest dosage morning and night. She was careful. It seemed he'd impressed on her the importance of following his instructions. Like a fool, I eased my supervision.

"September arrived, and still Geoffrey did not appear. Amelie did not look well. Her hands flew as she spoke, she jumped at the smallest sound, her eyes were too large in her head, and shadowed, as if she slept little.

"I thought it was the news from Calais. Robert wrote that King Philip had at last brought a great army to save the people of Calais, then ordered the army's retreat a few days later, without battle. Behind the city walls a great wail rose up. A year besieged, and now they knew themselves abandoned. Joyous for us, not so for Amelie. They were still her people."

"I served with men who were at Calais," Owen said. "It was a terrible time. When they opened the gates, there were no dogs, no animals but a few goats and cows for milking. All the rest had been slaughtered to fill the empty bellies. So many had died. It was a barren, silent city."

Lucie wiped her eyes. "Maman's convent had been raided by Edward's army. That is why she was at home when Sir Robert brought her father back and demanded ransom. She had been hidden by a sister in the flour bin in the larder. A soldier dragged one of her classmates in there, raped her, and slit her throat, right there in front of Maman. She could not scream, she could not move enough to hide her eyes for fear he'd discover her. She could just watch."

"She'd had her share of grief, to be sure," Phillippa said. "And the news that Calais had fallen to King Edward's army sent her into hysterics. My brother had sent word that as soon as the city fell, he would return to Freythorpe. What if he should arrive before Geoffrey? Merciful Mother. I kept asking her if she was certain the child had not yet passed. She was so thin, I doubted that so little flesh could nurture a growing child. She swore it had not passed. I warned her that as soon as she could, she must stop the physick. Every day she grew weaker. She fluttered like a caged bird, and her eyes were haunted.

"And then Robert arrived, full of himself, blind to her condition. King Edward had made him aide to the governor of Calais. He meant to take Amelie back with him. I saw that he hoped returning to France would make her happy. Happy enough to bear the son he wanted. And I suddenly realized how he must love her. To make the difficult Channel crossing and travel six days at a gallop to reach her, only to return with her in a short time. He was not a young man. And there was no question he must return quickly. The governor needed him then most of all.

"And I had helped her betray him. Holy Mother, I had encouraged Amelie in her unfaithfulness to my own brother, who loved her and was her lawful husband. I had been caught up in a romantic dream. Certainly he was a lout, he had no grace, no gentleness. He'd been bred to fight, later to lead men into battle. No one had taught him to be a husband. But he meant to try. He meant to give her what he believed she yearned for. Her country, her people.

"And then it all fell apart." Phillippa wiped her forehead with a trembling hand. Lucie gripped her own hands so tight her knuckles showed white.

"Amelie looked very ill when she came to dinner. I wanted her to lie down, but she insisted that if she played up to Robert's homecoming he would notice nothing. He was not so blind as that. He asked her forgiveness for bringing her to Yorkshire. Said he had not understood how difficult it would be for her. She sat straight, eating little, staring down at her plate or at her husband's hands. Her wimple was damp at the temples. Her color was bad. Gray. Robert ate and drank with enthusiasm. He thought her pallor, her trembling hands, must be her usual state. He looked forward to changing all that with the voyage to Calais.

"Suddenly she gave a cry and stumbled from her chair. Robert and I both jumped up. She clutched her stomach. He caught her as she fell. She hemorrhaged. Lucie, my love, you screamed at the blood soaking your father's arm, your mother's dress. I grabbed you and hurried you to your parents' chamber and yelled for Cook to stay with you.

"Amelie had overdosed, thinking to rid herself of the evidence of her unfaithfulness as quickly as possible, before Robert noticed. A toxic dose. She said she felt nothing in her hands and feet. They were like ice. She was terrified. I do not believe she meant to kill herself."

"But Nicholas had warned her," Lucie said. "And so had you."

"The arrogance of youth. She thought it might kill a weaker person, but not her. I think if she'd meant to kill herself she would have taken all that was left. To make sure of the job. But she left much of it.

"She died in Robert's arms. He looked so lost and frightened. 'What has happened here?' he asked me. What could I do? I told him.

"He was stricken by the betrayal. Geoffrey had been Robert's squire when he brought Amelie to York. He'd watched over Amelie on the crossing. Robert realized he'd brought them together.

"He asked me to leave him. He did not want me to see him weep. I went out to the garden. Geoffrey found me out there. He'd waited for Amelie in the maze for hours. Dear God, all the evenings she'd checked there to see if he'd returned. And this one. If she'd gone out there." Phillippa's voice broke. She stared at the fire.

Lucie still clasped her hands tightly. "When Cook fell asleep," Lucie said, "I sneaked down the ladder and found Sir Robert holding Maman and moaning. There was blood all over both of them. Maman's pretty gown was soaked. I touched her face. It felt wrong. Cold. Like a statue—not like Maman's face. And her hands were cold. I thought it was because they dangled down near the floor. I tried rubbing them. Sir Robert shooed me away. Like a dog. As if I had no right there. He did not tell me she was dead. Just shooed me away. I knew from the blood someone had been hurt. I thought he'd stabbed her. I thought he'd found out about Geof and hurt her so she would not see him anymore. I hated him."

"But I told you Robert was not the cause of her death," Phillippa said.

"You told me the baby killed her. And Sir Robert was her husband, so I thought it was his baby. Even when they whispered at the convent, I was sure they were wrong. Sir Robert hated her, and he killed her with his baby."

Her aunt sighed. "Geoffrey blamed Nicholas. He went to him, woke him in the night, beat him senseless, stabbed him, and left him for dead. Paul Wilton found his son on the shop floor. He did not want any gossip. He went for Magda Digby, knowing she would nurse Nicholas without comment. He had Archdeacon Anselm administer the last rites, knowing that he would not betray Nicholas. Between Anselm and Magda, Paul learned what had happened.

"He and the Archdeacon called on us at Freythorpe. Asked us what we meant to do about Nicholas's role in Amelie's death. My brother surprised us all by blaming himself for what had happened. He had already sent a messenger to the King to resign his post. He would go on pilgrimage to atone. He was a broken man. Nicholas, too. Geoffrey had disappeared, thinking he'd murdered Nicholas. Amelie was dead. It was too horrible. When Robert told me to take Lucie to the convent, I thought it best for her. To get away from the cursed house."

"Why in Heaven's name did you let her marry Nicholas?" Owen asked.

"Have I not made it clear? He made a youthful mistake. I could not condemn him for the rest of his life."

"But for Lucie he was a reminder of all this."

"No," Lucie said. "I knew nothing of his part in it. To me he was from the good times, when Maman was well, when I was loved. And he promised a life of purpose." She got up and opened the door, breathing in the chill night air. Phillippa and Owen watched her. After a while, Lucie quietly shut the door and turned back to them. "But you were wrong to deceive me, Aunt Phillippa. And so was he."

"You would never have accepted him if you knew."

"Perhaps that would have been best."

"No. He ensured a future for you, as I hoped he would. I wanted you to be free of the fears that bedeviled your mother. To marry in your class would have condemned you to the same life, fearing that you'd lose your husband's respect if you did not bear a son and heir. A second son for good measure. Fearing that should he do something treasonous or criminal you would lose everything, through no fault of your own. Fearing that he might die too soon and leave you as I was left, without a home, with no standing, always beholden. And to whom would you go for help? Once Robert was gone, you would have no home. You would be a ward of the court. Any money left you would be used up, and you would be sold to the highest bidder. That is the way." Phillippa rose, caught herself as she wobbled with weariness. "I saw Nicholas as a godsend." She touched a trembling hand to her forehead.

Lucie helped her aunt to bed. As Lucie was leaving, Phillippa said, "Do you see, Lucie? Nicholas is a good man."

"He is still a murderer, Aunt Phillippa. Thrice over."

23

OBSESSION

The reins were so wet they felt slimy in Anselm's fingers. But the unpleasant feeling did not last. The rain and cold numbed his extremities as the evening wore on. With every movement of his body he discovered a chill wetness. He shivered. He felt warmth only where his legs touched his sweating beast. His companion, Brandon, a burly novice from the border country, plodded on ahead, apparently unaffected by being soaked to the bone.

Anselm offered up the discomfort as penance for his sin of pride, his boldness in playing God by deciding who was to live and who to die. His Archbishop needed him, Thoresby was too great a man to be subjected to this journey, and Anselm would not complain.

In fact, his lord the Archbishop honored Anselm in no small way by entrusting him with this mission. The benefice he was to negotiate in Durham would bring a great sum to the cathedral fund. The negotiation must be handled with care. Sir John Dalwylie might change his mind, bequeath the money elsewhere, and they would be left with nothing. It was for Anselm to impress on him the importance of the cathedral, the faith and thanksgiving it embodied, the indulgences it would gain for those who contributed.

His companion would be tucked away in a monastery nearby. Brandon could not be trusted to say the right thing. Or to be silent. He would be a liability in such delicate proceedings.

It puzzled Anselm that Abbot Campian had assigned Brandon to be his companion rather than Michaelo, who was shrewd and well spoken. Anselm had asked for Michaelo. He would be useful, the second son of an old, landed family. He had aristocratic sensibilities, which would stand him in good stead with Sir John. Campian said that Michaelo had not wished to go, had begged to stay in York because of his delicate health.

He was delicate. Like Nicholas. Dearest Nicholas. What Anselm would not give to see him as he had been. To stand with him in his garden. Taste this, crush this between your fingers, smell the essence, look at the colors, is this not God's munificence in miniature? Can we not see the glory of His creation in this garden? Nicholas was so full of love for God's creation.

Delicate, sensitive, soulful Nicholas. What might he have become, had he stayed at St. Mary's, protected from the world? He would have outshone the doddering Wulfstan. He would have created his beautiful garden within the abbey walls, safe from the temptations of the French whore. All the evil with which she'd poisoned Nicholas's life would have been directed elsewhere. He never would have met Amelie D'Arby. Her child would never have lured him into her lair. Lured him and sucked all life from him, all beauty, all grace. Poor Nicholas lay now in that tiny, stinking room like a fly sucked dry and tucked away in the web for future consumption. Succubus. Evil, wicked woman. Anselm was glad he had given her a taste of her eternity last night. Now she was burning in the truly terrible fire, the eternal fire. The potting shed had been nothing to that.

Anselm. The name was whispered in his ear. The sweet breath caressed his neck. Anselm turned to see his love. But Nicholas was not with him on the moors. It was the wind teasing him. Anselm pulled his icy, rain-heavy cloak up tighter around his neck. *Anselm. Anselm.* A plaintive cry. A blaming cry. *Why are you not here? Can you have left me when I most needed you?*

Nicholas was dying. That must be the meaning of the phantom cry. He was dying, with Anselm far away on the road to Durham. Anselm had deserted his love. He had left him alone and terrified of what was to come. Fearful of Hell. Nicholas was afraid that God would not understand what he'd done, what he'd had to do, that God would not forgive him the murders that Amelie D'Arby had made necessary. Darling, gentle Nicholas was afraid because that witch had shattered his peace of mind with sweet words, downcast eyes. Bewitched him and led him into sin. It was not Nicholas's fault. God would know that.

But Anselm must be there to remind him. Nicholas must not die in fear. In terror.

Brandon paused suddenly and signaled Anselm to stop. The whites of the clod's eyes shone in the moonlight. "Horsemen behind us."

Anselm listened, but he heard only the wind. "Nonsense. You—" Brandon hissed at him to be quiet.

Anselm closed his eyes and listened beyond the wind. And there, more a feeling from the earth than a sound, were hoofbeats. It must be a messenger from York. Riding after them to tell them that Nicholas was dying and had asked for Anselm, could not die without Anselm at his side, would accept absolution only from him.

"Come. We must gallop," Brandon cried.

"No. It is a messenger sent to call us back."

"It's no messenger. Not with so many horses. Surely it's Scots. Our only hope is to run before they've seen us. Come on." Brandon took off.

Anselm shook his head. Young fool. But as the sound of Brandon's horse faded, Anselm heard that the lad was right. It was more than one horse. And the Archbishop would consider Anselm's mission far more important than his old friend's absolution. This was no messenger after them. Anselm spurred his horse after Brandon. But Nicholas was dying, he was certain of that. The farther Anselm traveled, the more impossible it was to be at his dear Nicholas's deathbed.

And then the Scots were upon him. Their hoofbeats shook the ground beneath Anselm. Their weapons gleamed in the shimmering darkness. Their inhuman cries terrified his horse. It screamed and reared, throwing Anselm, then bringing a shod hoof down on his forehead. All was dark.

• • •

Nicholas pressed on Anselm's head. *Wake. Wake, Anselm.* Anselm tried to brush away his friend's hands. The pain. Nicholas must not realize his strength. Anselm fought to open his eyes, but Nicholas pressed on the lids. "Why?" Anselm moaned. "What have I done that you should torture me like this?"

I was frightened. The Creator came for me, and I was frightened. I could not wake you.

Anselm fought harder to open his eyes. It was night. Wind moaned in his ears, rain cooled his throbbing forehead. He remembered.

He touched his right hand to his forehead. He thought he did. But the fingers had no feeling, although the hand throbbed. With the other hand he felt the forehead. Torn, abraded, and swollen. He tried the right hand again. The fingers did not respond as they should. He felt nothing in them. He pulled himself up to a sitting position, ignoring a hot pain in his stomach, and let the wet darkness spin around him. When it stopped, he stood up, wobbly on his legs, but they seemed uninjured. He walked a few feet, stumbled over some yielding lump, and fell. It was his horse, sticky with blood, dead. Anselm knelt and retched violently.

Anselm.

Anselm had forgotten. Nicholas was dying. He must get to him. But without his horse, what could he do? He began to walk.

Lucie sat in front of the kitchen hearth, the cat Melisende on her lap. Owen sat across from her, but said nothing. She appreciated his silence.

She was trying to understand Nicholas. He swore that he loved her. Phillippa believed that. Believed that all he had done, he had done for Lucie. To ensure her future. To ensure that she would not live with the fear that had plagued her mother, that had eventually killed Amelie. Dame Phillippa understood all that. She had lived with that same fear. Of displacement. Of being nobody. Having no home.

It was that fear that had driven her mother to take her own life. If Sir Robert had discovered she was to have another man's child, he would have cast her out.

Would he? Lucie did not know. She hardly knew her father. It felt strange to think of Sir Robert without hatred.

So if Nicholas was not to blame, and her mother was not to blame, who was? Someone had to be. God would not plan such an end for her mother. Someone had transgressed. Disturbed the balance of nature. They were to blame.

How different Lucie's life might have been, had her mother lived.

How different her life would have been without Nicholas. He had been good to her. He had taught her to be useful. She was respected in York for her skill, not for her marriage. But all that would be taken away now.

Lucie looked up at Owen. "When you tell all this to the Archbishop, what will he do?"

Melisende jerked awake with a fretful growl, pricked up her ears, dug in her hind claws, and pounced at something skittering across the floor.

Owen rubbed the scar on his cheek. "I don't know, Lucie. I'm sitting here trying to think of a way not to tell him."

"You must not compound the guilt, Owen. You must tell him. Your loyalty must be to him." Lucie went upstairs to Nicholas.

Owen watched Melisende toying with the mouse she'd cornered. He felt as helpless as the mouse. How could he avoid telling Thoresby what he'd learned?

Anselm stumbled along the pale ribbon of road, assuring Nicholas that he was on his way. The pain in his forehead dulled as he walked. It was the hand that brought the most agony. He tore a strip of cloth from his tattered cloak and wrapped the hand as best he could, then tucked it in his left sleeve. That helped. He did not consider the possibility that he would not make it back to York.

• • •

Lucie found Nicholas in a pitiful state, moaning and whimpering. She knelt beside him, praying that God might ease the pain, release Nicholas from his suffering. She imagined he dreamed of judgment, the dread moment when God would call him to account for her mother, Montaigne, and Fitzwilliam.

Once, Nicholas cried out and clutched her hand tight. Lucie kissed him and whispered words of comfort, hoping that he could hear. Later his eyelids fluttered, then opened.

"I forgive you, Nicholas," Lucie said. "Rest in peace."

He looked at her and whispered her name. Then, with a violent shudder, he died.

Dead. Lucie's heart stopped, her mind went blank. A numbing cold began in her fingertips and crept up her arms. She hugged her arms to her body. Nicholas was dead. She stood up, walked to the window. The garden window. She imagined him out there, his tattered hat, smudges on his face. In the summer, freckles sprinkled his nose and cheeks. "No. No more," she whispered. "He is gone."

Now she wept. Gentle Nicholas. She knelt back down beside him. She had loved him, he had been good to her, a gentle husband, always concerned for her welfare, her happiness. His pale blue eyes, which had followed her about lovingly, stared now at nothing.

She hesitated to close them, knowing that she saw them for the last time, those strange, beautiful eyes. Memories held her there, drew her down into the blue depths, her mother and she in his garden, his first visit to the convent, his hesitant, humble proposal of marriage, his patient training, how he had beamed at the birth of their son, how he had wept at Martin's death. All that they had shared she would remember alone now. Alone. She searched the familiar eyes, but his soul had departed, the flicker of life was gone. She closed them.

She should go down, tell Owen, send Tildy for Bess. No need for a priest, Anselm had already given him the last rites. There was nothing to do but prepare the body for burial, wrap it in a shroud. Bess would send her stable boy to Cutter's for the coffin.

Lucie would have liked to bury Nicholas in his garden—it was there he had been happiest—but it was not possible. He must be buried in hallowed ground. She must get up, go downstairs, take care of the details. But she lingered, feeling close to him even though his eyes were closed and his soul had passed on, knowing that once she left Nicholas's side, he would be truly, completely gone.

This evening her feelings for him had been confused. She had felt betrayed. Her mother had been poisoned by the man in whom Lucie had placed all her trust. All her hope for the future. The father of her only child. That brief joy, so sharp and pure. Nicholas had acted irresponsibly and handed her mother her death. He had sought out the advice of his former lover, someone bound to be jealous of Nicholas's feeling for Amelie D'Arby.

It was the Archdeacon Lucie should hate. She had lashed out at Nicholas, but it was Anselm she should hate. Anselm.

He must pay for all this pain.

Owen cursed as the shop bell rang. He needed to think. But he could not ignore the bell. No one came to them at this time of the evening except with an emergency. Melisende guarded her catch and watched Owen as he walked past her.

"God be with you." A young monk, flushed, out of breath, eyes shining with troubled excitement. "I must speak with Mistress Wilton." Brother Sebastian from the abbey.

"There is illness in the household. Mistress Wilton watches over her husband."

The young monk bowed. "My Abbot sends me to warn you that Brother Wulfstan has been poisoned."

Owen was surprised. Brother Wulfstan attacked, even with Anselm out of the way? "Is he dead?"

"The Lord spared him. But he is ill. And the Abbot worries that Mistress Wilton is in danger. He wants you to take the Wiltons to Freythorpe Hadden. They should be safe there with Sir Robert and his retainers."

"An odd choice. It would be easier to set up a defense in familiar territory. Why Freythorpe Hadden?"

Brother Sebastian shrugged. "I am just a messenger."

Such messengers often knew far more than the players. "Think. What could be his reasoning?"

"Perhaps he feels York is dangerous. Enemies could be anywhere. It was one of our brethren who tried to poison the Infirmarian. Brother Michaelo, acting for the Archdeacon. Perhaps my Abbot suspects he has more agents." Sebastian frowned, fearful he had said too much. "But I am only a messenger."

"And where is the Archdeacon now?"

"On the road to Durham."

"And if Anselm doubles back," Lucie asked from the doorway, "and finds us gone, will he not think to go to my father's house?"

Brother Sebastian bowed to her. "God be with you, Mistress Wilton. My Abbot is concerned for you. He says Owen Archer and Sir Robert's retainers can better protect you at Freythorpe."

"Owen can protect me here. My husband has just died. I want to bury him here, among the people who loved him."

"Nicholas is dead?" Owen went over to her.

Lucie held herself stiffly, as if any softening would undo her. Her face was pale, making her eyes look huge in her face. "Please thank Abbot Campian for his warning and his concern. Tell him that we will be watchful." Lucie excused herself and went back up the stairs.

Brother Sebastian gave Owen a worried look. "My Abbot will not like it."

Owen considered him. "Did Brother Michaelo say that the Archdeacon meant to kill Mistress Wilton?"

"I do not know."

"I understand the Archdeacon was sent to Durham. Surely not alone?"

"Brandon, a novice, accompanies him."

"And who else?"

"Just Brandon."

"That is all? One novice?"

Sebastian looked uncomfortable. "Brandon is strong."

Owen laughed in disbelief. He was surrounded by fools. "One strong man is no match for the Scots on the road."

Brother Sebastian shrugged.

Owen patted him on the shoulder. "I know none of this is your doing. I do not mean to badger you. But you must see that I cannot argue with Mistress Wilton on the night of her husband's death. I am afraid you must tell your Abbot what she said."

The messenger gone, Owen climbed the steps. Lucie sat beside Nicholas, studying him with a faraway look.

"I sent Brother Sebastian on his way."

Lucie shook herself, rubbed her forehead. "I will not bury Nicholas at Freythorpe Hadden," she said.

"Why not?"

"That place brought only sorrow to both of us. I wish I could bury him in his garden. But certainly not at Freythorpe. Sir Robert pushed me away. There is no love there for me or Nicholas."

"But it was your home."

She gave him a strange look. "You chose not to return to the place where you were a boy. Perhaps you were right."

Owen could think of no response to that. "What can I do to help you?"

"Aunt Phillippa must sleep. Ask Bess to come help me prepare Nicholas for burial."

Owen took her hands in his. "Your aunt is not the only one who needs sleep."

"I cannot sleep."

"Lucie, think what you've been through the past two nights. The fire. Now Nicholas."

"I will prepare him. Then keep vigil."

"Let someone else keep vigil."

"No. I will do it. I killed him. I will keep the vigil."

Owen's heart sank. Killed him? Had they come full circle? Was she the murderer after all? Had Nicholas been killed by a slow poison so he would never recover enough to remember and possibly accuse her?

Lucie laughed, a brittle, chilling little laugh. "You are shocked that I killed my husband."

"I'm confused. How did you kill him?"

Even lacking sleep and in the first stages of mourning, Lucie could look at him with those eyes of hers and make him feel that she could see into his soul. "I'm not a poisoner, if that's what you're thinking." Spoken without anger. She sounded merely tired. "I told him that his friend had tried to kill me. I blamed him for my mother's death. When he tried to tell me that he had killed Montaigne for me, I turned away from him. And then I came down here. I should have been with him." Gently she smoothed the grizzled hair back from Nicholas's forehead.

"He was already dying, Lucie."

She kept her eyes on her husband. "I was wrong to blame him. All of this has been the fruit of the Archdeacon's unholy love for Nicholas, a mean, suffocating love. It is Anselm who will burn in Hell for all this, not my Nicholas."

"Think about this tomorrow."

Lucie was not listening. "I came and found Nicholas whimpering in his sleep. I tried to comfort him. I told him I forgave him. But I don't know if he heard."

"I am sure he did."

"You say that because you want me calm. Then you can persuade me to take him to Freythorpe."

"That's not true, Lucie."

"Go fetch Bess."

Owen, seeing she would not be comforted, went for Bess.

24

CONFRONTATIONS

A cart came up behind Anselm, rumbling and squeaking. It was a farmer's cart. It trundled by, then stopped. The farmer looked back, took in the priest's garb and its state, tipped a greasy cap. "What is this, the thieves don't even respect the cloth now? Have you been overtaken, Father? Lost your horse?"

Anselm dragged himself to the man, steadied himself against a wheel. "We were attacked. My companion is dead. I must get to Wilton's apothecary in York, by the minster. Can you get me there?"

"That I can. I be heading there for market. The Lord is good to put me in the way of helping one of his priests. I'm sinner enough to need the indulgence it should get me."

Anselm soon lay among baskets and sacks, comforted by this sign of God's grace.

Bess shooed Lucie down to the kitchen after they had prepared Nicholas's body. Then she set a cup of brandywine in front of her friend, saying, "I'll send the stable boy for Father William at first light." He was their parish priest.

Lucie nodded. She stared somewhere beyond her hands, her eyes unfocused. Bess and Owen exchanged looks.

The shop bell jingled.

"Who in God's creation?" Bess went to see, scurried back with a flush to her face. "My Lord the Archbishop," she announced, her cap ribbons aflutter.

Thoresby strode into the room even as Bess spoke, making the sign of the cross to bless the house.

"Mistress Wilton," he said, taking Lucie's hand, "your husband was respected in York. Nicholas Wilton was a fine apothecary. He will be missed."

"Thank you, Your Grace."

"You must forgive me for intruding on your mourning. But circumstances force my hand. It is most unfortunate." He nodded to Owen, glanced at Bess. She excused herself to go sit with Nicholas.

Lucie took a sip of the brandywine. Her hands trembled. "Please sit down, Your Grace," she said quietly.

"I will not stay long. I meant simply to assure you that I have arranged everything. Two of my men will bring a cart and a coffin shortly. At dawn, I and four of my men will accompany you to Freythorpe Hadden."

"You need not concern yourself with us, Your Grace. The Wiltons have served your purpose."

"What are you talking about?"

"I know that Owen is your man. I suppose I am to be grateful that you allowed me to have his services for a time."

He paused, but only for a moment. "Mistress Wilton, this is not the time for injured pride. I am trying to prevent my Archdeacon or his young men from causing any more distress."

Lucie rose, flushed and trembling with anger. "I do not mean to sound ungrateful, my Lord Thoresby, but I cannot accept your gift. I do not intend to bury my husband at Freythorpe Hadden. That is not where he belongs."

Thoresby stood. "I chose a bad time, I can see. Forgive me, Mistress Wilton." He signaled for Owen to follow him out the kitchen door. Lucie eyed Owen darkly as he passed.

Out in the wet garden, Thoresby dropped the pleasant courtesy. "Damnable woman. Does she think we play a game, Archer? Does she not know how precarious her position is?" He pulled up his hood.

"I am not sure what Mistress Wilton thinks at the moment,

Your Grace. Last night Anselm trapped her in a burning shed. Tonight she lost her husband. Now you suggest that she bury her husband where she had never thought to bury him. And she wonders whether she can trust me. Whether she can count on me. You must not judge her by her words or actions tonight."

Owen felt Thoresby's eyes on him. "Mistress Wilton is more than an employer to you, that I can see. What does she know of all this?"

"She knows everything."

"And what is 'everything'?"

"That Montaigne held Nicholas responsible for Amelie D'Arby's death so many years ago. Montaigne was her lover. She died aborting his child with an overdose of a potion concocted by Nicholas. Montaigne tried to kill Nicholas the night she died. He thought he had succeeded. His return threatened Nicholas. He feared Montaigne would discover he was still alive and try again to kill him—or ruin his name, which would ruin all he'd tried to do for Lucie. So Nicholas poisoned him with the physick that was later used in ignorance on Fitzwilliam."

"I might have guessed a woman was involved. We can be such fools over them." Thoresby was quiet a moment. "Did Mistress Wilton have a hand in the poisoning?"

"No. She did not even know the identity of the pilgrim Nicholas had mixed the physick for. And because her husband fell ill the very night he committed the deed, she did not learn of the poison soon enough to save Fitzwilliam." Owen could make out an unpleasant grin on Thoresby's face. He had denied it too quickly.

"You would not tell me if she *were* guilty."

"My first allegiance is to you, Your Grace."

Thoresby chuckled. "I think not. But it is possible she is innocent. So I choose to accept your explanation." He shook his head. "The Lord's purpose in this mystifies me. Fitzwilliam deserved punishment, but not by the hands that meted it out. And now my Archdeacon seems possessed by the Devil himself. He influenced Brother Michaelo. Who else? You must persuade Mistress Wilton to accept my plan."

"She is not easy to influence."

"It's time you discovered how to move her, then." He said it with a chilling firmness, with finality. Thoresby departed, leaving a cold silence in his wake. Then Owen heard his horse trot off into the night.

Bess looked up as Lucie sank down on the stool by the door. "So, what ordeal does our lord the Archbishop mean to put you through so soon after you've been widowed?"

Lucie did not answer at once. Bess noted the shadows under her eyes and the deepened creases from nose to mouth, signs of little sleep and much worry. "Men never know when to be still."

Lucie sighed. "There may be trouble here. They want me to leave at dawn. The Archdeacon has gone mad, it seems. But the Archbishop is being kind, Bess. He is sending men and a cart with me to Freythorpe Hadden. And he will come with us to say the requiem."

"Travel to Freythorpe? In your state? With no sleep?"

"The Scots rarely strike so early in the day."

"But you've had no rest, my girl."

"I'll rest later. Aunt Phillippa will see to that."

"Oh, aye, as she's seen to you in the past. I've no confidence in her seeing-to."

"I could use a cup of your brandywine to see me on the road."

"You're trying to get rid of me?"

"It would warm me, Bess. And one of the blankets you use in the cart." But Lucie did not look at Bess. Her eyes were on her husband, silent and already strange in his shroud.

Twice widowed herself, Bess could see that Lucie needed time alone before all the fuss began over the funeral. "Well, you could use some warming. I'll fetch what you ask if you sit yourself down by the window and rest awhile."

Lucie promised to rest.

Bess huffed away. As she passed the shop door, she heard

Owen speaking with Tildy. Satisfied that the two would hear Lucie if she needed anything, Bess hurried out the kitchen door to fetch whatever she might think of to ease the strain of Lucie's journey.

Lucie came to with her head resting on Nicholas's arm in the dark room. She would not have believed she could fall asleep with her husband just dead. Such weariness frightened her. It muddled wits, caused mistakes. She shook herself and went to the window, opening it wide to let the chill air revive her. Nicholas was past caring about drafts. The breeze stung her face and worked like a slap, awakening her to the awful reality. Her husband had been taken from her. His kind eyes were forever closed.

And already the men around her tried to wrest her power from her. Tell her where she might bury her husband. What right had they to interfere? They claimed it was for her protection. But what could the Archbishop of York and Lord Chancellor of England care about her safety? All courtesy demanded was that he warn her. Perhaps suggest a means of protection. But not demand. Not prepare the way.

Thoresby and Campian protected themselves. She knew things they would prefer to have hidden. She might talk. And the folk of York would be only too glad to listen to her.

But that would gain her nothing. Folk would be intrigued by the tale of Anselm, Nicholas, and Amelie. Entertained. They would take the story home to their hearths and while away many a cold night whispering of it. But why would she betray herself? She had nothing to gain from it and much to lose. It was a story of bad judgment. It would reflect on her. An apothecary with poor judgment would not inspire confidence.

She had no cause to tell the tale, and the Archbishop should know that. She would speak with him tomorrow. Today. It must be close to dawn, though the rain kept the sky dark.

As she stared out into the wet darkness, the door opened behind her. She imagined Bess looking in, worrying over her, and smiled to herself despite her fears. Bess would be pleased to see her taking air. Stealthy footsteps crossed to the bed. A moan.

"I am too late? Oh, Nicholas, you are too cruel. Why did you not wait for me? You call me and then you do not wait. I have crossed through Hell this night to come to your side."

Lucie shivered. It was the Archdeacon, the architect of all her sorrow. Owen must have gone to sleep. And Bess. Lucie could count on no one.

The man's breath wheezed and rattled like that of one wounded or very ill. "I heard you, Nicholas. I heard. They tried to stop me. But I got away. Beautiful Nicholas. They have closed your eyes. They did not want me to see them again."

Lucie groped her way to the little table, holding her breath for fear she would kick something on the way. She felt for the little spirit lamp, turned up the wick. A bright flame flared out.

Anselm gasped as he was discovered and shielded his eyes with a twisted, swollen hand. Nicholas lay across his lap, peeled from his winding sheet. The Archdeacon looked hideous. Blood trickled down his forehead. He reeked of blood and the sweat of fever. A dark red stain spread across the winding sheet on his lap. He gave up shielding his eyes to hold Nicholas tighter, clutching his pale nakedness. "I burned you. How did your spirit get free? Get thee hence, she-devil!"

"This is my house, you monster. And Nicholas was my husband." Lucie moved closer.

Anselm bared his teeth and growled at her like a wounded cat, crushing Nicholas to him.

It was the stuff of nightmares. One dead, the other mad with pain and grief and looking as much a corpse as the dead man. The madman muttered something in Latin, pried open Nicholas's right eyelid with his swollen, twisted finger, and bent to kiss him on the mouth.

"In the name of Heaven, leave him alone." Lucie trembled with rage.

Anselm lifted his eyes to Lucie. "Heaven? What do you know of Heaven, she-devil?" He stroked Nicholas's hair, his stomach, his thigh, watching Lucie, enjoying her discomfort.

"Stop that!" she hissed. She tried to calm herself, to think of what she might use as a weapon. She remembered the knife she used for bandages. It was on the table beside the bed.

"I have a right to say my farewells." Anselm bent to kiss Nicholas again. "He loved me. I protected him."

"Love?" Lucie edged closer. "Nicholas feared you. He said you were mad. Evil."

Anselm screeched and put Nicholas down with trembling arms. Lucie grabbed the knife and held it behind her, backing away.

Anselm reared up. "You are the spawn of the evil that poisoned the soul of my Nicholas," he cried. "Nicholas loved me. It was a pure, innocent love. And then she turned him away. Amelie D'Arby. The French whore."

"And so you tricked innocent Nicholas into killing her."

Anselm grinned. "It happened just as I prayed it would."

"You coward. You had your beloved commit the sin for you. So Nicholas will burn for it. Not you."

"She will burn. Not my Nicholas. She died horribly. Hemorrhaging, life gushing from her. Such pain. Such fear. And she was unshriven, did you know that? Unshriven. She burns in Hell now, my little she-wolf. Do you think of her there? Writhing in the eternal fire?"

Lucie slashed out at his face with the knife. But she was inexperienced. She opened the side of his face, not his eye.

Anselm shrieked and lunged for the knife.

Lucie kicked at him, but her skirts hampered her.

He knocked the knife out of her hand.

She grabbed a chair and rammed his side with it. He tottered, but came back at her almost at once. He was bleeding from the stomach, the side of his face, his forehead. She could not imagine where he got the strength to continue.

He grabbed her. Got her neck in his hands. One hand pressed into her. The other did nothing. Lucie twisted in the direction of the bad hand. He drove her head against the wall. The impact stunned her, and her knees buckled beneath her. Anselm yanked her up and slammed her head against the wall again. She screamed as she felt her knees go out completely. He grabbed her up and pressed her against the wall, the good hand round her throat.

Footsteps came pounding up the stairs. *Dear God, give me the strength to kill him. For my mother. For my husband,* Lucie prayed. She dug her nails into Anselm's hand. He rammed his head against hers. Her ears rang. She could taste his sweat and blood.

"Stay back, Dame Phillippa," Owen called from outside the door. "Stay out of the way." The door crashed open.

Anselm hissed and clutched Lucie to him. Owen tore her out of the Archdeacon's broken hands. She crawled toward the knife.

Anselm, howling in anger and pain, lunged for Owen, who turned, caught him in his powerful arms, and threw him against the wall. Anselm hit it with a sickening sound of breaking bone and slumped to the floor, his head sinking down on his shoulder at an unnatural angle. Phillippa screamed.

Owen hurried to Lucie.

She knelt with the knife raised, staring at the broken body of the Archdeacon. "You have killed him?" A touch of breathlessness. Disbelief. "He was mine to kill. Mine."

Owen knelt beside her, touched her chin, gently turned her face toward him. "You put up a good fight, Lucie. He is dead now. He can hurt no more of your family."

She twisted her head to look back at Anselm. "He uncovered Nicholas. Kissed him and—"

"Let me take you downstairs," Owen said gently.

"He—" Lucie pulled away from Owen and struggled to stand by herself. "He snarled and snapped like a wounded animal. I did not—He did not seem human. And the way he held Nicholas, I—" she took a step toward Nicholas, his naked corpse lying on the sheet fouled by Anselm's blood. She put her hand to her mouth. "The way he held him. Touched him. Taunting me. I—Nicholas died fearing him. And that monster held him there when Nicholas could not fight him." Her body trembled.

"Lucie?" Owen touched her arm.

She backed away, went to stand over her husband's body, hugging her elbows to her sides, the knife trembling in her hands. "My God. Even in death the man clutched at him. Such a terrible, suffocating love. More hate than love. What was my husband's sin, that he should suffer so long?" She lifted the bloodstained sheet. "What right had he? What right?" All the blood. Her mother's gown had been heavy with blood, the skirt pooling on the rushes, so wet and cold. Her skin so smooth and cold.

Owen went to her. "Let me take you down to the kitchen."

Lucie shook her head. "Bess will have a clean sheet. She will have a clean sheet."

A door opened down below. Footsteps crossed the kitchen, mounted the stairs. Voices murmured on the landing.

Bess stepped through the doorway. "Merciful Mother," she whispered at the sight of Nicholas's nakedness against the bloody sheet. "What happened?" Her eyes searched the room, took in Lucie's blood-smeared face, the bloodstains on Owen's shirt, and rested on the body of the Archdeacon. "Holy Mary, Mother of God," she breathed, leaning down to him, then turning away as she caught the stench of his ordeal. "You cannot have done all this?" She looked Owen in the eye.

"He was wounded already."

Their voices seemed to wake Lucie. She dropped the knife. It clattered on the floor.

"Lucie?" Bess said. She dabbed at the blood on her friend's face.

"The brandywine and blanket won't be necessary now," Lucie said.

Bess looked at Owen. "It's the Archdeacon's blood on the winding sheet?" Bess asked.

Owen nodded. "Aye."

Bess was quiet a moment. "The Archbishop's men are here with the coffin. Phillippa and I will wrap Anselm in his own filth and get a clean sheet for Nicholas." She nodded to herself, turned to leave. Then turned back. "And you two must deal with the Archbishop's men."

Lucie had begun to shiver uncontrollably. Owen caught up her hands. They were like ice. He held them.

"I don't know what to do." Lucie stared at her hands in his, her eyes wide with the numbness that Owen had seen time and again in his men when they had fought too long on a battlefield with the dead all about them, slipping on the blood and entrails of their comrades and their enemies, and suddenly it all became too much, their minds and hearts could deal with no more. "I don't know what to do," Lucie whispered.

"For the moment we must go downstairs," Owen said, and led her by the hand.

The Archbishop's men rose, and Owen motioned to them to sit back down. "Mistress Wilton needs brandywine. I could use some, too."

25

AFTERMATH

Wulfstan heard a pair of boots and an accompanying pair of sandals on the stone floor of the chapel. They paused in the doorway, then both came forward. Gold chains rattled richly. Wulfstan withdrew his senses, returning to his meditation on the cross, which he echoed in his posture, lying prostrate on the stone floor before the altar, arms outspread. The cross, Christ's agony, mankind's salvation. Salvation. Because of that selfless act, man could hope for salvation, no matter how grievous his sin.

He struggled to keep his mind on the cross, but discipline did not come easily to Wulfstan. He floated, his thoughts drifting up, over, around him, never quite engaging him, just brushing him with random strands. It was a pleasant feeling that he found impossible to resist. But he tried. He had a vague idea that he should not be comforted, that he'd done something unforgivable, though at the moment he could not remember what it was. When he tried to remember, he became frightened and shied away from the effort.

"Brother Wulfstan, can you hear me?"

It was a quiet, unfamiliar voice. Deep, resonant. Wulfstan liked the voice. But he did not answer. To speak would break the bubble in which he floated. Why could they not leave him alone?

"Wulfstan, the Archbishop is here to speak with you."

His Abbot's voice. High-pitched with tension. An unpleasant voice. Wulfstan preferred the other.

"He wishes to ask you about Lucie Wilton."

Blue eyes. A gentle touch. A smile. Lucie Wilton. Wulfstan

shivered. The bubble in which he floated dipped precipitously, then righted itself. Lucie Wilton stirred an unpleasant strand of memory. He did not want to think about her.

"Wulfstan?"

Why would they not go away?

"Nicholas Wilton is dead, Wulfstan. We know he poisoned your friend Montaigne. Did Lucie Wilton have a hand in that?"

Montaigne. Gentle pilgrim. Darkness. Merciful Mother Mary, that was it. That was the horrible deed for which he could not be absolved. Not with any amount of penance. His fault. He should have known. It was his duty to know. He had murdered his friend. He had failed him. Arrogance. And dear Lucie Wilton. Could she have had a hand in the poisoning? Or known and not warned him? Could she have cold-bloodedly looked away as his friend was poisoned?

"No!" The bubble burst. His heart jolted. He clawed the stones, struggling to rise. Strong arms came to his aid. Wulfstan opened his eyes and stumbled, blinded by the flickering light of the altar candles. The strong arms steadied him.

"Come, sit down on this bench." It was the Archbishop who spoke with the pleasant voice and helped him so gently. Thoresby himself. The Lord Chancellor's chain of office shone on his chest. He smelled richly of scented oils.

"I must know the character of the woman, Brother Wulfstan. You must tell me about her."

Michaelo sometimes smelled like this. Spicy, musky, flowery all at once. A vain young man. But harmless, Wulfstan had thought. Until Michaelo had tried to poison him. Had come perilously close to succeeding.

"Why me? Why would he want to kill me?" Wulfstan wondered aloud.

"Wulfstan." Abbot Campian filled his vision. "You are wandering." To Thoresby, Campian said, "He is not fully recovered. But he begged to be allowed to come to chapel and do penance."

"Penance? For what sin, Brother Wulfstan?"

Wulfstan hung his head. "I should have recognized the nature of the concoction. I should have recognized the symptoms of aconite poisoning. Your ward should not have died. Or Geoffrey." He wept.

Dame Phillippa and Bess had persuaded Lucie and Owen to go and sleep at the inn. They would prepare Nicholas and sit with him. One of the Archbishop's men guarded the inn, another the shop. The other two had gone to inform Thoresby of the Archdeacon's death.

Owen looked in on Lucie before going to his own room. She stood at the window, her arms wrapped tightly around her, as if braced for the next blow.

"You must try to sleep."

"When I close my eyes, I see Nicholas in Anselm's arms." Her voice was full of tears. "I cannot bear it."

Owen stood for a moment, uncertain whether he was welcome. But he could not leave her. "Come. Lie down. I'll talk with you until you sleep."

She let him lead her to the bed. "Tell me how you met the Archbishop."

"No. That would keep you wakeful." Instead, he told her about his archers, naming each one and describing him. Lucie was soon asleep.

Owen nodded off in the chair beside her.

Lucie awoke at the cock's crow, disoriented. "What is this place?"

Owen jerked awake.

"What is this place?" she repeated.

"The best room at the York. We came here last night."

"The Archdeacon," Lucie whispered, touching her head gingerly. Bruises had appeared on her face and throat, revealing to Owen that they had struggled more than he'd guessed.

The sight of the bruises filled Owen with a rage that killing Anselm had not satisfied. He must master this. "Lie still." He pressed a cold, damp cloth to Lucie's head. "You fought bravely."

Her eyes looked beyond Owen. "I wanted to kill him," she said. "I was angry with you for stealing the kill from me."

"It is all over now."

"What am I to do?"

"Do?"

"I have lost everything. My husband. The shop. Everything."

"I have told the Archbishop you are innocent."

"That will not matter."

"I will do my best."

Lucie pushed the cloth away and sat up with effort. "You will continue in the Archbishop's service?"

"I may wind up in his dungeon in the Old Baile."

"Why? You came to my defense. Why would you wind up in his dungeon for that?"

"He did not want Anselm disposed of in the city. He wanted it to happen away from witnesses." And he'd already questioned Owen's loyalty.

"So you should have let Anselm kill me?"

"Of course not. It is a matter of whether His Grace believes me." Owen freshened the cloth and put it back on her forehead. "I saw the knife slash on Anselm's face. That took daring."

"I was driven. I wanted to blind him and then stab him in the heart. You see how successful I was. I'd never used a knife on someone before. It wasn't—His skull—" She coughed, doubled over. He held her head over a pan as she retched.

John Thoresby removed his chain of office and his cloak. Blood did not easily wash out of fur. Then he bent down to examine his Archdeacon. The neck had been neatly snapped. Archer was tidy and quick. It pleased the Archbishop. It also disturbed him. He had wanted this to happen, yes. But not in York. Not so close to the minster. Or if it had to happen in the city, then within his liberty, where he had jurisdiction. Not that anyone involved would talk. But in the middle of the city. Some soul, unable to sleep, might have seen the Archdeacon arrive. Seen the commotion. And for whom had Owen murdered Anselm? For his lord, or for the pretty widow? Thoresby knew how to deal with the widow. Wulfstan had said she expected to be made a master apothecary soon. He said she wanted that very much. And Nicholas had wanted it for her. That suited Thoresby. He liked Mistress Wilton's spirit. She would have made a good abbess. He would agree to her becoming a master in exchange for her silence about this affair. He did not doubt she would cooperate.

But Archer. What to do with him? He knew everything, had no loyalties, no handles to hold him down, keep him to his silence. Unless it was the widow. If Archer had murdered Anselm for the widow, that might be something. Thoresby would watch him.

The requiems were small and quiet, but not for any shame. Both Anselm and Nicholas were laid to rest in hallowed ground. In the apothecary's case, Thoresby blessed a corner of the Wiltons' garden. It was a small matter, but the widow was touchingly grateful. He wanted her that way.

Thoresby watched Archer at the grave. If the man was in love with the widow, he should be elated. She was now free, though of course a discreet period of mourning ought to be observed. But Archer stood there with a dark light in his eye, close to but never touching Lucie Wilton. As if he could not see through to that earthly reward.

After the ceremony, Thoresby drew Owen aside. "What is this gloom?"

Archer gave him a queer look. "None of it is right. All of York is making a martyr out of Anselm. They say he was ambushed as he returned to the city to give the last rites to his friend. That God saw his loyalty and let him live long enough to help his friend to Heaven."

"It is almost the truth, Archer."

"The people should know the whole truth. They should know what Anselm had done."

Thoresby looked down at his ring, discomfited by the fanatic glint in the man's eye. "It was I put the story of Anselm's noble death on people's lips," Thoresby said quietly. "If I were to correct it, tell people that my Archdeacon had killed Digby, tried to kill you and Mistress Wilton, then we have scandal at the minster. Folk do not bequeath money to churches connected with scandals. And the King wants York to be a grand minster, because his son is buried there, William of Hatfield, who died so young, still a babe, because he was too good to live. Edward likes that image. The Hatfield chapel must be in a church worthy of the little angel. Untouched by scandal. So you see, the romantic story of boyhood friends is the only story they must ever hear."

"It is a lie."

"You are a fool, Archer. Whom will it hurt?"

"Are you a man of God? Are you not to lead us on the path of righteousness? To show us how to choose between good and evil?"

Thoresby bit back a smile. Could Archer be so naive after all his years in the old Duke's service? "I am the Archbishop of York and Lord Chancellor of England. Good and evil I must judge in the light of the common weal."

Owen paced in front of him. "You sent your Archdeacon off to Durham hoping that he would be ambushed."

"Not hoping. I told you I had signed his death warrant. What did you think I meant? The ambushers were my soldiers."

"And Brandon?"

"I had to send someone from the abbey, or Anselm would have been suspicious. Young Brandon knew the plan. He rode off, but he didn't need to. My men knew not to harm him."

"It was dark out on the moors, Your Grace. How could they be sure they had the right man?"

"The lad is resourceful. He might think to identify himself."

"And what if the Scots had found them first?"

"I trusted in God. Brandon is a strong lad from the borders. He knows how to defend himself."

"Against Scots? What do you know about fighting alone? You, who have been coddled from birth. 'Tis the same in battle. You sit in your fancy tents and plot and scheme, then move us around the field mimicking tactics you read about in books. You find it exciting. A challenge. You make wagers. Clever tactician, that Thoresby, he lost only fifty men."

"As a soldier you would have valued such a man."

"Why did you send the novice? Why not Michaelo?"

"I could not trust Michaelo not to try to save Anselm at the last."

"You are too cold."

Thoresby chuckled. "I like your moral outrage, Archer. I want you to remain in my service. I can use a man like you."

"Why would you want me? I have made a mess of it."

"How so? You solved the riddle of Fitzwilliam's death. I am pleased his death was accidental. I do not feel such a failure with him knowing that he was not yet so evil that God struck him down."

"I don't understand you."

"You are not yet accustomed to the ways of the world, Archer. In battle the sides seem clear. They are not, you know. Out in the field you see none of the play behind the lines. Today's enemy is tomorrow's ally, sometimes over a mere strip of land along a river. You are behind the lines now, seeing the muddled truth of things. Nothing is so clear as you thought. You have lost your innocence."

"I fear I have lost my soul. You once gave me a choice between yourself and Gaunt. I chose you, thinking you were more honorable." Archer looked disgusted with himself.

"Dine with me tonight. We will talk."

Thoresby found Owen in the hall at the appointed hour, darkly watching some soldiers who hovered round a cask of ale, trading stories, comfortable in their brotherhood.

"You could return to that life. Would you like that?"

Owen shook his head. "The reasons I left have not changed. With one eye I am less reliable. I need to work alone. That way I risk only my own life."

"Good. I can use you in my household."

"I would rather find more honest work."

"Honest. Ah. What did you have in mind?"

"What will become of the Wiltons' shop?"

Thoresby cocked his head to one side. "You would be interested in it? But you're merely an apprentice."

"I would like to continue my apprenticeship with Mistress Wilton."

Thoresby raised an eyebrow. "I have not decided whether she will keep the shop."

"You would be a fool to take it from her. She may prove to be even more skilled than her husband."

"And hence your interest in apprenticing with her." Thoresby smirked.

Owen glowered at Thoresby. "You think I mean to bed her. But it is the life I want. It is honest work."

"You killed my Archdeacon for her, not for me, didn't you?"

"At that moment it mattered not a whit who it was up there, I could not let him hurt her."

Thoresby thought back to the funeral. There had been no signs of affection between them. "Have you discussed your plans with her?"

"No."

"What if she refuses to keep you on?"

"Then I will look for a similar post."

"I see. Either way, I am to lose you. Pity. I liked that you hated the work. It is what keeps a man honest."

"When will you decide about the shop?"

"Soon."

"I mean to spend some days at St. Mary's."

"Honest work and prayer. I wonder if your old comrades would recognize you?"

"Ever since you made up the story for me that I had lost the heart for soldiering…" Owen shook his head. "I don't understand it. But I cannot forgive myself for Digby."

Thoresby put a hand on Owen's shoulder. "We can never predict the losses that we find hard to bear. Come. Let us eat."

26

FORGIVENESS

Bess sat on the bench in Owen's room, watching him assemble his belongings to take to St. Mary's. "'Tis a good thing to do, pray and think, after what's happened. You have a head on those broad shoulders, Owen Archer." He had told her everything. Even his hope for the future. "And when you get back, Lucie may be ready to think about you in a different light."

"I cannot hope for that so soon, Bess. But you're a good friend to say it." Owen put his pack down beside Bess, lifted her to her feet, and hugged her hard.

"My." Bess took a step backward, flustered. "If she doesn't look forward to that, my friend Lucie is not near as smart as she seems."

"Look after her, Bess." Owen hoisted his pack.

"The room will be waiting for you," Bess called to his departing back. But would Lucie Wilton, she wondered. The young woman had a mind of her own, and a stubborn will. Bess could not predict her reaction to Owen's plan.

Lucie rose to get more mulled wine for the Archbishop. He waved her down. "I cannot stay longer. You are satisfied with the terms?"

She examined the paper with what seemed inordinate care, but he wondered how much of that was show. Her pale, drawn face spoke of her grief and her ordeal. The bruises were dark against her white wimple. It was too soon after her husband's death and her confrontation with Anselm to bargain for her future. And that was precisely why he had chosen the day after the funeral. No time to stew over it, begin to question any of it. She would have what she wanted as long as she vowed to remain silent. That was where he wanted her.

"I am happy with it. What does Guildmaster Thorpe say?"

"He intended you to take over the shop. He need not know that his plan would have been blocked had you refused to cooperate."

Lucie studied Thoresby's face far longer than he found comfortable. "I think I am right in trusting you," she said. "I hope I do not find I was a fool."

"As long as you keep your side of the bargain, all will be well."

"And what of Owen Archer?"

"He is disillusioned by his service in the Church. He means to find honest work."

"Can you let him do that?"

"It depends. Has he said anything to you?"

She shook her head. "We will talk when he returns from the abbey."

"Ah, yes. He is praying over it." Thoresby rose.

Lucie rose. "Your Grace, his eye. Could he still be Captain of Archers with one eye?"

Odd question to ask him. "Certainly. An archer closes one eye to aim. The sighting is not the same, but the old Duke said Archer had almost attained his old accuracy."

"So why did he leave that life?"

"He did not trust himself anymore."

"That is what he says. But what do you think, Your Grace?"

Thoresby smiled. He liked her. "I believe him. And I think he was done with killing. He lost that eye because he saved someone's life who did not find his life anything to be grateful for. Archer is an innocent. Was. I think he has learned something in my service."

"He saved my life."

"It's fortunate that Archer still has the reflexes of a soldier, if not the heart. God be with you, Mistress Wilton."

"You will not punish him for your Archdeacon's death?"

Another odd question. "I did not become Archbishop of York

and Lord Chancellor of England by being a fool, Mistress Wilton."

Lucie sat long into the evening. Melisende came in, drank some water, napped in Lucie's lap, Tildy put food before Lucie and took it away cold, Bess looked in and decided to leave her in peace, the cat left for her night revels, and at last, cold and stiff in all her joints, Lucie dragged herself up to bed, where she buried her head and wept.

Owen tossed on his cot, holding his ears. But still he heard the bells, felt them vibrate through his body. Damnable bells.

A timid knock. "Pilgrim Archer. It is time for the Night Office."

Owen sat up, realizing why the bells had sounded so loud. He was at St. Mary's. He groped for his eye patch, put it on, and opened the door of his cell.

A novice bowed to him. "Follow me."

The bells stopped. In the echoing silence, his and many other sandaled feet whispered along the dimly lit stone corridors. The black-robed company filed into the candlelit chapel and flowed into the rows of seats, all without speech, with few even looking up. The novice led Owen to his place. He looked round at his companions, most with their hoods up, heads bowed, no one bristling with resentment, no one jostling for a better seat. All these men moving with humility and quiet obedience. It filled Owen with a sense of peace. In this he could see the appeal of monastic life. As they began to chant the office, he felt lighthearted.

Until his eye rested on Brother Wulfstan. Gentle Wulfstan. Since the attempted poisoning, there was a vague cast to the old Infirmarian's eyes, as though his thoughts were fixed on the next life. Owen wondered how long Michaelo's poison would linger in Wulfstan's body, and whether the novice Henry had thought to bleed the old monk.

Owen's feeling of peace was gone.

After he had broken his fast the next morning, Owen wandered to the infirmary to speak with Henry. But he found Wulfstan alone at his worktable, dripping various essential oils into a salve paste. As each oil touched the warm paste, it released its intense perfume. Owen understood why the old monk stood near a slightly opened window.

"May we speak?" Owen asked. He was not sure how closely they followed the Rule of Saint Benedict here.

Wulfstan motioned Owen to a seat near him. "The infirmary is necessarily an exception—and, as our Savior knows only too well, I have grown lax in my vow of silence over the years."

This morning the old monk's eyes looked clear. "You seem much recovered," Owen said.

Wulfstan thought a moment, then nodded. "A bad business. Who would have thought Michaelo would do such a thing?" He gave a little laugh. "I find it quite miraculous that he had the energy."

The laughter surprised Owen. "You have forgiven him?"

Wulfstan shrugged. "He has confessed and performed penance." He squinted while he measured another drop. "And if in his heart he truly repents, the Lord God will forgive him. I can do no less."

"And Nicholas Wilton. Do you forgive him?"

Wulfstan sighed, wiped off his hands, sank down beside Owen. "That is more difficult. He used me to poison my friend. Abbot Campian explained that it was because Nicholas feared Montaigne. But he need not have done, of that I am certain. Geoffrey had come to make his peace with God. He would not have put his soul in peril. He would not have attacked the Wiltons." Wulfstan brushed tears from his eyes.

"I am sorry for the pain this has caused you."

The Infirmarian studied Owen's face. "I believe you. I did not like you at first."

"I know."

"You knew too much for a stranger. Asked too many questions." The old monk shook his head. "Poor Lucie. Will the story be told? Will she lose all that Nicholas tried to give her?"

"The Archbishop has no desire to publicize a scandal involving his late Archdeacon. But whether he will let Mistress Wilton keep the shop, I do not know."

"You do not approve of the Archbishop's silence?"

"I am pleased for Mistress Wilton. And for you. But the people have been misled about Anselm."

Wulfstan shrugged. "He was a benighted soul. As are we all, more or less. Let him rest in peace."

Owen was quiet.

"What will you do now?" Wulfstan asked.

"I would like to continue as Mistress Wilton's apprentice."

Wulfstan sighed. "I see." Owen would bide his time, work his charm, ask for her hand. And who could blame him?

Early one morning two weeks after the funeral, Lucie woke to a fresh scent that reminded her of spring. She smiled when she turned toward the garden window and saw the quince branches she had brought in two days ago. The warmth in the room had coaxed them into bloom. A good omen on her first waking in this bed alone. She had dreaded this first night. She had put it off, sleeping in the smaller room with her Aunt Phillippa while they aired out this room and scrubbed away the illness and death.

Phillippa had left the day before, with misgivings. "I should not leave you so soon. You have not even tried a night in the room they died in. Some people find it frightening. Though Heaven knows, others must have died here before Nicholas and Anselm. It is knowing it. Having seen Nicholas here in his shroud—"

"Please, Aunt Phillippa." Her constant chatter would drive Lucie mad. "You have been here when I needed you most. I can tell you're worrying about Sir Robert and Freythorpe. A fortnight is long enough to be gone."

Phillippa sighed. "You do seem to have things under control." She looked round the tidy kitchen with satisfaction.

Lucie smiled. It was Phillippa and Tildy, not she herself, who had thoroughly cleaned the house. "I am sure that Tildy will keep this room clean now you've trained her."

Phillippa straightened a bench. "She's a good girl. Your Guildmaster has done right by you."

"And the Archbishop."

"Hmpf. It was in his own interest to keep silent about the matter. I would not waste too much gratitude on him, child."

"Will you tell Sir Robert about Nicholas and Geoffrey?"

"I have prayed over that. I fear it might send Robert off on another pilgrimage. But I think he ought to be told. Who knows? A sense of the circle closing might wake him up to the world again. He might even think to come see his daughter."

Lucie thought of that this morning, and did not know how she felt about the prospect. She had banished Sir Robert from her thoughts fifteen years ago. And before that he had been more of an ogre than a parent.

But the thought of him and Aunt Phillippa at Freythorpe Hadden, thinking of her, made her feel less alone.

She had never been so alone. As a child she had slept with her mother or her aunt. At the convent she had shared a room with other girls. And then she had come to Nicholas's bed. Suddenly she was all alone. And would be so indefinitely.

Dreary thoughts. Perhaps Phillippa had gone too soon. But Owen was to return from St. Mary's today.

Owen. The thought of his return cheered her. Silly. She could hardly expect him to keep up the ruse of apprenticing to her. Some pilgrim to the abbey may have offered him a post already. He might not even stop in to say good-bye.

More dreary thoughts. Even the quince blossoms could not cheer her. Lucie scooped Melisende up from the foot of the bed and cuddled her. The cat had been sleeping peacefully. Now she opened an eye to see why she had been disturbed. And, seeing her mistress's teary face bent over her, applied a rough tongue to the tears.

"I thought if I had the shop I would be quite content," Lucie whispered into Melisende's warm fur, "but I had not thought what it would be like all alone." She put the cat down and got out of bed. "The best antidote for this sort of mood is hard work."

She had just poked the fire to life and started breakfast when Owen came in with a load of wood.

Lucie's heart skipped a beat. "I hardly expected you so early." She turned away from Owen to hide the relief on her face.

"I am sure there is much to be done."

"I have managed."

He stacked the wood by the hearth while she prepared the porridge. They ate for a while in silence. Lucie tried to think how to ask Owen what his plans were, why he was here.

Owen broke the silence first. "Jehannes is to be the new Archdeacon of York."

"Is that good?"

"I think he is an excellent man."

Lucie nodded, staring at her bowl.

"And Michaelo is replacing Jehannes," Owen said.

"That does not seem such a wise choice."

"I would agree with you there. The Archbishop says that Michaelo feels he has been given a second chance at Heaven, and that will make him loyal." Owen's tone said the Archbishop was a fool.

Lucie was surprised. "You do not care for the Archbishop."

"No." Owen looked angry. "Michaelo's family bought him."

At the moment Lucie did not want her trust in the Archbishop undermined, so she changed the subject. "Did you while away all your time at the abbey in gossip? Were you not to decide what to do with yourself now?"

Owen looked guarded. "Has the Archbishop spoken with you?"

"Yes. I am to have the shop for my silence. And you? Has he spoken to you?"

"He told you nothing else?"

"What else was there to tell?"

"Anything about me?"

"He said you wanted to find honest work."

"That is all?"

"Yes, Owen. What did you think?"

"I want to remain here. As your apprentice."

Her eyes opened wide, then her face lit in a grin. "You are joking."

"No."

"I cannot imagine you being content with that."

"I can imagine it."

"You are running away from life."

"From my old life, yes."

"You will itch for action."

"Then I will go out in the garden and work up a sweat. Chop wood. Dig holes. Move trees."

Lucie laughed.

Owen was disappointed. He'd been a fool to hope. He should have known she would not agree. "You still think of me as a soldier. You have condemned me to that life forever."

"I'm sorry."

"People can change, but you'll never believe it. Where would you be if Nicholas had assumed you could be happy only as lady of the manor? Would you have liked spending the rest of your life in a convent?"

Lucie blushed. "Someone else might have asked for my hand."

There he went, insulting her. Jesus Lord, he had an unlucky tongue. "That is not the point. I have told you more times than I can count that I am finished with soldiering. Why won't you believe it?"

"Why should I believe anything you say? You insinuated yourself in my household with a lie. You sneaked around and lied about what you were doing. Oh, surely, now you say that you want to be my apprentice, but how do I know that you're not still in the Archbishop's employ? Keeping an eye on me, perhaps? Just in case the widow Wilton was a poisoner after all?" She was shouting at him, as if her voice were a whip with which to hurt him for hurting her.

Owen stood up. "I never wanted to lie to you."

"Nevertheless, you did."

"I also saved your life."

Lucie bit her tongue.

"I'm a fool to keep trying to make you believe me. You rejected me the moment you saw me." Owen walked toward the door.

"Please sit down, Owen. I don't mean to argue with you

whenever we speak."

He turned. "Perhaps it's a sign that my apprenticeship is a bad idea."

"What would the Archbishop think of this plan?"

Owen realized that she was stalling. She did not want him to walk out the door. All right. He would see where this led. He returned to the table. "I told him what I planned. He did not object."

"He did not tell me."

"I thought he would."

Lucie picked up the dishes, wiped off the table, then sat down across from him again. "Aunt Phillippa left yesterday. I could use help. At least until the Guildmaster can find another apprentice."

"Try me out."

She sighed. "I have to, don't I? I signed a contract. The Guildmaster witnessed it."

"When I lied, I forfeited any right to hold you to the contract."

"You have been far more helpful than an ordinary apprentice."

And he continued to be, on through the spring. At first Lucie watched him, wondering why he stayed, and if perhaps the Archbishop had actually planted him there to watch her. But Owen stuck with his work all day, accompanied her to Mass on Sundays, and, according to Bess, met with no suspicious drinking companions at the tavern. Unless he did not sleep, Owen had no time to work for anyone but her. So Lucie relaxed. She let him work on his own more, and accepted his suggestions when she agreed with them. There even came an evening—it would have been Nicholas's birthday—when Lucie needed company and invited Owen to stay after the meal and sing to her. As before, his voice moved her. Cheered her. She realized how fond she'd grown of his crooked smile, the birdlike way he moved his head to see everything with the one eye, even the way he argued with her when she was being stubborn. She liked having him here in front of the hearth with her at the end of the day.

She did not confide any of this to Bess.

...

The Breton jongleur haunted Owen's dreams. The wild-eyed man crept toward him from the shadows. His leman crept up behind. Again and again Owen caught her arm as she reached for his eye and yanked the arm behind her. At dawn his comrades congratulated him on the corpse. And he was whole. He was Captain of Archers. Across the Channel his wife waited in his bed, dreaming of him, longing for his return. He could see her there, her white skin, her silky hair spilling down her naked breasts...

Owen woke in a sweat, as he had many nights through the spring. He slipped out of the York and walked. Walked fast. Walked until the tenderness of the dream, the joy, was sweated out of him, cleared from his head. It would not do to dream of Lucie Wilton as his wife. She had shown no such inclination. But this night he could not shake the feeling of tenderness. He returned to Davygate still disturbed. He opened the gate beside the shop and went back to the garden. There was a pit for compost to dig. He stripped to the waist and worked in the moonlight.

Lucie woke at the sound of the gate, terrified. It was too late to be Owen or Bess. The intruder passed under the window, and then silence. She held her breath. Then she heard someone shoveling, far back in the garden. She threw on a shawl and picked up the walking stick Owen had cut and shaped for Nicholas.

The full moon lit up the garden. Lucie kept to the shadows, tracking the intruder. But it was no intruder. Worse, perhaps. It was Owen, stripped to the waist, sweat shining on his back and arms. The muscles in his back flexed and rippled as he worked. Geof had once told her that archers had to be very strong to make an arrow fly all the way to the enemy. She remembered the feeling of Owen's arms around her. He was as unlike Nicholas as a man could be. She wondered if those muscles were hot to the touch when he worked like that. *God forgive me for such thoughts.* She should go back inside. But she could not take her eyes off Owen. Moon-mad, both of them. He for digging a hole in the middle of the night, she for staring at him. She shivered, although her body was uncomfortably warm.

Owen sensed he was being watched. He looked around, saw her. Dear Lord, all his work to put her out of his mind, and there she stood in her shift, her hair tumbling down around her slender shoulders. "You should not come out here like that."

"I thought you were an intruder."

"All the more reason."

"What are you doing?" She stepped closer. He smelled of sweat and rich earth.

Owen stabbed the shovel into the pile and used it to climb out, staying on the side of the hole farthest from her. "I could not sleep."

"Something troubles you?"

He thought of some innocent lies, but it was no use dissembling with her. She obviously had no idea how he felt about her, to let him see her like this. "Lucie, our arrangement is not working. I was a fool to think I could work so close to you and not want you." He wiped himself down with his shirt.

"You dreamt of me?"

"Aye. A scoundrel, eh?" If he made light of it, perhaps she would not notice how he was trembling on this warm night.

Lucie stepped around the pit to him, coming so close he could see the moon in her eyes, feel the heat of her body. "You're shivering," she whispered, and opening her shawl, she pulled him to her, wrapping them together, and pressed herself to him. It felt good to touch flesh. And when he put his arms around her, she felt the life in him, the warmth. She kissed him.

"Do you know what you're doing, Lucie?"

"I dreamt of you once. It frightened me."

"Why?"

"I don't know. I never dreamt such dreams about Nicholas."

Their bodies moved against each other.

He pressed her to him, delighting in the scent of her. "I cannot trust myself, Lucie."

Nor could she trust herself. Perhaps she was wrong. She thought of running, but the empty room and cold bed were uninviting, and he was warm and alive and he wanted her. "Kiss me."

They slipped to the ground entangled in each other and made love, Lucie with a passion unlike anything she had experienced with Nicholas, Owen with a tenderness he had never before known.

They woke chilled by the dew.

"I love you, Lucie," Owen whispered, kissing her.

She propped herself up on one arm and looked at him. "Did you really think I might have poisoned Geof for my family's honor?"

"Why bring that up now?"

"I want to know."

"You were strong and proud. I thought it possible." She looked beautiful with her damp hair clinging to her face.

"You are certain now that I was innocent?"

He smiled. "Innocent in that instance, yes. But you are still strong and proud. I cannot say what you might be capable of."

"Soldiers prefer their women meek and obedient."

"Then 'tis a good thing I'm no soldier, eh?"

She brushed his hair off his forehead and touched his cheek gently. "I think I could love you, Owen."

Could. Merciful Mother. "You could not lie, just for this moment, and say you love me?"

Lucie gave him that damnable level gaze. "That would not be a good way to begin."

Instead of arguing, he gathered her to him and held her close. She clung to him. And he thought perhaps he had not been a fool to save the jongleur. Perhaps the blinding was God's way of leading him to Lucie.

"We will marry," Lucie said at breakfast. "And you will remain my apprentice."

"Have you decided you love me, then?"

She smiled. "I think I will."

"I will have to work at convincing you that life is sweeter when I'm about, I see."

Her eyes softened. "You have made a good beginning." She bent to pet Melisende.

When Lucie straightened up, Owen reached across the table

and took her hand. "I mean to make you love me."

Lucie looked at Owen, and already his scarred face was dear to her. "I think you just might, Owen Archer."

Bess found them in the shop, working side by side. Something about the way they moved together told her what had happened. She hurried back to the York Tavern for a pitcher of the Archbishop's brandywine.

"What's that for, then?" Tom asked. It was but midday.

"Lucie and Owen. Just as I told you it would be."

"Well, then, Bess, so you were right. Patch and all."

"That eye was never his problem, Tom. I don't even know why you would think it."

AUTHOR'S NOTE

England in the reign of Edward III (1327-1377) was an exciting, dangerous place. Change was in the air, as momentous as a stronger Commons voice in Parliament and as frivolous as the greatest advances in fashions in centuries. The proud, ambitious son of a deposed king and a ruthlessly ambitious queen, Edward embroiled his country and France in a war that would drag on intermittently from 1337 to 1453, at first in an effort to save the last piece of the Plantagenet empire in France, Gascony, but later as the self-proclaimed "King of England and France." His constant requests to Parliament for new taxes to finance the war led to the stronger voice of the Commons; the wealth brought by the spoils of the war led to the frivolity of fashions.

It was in this war that my main character, Owen Archer, lost the sight in his eye, defending French nobles who were being held for large ransoms. As Captain of Archers for Henry, Duke of Lancaster, Owen had been in the service of the military hero of the age and an expert with the weapon that brought the English their resounding victories at Crécy and Poitiers, the Welsh longbow. In losing this life, Owen Archer mourned much more than his left eye. The longbow was the weapon of the day. It was fortunate for Edward III that his grandfather Edward I saw the value of putting aside the crossbow for the simpler but deadly Welsh weapon. A good longbowman could shoot 10 or 12 arrows/minute to the crossbowman's 2. Even though the range of the crossbow was greater, by the middle of the 14th century the 6-foot longbows of yew, maple, or oak were capable of penetrating chain mail and had a range of about 275 yards, although above 165 yards they were less effective. Edward III combined cavalry and archers, the archers literally darkening the sky with their arrows, the horsemen then rushing in to take advantage of the bloody confusion of the enemy. It was a deadly combination. The archers proved so critical in battle that in 1363, Edward ordered that regular archery practice should take the place of football on Sundays and Holy Days.

This long war was fought on French soil, particularly in the north of France. In the book, Lucie's mother, Amelie D'Arby, is the daughter of a Norman noble whose land was so devastated by the armies that he could not raise the money for his ransom. He offered his marriageable daughter to Sir Robert D'Arby instead. She was brought to Yorkshire while still in shock over the horrors of living in a war zone. She had seen her brother's head on a pike, watched a schoolmate raped and murdered by an English soldier, and was now wed to the enemy and brought to a country in which Norman French was being replaced by English. Today, Normandy and Yorkshire don't seem so far apart; then the two were separated by long, dangerous journeys and cultures in no way homogenized by media coverage. Without the war and its consequences there would have been no Amelie, and no story.

All was not safe on the island of England. Edward was also embroiled in intermittent wars with the Scots, who were in league with the French and often cooperated by distracting Edward from his empire building. Yorkshire was not out of the range of the skirmishes with the Scots. Edward actually moved the government up to York in 1327 and 1333-38 to have it handy while he was busy at the borders. He and Phillippa of Hainault were married in York Minster. It was in the 14th century and because of the Scots threat that York's city walls were repaired and completed in stone. Today the city center is still within the walls, but the city spreads out beyond them. In the 14th century, it was the unfortunates who lived outside the walls. The Forest of Galtres to the north was the haunt of thieves, there were roving bands of outlaws, including Scots, on the roads, and it was a practice in the Middle Ages to burn the "vermin cities" and other shanty communities that grew up outside the city walls in preparation for defense. So although the population might rise, the physical dimensions of a city remained the same, causing crowding and taxing the sanitation systems beyond their limits. Periodical and inevitable fires made room for new buildings, often the stone houses of wealthy merchants.

York, situated on the tidal River Ouse (no longer tidal because of a dam), and halfway between Edinburgh and London, was considered the capital city of the north politically and financially through the 15th century. It was an important city to the Romans, who called it Eboracum and housed a legion there, to the Vikings, who called it Jorkvik and settled there, and to William the Conqueror, who burned much of it to convince the rebellious northerners that he was indeed King. He built twin castles to guard the river, York Castle on the east bank, and what is known as the Old Baile on the west bank.

As a crossroads, York became an important market town and trading center. Two rivers join to the south of the city walls, the Ouse and the Foss. Ouse Bridge, with its city council hall, city jail, St. William's Chapel, maison dieu (hospital for the poor), public privy, and assorted other buildings, was the only bridge between the Ouse and the sea large enough for carts to pass over it. Upriver, a chain stretched between Lendal Tower and what is now called the North Street Tower to prevent the movement of ships without the payment of a toll. In the 14th century the York quays bustled with the wool trade that financed Edward's war.

York was also an important ecclesiastical center. One must never underestimate the power of the Church in the 14th century. In York alone there were 10 religious houses, 47 churches, 16 chapels, and the cathedral. York was the seat of the second most powerful Churchman in England, the Archbishop of York. All of England was divided into two metropolitan provinces, Canterbury and York, which were further divided into dioceses (about 21). The Archbishops of Canterbury and York sat in the House of Lords, at this time known as the Great Council. The Abbot of the Benedictine monastery of St. Mary's in York also sat on the Great Council.

When Abbot Campian and Archbishop Thoresby discuss Owen's inquiries over a flagon of wine, two great men are protecting their considerable interests.

In fact, they were lords of their own liberties in York. Although the city had a mayor and two councils, there were areas of the city under separate rule, called liberties. York Castle was one such liberty. Abbot Campian was lord of the liberty of St. Mary's, and Archbishop Thoresby was lord of the liberty of St. Peter's, or York Minster. A liberty represented an immunity from royal administration because the officials of the liberties, not the King's officials, carried out royal orders. Each liberty had jurisdiction for crimes committed in it and contained its own courthouse, jail, and gallows. Hence the deaths at the abbey occurred in Abbot Campian's jurisdiction, and Thoresby's inquiries were intrusive.

But Archbishop John Thoresby was much more powerful than Abbot Campian because he was both Archbishop of York and Lord Chancellor of England, one of the chief officers of the state. This was not an unusual dual career. In fact, because archbishops and bishops were politically active, it was understood that they depended on their archdeacons to carry out most of their duties. York was divided into five archdeaconries: York, East Riding, Cleveland, Richmond, and Nottingham.

Writing a historical mystery novel requires the author to wear three hats, novelist, historian, and mystery writer. The novelist guards the integrity of the form, the growth of the main character, and glories in the creation of the character's world, freely using the imagination. But the historian groans at anachronisms, agonizes over chronologies, and corrects descriptions according to archeological studies from city plans to the heights of the people. The mystery writer doesn't want too much superfluous historical description to confuse the clues, has to postpone some of the revelations of the novelist in order to maintain suspense, and yearns to move things around in time and place to serve the mystery. Compromises must be made in order to finish the book in one's lifetime.

I have chosen not to dwell on the filthy, unsanitary conditions in 14th century York, how narrow the streets were, how dark because of the overhanging upper stories. Owen notes that it stinks like Calais and London when he first enters the city, and wonders why anyone would live there. But the rest of the characters are residents of York and would take no more notice of the conditions than we do of our own cities. To the city dwellers, the much discussed filth of the medieval city was like our modern day pollution, something that was part of urban life.

I chose York as the base for my series character because of its varied importance in the period. I made Owen an outsider because the best detectives have been people outside the immediate society, never quite a part of the community, and because his past experiences and connections would make him more flexible. A Welsh archer who climbed so high in the household of the Duke of Lancaster would be intelligent and resourceful. And, of course, physically strong.

I had similar motives of isolation and flexibility in creating Lucie Wilton's situation. I wanted her to be as independent as a woman could be in the Middle Ages, and a strong woman so unlike the court and camp women Owen had known for so many years that he must go all the way back to memories of his mother to have a clue to how to please her. She is an ambitious woman, and one much like Queen Elizabeth I who learned in childhood that a woman must learn to count on herself. Unfortunately, apothecaries did not become regular members of a guild in York until the 15th century, when they appear on the rolls of the Merchants' Guild. Guilds developed differently from city to city. In Paris, apothecaries were part of the Brewers' Guild. And in 14th century Paris, Lucie might very well have taken over the shop at her husband's death. So the novelist used Paris guild rules in York, but the historian made sure they were historically accurate rules. The mystery writer made Lucie a woman outside the hierarchy, the daughter of a lord but the wife of a master apothecary, with a troubled past and the skill and ambition to make her satisfactorily suspicious.

Most of my characters are fictional, but the old Duke, Henry of Lancaster, was indeed a powerful military hero who died in 1361. John of Gaunt, third son of King Edward III, did become Duke of Lancaster on Henry's death. John Thoresby *was* both Lord Chancellor of England and Archbishop of York, although he had resigned his post as Lord Chancellor by 1363. I postponed his resignation in order to consider the two sides to such a statesman/Churchman, a common coupling in medieval England. In this book he is still comfortable with his dual role, but later he will find it intolerable. Archdeacon Anselm is my own creation. His obsessive character was necessary for the story.

And what of the Digbys? Chaucer sketched a sordid, unlikable Summoner in *The Canterbury Tales*. What kind of person chooses a career as a snoop? Owen sees an unpleasant similarity between his job and Potter Digby's. But Digby saw the post as a legitimate way to climb out of the vermin city that clustered on the ever flooding river bank north of the abbey walls. The Ouse still floods after winter storms up on the moors. In December of last year I woke one morning to discover that the riverside street below my townhouse was a frozen lake. Overnight, the river had risen several feet. In the morning, as the day dawned sunny and cold, the lake froze. When the river receded, frozen, rutted mud remained. Gradually it thawed into a muddy mess. What must it have been like in the 14th century, when your house was mud and sticks?

Magda Digby, Potter's mother, lives in a world of her own. An old Viking boat from York's past crowns her house. Her speech is the old speech. Magda is purely the novelist's creation, and perhaps to me the character most real. Like the juxtaposition of pagan and Christian England in *Beowulf*, Magda encapsulates the past and present. She is outside time, like the city of York, part Roman, part Viking, part medieval, part Victorian, part 20th century tourist town. And therein lies the intrigue.

THE OWEN ARCHER SERIES

THE LADY CHAPEL

Perfect for fans of both Ellis Peters and CJ Sansom, *The Lady Chapel* is a vivid and immersive portrait of court intrigue and a testament to the power of the medieval guilds.

Summer in the year of our Lord 1365. On the night after the Corpus Christi procession, a man is brutally murdered on the steps of York Minster. The next morning his severed hand is found in a room at the York Tavern—a room hastily vacated by a fellow guild member who had quarreled with the victim.

Archbishop Thoresby calls on Owen Archer to investigate. As Owen tracks the fleeing merchant, he uncovers a conspiracy involving a powerful company of traders, but his only witness is a young boy who has gone into hiding, and his only suspect is a mysterious cloaked woman. When Owen discovers a link between the traders and a powerful coterie in the royal court, he brings his apothecary wife Lucie into the race to find the boy before he is silenced forever by the murderers.

THE NUN'S TALE

Based on an enigmatic entry in the records of Clementhorpe Nunnery, this authentic, gripping mystery conjures a 14th century ripe with forbidden passions and political intrigue.

When young nun Joanna Calverley dies of a fever in the town of Beverley in the summer of 1365, she is buried quickly for fear of the plague. But a year later, Archbishop Thoresby learns of a woman who has arrived in York claiming to be the resurrected nun, talking of relic-trading and miracles. And death seems to ride in her wake.

The archbishop sends Owen Archer to retrace the woman's journey, an investigation that leads him across the north from Leeds to Beverley to Scarborough. Along the way he encounters Geoffrey Chaucer, a spy for the king of England, who believes there is a connection between the nun's troubles, renegade mercenaries, and the powerful Percy family. Back in York, however, Owen's wife Lucie, pregnant with their first child, has won the confidence of the mysterious nun and realizes that there are secrets hidden in the woman's seemingly mad ramblings...

THE KING'S BISHOP

From the marshy Thames to the misty Yorkshire moors, murder stalks Welsh soldier-sleuth Owen Archer and one of his oldest friends.

On a snowy morning in 1367, Sir William of Wyndesore's page is found in the icy moat of Windsor Castle, and some whisper that the murderer was Ned Townley—a former comrade-in-arms of Owen Archer. Burdened with a reputation as a notoriously jealous lover, Ned cannot hope to clear his name; even Mary, his ladylove, is unsure of the truth. Hoping to put Ned out of harm's way while solving the murder, Owen places his friend in charge of a mission to Rievaulx Abbey at the edge of the moors. But when the travelers receive news of Mary's drowning, Ned vanishes into the wild.

Riding out in search of his old friend, Owen does not know whether he will be Ned's savior or executioner. With his one good eye, Owen sees more than most, but now he must find a way to penetrate the curtains of power that surround the Church and England's royal court and discover the truth of Ned's innocence or guilt...

THE RIDDLE OF ST. LEONARD'S

In the year of our Lord 1369 the much-loved Queen Philippa lies dying in Windsor Castle, the harvest has failed, and the pestilence has returned. In York, the atmosphere of fear and superstition is heightened by a series of thefts and violent deaths at St. Leonard's Hospita, as well as rumors that these crimes are connected to the hospital's dwindling funds. The Master of St. Leonard's, Sir Richard Ravenser, hurries north from the queen's deathbed to summon Owen Archer, soldier-spy, to investigate the scandal before it ruins him.

While his wife Lucie faces the plague-panicked townsfolk at the apothecary, Owen encounters a seemingly random series of clues: a riddle posed by one of the victims at the hospital, a lay sister with a scandalous past, the kidnapping of a child from the hospital orphanage, and a case of arson. The answer to the riddle of St. Leonard's lies in the past, and as Owen's family is caught up in the sweep of the pestilence, he must abandon them to race across the countryside to save the next victim.

A GIFT OF SANCTUARY

Under the pretense of escorting his father-in-law and the archbishop's secretary on a pilgrimage to the sacred city of St. David's in Wales, Owen Archer and Geoffrey Chaucer, in truth, are carrying out a mission for the Duke of Lancaster. England and France are at war, and the southern coast of Wales is vulnerable to invasion—Owen and Geoffrey are to recruit archers for the duke's army and inspect his Welsh fortifications on the coast, while quietly investigating whether the duke's steward at Cydweli Castle is involved in a French plot to incite rebellion in Wales.

But trouble precedes them in the cathedral city of St. David's. On Whitesands Beach beyond the city a young man is beaten and left for dead, then spirited away by a Welsh bard. Shortly afterward a corpse clothed in the livery of the Duke of Lancaster is left at the city gate, his shoes filled with white sand. Meanwhile, at Cydweli Castle, a chain of events begun by the theft of money from the castle's exchequer ends in a violent death and the disappearance of the steward's beautiful young wife. Owen and Geoffrey begin to see connections linking the troubles in city and castle, and learn they must unravel the complex story of betrayed love and political ambition to prevent more deaths. But in the course of his investigations in the land of his birth, Owen is haunted by doubts about his own loyalties...

A SPY FOR THE REDEEMER

Late spring in the year of our Lord 1370, and Owen Archer is anxious to leave Wales for home. His mission for the Duke of

Lancaster complete, he attempts to arrange safe passage on a ship sailing for England, but the hanging of a stonemason interrupts his plans. On the surface it appears the young man was driven to suicide by a broken heart, but to Owen the signs all point to murder. As his investigation stretches on, however, Owen finds himself drawn into the influence of the leader of a Welsh rebellion whose manifesto speaks to his heart, and a choice is offered to him: join or die.

Meanwhile, at home in York, Owen's wife Lucie is troubled by rumors that her husband's long absence is permanent, as well as threats by a customer who claims she was poisoned by a physic from the Wilton apothecary. Meanwhile, Lucie is tempted by the attentions of a friend's steward, even as she uncovers a shattering betrayal in her own household.

THE GUILT OF INNOCENTS

Winter in the year of our Lord 1372. A river pilot falls into the icy waters of the River Ouse during a skirmish between dockworkers and the boys of the minster school, which include Owen Archer's adopted son Jasper. But what began as a confrontation to return a boy's stolen scrip becomes a murder investigation as the rescuers find the pilot dying of wounds inflicted before his plunge into the river. When another body is fished from the river upstream and Owen discovers that the boy Jasper sought to help has disappeared, Owen Archer convinces the archbishop that he must go in search of the boy. His lost scrip seems to hold the key to the double tragedy, but his disappearance leaves troubling questions: did he flee in fear? Or was he abducted?

On the cusp of this new mystery, Owen accepts Jasper's offer to accompany him to the boy's home in the countryside, where they learn that a valuable cross has gone missing. A devastating fire and another drowning force Owen to make impossible choices, endangering not only himself, but the two innocents he fights to protect. The bond between fathers and sons proves strong, even between those not linked by blood.

A VIGIL OF SPIES

Archbishop Thoresby of York, the second most powerful cleric in England, lies dying in his bed. The end of his life is seen by the great families of the North as a chance to promote one of their own as his successor, and Thoresby himself announces he will leave the matter to the dean and chapter of York. On the eve of this decision, the dying archbishop agrees to a visit from Joan, Princess of Wales, wife of the Black Prince, heir to the throne of England. Thoresby's captain of the guard, Owen Archer, has no doubt that trouble will follow.

As soon as the company rides into the palace yard he is proved right: they arrive burdened with the body of one of their party, and Owen finds evidence that the man's death was no accident. Within days of this discovery, a courier carrying an urgent message for the archbishop is found hanging in the woods. With guards surrounding the property, it is clear that the murderer walks among the palace guests. The powerful Percy and Neville families are well represented in the entourage, including a woman who remembers an afternoon tryst with Owen as much, much more. Even the princess' son is suspect. As Owen races to unmask the guilty and rid the palace of the royal party, his final wish for his lord is that he might die in peace.

THE MARGARET KERR SERIES

A TRUST BETRAYED

In the spring of 1297 the English army controls lowland Scotland and Margaret Kerr's husband Roger Sinclair is missing. He'd headed to Dundee in autumn, writing to Margaret with a promise to be home for Christmas, but it's past Easter. Is he caught up in the swelling rebellion against the English? Is he even alive? When his cousin, Jack, is murdered on the streets of Edinburgh, Roger's last known location, Margaret coerces her brother Andrew, a priest, to escort her to the city.

She finds Edinburgh scarred by war—houses burnt, walls stained with blood, shops shuttered—and the townsfolk simmering with resentment, harboring secrets. Even her uncle, innkeeper Murdoch Kerr, meets her questions with silence. Are his secrets the keys to Roger's disappearance? What terrible sin torments her brother? Is it her husband she glimpses in the rain, scarred, haunted? Desperate, Margaret makes alliances that risk both her own life and that of her brother in her search for answers. She learns that war twists love and loyalties, and that, until tested, we cannot know our own hearts, much less those of our loved ones.

THE FIRE IN THE FLINT

Scots are gathering in Murdoch Kerr's Edinburgh tavern, plotting to drive out the English forces. Margaret takes her place there as innkeeper, collecting information to pass on to William Wallace—until murder gives the English an excuse to shutter the tavern. The dead man was a witness to the intruders who raided chests belonging to Margaret's husband and her father, the latest in a string of violent raids on Margaret's family, but no one knows the identity of the raiders or what they're searching for.

Margaret's uncle urges her to escape Edinburgh, but as she flees north with her husband Roger, Margaret grows suspicious about his sudden wish to speak with her mother, Christiana, who is a soothsayer. Margaret once innocently shared with Roger one of Christiana's visions, of "the true king of Scotland" riding into Edinburgh. Now she begins to wonder if their trip is part of a mission engineered by the English crown...

A CRUEL COURTSHIP

In late summer 1297, Margaret Kerr heads to the town of Stirling at the request of William Wallace's man James Comyn. Her mission is to discover the fate of a young spy who had infiltrated the English garrison at Stirling Castle, but on the journey Margaret is haunted by dreams—or are they visions?—of danger.

He who holds Stirling Castle holds Scotland—and a bloody battle for the castle is imminent. But as the Scots prepare to cast off the English yoke, Margaret's flashes of the future allow her to glimpse what is to come—and show her that she can trust no one, not even her closest friends.

A Cruel Courtship is a harrowing account of the days before the bloody battle of Stirling Bridge, and the story of a young woman's awakening.

Printed in the USA
CPSIA information can be obtained
at www.ICGtesting.com
LVHW041619030124
768082LV00005B/9